THE LEGACY

ELLEN L. EKSTROM

Whyte Rose & Violet, Scribes

THE LEGACY

ISBN: 978-0692348567

Published in the United States of America

This is a work of fiction. Names, characters, places and incidents
either are the product of the author's imagination or are used
fictitiously and any resemblance to actual persons, living or dead,
business establishments, events or locales is
entirely coincidental.

Cover design: Whyte Rose & Violet Artists
Images courtesy of Adobe Stock and
iStockPhoto.com

Whyte Rose & Violet, Scribes

www.whyteroseandviolet.net
queries@whyteroseandviolet.net

Once a thing is done, it is finished...

AUTHOR'S NOTE

This is a work of fiction based on real persons from the fourteenth century in Tuscany, the ancient Guidi family and its various and many branches. *While the names are historical, the characters are not.* This is purely a work of fiction.

For ease of reading, I've used English names and conventions for clothing, as Italian clothing of the fourteenth century had various names for the same garment depending in which city state one lived. For armor, I've used the traditional French names.

I have used the Italian convention for titles, *i.e.*, 'sir,' 'miss,' etc. 'Signor' meant 'sir,' 'Signore/Monsignore' meant 'lord' or 'my lord.' There were various titles for women with the same convention. 'Dona' meant 'lady,' 'Madonna,' 'my lady,' 'monna' and 'mona' were also used to mean 'lady.'

THE
LEGACY

PART 1 – THE JOURNEY

CHAPTER 1

FRANCESCO WAS AWAKE; truth be told, he'd never slept the night before. So many ghosts, so many demons lurked in the purple shadows. He knew every one of them. On this particular morning, one demon lay in wait.

Today would bring certain death.

The waning moon loosed arrows of light through chinks in the bed curtains. Francesco focused on the outline of furniture and things beyond the linen panels. It was like viewing his world through the opaque fiber of a death shroud. If his plans were foiled today, these images would be among his last. This bower would be a bier; a shroud would mask his dull, lifeless eyes.

It must be done.

"It is what I must do. It must be done. There is no other way," he whispered aloud.

Having said this, Francesco turned in bed and brushed his lips against Gismonda's brow. She didn't stir and for that he was thankful. Goodbyes were the hardest in the morning. He shifted again and tried to rise, groaning in pain. He was unused to the luxury of a featherbed, accustomed by necessity to the hard earth of the Tuscan mountains. Days spent in full harness and in the saddle gave him less discomfort. Francesco eased his way out from under the pile of soft coverlets and blankets, picked apart the trail of clothing from bed to stairwell and dressed as he went, made his way down to join the household guard.

Foot soldiers staggered to attention as Francesco rounded the herb garden and baking house, then entered the stable yard and made straight for a brazier where mulled wine steeped and meat pies sizzled—fine fare to break fast after days of nothing but dried meat, bread, and cheese.

Francesco accepted a cup with thanks and gulped down a mouthful.

1

The hot liquid scalded his tongue and he swore as he flung the wine in a wide arc, men and dogs scattering out of its path.

"He's in fine mettle for a fight," said one soldier to another.

"That's what we want, isn't it?" was the reply.

Francesco heard the comments and glared at both men. He took a few steps towards them to share his opinion of their comments when one of the sergeants caught his attention.

"Monsignore! Riders! From the east!"

Francesco brushed past the men and went to see for himself.

A sun that turned from pink to yellow gold as it rose over the landscape burned away mists from the Arno and reflected off the mail shirts worn by the riders, shimmered against the silver falcon on the fluttering Romena standard carried by one of them.

On any other morning, Francesco would have given thanks for such a day and for such a place. The horizon was sketched with softly rolling hills and the sharp outline of the Tuscan Apennines. Laid out before him like one of maestro Giotto's paintings was a myriad of greens, from the richest and darkest forest to the dull olive of orchards and farms together with the gold and russet of turning leaves and summer grass dying. The fragrant familiar air had the tang of morning dew and earth, a good sharpness.

But all that held Francesco's attention now was his standard as the riders approached.

"This is one hell of a fine morning to pick a fight."

Francesco turned at the sound of Edmund Clifford's voice. The Englishman nodded in greeting and approached.

"Well the sooner it's started, the sooner it's over and we can enjoy the rest of the day," Francesco replied and after a moment's reflection added, "God willing."

"The day will be ours; it couldn't go any other way," Edmund said and he stepped aside to allow the riders into the yard.

They watched silently as riders circled and dismounted, as one of them dropped to his knees before Francesco and handed him a letter that was opened and read quickly. The gray pallor of his face told Edmund that perhaps the Wheel of Fortune would not turn in Francesco's favor. Not yet, at least. Edmund waited for news and wasn't surprised when Francesco ignored his question of the message.

"The army waits at Poppi," Francesco said. "We should be away from here soon—before Gismonda's husband returns. That's not a fight I'd win today."

Francesco then took a meat pie from the brazier and walking past the stables to the orchard, sat under a plum tree to break his fast.

Beyond the nut trees and fruit trees, beyond the gently rolling hills etched with vineyards, he could see the rooftops and towers of the castle of

Raggiolo and its abbey, San Proculo il Soldato. From here to Raggiolo was a short distance, yet he was loathing the journey.

It is what I must do. It must be done. There is no other way, he thought.

༂

BY THE TIME Francesco and his household guard were on the road to Poppi, the monks of San Proculo il Soldato were bustling and Abbate Giordano was already settled into the day's work. He carefully took a knife to the new parchment before him, turning a mundane ritual into a sacrament. At every pass of the blade, he made precise turns and elegant strokes, scraping, sanding, until the page was smooth and ready for a quill and ink. This continued for several minutes. The abbot's thoughts were elsewhere as he worked. This was apparent when he raised the sheet to the morning sun and squinting with farsighted eyes, found a gaping hole where the knife had been applied time and again.

"From constant meditation on the missteps and blunders of our young benefactor, Good Lord deliver me!" Giordano sighed. With fresh parchment before him, he took pen in hand and wrote the date.

October 14, 1327.

He hesitated, looked out into the abbey gardens upon hearing shrieks of laughter.

Two novices scrambled for an overturned basket of apples. Fruit rolled under habits and the novices with it. There were shouts of indignation, outrage, and laughter as apples were reclaimed. The game ended when the brothers making harvest suddenly stopped and looked upwards. So did Giordano, watching the sky for storm clouds. He turned then, hearing what they heard. Rolling thunder.

No, not thunder, and far from it, too—the unmistakable metallic clank of harness, the pounding of hooves. Only war horses armed to the teeth could make the ground quake as it did now. His suspicion was confirmed when the governor of Raggiolo, Fulvio Calo, burst in with the abbey prior on his heels.

"Pardon abbate! We told, we told . . . him . . . you weren't . . . to be . . . disturbed!" Fra Uzzano apologized, still sucking for air.

"Ser Fulvio, Benedicte. I can only guess what's brought you here," Giordano addressed the governor, who stood over him sweating and heaving in a scarlet robe of office trimmed in ermine. He wrote something on the parchment, sighed, and made another entry, squinted at that, frowned, and scratched it out. Tortuous moments slid through the hourglass before he spoke again.

"Is there an army on the road?" This last spoken no more seriously than a query about the price of eggs.

"Just so; from the north," Fulvio answered, mopping his brow with his sleeve.

3

"North? From Poppi or Stia?"

"Poppi or Stia? What does it matter? An army's an army!" Fulvio sputtered.

"Poppi or Stia."

Giordano needed to know. In these his last days as abbot of San Proculo il Soldato, he wanted a clean record, nothing to besmirch twenty-four years of service to the German Emperor, the Guidi, and God, in that order. The Imperial Abbey in Florence waited for him. He'd worked his whole life for it.

"Poppi or Stia?" Giordano repeated himself.

"Poppi!"

"Hmm . . . not surprising,"

"You must open the abbey to the town!"

Giordano pointed toward the church.

"Good God! Do you want to pray right now?" Fulvio exclaimed, his voice rising painfully.

"This way," Giordano said, and waving off the nervous brothers clustering at the door, led on.

They scuttled between pink marble colonnades around the cloister and to a path skirting the church, up a winding casement that was like a corkscrew and just as deadly, to the top of the bell tower.

The view was worth the perilous climb. Before them lay the northern end of the vast High Casentino—an expanse of mountainous, forested, land dotted with farms and castles, unequaled in Italy for beauty or wealth. Directly below them lay Raggiolo.

"Is this, is this what you've dragged me up here to see?" Fulvio groused, still laboring for breath. "Abbate, it's nothing I haven't seen before!"

Nothing seemed amiss, nothing, really, until they glanced northeast.

There!

A silver thread—a glistening stream? Nothing of the sort. It was, as Giordano surmised and Fulvio dreaded a great army. This army came rapidly, too, for what might be mistaken for mist or clouds was dust stirred up by the advance of a mighty force.

Giordano studied the horizon and then nodded, holding back a smile. He knew; he only wondered why it had taken so long.

"Christ's body and blood! Why do you wait?" Fulvio demanded. "Will you open the gates?"

"I'll open them to Francesco Guidi, conte di Romena, for this is his army."

"Romena—!"

Giordano watched in satisfaction as the sweat beaded on Folio's upper lip and his skin blanched like a boiled pear. "No doubt he'll want to exact a price from you. Am I right, Fulvio?" A moment passed, and then, "Let's go."

As they went down, Giordano turned abruptly on the casement and Fulvio grabbed hold of the rough stone wall. "Are you trying to kill me?" Fulvio demanded as he regained his footing. In the dimness of the stairwell Giordano's smile gleamed white and menacing, the silver curls of his tonsured head caught thin rays of sunlight trying to break through the stones, turning them into horns. His dark eyes were like copper coins.

"When you choose loyalties, Fulvio, it's best not to take store in promises from those who won't deliver! There's not an enemy of Romena who hasn't dearly paid his piper!"

"What would you have done?"

"I'd have turned the man out! You know this quarrel between Romena and his uncle Porciano! You know it better than most since you've seen fit to harbor the fool. There's always one malcontent in a family, one cousin or brother dissatisfied with the bread on his table!"

"I didn't think,"

"That's right. You didn't. Be ashamed for your stupidity! If you live—if we all live—to see the end of this day, maybe you'll take a moment to ask the Lord for the common sense he gives sheep!"

"No one expected he'd come after all this time."

Muttering a prayer, Giordano shoved Fulvio on his way.

❧

THE TOWN FATHERS met Fulvio on Raggiolo's walls. They turned as one when Fulvio appeared on the parapet. "Well?" asked Tancredi the apothecary. "Where's Giordano? You said he'd open the abbey."

"He thought prayer the best solution to our problem," Fulvio grumbled. "He's not coming."

"What? What was that?"

"I said, he's not coming."

"Saints in heaven, we're going to die!" Tancredi moaned, the parchment-like skin on his skeletal face turning as gray as the matter fur cuffs of his overgown. He spun about and pointed a finger at the captain of the town militia. "You see? This is what happens when you send an idiot to do a soldier's work!"

"There's still time," Fulvio said.

"Not much."

"Do you have any ideas?" Fulvio hissed. "I didn't hear you offering to come with me or listen to what I suggested in the first place!"

"Well, what have you come up with?" the captain demanded. "C'mon! Tell us."

Fulvio avoided the captain glaring at him from his one good eye. "We wait," he answered after a time.

"What?" several council members cried at once.

Maestro Ornello, the town's fat goldsmith, pushed his way forward. "I didn't delay a trip to the fairs of Burgundy to stand here and wait for the conte di Romena to slaughter us all!" he growled. "You'd better do something! You've put us all in danger!"

"There's nothing much we can do!" Fulvio cried, exasperated. "And we don't know if Romena is going to murder us."

The town notary, Lachine, snorted. "We know of at least one man who ought to make his confession before Romena gets here! And don't forget the eight florins you owe me!"

"Where's the priest?" Ornello laughed. "Someone find the old chaplain from Santa Trinita!"

Nervous laughter made the rounds and fell away, as brittle as the silence that followed. The council members eyed one another, making sure there was an accord on at least one matter. Fulvio was a dead man.

"You don't know," Fulvio complained. "None of you know what it's been like!"

"That's not our concern," the captain said, leaning in so that Fulvio could only see the hideous scar that closed his left eyelid forever. "It's all the same to me, Fulvio, whether you, Romena, that prick Porciano, or all of you! Are dead by nightfall. It's all the same."

Fulvio shrugged him off and then moved away as far as he could without falling down the stairs. "We wait until Romena comes," he stated. "And then we'll talk to him."

❧

WHEN ROMENA'S ARMY crested the horizon, it was a sight to give the most hardened soldier pause. Fulvio ciphered the number of armed horse and men and lost count after five hundred and twenty. Romena had contracted four great companies of soldiers for hire and flying with Romena's personal banner was that of the most feared of English mercenaries in Italy, Edmund Clifford of York, who led the Company of the Rose.

"Clifford!" someone swore.

"The Rose - the greatest company!" another whispered.

"*Diavole Inglese!*" spat another.

The horizon filled with the flash of armor and bright heraldic pennants. Raggiolo's defenders looked to one another for advice as the army drew up and held silently but for the neighing and snorting of horses and the shouted commands from the knights in the rear lines. A herald bearing the Romena colors of *murrey* and *or*, mulberry and gold, rode forward and paused, waiting for a standard bearer to join him, and together they galloped up to Raggiolo's walls, stopping below Fulvio.

"What say you, herald?" Fulvio opened.

"My lord Romena says this. He commands you give up his kinsman

Tommaso Porciano and any of his you may harbor in Raggiolo. Do this, and no harm will come to any man here today," the herald called up.

"Send to conte di Romena that I offer my thanks for his generosity but we cannot give what we do not have," Fulvio replied.

"Signor, he knows!"

"Knows what, Herald? That could be any number of things!"

"He knows that Porciano came into the town last night."

"Does your lord know that he left? On your way, Herald! There's nothing for you here!"

Fulvio grinned when the herald nodded and wheeling about, rode back to the army.

Again, there was a standoff and silence. Fulvio and the men on Raggiolo's walls conferred and congratulated themselves on a victory, small that it was, even though the Romena army kept its lines and stood at attention, waiting, as the sun rose higher in the sky.

The front line broke just as the abbey bells rang at midday. A knight burst through the ranks with two heralds in his wake.

The sun caught his armor, blinding curiosity seekers who scrambled out of the way. It was a reckless gamble, not knowing what defenses Raggiolo had, but praiseworthy and daring all the same. His handling of the restive warhorse beneath him caused more excitement, even praise. These powerful animals called destriers were known for crushing a man's head in their jaws, for attacking with the ferocity of a lion or wild boar, yet the knight controlled his mount as easily as a palfrey.

"Make way!" one of Raggiolo's guards shouted as the destrier loomed, cantering first to one side and then another, snorting and straining at the bit.

The knight pulled up rein and removed first his great helm and then the bascinet, a smaller, form-fitting helmet, tossing each to a herald. He sat, waiting, and then rode forward.

The captain guffawed and all turned to look at him, wondering what was so amusing. "Romena surely knows how to create excitement by his arrival. He learned that from his bastard kinsmen!"

Fulvio glanced at the tall young man riding slowly towards them, then cast a nervous look at the captain.

"What's the matter, Fulvio?" the captain teased, noticing how Fulvio's mouth dropped. "You didn't know he was taller than most men? Take comfort knowing his temper doesn't match his size; they say he's nothing like his father."

"*They* say! We don't know that for certain!" Fulvio snapped.

"I've heard he's an honorable man and well-liked."

"He's Alessandro da Romena's son! He's one of the conti Guidi!"

"So? He's not Alessandro."

Fulvio wiped his sweating brow, hissing, "He's one of the conti Guidi of Castello di Romena; surely you know about them?"

"Nobility bleeds like the rest of us," the captain said.

"They always manage to cheat death!"

"Unless they can raise the dead and change water to wine, I don't think there's a difference."

"Merchant lords!" Tancredi spat. "Castles and lands aren't good enough! They want to control what we do in the towns and cities. They want to dye wool and spin it, weave it into cloth. That's how they've managed after Alessandro lost everything. It'd be a rare day if any one of them got out of bed to strap on harness for a good fight!"

Six pairs of eyes burned into Tancredi, who merely shrugged and took a sword from one of the guards, wielding it expertly.

"When were you ever in a good fight, Tancredi?" Ornello demanded.

"If the occasion calls for it,"

"Enough!" Fulvio shouted. "I know them! The Romena hold the High Casentino, the lands of the Pratomagno, the Mugello Valley and every trade route that leads into Florence. If you want to know why it costs so much to trade with Bologna and Venice, it's the tax Romena put on the roads! That makes them the most powerful and dangerous of the conti Guidi, and Alessandro, may God rest his immortal, black soul, was the worst. Oftentimes the apple doesn't fall far from the tree! And *that's* Romena cloth you're wearing, Tancredi!"

Tancredi studied the sleeve of his overgown and shrugged.

"I heard it told when Alessandro was murdered, the bells of Florence rang in thanksgiving for three days," Ornello said.

"At least he didn't rise from the dead!" the captain guffawed.

"Found him butchered in a brothel!" another snorted.

The men began to laugh and exchange stories of the infamous Alessandro Guidi, conte di Romena. No tale was identical, but it was agreed that Alessandro's boy was cut from a different cloth altogether.

This posthumous son of Alessandro's was an enigma. Born under the worst of circumstances and in the worst of times, no one knew him personally, only to speak of, and the stories were legion.

"Here he comes," the captain said, jerking his head toward Romena.

Whispering a prayer, Fulvio went down, signaling the captain to join him. The council members followed, muttering their displeasure at odds so apparently against them.

Francesco da Romena halted a pike's length from Fulvio and dismounted swiftly and easily, as if the oppressive weight of his highly polished, white silver, armor was nothing. And then he overshadowed Fulvio, blocking out the autumn sun.

"Good morning, ser Fulvio."

Fulvio caught his breath. Francesco da Romena was the most impressive man he'd ever seen.

The smile was dazzling, if not deadly. He was truly an imposing spectacle: six feet and seven in height, and in full battle harness, taller still. His tawny, curling hair was streaked with copper and gold and cut in the English fashion, cropped almost to the shoulders. His large green eyes were compelling, set wide on a fair complexioned, yet sunburned face. He had a straight nose, a square face that narrowed at the chin, and a thin, sharp, mouth. Francesco da Romena was extraordinarily handsome and he was extraordinarily young.

Bowing low, Fulvio said, "Welcome, Signore Romena; you do us honor!"

"Let's wait on praise until the end of the day," Francesco stated quietly in a voice as equally mesmerizing as his appearance. "I understand my kinsman Porciano is your guest. Bring him here; I'd like a few words."

"Signore, how should I do that? Conjure him out of clouds or smoke?" Fulvio laughed nervously. "I'm sorry, but he's not here."

"You'll have to be more convincing than that," Francesco replied. "My herald saw him enter the town last night."

"And then he left. I'm told he escaped after the watch changed."

"Do better, Fulvio. I had men posted at every gate and no one left, and no one came in," Francesco said, and stepping forward, said, "You know what's at stake; you know what is expected. You know what you have to do."

"It would be next to impossible!"

"Bring him out. Now."

Behind them, Raggiolo's council members shuffled impatiently and offered their opinions in none-too-quiet whispers. It was a reasonable request! Tommaso di Porciano had a lot to answer for. He'd spent the last twenty-four years taking Francesco's castles and towns one by one so that almost nothing was left of his inheritance.

"Signor, perhaps you didn't hear me,"

"Bring him and I'll withdraw."

"Forgive me, but I believe you do not understand . . ."

"I understand more than you would credit me. Must I ask again?"

"If he was here, he would have to come of his own will. Raggiolo could not afford such a betrayal."

"It depends on who would be most offended. Now again I ask you, where is Porciano?"

"Signore il conte, I have a proposition for you to consider." Tancredi blurted out, shoving forward. "Raggiolo would most happily come to terms, should there be an offering of a hundred florins?"

"Be silent!" Fulvio hissed, pushing Tancredi aside. He smiled at

Francesco, saying calmly, "And if Porciano doesn't wish to come? If he was here?"

"He'd want to come. If he was here."

"Understand me, messer conte, if I asked him to come, and if he was here, which, I cannot tell you for certain, if I brought him forward—"

"Enough!" Francesco bellowed. Even the kestrels grew silent as every man waited to see what would happen next. Francesco took Fulvio by the throat. "Don't play games and don't take me for a fool!" He snapped in a voice that darkened with menace. "I can tear this town asunder, stone by stone, castle to manger, barn to blacksmith's, all of which, if you know your history, is mine!"

"By Christ's body and blood, you would not!" Fulvio cried. "The women and children,"

"Do you not hear? Bring him to me. Now!"

"But the women and children, monsignore!"

"*They will be spared!*"

Francesco's shout rent the frightening silence and echoed past the town walls, was heard by fleeing soldiers, merchants, and politicians. It was only a matter of minutes now.

This *parle* was interrupted by a monk who suddenly appeared and knelt before Francesco, thrusting a letter at him. A message from the Abbot, Fulvio surmised, recognizing the seal. Francesco tore it open, read quickly, and handed it back to the exhausted monk with the force of a bolt. The fellow reeled and had to grab the destrier's withers for support. His actions made the warhorse uneasy and eager for blood. Francesco was oblivious to the little drama that was sure to cost a life. Whatever the message, it held no interest for the time.

After a moment of deadly quiet Francesco said, "Ser Fulvio, I mean to exact a price from Raggiolo if you refuse to deliver Porciano. Do as asked and I'll forget your poor judgment."

"I tell you, Signor, he's not here!"

Francesco glanced at Fulvio and his men, looked as if he would speak, then signaled to his heralds, who wheeled and started back to the army.

෴

RAGGIOLO WAS A pretty town in the western marches of the High Casentino, a cluster of ochre-colored houses on a forested hillside between the abbey and the Romena castle. From a distance, it all resembled one great fortress shimmering pink and gold in the Tuscan sun.

In an hour or less, it would be a pile of useless stones.

"We're going to die; that's the truth of it," said one guard on the town walls to another.

Every man who watched Francesco da Romena mount up and gallop back to the waiting army owned that sentiment.

Then it began.

With the roar of a lion, Francesco pronounced the death sentence.

"Damn you, Fulvio!" Tancredi hissed struggling with the coat of mail he pulled on over his ceremonial robes. He was a man unused to warfare, knew this mail would be nothing against the advancing army. Tancredi's fingers trembled violently as he pulled at the straps though he couldn't be sure which shook more, the ground or his hands. He released an involuntary cry when kestrels suddenly rushed from the sweet chestnut trees and scattered in all directions.

The captain grabbed his arm, shouting, "Make no move against them! Romena's an honorable man. It isn't us he wants! Make a brave face, I tell you! It's not us he wants!"

"D'you know that for certain?" Tancredi shouted over the din of battle preparations. "Can we be so sure?"

The captain had no time to respond, for Romena's foot soldiers crossed the stream and with a deafening shout surged toward Raggiolo.

"Christ in heaven!" Tancredi screamed, falling to his knees as they approached, mindless of the captain's orders to get up and fight. He waited for the sharp, burning stab of a sword to end his life and started muttering bits of prayers, jumbling *Pater Nosters* with *Ave Marias*. Tancredi was surprised to be only kicked out of the way and stepped over as the soldiers made their way to the walls. Opening his eyes, he saw the dull, lifeless face of the captain, felled by a single swipe of a sword across his neck. He rolled to safety and then ran to the abbey churchyard where he crouched behind a tomb and watched what he was unable to prevent.

Raggiolo's defenders were ranged along the wall: a handful of archers, a trebuchet, three score armed men and frightened townsmen wielding pikes, staves, and pitchforks. Their flame-tipped arrows and oil pots, missiles of burning pitch and stones failed to slow the army's advance. When men fell, others stepped in place and they too were replaced when they fell off the walls or were hit by Romena arrows and bolts. When the siege ladders were placed only a dozen of Raggiolo's men were there to push them back on Romena's soldiers.

And then the armored horses came, their approach shaking the foundations. As soon as the knights thundered over the stream and came upon the town, what was left of the defenders fled. That great fool Fulvio was still at the gates, screaming at men to hold fast but his words were lost amidst the victorious shouts of the army falling upon the town. Like a great tide, it surged forward, cutting down Fulvio and everyone in its wake.

Tancredi had seen enough and made for the abbey gate. He was almost there when a cadre of soldiers rounded a corner and saw him.

"Open! Open, I am a friend to Romena! Open!" Tancredi screamed, but his cries for help were lost in the blood that strangled him to death.

✦

WITHIN THE SAFETY of the refectory, the abbey community listened to a scripture reading while they dined and the battle waged outside their walls.

"Fra Timeo, louder if you please, I cannot hear you," Giordano said. He ignored the frightened glances and stares every time a death scream or victorious shout rose above the din, choosing to contemplate a small crust of bread or vegetable floating on the surface of his stew and ignoring the frightened whispers of his flock.

"We cannot give the right of sanctuary to everyone!"

"We'll be slaughtered!"

"Someone should send word to the Bishop of Florence!"

"Not Florence, Arezzo! The Bishop of Arezzo is a vassal of Romena! Romena will listen to him!"

"We must book the dead and bury them, send word to the families."

"The Emperor would never countenance this!"

"Damn Romena to hell!" Giordano cursed softly and threw his spoon on the table.

"Perhaps we should send another emissary to Romena, or go ourselves. Perhaps he never received your letter," Fra Uzzano said.

"Only a week ago I urged reflection and patience in this endeavor," Giordano whispered angrily. "Another week, a month! All that mattered was patience and trust in the Lord! Now see what has happened!"

"Then we should go and stop him. Tell him to call back the army!"

Giordano assembled the brothers for prayer and then, summoning Fra Uzzano, hurried over wheat fields and vineyards to Raggiolo. Upon entering the market square, they exhaled ragged cries of anguish, followed swiftly by prayer.

"Madness!" Giordano gasped. "This is nothing but madness!"

"Gesu save us!" Fra Uzzano whispered. He knelt beside a corpse before him still oozing blood into the dirt.

Keeping his eyes fixed on that trickle of blood, Giordano began a Pater Noster. He tried to ignore a woman's screams from the blacksmith's; tried to block the laughter of men followed by shouts of release; tried not to stare at the bright silk tatters of a once-expensive gown as a young, defiled girl staggered up the lane, followed by drunken soldiers too spent and drunk to inflict more harm; tried not to see the wailing toddler crawling out of a burning house; he averted his eyes from the sight of a small boy being strung up from the well head and his cries for his mother and mercy ignored by laughing soldiers.

"Damn him! Damn them all!" Giordano spat.

"Abbate, our prayers to God—"

"Oh, shut up, you fool! There is no God! No God would condone *this!*"

❧

RAGGIOLO AND ITS castle was in ruins by nightfall. The smoke and fires were visible from as far away as Arezzo. When it was over, Francesco rode in alone, his horse's hooves plodding softly through streets littered with bodies and plunder.

He dismounted at what was left of the market and walked in disbelief through the town. Francesco was an experienced soldier and had seen and done unspeakable acts in the name of war, but nothing as disturbing as what lay before him.

Nothing was whole, not a shop or cottage had been spared. Buildings smoldered, bodies bled in the streets. Francesco saw the shocked stares and heard wails of children as they knelt over mutilated bodies once their parents and knew he was to blame. His anger had done this.

His sin.

"Porciano escaped."

The German commander of the White Company repeated himself when he realized Francesco hadn't heard what he'd repeated twice.

Francesco was preoccupied with a young woman cowering under a hay wain rammed up against the church steps. His efforts to coax her out were futile until he tendered a loaf of fine white, bread called wastel, snatched from a drunken soldier coming out of the ruins of a baker's shop. Francesco held back a wave of nausea when he saw that the woman had been beaten, raped, and miscarried of a child.

Francesco swung round to face the German commander and the soldiers who were sober enough to join rank.

"Call back the army!" he growled. "Immediately! Find the men responsible for this and execute them!"

The commander exhaled an exasperated sigh and said in German, "My lord, what can we do? It's not possible now. It would take hours at least."

"Then the entire army is responsible! I did not give license for this!"

"But—"

"Those are my orders. See to it!"

"Your command was to take the town, stone by stone, to take the castle stone by stone."

"I know what my orders were! Another word and you'll answer for all!"

"It's war plain and simple and the men haven't been paid for weeks. What do you expect?"

"You!" Francesco shouted at a sentry nearby. "The commander is under arrest. Escort him to camp and await further orders."

The remaining soldiers took cautious steps rearward when Francesco stared each one down and hissed, "Does anyone else have anything to say? Well?" A moment then, "Good. I thought as much."

Francesco pivoted and was face to face with a sergeant whose face had gone the color of whey. Their eyes met; the poor sergeant was sure Romena was going to kill him where he stood.

"Find Clifford so we can get out of this miserable place!" Francesco barked at him.

"Edmund Clifford is with the foragers," the sergeant said. "He took some men and went looking for Porciano when they couldn't find him in the castle."

The sergeant mouthed a prayer for salvation when Francesco's face lost its color and the green eyes had hardened to glass.

"A florin to the man who brings me his vitals!" Francesco hissed as he pushed men out of his way and stalked off. No one moved until he was safely out of sight.

∿

EDMUND CLIFFORD WAITED for a reply to the Bishop of Florence's letter. The silence was so complete one could hear conversations at the other end of the siege camp, the barking of dogs scavenging around campfires and the oaths of weary soldiers chasing them off.

Francesco turned the letter over in his hands as if looking for something he might have missed, turned it over again, and sighed.

"Will you send word?" Edmund inquired.

Francesco shot him a glance that warned to keep silent.

"Monsignore, if we send word . . ."

"I ought to send your heart on a salver! Gesu, Edmund! You might have taken better control of the army! I told you to pay every man a *soldo* before we marched to prevent this!"

"With what money, monsignore?"

Francesco frowned. "What happen to the strongbox from Rimini?"

"There was a box?"

"God's Teeth! What happened to the box? I had enough money in it to pay every man for a month."

"It never came. Still, the men did expect their wages, and you said to take the town and castle,"

"And so they took their pay in rape and murder of innocents, those things I expressly forbid time and time again!" Francesco shouted in reply. A moment passed, then more quietly, "Take ease, Edmund. You'll not go the way of the rest. If anyone's to blame, it's me."

Edmund let his massive shoulders relax, knowing his body wouldn't be dangling from a gibbet by morning. He now motioned toward the bishop's letter, repeating his question, "Will you send word?"

"It wouldn't help." Francesco reached across a table cluttered with maps and found the wine flask, emptying it into his goblet and gulping it down, spilling the wine on a map of Tuscany already stained with blood. He looked at Edmund squarely and said, "The bishop has withdrawn his support."

"How? I don't—he made a promise only last week!" Edmund sputtered.

"He doesn't think an ecclesiastical sanction of carnage and destruction a proper means for advancement to the Curia!"

Edmund scratched his head, wondering. "How could he have known?"

"How do you think? Abbate Giordano! There's no other way he could have received news so quickly. Giordano must attend to his political future, what with the imperial abbey of Florence his for the asking. He asked me to withdraw and I did not."

"Signor!"

The shout came from across the camp. There was sudden activity outside, the clank of steel and scuffing of leather, voices rose in shouts, and then a messenger burst through the tent flap. Every man around Francesco grabbed for a sword and relaxed when they saw Romena's colors on the messenger's back.

"Porciano?" Francesco demanded, adding silently *if the angels and saints so will it!* Whatever the news, it wasn't good.

The messenger was nearly dead from exhaustion and Francesco proffered drink himself. "Tell me when you've breath to speak," he said gently. There was no use in frightening the man in his state. Not after today.

"Monsignore," the man spoke at last. "You must come at once. Ortignano . . . they begged me . . . to come and fetch you as quickly as I could . . ."

Francesco didn't stay to hear the rest. He made for the horse park in the clearing by the river. Before the others could prevent him, he rode at a break-neck pace east through the mountainous country of western Tuscany to Gismonda's hunting lodge at Ortignano, guided by the flames of burning buildings lighting the night sky.

The magnificent lodge had been sacked. Nothing was left to salvage. The priceless relics and carpets from the Holy Land, the illuminated books, all gone or destroyed. Furniture had been broken up and lay strewn everywhere.

Stepping over splintered and broken doors and climbing staircases, Francesco wandered the lodge as if under the spell of a powerful herb. The sights before him were surreal, like gazing in highly polished metal—distorted, monstrous, exaggerated. He found nothing whole and found no one alive. Even the animals were slaughtered.

"Gismonda?" Francesco called.

Up a flight of stairs and through a passageway to the bower.

"Gismonda, where are you? Answer me!"

The bodies of her ladies were strewn on the floor with clothing and jewels. A tapestry half-finished had been shredded and the strips now blew in the wind coming through a broken window.

"Gismonda!" Francesco screamed and took another passageway behind a secret door, up to the tower and the bedchamber he shared with Gismonda only that morning.

The door had been forced and Francesco drew his sword as he pushed aside the broken wood, stepping across the threshold to find the bedchamber in a worse state than anything he had seen thus far.

Agnolo Cavalleri was sprawled across the bed. Francesco had never set eyes upon him until now. Gismonda had always called her husband the 'wolfhound,' and he looked just that—long, elegant face, with an even longer nose. His hair was liberally dusted with gray. He had been nothing but an inconvenience to Francesco, who checked for signs of life and finding none, closed the man's eyes.

"Sweet blood of Christ!"

Francesco looked up when he heard Edmund's oath. The men were scrambling forward, obeying whispered commands. He took a step forward only to be blocked by Edmund's lieutenant, held back by a gentle hand on his shoulder.

"What is it?" Francesco demanded.

The whispering was more frantic now and the men were ripping sheets and coverlets off the bed, tossing them at Edmund.

"Edmund! Damn you, let go!"

Francesco stumbled over the broken furniture and pottery, tripped on clothing and bed linens to come around to the other side of the enormous bed.

"Signor, I don't think,"

"Let go of me!"

He pushed aside the soldiers in his way and stumbled on an overturned stool to land at the feet of a body Edmund was trying hard to shroud.

And then he saw her

FRANCESCO HAD NO idea how long he'd been screaming; he was amazed to find himself surrounded by armed men. Porciano's knights, were they? He'd pay them in kind for what happened here! He raised his sword for an attack only to be wrestled to the ground.

"Drink!" Edmund ordered, forcing a cup past Francesco's lips.

He drank, aware of Edmund's presence, of the soreness of his throat, of the chill of the morning. He was in the stable yard. Had he been there all night? The sun was rising behind a heavy fog.

The cup was offered again. The liquid was thick, sweet, and burning, coating his mouth and tongue as it slid down his throat. Francesco grabbed the cup a third time and drank deep, then heaved.

"Come, man! Get your courage back! You've seen worse, done worse!" Edmund murmured.

Francesco staggered up and drew water from the well. He rinsed his mouth and then poured more of it over his head. The biting cold shocked him back to his senses. Sympathetic stares met his quizzical gaze.

"What happened?" Francesco gasped.

"We found survivors. A serving girl hiding in a garderobe, monsignore," one of the captains spoke up.

"Tell me."

The captain's eyes slid in Edmund's direction.

"Damn you! Tell me!" Francesco shouted so that his echo startled birds nesting on the courtyard eves and the rustle of flight broke the silence that followed.

"Ser Agnolo arrived after you'd gone this morning. The girl said he'd seen you riding out,"

"And?"

"He quarreled with your lady."

"Did Agnolo murder her?" Francesco demanded, incredulous.

"No; but he was threatening her, shaking her, when Cavalleri suddenly groaned and fell on the bed."

"Ah, his heart stopped then," said Francesco. "And his wife?"

"It was Porciano's men. They rode up in great numbers. There was no time to escape." The captain paused, looked at Francesco's pallid face, and wanted to go no further.

"You might as well tell me; it isn't hard to guess," Francesco said.

The captain nodded and swallowed hard as if a pebble caught in his throat. He then relayed what was known about the sordid end of Gismonda Cavalleri. Francesco nodded silently when was he done.

"Monsignore?" Edmund queried after a while. He reached up to place a hand on the younger man's shoulder affectionately. "Cecco?" Francesco reeled a bit, still unsteady on his legs. He brushed away Edmund's helping arm. "Porciano's bastards are still within reach," Edmund said. "We can send a party of foragers and return favor for favor."

"No." Francesco stopped Edmund in a voice surprisingly calm and assured. "It's what he wants and I've no mind to ride into a trap." He splashed more water on his face and then leaned against the well head, watching clouds float in the cobalt sky and wondering how anything could still claim the right of beauty on such a day.

"It's best not to let the men see you like this," Edmund murmured.

"Why not say she was just another girl, Edmund, and be done?"

"I . . . Forgive me,"

"There's nothing more to do here save honorable burial of the dead,"

Francesco ordered as he walked away. "When that's done, we'll go to Florence. You, herald!"

"Monsignore?"

"Go ahead of us to Florence to the bishop and remind him that he owes Romena a great deal. He is asked to make good of a promise. He'll understand the meaning of this, or if not, we shall come to terms."

Edmund and the men glanced at one another skeptically, but when Francesco spun about and looked at each, in turn, waiting, they all came to attention and followed.

CHAPTER 2

"MONSIGNORE? MONSIGNORE, IF you would come with me now. The bishop waits."

Francesco looked away from his study of the cloister wall and waved at the young Cistercian monk, beckoning him closer.

"Tell me, if you would. Who wrote that?"

"Pardon, signor?"

"Here," Francesco now traced ancient graffiti slowly with a finger. "Someone wrote, 'Only fools enter this house.' Do you know who put it there?"

He leaned forward, hands still enfolded in yards of brown wadmal. Francesco caught a scent of soap and clean linen as he moved and for the first time in days wished he'd taken the time for a bath and shave, and a change of clothes for this audience.

"Ah!" the monk said, nodding. "Yes, it's quite plain, isn't it? I'm sorry, signor, but I don't know. But here it says, 'The victorious walk away.'"

"After taking knives out of their backs, I imagine."

"Pardon?"

"Nothing important; a little joke."

"A very little one. The bishop waits, signor."

The monk pushed open the bishop's door to the nave of San Miniato al Monte and allowed Francesco entrance.

Francesco paused before going further, letting his eyes grow accustomed to the dimness. He could make out the shapes of a dozen people in the sanctuary, the symmetrical lines of the choir screen and pale rectangles of colored light from the windows. Mists of soothing incense followed the draft from the cloister.

As Francesco headed toward the sanctuary, Edmund materialized from the shadows.

"Are you certain about this?" Edmund whispered.

"I wasn't aware of any choice."

"Cecco, you treat with the devil!"

"It's what I must do. Be at ease, Edmund."

"Then here." Edmund took Francesco's sword from within the folds of his cloak and passed it over.

Francesco smiled and hid the weapon under the cape he wore. Even when treating with a man of God, it was best to go prepared. Even more so with this man.

Gandulfo di Palmieri, bishop of Florence, waited for Francesco at the foot of the sanctuary steps. With him were secretaries and chaplains who made a splendid show as if posing for a fresco or a Byzantine mosaic. Francesco's uncle, Simone Guidi da Battifolle, Simone's eldest boy, Manfredo, and other relations from the Guidi castle of Davidolo, stood behind the rood screen. These kinsmen were shadowy and useless figures in Francesco's life; all had come for one selfish reason or another.

"Holiness," Francesco greeted when he arrived at the sanctuary steps. He sank to his knees and kissed the hem of the bishop's jewel-encrusted cope, then looked up at him with the most engaging of smiles. "How glad I am we have an accord."

"Do we?" the bishop asked, smiling back.

"I would not be here if it were otherwise."

"That much I know."

"Even so, I am glad to be here."

"I'd be impressed if I thought you were in earnest," the bishop sneered.

"I'm pleased to see you, too," Francesco said and was glad when he heard laughter from the spectators. Perhaps this would not be so difficult after all.

"You've had time enough to think. What is your decision, Romena?"

Francesco hesitated and then sat back on his heels. "Holiness, what you ask of me is impossible."

"You seek the episcopacy's assistance and I want a town that will protect my interests in the Casentino. I don't think that's too impossible."

"I cannot give you what I do not have."

"I know for a fact you've got more than you admit. And had you not destroyed your own town of Raggiolo, you'd still have the best vineyards and one of the strongest castles in Tuscany!"

"I had no choice!"

"Don't raise your voice to me. You came to me for help; I did not come to you! Again, I ask: what is your decision?"

"You know it. Why do you dissemble?"

The Bishop struck Francesco across the cheek, the great ruby of his ring cutting flesh. Francesco winced but made no move, not even to wipe the blood he felt trickling down to his chin.

"Think before you speak again, Romena. And don't raise your voice to me!"

"I cannot give what I do not have. I say no. That is my decision."

The Bishop struck him again.

Again, Francesco was immovable. The pain and heat in his face notwithstanding, he focused on the weave of the fabric in the Bishop's cope. Finest silk woven with golden and silver threads, the Roman cross just visible in relief against the ivory ground. He tried not to smile when he recognized the fabric as Romena cloth, manufactured in one of the Florence shops.

"I pray you think harder, Romena," the Bishop said. He grabbed Francesco's chin in his gloved hand and jerked it upwards so that they were eye to eye. He grimaced when his glove of white kid came away with blood, dirt and sweat.

"I'll do nothing until you keep your part of our agreement," Francesco said quietly. "Of all the men here, can you name another as desperate of circumstance or as deserving of your beneficence?"

The bishop was hard put to think of one. Nevertheless, he was not in the mood to give in so easily, especially when every man present expected him to.

"Born of a whore and a sodomite," the bishop hissed. "No, I think not!"

The insult passed unnoticed over Francesco, who spread his hands in supplication. "Bishop Gandulfo, I only ask for what you did promise me months ago. I want what is owed to me. I want what we agreed upon. No man in this church would dispute the legality of our agreement. You swore before these men here—"

"You've come at a bad time." the Bishop sighed and he waited, hoping Francesco would lose his temper and do something stupidly violent, give him a reason to back down on the promises they'd made at this very altar.

Francesco pushed himself to his feet. "Then I shall return tomorrow, and if it is again a bad time for you, I'll come back the next day,"

"You'll not be received."

". . . and the next until you receive me or you've died of old age. I only ask for what is rightfully mine, and that those more fortunate in their present circumstance keep their word and give me the men and arms I need to take what is mine by birth. You understand me. You were once part of my struggle. It is how you bought this episcopacy."

"Liar!"

"Tell me, where did I get the money to pay for the war against my uncle? I can't believe you've forgotten. I may have been a boy, but I remember my mother's persuasive arguments and how willing you were to accommodate her."

"Maybe she was willing to accommodate him!" someone in the shadows spoke up and brought laughter. The Bishop raised his hand for silence.

"If you want a war with me, Romena, you've got one!" he hissed.

"I know of forty noblemen, all struck knights, who would not hesitate a moment to join me in battle against you. I would not hesitate to call upon them."

"If you want a war, Romena—"

"By Christ's holy and blessed wounds, I do not!"

"Say another word and you will be reduced to nothing! I shall tear down every castle and town you have!"

Francesco drew his sword and before anyone could move, he had pressed the blade against the bishop's muscular throat. Just as quickly, four ecclesiastical guards appeared and, in a quick but violent altercation, stopped Edmund from coming to Francesco's aide while they wrestled the sword out of Francesco's hand and almost beat him senseless until the bishop put an end to it.

"You might have murdered me," the bishop sneered, pressing Francesco's chest none too gently with the toe of his purple shoe.

"I'd call it divine justice . . . but you can call it murder."

"Sorry to disappoint you!"

Francesco lay on the pavement for what seemed an inordinate amount of time, watched by twenty pairs of eyes. He finally rose, moving slowly and carefully, struggling to show neither pain nor embarrassment as he pulled himself up to his great height.

"Bishop Gandulfo, you must do what you know in your heart to be right and by oaths sworn to me before this altar and on the holy relics there. Relics my grandfather brought from the Crusades and gave to this church!" Francesco pointed to a golden reliquary on the credence table behind the altar. A jewel-encrusted golden foot of some unknown saint.

The bishop barely glanced at the reliquary and then stared at Francesco. The suffering Christ came to mind. Tears glistened on his lashes and spilled down his cheeks, the bruising and blood starting to disfigure what some people called the most handsome face in Tuscany. That he was in pain was evident; that Francesco chose not to reveal it was infuriating. The Bishop was about the lecture him on vanity and self-importance when he saw Maestro Giotto, the famous painter, sitting off in a corner sketching something in a book. So he was back from Rome, was he? No doubt Francesco da Romena would be the subject of a fresco in the months to come. Christ before Caiaphas or Pilate! Everyone would know who it was. He was already depicted as the Archangel Gabriel in a painting at Santa Trinita. No one truly came out victorious over the Guidi lords of Romena.

"Monsignore?" one of the chaplains whispered, bringing the Bishop out of his thoughts. The chaplain nodded towards Francesco.

"Well?" snapped the Bishop at Francesco.

"I can do nothing more," Francesco said quietly. "I have done your bidding. Please,"

The bishop bowed his head then. Many in the church thought he was praying. He was, in fact, looking at the scuff marks on his new leather shoes and avoiding Francesco's unflinching, uncompromising stare. Finally, he glanced up and nodded almost imperceptibly.

"It is done. But not without a price!" the Bishop whispered, and then aloud declared, "Francesco Guidi da Romena, *te absolvo; Benedictus; in nomine patris, et fili, et spiritu sanctu.* The sins of your father are forgiven. The sins of your mother are forgiven. Your sins are forgiven. We welcome you back to the Holy Mother Church. We offer you in Christ's name absolution and entreat you to receive the Holy Sacrament."

Saying this, the bishop snapped his fingers and his chaplains and acolytes prepared the holy table for Communion watching Francesco carefully as if he would walk away with one of the chalices or patens.

It seemed like centuries, waiting through versicles and canticles, but finally, the moment arrived. For the first time, Francesco received the sacrament of Holy Communion. All his life Francesco had wondered about this holiest of mysteries, the partaking of the consecrated bread, the transubstantiated body of Christ. This bread of heaven should have tasted like the sweetest of cakes. Instead, it was flavorless and stale; the wine was sour and tasted of mildew.

Another parallel to his wretched existence.

He stayed kneeling at the communion rails until the altar had been stripped and the sacrament locked away in an ambry.

Edmund quietly knelt beside him. "Save some prayers for tomorrow, Cecco, you may have need of them," he jested.

"I'm praying for the pain to stop. It hurts to move. Help me to my feet," Francesco admitted, a weak smile turning to a grimace.

"Your man Lorenzo is fretting and thinks you should go to the infirmary. I'm of like mind," Edmund said, offering Francesco an arm to help him up.

"Take me there." He now clutched Edmund's shoulder for support and limped out the nave.

"Anything broke?" Edmund queried when they were in the sunlight.

"My will."

❧

THE PHYSIC TUT-TUTTED and sighed as he washed the scrapes and cuts Francesco received in his audience with the bishop and bade his patient sit still while unguents and poultices were delicately applied and bandages wrapped. His work was made more difficult by the fact his patient wanted to conduct business as usual.

Francesco motioned to his servant Lorenzo, a sweet, moon-faced boy of thirteen, and whispered something in his ear. Lorenzo nodded and returned moments later with a small coffer, which was given to Edmund.

"Your back wages. The Bishop kept his word after all," Francesco said between his teeth as the physic poked and prodded at an open wound with a stylus. "It's mostly for you, but if you would use some of it to buy masses for those who died at Raggiolo and Ortignano. *Gesu!* You'll have to buy masses for me if this physician kills me with his cure!"

"Will you not save even a florin to help your kinsmen?"

It was Simone da Battifolle. Aided by a cane, the old man tottered and weaved as he entered the infirmary. All save Francesco bowed low in deference to the eldest of the Guidi counts.

"What do you want, Uncle?" Francesco asked. It was always better to come to the point with this one.

"Now that your situation looks to improve, we ask that you consider your family. Our Guidi kinsmen require your help against Charles of Calabria. He makes claims upon our bishoprics and towns."

"Do you think I humiliated myself before the bishop to stay a soldier for hire?" Francesco demanded. "You're mistaken."

"We ask only—"

"Charles of Calabria was recalled to Naples by a threat to his birthright. I have it on good authority that he lies with a fever somewhere north of Rome and won't last another month. He is no more a threat to your interests than mine."

Battifolle laughed nervously as he stroked the bombastic crucifix suspended from a gold chain around his neck, hanging like a millstone and just as heavy. He rocked on his heels and waited patiently, for what, no one knew, until the bishop's chaplain mercifully interrupted and whispered to Lorenzo, who in turn conveyed the message to his master. Francesco nodded and excused himself, signing Lorenzo to accompany him and Edmund to wait. The physic sputtered protests as Francesco, using the boy as a crutch, limped out of the infirmary. Francesco made a slow progress to the cloister where a messenger waited.

"You have a letter for me?"

The fellow jumped to his feet. "Francesco Guidi da Romena?"

"The same."

"I come from Gian Maria Guidi da Porciano."

"You've come for nothing because we've nothing to say to one another. Here's for your trouble, take it with my thanks." Francesco tossed him a coin. "God keep you and farewell."

"Wait, signore! My master bids me say thus. He bade me say he is not his father." Francesco turned and waited. "He seeks a kinsman, but mostly a friend."

Francesco's eyes flickered. "Does he mean to betray his father?"

"Make of it what you will."

A smile crossed Francesco's lips and the messenger relaxed, stepping forward as he took a sealed letter from his satchel and handing it to Lorenzo.

"Does he offer his sword?"

"Make of it what you will, signore."

"Does he wish to treat?"

"Again, make of it—"

"—I make of it that my cousin Gian Maria knows how to speak volumes with as few words as possible."

"Yes, monsignore," was all the messenger could say.

"Say the time and place; perhaps I'll be there. If he offers his sword -- that is a matter altogether different."

Francesco gestured abruptly that the audience was over.

"Take him at his word."

The sound of Battifolle's voice didn't surprise Francesco. The old man had followed and listened to the entire conversation. At eighty-six, Battifolle was weary of conflict, but not averse to stirring it up. This odious quality was undoubtedly the reason for his longevity.

"Wouldn't you think it strange? The boy may be Tommaso's man to the teeth," Francesco said after a moment of reflection.

"Gian Maria? Not that one." Battifolle chuckled and then snorted happily. "Any of his brothers, yes, but they're all dead! And for that reason. He's never been influenced by his father. He's never been his father's man. You need him for that reason. What better weapon do you have against Tommaso di Porciano but his son?"

"Still, he's Tommaso's son."

"I'm Tommaso's uncle; he's my nephew, as you are. We're all different and we're all useful in different ways. And now, Nephew, since we've sorted out our family tree, you have to look to those kinsmen who can prove useful."

Francesco studied the dappling shadows moving across the garth and spied a cat silently watching its prey, just close enough to pounce and have the bird for supper. Francesco suddenly felt like that poor bird.

"I'm sure when the time comes you'll want something for your advice. Experience doesn't come cheap," Francesco remarked quietly.

Battifolle scoffed. "I've yet to ask!"

"Haven't you? Your memory is short. Don't worry; you'll be rewarded. I've never yet gone back on my word though it may take some time."

"I never thought!"

"But you made it apparent, Simone."

Battifolle's rage came to a boil, his face turning purple and red in fits. He frothed like an overworked stallion, even snorted his displeasure. What galled him more than Francesco's indifference was his smile. Ever like a Romena, enjoying the discomfort of others!

"I came to champion you and this is how I am repaid!" the old man snapped.

"Good day, Simone. Thank you."

Francesco sat heavily on the parapet. "Get me some wine, Lorenzino?" he asked and when the boy left to do his bidding Francesco leaned against one of the columns and tried to relax.

He wasn't concerned about Battifolle. The old man had never been a threat. Of the Guidi, he was the laziest. Tommaso di Porciano, however, replaced Alessandro as the deadliest, and what man wouldn't be in his enviable position? It had been easy to seize the Romena lands when there was no adult male to hold them. And Tommaso's grasp showed no indication of loosening. Francesco considered his family relations and set each in his mind like chess pieces on a board. None were truly useful; all were dangerous.

It would be a matter altogether different if the son of Tommaso di Porciano indeed offered his sword to Romena.

❧

"SO. WHAT DID Romena say?"

Simone da Battifolle was more interested in the savory roast capon floating in butter sauce on the bishop's trencher than the question presented. The bishop dipped a slice of wastel bread in honey and made a great noise over it. The butter sauce looked like molten gold and its scent was an aphrodisiac. When Battifolle made a move to swipe the trencher with a crust of bread, the Bishop moved it out of reach.

"Tell me. What is your nephew's mind?"

"You should have killed him while you had the chance."

"You forget to whom you speak!"

"The man whose spotty bottom I've kept on ecclesiastical cushions the last thirty years. You forget whom you owe and who owns *you*, Eminence! I've got much to lose if Romena manages to win."

The bishop now turned to the priest at his left, a dour man appearing much older than his sixty-seven years, and whose plain features weren't helped by the wavering candlelight casting devilish patterns on his face.

"You promised there'd be no trouble from him, not after Ortignano," the bishop chided.

Abbate Giordano took the bishop's knife and cut through the pomegranate on his trencher. He pulled the knife out of the fruit and licked the blood-red juice that trickled onto his fingers, then picked at the seeds, one by one. Glancing at Battifolle and then at the bishop, he shrugged. "Eminence, surely you must know by now that young Romena is not his father. Granted, like for like, they are one, but only in the flesh. Francesco has a deadly charm and spirit. We've all seen it. He'll not be swayed easily."

"But he's broken easily. We've all seen how easy that is. Christ's body and blood, the way he carried on about his mistress!" the bishop scoffed.

"Any other man would have found another whore!"

"But we're not dealing with any other man. We're dealing with Romena, Eminence. His strange proclivity for devotion to one woman aside, he is still who he is. Francesco, not Alessandro."

"And what's that supposed to mean?"

"If you a push a man, particularly one like Romena, to the wall. . ."

"We can see that another horrible incident, such as Ortignano, ruins his plans," the bishop replied, and continued stripping meat off the capon until bones glistening with oil and sauce were all that was left. "Besides, I've sent a letter to Tommaso da Porciano. We may be assured of his support."

"What happens if Porciano doesn't agree to our proposals?" Battifolle demanded.

"Porciano? Oh, he's a small fish. We are most concerned with Romena."

"Eminence, this is madness—to deny a man what is rightfully his—"

"Have a care, Giordano. You cannot have lost interest in the imperial abbey so quickly that you must champion the wrong man."

"Francesco da Romena the wrong man?"

The bishop smirked at Giordano and shook his head. The truly devout were such fools. When would they learn that prayer alone never helped? The greatest commandment was 'choose your enemies wisely; never trust your friends.' The bishop knew if Abbate Giordano lived by that creed, he would be sitting in Rome, and not waiting patiently for an abbey as inconsequential as a parish church in the Oltrarno.

And if Francesco da Romena lived by that . . .

The bishop burst into laughter.

&

A COSTLY TAPESTRY from Zeeland had been stretched across the only window in the bedchamber and blocked the last rays of moonlight. The finely woven piece illustrated the life of Parsifal and gave the sanctuary house a little cheer, as did other pedantic touches of comfort used to decorate a room accustomed to austerity. The stone bench carved out of a recess in the wall was covered with velvet pillows. A lute had been tossed there, along with a pair of riding gloves. A table shoved up against the window was draped in a length of mulberry and gold brocaded silk. A helmet, stacks of books, and a statue of The Archangel Saint Michael obscured most of the cloth. Across the room, a narrow bed was made up with plump pillows filled with goose down, linen sheets and a fur-lined coverlet of mulberry and gold wool.

Amid this opulence sat Francesco da Romena, staring at the little polychrome statue of Saint Michael.

Francesco traced the chipped paint of the archangel's tabard, harness and magnificent wings, with a languid finger. They were old friends,

Francesco and the Archangel, and now he considered this companion of a desolate childhood while Lorenzo applied new compresses of comfrey and mint to a wound on his forehead that still oozed blood.

"Did that hurt much?" Lorenzo queried when Francesco flinched and swore softly.

"I don't know what could be worse, the bishop's insult and humiliation of me or a few weeks of discomfort."

"At least you know the wound will be gone in a fortnight. But the bishop?"

Francesco tried to laugh at this, but the pain once again caught him. He clutched the base of the statue so tightly Lorenzo thought it might break and gently eased it from his hand. Francesco had so few friends; it would be a shame to lose this one.

"Begging your pardon, signore, you should have stayed in the infirmary tonight. The brothers have better medicines than I do. This gash looks to be infected already."

"Should I have killed the bishop?" Francesco murmured now.

"Kill the bishop? Ah . . . no. There'd be no end of your trouble. Though you'd have a few new allies, I'm sure."

There came a knock at the door and then three raps in succession; Edmund Clifford came in uninvited. Lorenzo knew that whenever Edmund Clifford was present, Francesco's easygoing humor turned dark. By the look on the disagreeable Englishman's face, it would be another night of solitary brooding for his lord. Another night of drinking alone by the fire. As much as Lorenzo wanted to stay, he knew better than to ask.

"Signor Clifford," Lorenzo greeted with a bow. "I'm just going. I bid you a good night. Oh, and make sure monsignore il conte does not rip off the poultice. As much as he hates the smell it would do him a world of good to put up with the inconvenience."

The door creaked open then closed with a whisper.

Out of the corner of his eye, Francesco saw Edmund's massive hand reach for the flask of wine, the glitter of his ring as it passed.

"Well, Edmund?" Francesco asked, keeping his vigil on Saint Michael, "Do they mean to betray me?"

"Hard to say, Cecco; I saw Battifolle in the bishop's chamber."

"I owe you a florin; you said he'd turn."

"It was a stupid wager, signor. We all knew."

"It doesn't matter. We'll be ready if and when the time comes."

Francesco now traced the serene, painted smile of Saint Michael the Archangel.

He would be ready.

CHAPTER 3

TWELVE KNIGHTS SURROUNDED Francesco and waited for orders. Joining the cadre, Edmund glanced up at the sky and judged it was ten o'clock. They'd been at it since Lauds. He'd fought harder campaigns in Scotland and in less time, but Castello di Romena, with its fourteen great towers, three rings of walls, and massive donjon, still held for Porciano on this, the sixth day of the siege.

Francesco and his men crouched on the northern side of the hill below the first curtain not far from where the assault began. They had advanced this far, but it had taken five hours to gain so little ground.

Someone handed Francesco a flask, but rather than drink, he removed his bascinet and poured water over his already damp head, washing away sweat and blood from his encrusted face and hair. The water made tracks across his bloodied armor, pooling in dents made by soldiers he'd either fought against or killed to get safely to this hill.

The captain of the right wing suddenly burst into laughter and pointed below them: the front lines of Porciano's vanguard lost footing on the hill as they tried to reach Francesco and his captains, sliding down into their own ranks to be skewered on pikes and swords.

"Another hour of this and they'll send their own lines back!" Edmund laughed.

"Why wait?"

Edmund looked up when he heard Francesco's question and saw that he was going for his horse and followed, trying to match his strides. "Francesco, you can't!" Edmund protested. "It's what he wants! It's what he expects!"

"I want an end to this. Now," Francesco said and swung easily into the saddle as if the last five hours, the last six days, had been nothing.

"That penchant you have for recklessness is going to get you killed!" Edmund shouted at him. "It's a fool who would try to take the castle with the odds stacked against him! Not even your father would risk so much!"

Francesco shrugged and put on his bascinet, then turned to his squire. "My great helm," he said and fitted the helmet himself as the squire backed away.

"Francesco, damn you! Francesco, you can't do this— Shit!"

Couching low, Francesco waited as men joined him and when they were ready he drew his sword and led the charge. Edmund continued to swear a litany and shouted at his men to follow.

The Romena vanguard thundered back into hell, smashing through Porciano's front lines and mowing down men and horses. Only a fool would have charged down that hill into the hellish terrain—gullies, shrubbery, and bracken—and expected to live. They pushed further into the lines, Francesco at the lead. Men were skewered with sword and pole-axe as easily as if they were straw-filled mannequins. It was hard to tell body from body; the field was mired in slimy blood, bodies sprawled in every imaginable pose and those impossible and inconceivable in life.

Martial lessons learned in childhood became automatic for Francesco. He answered every challenge with a thrust in the gorget, a stab under the arm, a clean swipe with the battle-ax across the head. He had no time to consider that an iron helmet could be breached as easily as an apple's skin and its ripe fruit once containing a soul, a life, was nothing more than bloody tissue.

Francesco charged blindly, was heedless of the man he attacked next though it might have been one of his own. All sensation in his sword arm had gone. His survival demanded more, however, and he unhooked a deadly mace, a "holy water sprinkler," from his belt and applied it to a knight's skull. What an hour before had been effortless now took every sinew in his body. It was becoming more difficult to breathe; his sight was blurred by bloody sweat stinging his eyes and dripping down into his helmet; he felt in danger of strangling. Within the restricted space of the great helm, Francesco's labored attempts at taking breaths sounded like the growling of a wild beast inside a cage.

The lines fell back, but not far enough. He signaled to his captains and with a wave of an arm and a hand movement they understood. Better to push Porciano around the curtain and out into the open, rather than back into the castle.

The advance of the Romena vanguard, however, had thrown Porciano's left and right wings into confusion. For most of this campaign they'd striven to join their van and overwhelm Romena. Now Porciano's trumpets sounded retreat and the army fell even further back and at last gave ground.

"Come with me!" Edmund shouted at his wing. With swords raised and shouting Romena's *raison d'être*, "Honor above all" and "*à Romena!*" they pressed through a wall of bodies to reach Francesco, who was still mounted and rallying his men to hold their lines.

Edmund's left wing was now less than a half-mile from the Romena vanguard. Another assault as easy as this and they would join, attack Porciano together in one monstrous force, and end the campaign. He praised God when he heard the unmistakable roar of reserves committed to this last stand.

But they were the bishop of Florence and Battifolle's men and they were attacking the Romena vanguard and heading straight for Francesco.

"Francesco! Behind you!" Edmund shouted.

Francesco wheeled about to see Battifolle's archers draw and shoot into his vanguard. The Romena lines began to waver and then disintegrate as shouts of betrayal rose among the men. Any man left on the field wearing his colors would be slaughtered. He gave his destrier its lead through a body of knights only to see a cadre of the bishop's men charging to meet him. Swinging to the west, he met a wave of knights coming down fast and hard. Behind him, Battifolle's soldiers were closing in. Francesco jerked hard on the reins and dug in his spurs. The destrier screamed and rose up on hindquarters, flailing at the air. It was a gamble worth the risk of being thrown; there was just enough room to escape. No one was foolish enough to approach a destrier full of blood lust.

"Fall back! Retreat!" Francesco screamed at his men. "Fall back! Save yourselves!"

A rout was imminent. Francesco dug rowels into the lathered sides of his destrier and followed after he was certain that what was left of his army and captains were out of Battifolle's reach.

They were pursued onto a bridge fording the Arno. The weight of armed men and horses sent the bridge crashing into the turbulent water. Francesco's destrier went down with it and sent him spiraling deep into the ice-quartered river. The screams of dying men and those trying to swim away from Porciano's archers rushed into his ears and exploded when he resurfaced, heaving for air.

Francesco struggled against the current, spared drowning with his men by his uncommon height and strength of body. He found his mount and clung to the saddle until he was safely ashore, never once looking at the bodies littering the water like so many leaves. He led a band of survivors over narrow footpaths obscured by bracken and overgrowth, over hillocks, and into woods wet with rain. The seemingly endless flight halted at a parish chantry, the Pieve di Romena.

Francesco was the first to dismount as the chantry door opened and a frightened priest peeked out. "Padre Angelico?" Francesco greeted. "I am Francesco Guidi da Romena. My men and I seek sanctuary."

Eyeing Francesco and his party suspiciously, the priest Angelico opened the door just wide enough to see for himself. He recognized the silver falcon enchained on the tabard of one of the knights and then opened the door wider. Once they were all inside, one of the men threw the bolt.

"The doors must stay open for any who wish to enter," the priest insisted. "The Guidi counts of Romena would never allow such action! If you are who you say you are, signor—"

"I am the conte di Romena!" Francesco hissed.

The priest took a step backward and gulped down his objection, staring at this shivering creature, soaked to the skin and covered in blood and filth.

Francesco wiped his face to make himself recognizable and added more softly, "Truly. I am Francesco Guidi da Romena. I have no desire to be killed in my sleep tonight. Let the doors stay locked. At least until nightfall."

The doors of the chantry remained bolted.

Having placated the nervous priest with the gift of a ring, Francesco addressed his exhausted men. "Find places to sleep; then decide among you who will take the first watch. We'll leave at compline."

At six in the evening, someone pounded on the doors.

"I beg of you, monsignore, no bloodshed!" Angelico implored.

"I'll not be the first to draw," Francesco vowed. "I cannot speak for those outside."

The pounding subsided momentarily and then a man shouted, calling Francesco by a pet name.

"Open the door; Edmund Clifford is outside," Francesco commanded, scrambling to his feet. His sword was ready, nevertheless.

Outside, Edmund and five men who had survived the rout leaned against the doors, gasping for breath and shivering with cold. Edmund turned sharply when a golden light shone through the gap at the bottom of the door.

"If you're Clifford as you say, then what is the name of ser Francesco's hound?" one of Francesco's men shouted out.

"Which damned dog? Open, damn you! Romena knows me! I'm Clifford of York!" Edmund growled back.

Francesco nodded and the door was opened just wide enough to allow sanctuary to Edmund and his men. They rushed inside and collapsed at the font.

"God's life, you're whole!" Edmund swore when he looked up and saw Francesco above him. He rose stiffly and embraced the other man.

"And you. How many dead?"

"No one has booked the dead. Porciano's taken the castle," Edmund said. "He's sent a man to Poppi. Can't go there."

"What of Battifolle's men?"

"Scattered like leaves they did! We gave them a good chase, though." Edmund took the water Francesco offered and drank, then glanced round the nave as if looking for someone in particular. He said low, "If ever a man deserved to burn in Hell,"

"Just as you say. Simone da Battifolle blows where a favorable wind takes him. Eventually, he'll pay for his travels, as will Bishop Gandulfo."

Edmund wiped the sweat from his face and looked up at Francesco, as concerned as a father for his son. They were almost of a height though Edmund still had to incline his head to face the younger man. "Porciano doesn't have the advantage of time," he said. "He can't last forever."

"But can I?"

The Compline bell faded in the wind by the time the men settled down and fell to sleep. Francesco and Edmund were stretched out on the floor of the nave, side by side, with swords in hand like two funerary monuments. They were awake while the others snored. Once in a while, Francesco would exhale a sigh, then Edmund, their breath making clouds midst the candle and incense smoke.

"For king, country, and the best whores in London," Edmund muttered, and as he hoped, Francesco laughed.

"You remember that! It wasn't so long ago, meeting up in that brothel."

"I thought you were mad, Cecco. Here was a boy of sixteen at most, selling yourself as a man of arms."

"You agreed to my price, didn't you?"

"Only because you proved yourself against my best knight—and I wasn't about to disappoint you. You're a fine soldier when all's said and done."

Francesco turned to look at Edmund. "Yet here we are, Edmund. I've lost Gismonda, my lands, my title. What kinsmen I have left are traitors." He turned away and pulled his violet cloak tighter, thumping the habergeon he used for a pillow to make it more comfortable.

A flickering above the sanctuary lamp caught Francesco's attention. A moth hovered above the flame in its ruby glass. Shadows stretched and fell across the faces of the Christ in glory and His heavenly host watching from above the altar. The dancing light made them obscene, if not frightening. Francesco looked away. He half-expected the family ghosts to materialize like the morning mists on the Arno River, kinsmen come to flesh and bone from gray vapor. He imagined his father standing in the shadows behind one of the chevron-latticed pillars near the sanctuary screen.

". . . Bad luck always did follow you about, Cecco." Alessandro murmured, almost in his ear. "First, your wife dying in childbirth, the baby, and the business with your uncle and the Bishop, then that awful mess at Ortignano with your mistress . . ."

Francesco sat up and nervously looked around, searching.

"Something the matter?" Edmund asked.

Francesco reached out and patted Edmund's face, felt his brow, nose and mouth. "What are you doing?" Edmund laughed.

"I thought I heard something about bad luck and Gismonda."

"It was nothing important. Just thinking aloud."

Francesco settled down for only a moment. He was sitting up again, reaching for a votive candle on the shelf above them. The candle was held to Edmund's sleeping face. "Are you awake?" Francesco asked.

Edmund grunted and opened his eyes. "I am now. Hey now, move the light before you burn someone! Here I was just getting to sleep," he grumbled.

"No, unkind is taking a girl; unfair is cheating at dice."

"What is it?" Edmund yawned.

"You ought to have stayed in London,"

"I had nothing there worth keeping, truth be told."

"The girl and the dice game, if memory serves."

"I was attainted for treason and disowned by my father. You were there. You saw."

"I owe you much. Ask anything of me, Edmund; it is yours," Francesco whispered.

"I have my life; it is enough. You've given me what I thought I lost."

"I'll give you Focognaio."

"Truly? Cecco, it's a castle. I'd as lief take a horse, some armor,"

"And where would you put the horse and armor?"

"It's just—has it a garrison?"

"Sixty men, last I heard, and all sworn to Romena. More will pledge their swords once you're known to the country."

"Are you sure?" he dared to ask.

"Never surer."

৵

BY MIDNIGHT IT was safe to leave. Once the men were scattered in all directions, Francesco, Edmund and what was left of Francesco's household guard rode out of Tuscany into more favorable country, the Romagna, to his mother's castle of Benchiaro in the Senio Valley east of Florence.

A lone sentry heard their approach and looked out over the parapet of the keep. "Who approaches Benchiaro?" he shouted, waving a torch in order to see how large a host it might be.

"Francesco Guidi di Alessandro, conte di Romena! Open for your lord!" Edmund called back.

The sentry hedged, watching the last of the riders join with the front line. "Francesco is dead the last I heard," the sentry answered. "Else he's in England and that's as good as dead. Be off!" he ordered and would have turned his back if Francesco hadn't approached the spot of wavering torchlight and threw back his hood.

"Let down the drawbridge, whoreson! Don't make me wait a moment longer!" Francesco demanded. He did have to wait, though, for Benchiaro had fewer than twenty men in its garrison.

"The moat is dry," Edmund said as he walked his horse to the edge and threw a coin down, hearing the ping of metal on stone, rather than a splash. "We could use those big stones over there to reach the bridge and then hack the damn thing to pieces."

Francesco glanced over to where Edmund pointed and counted a dozen stones cut in perfect squares and then at the crumbling walls. They were for repairs to the outer curtain, which showed gaping holes towards the parapets where missiles reached their target not long ago, judging by the damage. He was ready to agree to Edmund's idea of laying siege when the sentry reappeared and waved the torch. The creak and groan of gears seldom used echoed now through the valley, followed by the clatter of horses as the Romena party rode over the moat and up into the castle.

Nothing had changed, not the gargoyles keeping watch from the crenellations, nor the reproachful stares of saints and ancient ancestors carved into the sandstone parapets. Like the curtain, repairs had stopped and some of them Francesco remembered from his boyhood. An oiled rag hung where the rose window should have been on the eastern side of the chapel, a ladder propped against the wall. No one had climbed it for months, perhaps years. Beneath it more piles of cut stone and buckets of mortar sat untouched. A mason's tools lay on a bench. The once-fine instruments were covered in moss and dirt.

A light flickered from window to window, passing through the many rooms and galleries of the donjon. The great doors creaked open and the steward of the castle, Drogo, peered out with a cresset lamp, staring at the black horizon. His wizened face creased into a broad smile when Francesco galloped into the courtyard.

"Signore! Thanks be to God!" he cried as Francesco slid out of the saddle. He bobbed over Francesco's outstretched hand and kissed it.

"How is my mother?" Francesco asked, glancing about the empty yard.

"As best can be spoken of. The humors come and go, monsignore."

Francesco nodded in understanding, clapping Drogo's gnarled, bent shoulder affectionately. "We can only hope for the best."

"Even that is more than we should hope for!" the old man whispered to himself.

Women's voices, shrill, hysterical, rose and fell and one in particular, louder and more frightening, caught their attention as they entered the donjon's great hall. "I suppose it won't do any good to hide there tonight!" Francesco jested, cocking his head in the direction of the musician's gallery above them.

Drogo shook his head, remembering how he found the child Francesco cowering there in dark shadows, sobbing miserably. It had been Francesco's fifth birthday and there was nothing to eat. There were no cloaks or furs to keep him warm, nor boots for his feet. Francesco had wet himself and in his shame, hid from his mother and the cruel, abusive, servants. Now the young master is home, Drogo thought, and there is no use in brooding over past times. Even so, he crossed himself and muttered a prayer, trying to dispel the unhappy, unpleasant memories. When he looked up, Francesco was smiling down at him, tears in his eyes.

"The past doesn't need our prayers, Drogo!" he whispered.

❧

AS SOON AS Albera da Susiana heard her son Francesco's low, pleasant voice she squeezed her flaccid body into her bridal gown and donned what was left of her jewelry—a wedding band and a cross—and pinched some color into her cheeks. No matter that the seams of her gown strained to the point of bursting, or that her gilt beauty was tarnished by premature age. Standing in the harsh light of the musician's gallery, she looked like the aging whores who glanced into their mirrors and saw youth while others saw monstrosities.

"Alessandro!" she cried happily at the sight of Francesco. "You've come back! I knew you were still alive!"

Albera's brilliant green eyes clouded when Francesco did not respond. She took cautious steps down the staircase to meet him halfway, tossing her head seductively to the left and then to the right in a slow, rhythmic motion with each step, waiting. A smile parted her lips and she ran the tip of her tongue over them, tasting her own rouge. Never once did she take her eyes from Francesco. She started to giggle and ran an exquisitely beautiful hand, the only evidence left of her youth, across her breasts as if inviting exploration.

Then she pounced. The force of the assault hurled Francesco and his men down the stairs, one on top of the other. There was a scramble for Francesco's dagger, torn from his belt in the struggle to gain control of Albera.

"You foul, loathsome, creature! You bastard!" Albera spat at her son. "You didn't think I'd hear about the boys, the little girls, the disgusting behavior? You didn't know I had you followed, did you? Don't stay here if you're not going to mend your ways! Go back to Florence, to your brothels and pimps, your whores!"

"Albera!" Francesco shouted. "I'm your son! I am Francesco. Not Alessandro."

Albera spat again and was ready for a second attack when the servants surrounded her, more for Francesco's protection than anything. He smiled at them and nodded, continuing. "Think back. Think hard on the days after discovering you were with child. When my father Alessandro returned from France, you promised not to cause trouble, but you did. You incited his sons to rise against him. His grown sons! My brothers! You made Alessandro execute them, Mother, to make room for your son. For me. He had his boys killed so that nothing would stand in your way. But you didn't think about Porciano and what he was up to. You didn't think about the pig farmer. See what your anger has done! You've made it possible for him to take everything because you wouldn't listen to your advisors, or even me. Someone will have to pay. Someone always has to pay. Should it be me, or should it be you?"

Albera seemed to grasp this argument and nodded.

"If you only knew, Francesco," she said.

"But I don't. And that's why I'm here. I've come for answers and your help. I need your help to end this war. I'm tired of it. I want my legacy and you can help me get it."

"You would never understand."

"We'll talk in the morning. For now, you must get sleep. Tomorrow we'll start all over," Francesco said. "Go now. Say your prayers and then off to bed."

Albera offered a weak smile and then nodded her agreement. She took the arm of a handmaiden and quietly retired.

The men relaxed as soon as she was gone and Francesco nodded and waved them off, whispering thanks. Drogo now approached Francesco timidly. "Will you stay the night, monsignore?"

Francesco suddenly realized how tired he was and sat on the courtyard steps, raking his hands over a day-old beard. "I've nowhere else to go," he yawned. "Moreover, I've got men after me . . ."

"Not again,"

"No more than usual, Drogo," Edmund said.

"Oh, well then, shall I send for men from the village?"

"Yes, Drogo," Francesco yawned. "A *soldo* each if they will come."

Drogo bobbed his head. "I can get at least ten men. Now I'll see that your rooms are prepared, and send supper."

"Thank you. Is there any wine?"

"I'll check the cellar, Monsignore. Signor . . . if you will pardon my saying so, I didn't think you knew about that awful business at Castello di Romena. It was before you were born, you see, and no one spoke of it,"

Francesco sighed. "There isn't much I don't know about my mother, and most of it, I wish I didn't."

"God keep you, monsignore. God keep you."

"Well," Francesco said to Edmund when the old man shuffled off, "it's always good to be home.

ॐ

THE FACES CAME to Francesco, appeared just as night faded into day, that enigmatic, peculiar hour before dawn when things familiar and comfortable during the day took on horrifying aspects in his mind.

The faces belonged to two young men. One had dark eyes and hair, his face handsome, haughty, and careworn; the other youth was circumspect, with light eyes and fair hair, a youth Francesco thought was himself, but a youth kind, gentle, and welcoming. In life, Francesco had never known them; but he knew they were his dead brothers.

And then the faces were replaced by vivid dreams. Dreams of soldiers armed to the teeth; of great warhorses shaking the ground as they stormed the village; of the army that plundered, took away or destroyed almost everything Francesco had known. The cries of mothers and children dissolved into the howling of the wind on the open sea and Francesco found himself tossed about in stormy water, traveling into the unknown.

Now the horrors of the battlefield encroached on the sanctuary within the bed curtains and Francesco was caught in the thick of it, beaten to the ground by men with swords and pikes. He cried out as he had on so many mornings, waking the servants who had grown accustomed to the night terrors and now scrambled to find something to ease the beating of Francesco's heart, to calm his nerves.

Francesco lay quietly until the terror subsided and he could relax. Turning to the left, he saw the portraits of his dead wife on the bedside table. Francesco picked up the diptych. The central figures of Mary Magdalene and the Virgin were modeled after Caterina. No one had bothered removing her personal effects, and here it was a year almost to the day. Easing back on the pillows, Francesco contemplated his pretty wife's face.

Their marriage had been a political necessity borne of Francesco's desperation to fund his war and muster support. Caterina Malatesta was a daughter of the tyrant of Rimini and brought a marriage portion that made life more than comfortable for Francesco after years of exile and penury.

It was pleasant enough, his two years of marriage. Francesco and Caterina understood the need for their marriage and each other's need for something else. For Francesco, it had been Gismonda; for Caterina, to be professed in holy orders. Caterina allowed Francesco the freedom to sleep with Gismonda whenever it pleased him, and in return, he gave her a magnificent chantry in which to spend her days. Vocation notwithstanding, Caterina took her marriage vows just as seriously and gave Francesco an heir.

Her death in childbirth had been a shock. True, women died every day, but Francesco thought death would never touch his sweet, gentle wife or their infant son. Francesco stopped taking the rising of the sun for granted and waited for his own end. Yet here he was. It was as if God was whispering every morning, *not today*.

Francesco conjured Gismonda beside him to dispel the more unpleasant of his ghosts, tasting her kisses and marveling at the smile that always greeted him upon waking, feeling her exciting body beneath his . . .

"God damn you, Alessandro!" Albera screamed. "You've left me at the mercy of your family! Damn you! Damn you!"

Now there was wailing. Animal-like growls and grunts as Albera paced and knocked over furniture and sent servants from mattresses and into the passageway. Francesco cursed his mother and pulled the blankets over his head to muffle her ranting. Edmund found him still cowering in bed hours after the Lauds bell.

"Are you all right?" he asked, trying not to smirk.

Francesco tossed the blankets off and glared at his friend.

"It's time to talk to your lady mother."

࿇

IT WAS ONCE the greatest castle in the Romagna, a fine donjon with six great square towers and a massive round tower jutting out of a rocky outcropping that faced the Senio Valley. The castle protected the Susiana lands and towns in the region and was a beacon for travelers en route to Florence from the east. Today, the fortress of Benchiaro was as pathetic as the ruins of the Forum in Rome, as haunting as the Acropolis in Greece.

The galleries Francesco passed through were barren and filthy. One of the servants had taken fair linen from the Lady Chapel and hung it on a northern wall for decoration so that the embroidered silk crosses were stained by water and mildew. A pottery ewer with a broken spout was filled with flowers and placed in a dirty basin on a credence table, also taken from the chapel, for everything, from English oak tables to Turkish carpets, had been sold at one time or another. The Romena wealth had been squandered on Albera's quarrel with Tommaso di Porciano and the rest of the Guidi family.

The master carver was pissing against a wall in the stairwell and barely acknowledged Francesco as he passed by. Up a second flight of stairs littered by food and offal a couple in the throes of copulation took no notice of Francesco, who ignored them and continued his way through the donjon, past his nursery and over a wooden bridge to the southern tower where Albera kept apartments.

Splinters fell from the rotten wood of the door when Francesco knocked. His raps echoed hollow and it was some time before the latch came up and a girl appeared.

"What do you want?" she asked rudely, raking him up and down with her eyes. "I'll tell you what I told the others. Madonna cannot pay today. Come back tomorrow."

"Pay what? I am Francesco."

"Pah! He's dead. Killed in the Casentino."

Then I'm a ghost. Let me in. I'm here to see the contessa."

"That's as you say. Go."

Francesco shoved the toe of his boot against the door. "I'm not going anywhere, girl. Tell your mistress Francesco has arrived."

She hesitated only a moment and then slammed the door. Francesco raised a fist to pound again when the door was wrenched open and he nearly struck the woman now staring up at him, pulling his hand back when she gasped.

"Monsignore, you will forgive us. We didn't have word."

"Where is the contessa Albera?"

The woman pointed her chin behind them to a bed raised up on chests. The moth-eaten curtains were tied back for the day and there in the midst of a bed cluttered by clothing, caps and veils was the contessa, rocking against the bolster and humming a cradle song as the headboard slammed against the wall, the jars and bottles, the coffers of trinkets clattering and keeping time. Cradled in her arms was a pillow swaddled in an expensive cloak, a cap balanced on its edge. Albera unloosed a withered breast from her chemise and pressed it into the pillow.

"Here's your supper, *mio principe, mio Francesco*," she crooned. When the pillow would not suck, she began to pound on and twist it until the goose feathers escaped from the ticking and flew about the room.

"Will you betray me as did your father, *il conte mio?* You hold no sway while I still breathe!" she shouted at the pillow. Albera now began to whimper and then growl as she pressed her thumbs into the ruined pillow. "No good, no good! He won't die!" This was followed by hysterical laughter. Gone were the authority and regal manner, the coolness in the face of adversity.

"Mother," Francesco said.

She pointed at him and hissed, "*He* wants a beating! *He* doesn't know how to behave! Take him to the stables! Let him sleep with the rats and dogs up in the loft! Or lock him in the cellar!"

"How long has she been this way?" Francesco demanded of the serving woman.

"Weeks, days," was the tired reply.

He threw her a look and approached the bed.

"Mother, I'm home," Francesco told Albera.

"What do you want, boy?" Albera growled.

"At least you know who I am. There is much we have to discuss."

Albera turned and stared vacantly as if seeing through him into the next room. It was some time before she responded to his gentle calls and she spat violently.

Francesco merely wiped his face. Turning to the servants, he said. "Good ladies, if you wouldn't mind?" He gestured to the door.

As soon as the door closed and the bolt was thrown, Albera threw herself into Francesco's arms. "I've missed you, Alessandro! When I heard you were through with the Salvemini whore I knew my prayers have been answered. Come to bed, Alessio; one son isn't good enough, not the one we have. I can give you more—"

"I'm not Alessandro," Francesco said as he gently pushed her away and sat her in the only chair in the room. "I'm here to talk about my future, what's left of my inheritance, and what you can give me."

"No!" Albera said. "How many times must I tell you? There will be no marriage for the boy! He will not marry Malatesta's brat!"

"What is the boy?" Francesco asked. "He is nothing. He is without land, holds a meaningless title, has no income save the benefice of friends. He needs the bastard daughter of a prince because she has a bit of land and property. Her dowry is handsome. One can't argue with that."

"The girl's a whore!"

"Caterina was my wife, Mother. She was my contessa."

"Was? Then Malatesta heeded my warnings. The marriage was prevented."

"No; she died a twelvemonth past giving birth to my son, who is also dead."

"Death was better for her!" Albera chuckled to herself, and then after a moment, "How you stare!"

"There's not a man in Tuscany who does not admire you," he whispered. It was the truth, for her exquisite loveliness shone through the madness at times, as it did now.

"I was the acclaimed beauty of Tuscany," Albera sighed. "Even when men heard the stories, they still came to my father's house or stood under my bedchamber window to win a glance or favor. Even when they heard the stories." She stopped and looked at Francesco. "The Holy Roman Emperor is my kinsman, you know."

"I know."

"So many gentlemen came to my bedchamber window, even though the stories…"

"I know what was said and I heard the stories. I have no interest in them," he replied. "I'm going to Florence, Mother. I'm going to take charge of my father's castles and lands, his wool and silk trading companies. But I will need your help." He paused, listening to her steady breathing. She turned suddenly and seized his hand. Albera was unexpectedly radiant at the sight of her only child. Francesco took the opportunity lent him and drew close. "Will you help me?"

"What may I give you, Francesco?"

Hearing this, Francesco breathed easier. "I need your garrisons," he said. "I need what's left of the men and arms you have at your disposal—no, I know that look—don't pretend not to understand, Mother. You still have at least a hundred men." Francesco now pulled a document from his sleeve. "I've asked the Peruzzi to draw up a contract memorializing our agreement today so that all terms are judged to be fair. Here is the contract."

She took it in her hands and dropped it on the floor. He was undaunted and forced it into her lap. Albera was staring at nothing in particular when her hands closed around the contract and her fingers ran over the wax seal.

"Ask, ask, ask! That's all you seem to do!" Albera snapped. "You don't care about my worries and problems. You were always a troublesome child!"

"I had a troublesome childhood if you remember."

"Poor you! Whining and mewling about your troubles. Just like your father!"

"There's a difference between us. I'm alive and he isn't. I can restore you to honor. I can regain our fortune if you would just listen to me and do as I ask," Francesco said with growing impatience.

Albera picked up the contract, glanced at it, then crumpled it into a ball before throwing it back onto the floor. "Contracts are unnecessary between mothers and sons. In exchange for my garrison, I want fifteen hundred florins and the castle of Montefiore Conca. I cannot live here another day. I cannot bear it! I want to go home to Faenza. You have my terms."

"They are accepted. I'll have your clerk draw up the contract. We can sign it this evening."

"You have what you want; go." As Francesco bowed and turned to leave, Albera said, "You won't return from this venture alive, Francesco. You cannot win. I've tried, and see where it's put me! We'll say our farewells now, for you'll die in your attempt."

She began to laugh and weep intermittently with her keening, howling and shrieks following Francesco as he went swiftly in search of Edmund and the men, pretending that it didn't bother him, that this was just another day for the Romena.

❧

"PRAISE BE THE saints, all's quiet again."

The pair of watchmen on the battlements nodded in agreement as their brother in arms arrived just as the midnight bell rang.

"How are you this night, Piero?" asked a fellow called Matteo.

Piero shrugged and opened a parcel of food on the parapet, dividing bread, cheese, meat and eggs equally between them. "Well enough; better than some," he said. "I took this from the pantry when the cook wasn't around. They're still up. Drinking and celebrating."

"Who?" asked the third watchman, Marco.

"Signor Francesco and his English friend," Piero answered. "The contessa has agreed to give him her knights to fight Porciano."

"We're going to war? God be praised!" Marco exclaimed. "I hope we go to the Holy Land and kill infidels. There's money in that."

"I doubt it. The young count's been to Jerusalem," Matteo said. "Much good did his prayers do. The real fight is with his uncle and the rest of his Guidi kinsmen. Soon he'll have enough money and men to take what's his."

"With the young count home, we won't have to steal our food," Marco added.

"Perhaps now we'll see our wages, and things will improve. It couldn't get any worse," Piero said hopefully.

"Don't count on that!" Marco coughed and spat out the moldy bread he almost swallowed. He started to throw the rest of the food over the parapet and stopped when he saw a woman coming up the stairs. "God give you peace, sweetheart!" he greeted, thinking it was one of the servants. "Come to keep me warm tonight—Donna Albera! Pardon!"

The men braced themselves for a scolding and were relieved when she merely skipped by them, humming a tune and taking sips from the goblet in her hands.

"Is everything well with you, madonna?" Piero queried, following as she danced closer to the wall. "Sweet Gesu! Come down!"

Albera was now tiptoeing on the parapet, skipping lightly on the stones one moment, down on the pavement the next. She balanced the goblet as she danced, never spilling a drop.

"He didn't think I knew about the little boys or the whores! He didn't think I knew about the little Salvemini girl! She was old enough to be his daughter! It's too late now—everyone knows! Alessandro, Alessandro! You're a fool and a bastard! You didn't think I'd find out, did you? That's what money is for. To pay for spies! Not to lose at dice, or give to whores, or to keep stable boys quiet!"

"Madonna, you should come away from there," Matteo called.

"And what have you left me but a boy that can't win battles! He's as pretty and gentle as a girl and when did a girl ever win a battle but by spreading her legs? Hah! Maybe he's knelt down or bent over enough to make it worth his while. He should have been the priest, not his uncle Tommaso! No good, no good, he won't die!"

"Come away, I beg of you," Piero insisted and motioned to the others to come with him. They tried to surround her, but Albera began a frenetic dance, spun faster, closer to the edge. Her robes caught on one of the cornerstones and she stopped suddenly to free herself. Matteo and Piero were at her side but too late. When she tugged at her robes she stumbled and fell. She was strangely quiet as she hurled to the ground.

જ

"SHE LOOKED PEACEFUL, you said?"

Matteo barely nodded in response to the question. Francesco, Piero, Matteo and Marco stood at the place where Albera fell to her death and stared at the muddy patch of blood marking where her body had lain.

Francesco put down the cresset lamp he held and stooped to pick up his mother's cross lying on the ground. He studied it for a moment, turning it over in the light so that the rubies and sapphires at the points and intersection shot sparks of color. He gave it to an amazed Piero.

"That's your mother's!" Piero sputtered.

"I don't want it. It's worth three florins. One for each of you." Francesco looked each man in the eye.

"It was an accident. Truly, it was," Matteo said. "You don't need to buy our silence."

"I know, but what man in the Romagna would believe the truth? Much is whispered about my mother. All of it unkind."

The men nodded silently.

Francesco turned and paused as the cart carrying his mother's body lumbered out of the courtyard. He hesitated, and then spun about to face the men. "You're absolutely certain she stumbled and fell?" he asked.

Piero and Matteo glanced at one another. "Signor, her dress caught on the stone, up there, you see, and she tried to free herself," Piero said, pointing to the torn fabric wedged between the stones.

"She didn't throw herself?"

"No, Signor!"

"Remember, one florin each," said Francesco as he walked out of the courtyard.

On his way to his chamber, he crossed paths with Edmund, who held up a letter. "This came from Florence."

"We'll talk in the morning," Francesco murmured.

"I paid the priest two florins to have masses said," Edmund added. "They will bury her in the churchyard tomorrow evening."

"Thank you. The letter?"

Edmund handed Francesco the letter and looked crestfallen when he merely tucked it into the pocket of his overgown and said good night.

Francesco locked the bedchamber door and sat on the window seat, staring at the letter for some time. He finally broke the seal and unfolded the letter carefully, as if something might leap out at him, and then smiled when he read the message from Gian Maria di Porciano. When times were the darkest it always surprised him when a ray of hope shone through the clouds

❧

HE WOKE IN the best of moods, the first in many weeks. Francesco sought out Benchiaro's chaplain and heard mass and received the sacraments alone. The ruined chapel was a comfortable place and the chaplain seemed awed by his presence, for it had been years since he'd administered the rites to any of God's children, let alone the infamous Conte di Romena.

"When I come into my own I'll send carpenters and masons to repair this chapel. A glazier to put in a proper stained-glass window," Francesco said as he watched the chaplain clear away the vessels and elements.

"The Lord bless you for your charity, monsignore," the chaplain said when Francesco offered a florin.

"Not charity, but an obligation. I'm going to meet my cousin Gian Maria in Prataglia and with any luck, we shall have an accord that will bring this war to an end. Your blessing, then?"

Francesco knelt and felt the chaplain's cool smooth fingers as the sign of the cross was traced on his brow and the words were spoken. As he rose he was met by the three watchmen. They bowed as one and knelt, drawing swords from under their cloaks, placing the weapons at Francesco's feet.

"Monsignore, we did as you commanded," Marco began. "Three florins between us. We have new armor, new swords, new cloaks."

Piero took some coins from the purse at his waist and held them up. "We didn't spend all. This we give to you."

"We are three sworn brothers to Guidi of Romena. Our swords are yours, signore Francesco," Matteo said.

He didn't know what to say. Men had never come to him voluntarily; they were foot soldiers in mercenary armies promised nothing but the spoils of war if they were free to offer. Francesco looked at the coins in his hand—all total, one *fiore d'oro*, a gold florin. Enough to buy ten men bread and ale.

"We are four sworn brothers," Francesco replied. "You will accompany me to Prataglia."

CHAPTER 4

GIAN MARIA DA PORCIANO PACED the cobbled floor of the abbey refectory like a caged lion and glanced for the hundredth time at the hourglass. When the last grains of sand slipped down he flipped it over with a thud.

"Son of a poxed whore!" he cursed.

Two miserable hours. He had waited for two hours and was ready to leave. Sometimes the best of intentions was not. Gian Maria scooped up bread and cheese and ate, then tossed bread crumbs at the mice studying him from their safe haven beside the hearth.

"Are you as scared me as I am of Romena?" he asked them. He'd never admit that aloud to anyone, and not after all the trouble he'd taken to arrange this meeting. Enough florins had been passed between hands to ensure the secrecy. Now he wasn't so sure.

A blast of freezing air shot through the refectory and Gian Maria pulled his cloak about him, cursing again, this time at the bastard that opened the door.

"Signor?" Gian Maria's man stood before him now dripping snow and sleet on the floor and into the hearth so that the meager fire sizzled and sputtered. "A party of riders entered the monastery. It must the conte di Romena."

"He's late!" Gian Maria snapped. "Though I suppose the Romena have more important things to do all day than spend two miserable hours in a flea and rat-infested monastery!"

The man went to the window and rubbed away the frost to look out. "Ah! Yes, it must be him. Someone in the cloister addressed him, though the snow is so blinding it's scarcely possible to see," the servant reported. "Ah! Those are the Romena colors, but I can't get a look at—holy 'evangels! *Look* at him!"

Now Gian Maria laughed, but nervously. "Is he a monster? My nursery tales were of how the conti Romena sacrificed little boys to pagan gods and ate their hearts."

"I gave it up for Lent; never got back into the habit."

There Francesco stood at the threshold of the refectory, or rather, filling up the doorway with his great height, and though near impossible, looking quite ordinary.

Staring up at him in awe, Gian Maria was surprised by the absence of trumpets and heavenly host.

Francesco strode in and went straight to the hearth. "Your nursery stories were more inventive than mine. Hello, I'm your cousin Francesco." He turned with a hand outstretched towards Gian Maria, who took a cautious step back. "Why does everyone I meet do that?" he chuckled.

Gian Maria watched his cousin shake the snow from an expensive and obviously cherished cloak that was lovingly draped over a bench. How should he commence? Should he say, *Sorry about my father; you know how fathers can be pricks?* Should he remark on Romena's good fortune in managing to stay alive against such terrible odds?

"Pardon?" Francesco asked, amused.

Gian Maria had made a noise; something akin to a squeal and a cough.

"Thank you! Thank you for coming, monsignore."

"I do not hold to ceremony. Call me Francesco," he said, plopping down in front of a table spread with supper. He helped himself to the pitcher of ale. Taking a drink, he added, "You're as much Romena as Porciano, and from the look of you, at least Romena won that battle."

He drank a full cup in three gulps and poured another. Gian Maria watched as the amber colored liquid frothed and swirled; he slid his tongue across his lips at the sight of it, watching as Francesco drank.

When Francesco offered him a cup, Gian Maria snatched it up gratefully and took the ale in one swallow, then reached for the pitcher and poured another drink, taking it just as quickly. He was aware that Francesco's eyes burned into him and saw that his hand was none too steady, saw how the ale spilled on the rushes. Gian Maria wiped his mouth on the back of his hand and drank from the pitcher. He wasn't ashamed; there were plenty of men who found their courage in drink.

"Be easy; I don't bite!"

Gian Maria was startled by Francesco's voice low in his ear. When he leaped away, Francesco laughed heartily. "Thank God I didn't sneeze! You'd have wet yourself!"

"Go to hell, Romena!"

"I thought everyone knew I'd been there more than once."

"Clever. But then, everyone says you're clever. Just unlucky."

They stared down one another and Gian Maria was the first to look away.

"Let's get down to business, shall we? I wouldn't have come out on the coldest day of the year if I didn't think your proposal interesting," Francesco said. "What do you require?"

"Nothing,"

Francesco relaxed and stretched out his legs so that they were nearly in the hearth. "I'd sooner believe you don't like ale. So. Have you something to offer?"

"I must think about that—if you would give me another day,"

"You don't offer to go to war unless you're willing to shed some blood. What shall it be? You know my condition and my state. However much I have and don't have, I can offer you something your father won't."

"What might that be? A castle? A town?"

"Perhaps. If it's that important. I can give you loyalty and my word. When were they last offered to you?"

"Never."

"I'm offering now."

Gian Maria reached for Francesco's cup, which was now tendered. Drinking slowly, he held Francesco's gaze.

❧

IT NEVER OCCURRED to Gian Maria that he would leave the abbey sure of himself in anything and friends with a man he thought the most dangerous in the world. Yet here he sat in a tavern near Prataglia with food enough for an army spread over the table and more wine than he could ever wish for and pretty girls his for the asking and price. His cousin Francesco was indifferent to their surroundings and ignored the man who stumbled against the table and made his pen skid across the letter he was writing, paid no attention to the pretty wench hanging on his shoulder.

Francesco held up the letter to the candlelight and squinted to read his work. Satisfied, he blew on the ink to dry it and then folded it carefully into a neat square and sealed it with a lump of wax taken from his satchel and melted over the candle flame. Having no insignia, Francesco used the hilt of his sword to press the blood-red wax into the parchment.

"For God's sake, no more letters tonight! You said we would celebrate," Gian Maria laughed.

Francesco winked at his cousin and then turned to the pretty wench still hovering. He pulled her down for a kiss that had even Gian Maria speechless, and then tucked the letter and a coin into her bodice, letting his fingers glide over the silky breasts topping the exposed chemise. "See that this is delivered to Tommaso da Porciano in Florence," he whispered, "and you'll get the rest of your wages at my house in the Borgo Santi Apostoli!"

The girl was gone in a second, turning back once to blow Francesco a kiss, which he returned.

"I hope that wasn't the last of your money," Gian Maria said nervously, studying every woman in the room and ciphering his chances with them. A pretty dark-haired girl was smiling provocatively and gesturing toward the stairs.

Francesco reached into his purse and spilled coins onto the table. "You've earned it. Off you go. I'll see you in the morning."

The coins were scooped up with the flask of wine and Gian Maria disappeared into the crowded common room in search of the night's misadventures. As soon as he was gone, Francesco took a letter from his satchel and held it up to the light. He studied it for a moment and then tapped the table with it, as if deep in thought. Crooking his finger, Edmund appeared out of the shadows and sat down at the table. Francesco set the letter before him.

"Everything ready?" Francesco asked, picking up his quill to start another letter.

"Once a thing is done, it is finished, as you always say."

"Thank you. Oh, and send the Bishop a basket of figs from my orchards at Poppi. I hear he is particularly fond of figs."

"I'll see it done myself."

"Amazing how everything's just fallen into place."

Edmund smiled. "It is, isn't it?"

ॐ

TOMMASO DI PORCIANO THREW Francesco's letter into the fire and watched the flames lick at it, then finally devour it. The smoke rose in a white column, twisting and curling up the chimney of the wall hearth, the first of its kind in the quarter. Some of it blew back and filled the room.

"Tommaso! God's life, you'll burn the house down! What are you doing there?" snapped his wife as she entered, waving her veil frantically at the billowing cloud of smoke.

He pivoted, the color rising in his face as he tried to cover what was left of the letter under a pile of soft gray ash.

"What's that?" Elisabetta da Romena asked. She sat in her usual place on the window seat and took a basket of needlework from a servant.

"Nothing," Tommaso muttered. He glowered at her in his usual manner and said nothing, clamoring up from the grate and sitting in his great chair before the hearth.

For two hours husband and wife sat in silence. Tommaso di Porciano and Elisabetta da Romena had been married long enough to know conversation was unnecessary and unwelcome. Elisabetta absently took stitches while she glanced ever so often at Tommaso as he watched the prettiest of her handmaidens walk across the chamber in search of more wool for her embroidery, or run after one of the dogs, or arrange flowers in vases.

"Do you know what day it is?" Elisabetta asked of a sudden.

"Wednesday, by my count," he answered.

"Today is the feast of Saint Andrew, the day on which we first met," Elisabetta said. "Do you remember?"

"Of course I do," Tommaso grumbled. "Your father beat me within a breath of my life."

"Only because you mistook my sister-in-law for me!"

"How was I to know? I'd never seen you before, and your father locked the doors so I had to climb over the garden walls. There she was in the garden."

"We all thought you were a thief come to rob us—we didn't know you were our cousin from the Casentino."

"I've heard the story before, Elisabetta. . ."

"How were we to know? Here was this boy, his clothes practically rags,"

"They weren't the latest fashion, but they were new and cost my father eight florins."

"You remember the cost? That doesn't come as a surprise. Do you remember that you didn't want to get married? You'd come from studying for the priesthood in Athens and there you were thrown into our midst to keep the peace in the family."

Tommaso snorted with pleasure. "And you didn't think I'd come with the castles and land. You thought I was just a *contadino* with nothing but the clothes on my back!"

"Well, your father was the poorest of the Guidi," Elisabetta laughed, remembering, and took a few more stitches. "He kept his word, at least. And we still have the castle, though what we should do with it now that Gian Maria and you have fallen out. Perhaps we can enjoy its pleasures as we did once before?"

She was aware that Tommaso was watching her now. And why shouldn't he? Even after so many years, she was proud that she kept her figure and looks. She was still proclaimed one of the great beauties of Florence. He said as much in their last meeting at the castle and would have reminded her husband of that had he not been leering at one of the handmaidens as she bent over to retrieve a ball of embroidery wool.

"Isn't it odd how strangers are thrown together and expected to live in love as in the old romances?" she said now. "Marriage is for the convenience and honor of the family. You and I have honored and made things convenient for the Guidi for many years, don't you think? Do you ever wonder what you would have done if we'd had the chance to marry other people?"

"Not really," he grunted.

Elisabetta concentrated on her needlework for a time so that the only noise in the room was the push and pull of thread through canvas, the crackle of the fire and her sighs.

"Did you hear that Lisetta da Bicci was found in the garden of San Marco with some man ten years her junior?" Elisabetta said to her women. When they all giggled, she added, "They were both naked! Of course, the brothers of the monastery were scandalized, and who wouldn't be?"

"I'm too old for this," Tommaso groaned all of a sudden.

"Too old for what? No one found you in the San Marco garden with a girl, I hope!" Elisabetta asked. "But then, that would be surprising . . . or perhaps not. I remember how you were found with my sister-in-law in the garden. You were still explaining the tear in her dress months later . . ."

"Oh, woman be silent!" he shouted. "I'm too old for intrigues!"

"What are you talking about?"

"Alessandro's boy is making demands we must consider."

Elisabetta stopped her needle midstitch and glanced up. Her expression and the lighting made her resemble the delicate madonnas worshiped in the churches of Florence. Tommaso looked away; the Romena always made him painfully aware of how lacking he was in appearance. What could compare to the perfection of deep blue eyes and golden hair, smooth, pale skin and dimples? Certainly nothing his parents had given him. Ruminating on what he didn't have gave Tommaso an excuse not to answer the question Elisabetta had posed.

"What demands? Surely they are reasonable."

Tommaso stared down at the worn points of his shoes and pushed himself out of the chair. He began to pace and when he passed Elisabetta, she placed a hand on his sleeve, preventing him from making another tour of the large room. It was not an endearing touch, but cold and defensive.

"We have enough now to content us. We lack for nothing. I ask you this one favor: make peace with Francesco and return all that you have taken."

He glanced sideways at her with the suspicion usually reserved for a stranger or a competitor. "What do you think will happen to us if I give in?" he demanded. "Who's to say he won't exact retribution for my sallies into the Casentino? Elisabetta, you know what happens to usurpers and wicked uncles when all is said and done!"

"It wouldn't surprise me if he is a forgiving man. There are a few in the Guidi family. And there's always the bishop. You can ask for the ecclesiastical court to hear your grievance again—though what wrong Francesco has done to you will be hard to prove."

"Wicked uncles, Elisabetta!"

The evening ended as it always did. Elisabetta reached the end of her patience with Tommaso and retired quietly to her bedchamber in the tower of the townhouse, while Tommaso went off to his suite of rooms, or down to the shop to study the account ledgers. Much later, however, Elisabetta sought out ser Michelino, Gian Maria's tutor, who was surprised to see her in Tommaso's library and more surprised when she closed the door and locked it.

"I must send word to my son," Elisabetta said as she lit two more candles and placed new parchment and a quill before him, shoved aside the codices and scrolls. "He is still in the Casentino and will not have left for Florence. May I trust you to deliver a letter?"

CHAPTER 5

FORTUNE HAD SMILED on Tommaso too long for this day to go awry. How could he not take the field and advantage from Francesco with so great a company? With him that morning were eight of the best captains in Tuscany that his money could purchase with foot soldiers, knights and engineers ranged with trebuchets and mangonels. Behind him, the castle of Fronzola was well provisioned for a siege. He'd taken it several years ago and now it was the most formidable of his castles. Today ten of his strongest knights waited in the courtyard behind the barbican with fifty soldiers to hold the castle if, and Tommaso laughed to himself at this, Romena was able to get past the vanguard. Archers and crossbowmen filled crenels and arrow slits on the battlements. Before him with the vanguard was his son Gian Maria, ready to attack as soon as the Romena army appeared.

That Gian Maria was with him was near to a miracle for when did the boy ever do as he was commanded?

What a day that had been when Gian Maria suddenly appeared from God knew where and said his mother persuaded him to honor the Porciano and stand with his father. Gian Maria's support didn't come with an army or gold. It was enough for Tommaso that his son was with him.

From where he sat, Tommaso could look down in the woods that encircled the castle and the road to Florence. In an hour, perhaps two, one of them would know whether to take the road to Florence or flee into the woods. Tommaso was feeling confident; it would be Romena running with tail between legs. With any luck, he'd run all the way to England or France and die there.

"How is my son this morning?" Tommaso asked the captain to his right. "The boy was silent the entire ride from Florence, and it's not like him to be sullen or quiet. He didn't drink and whore all night?"

"It's his first battle, signor."

"Never easy." Tommaso murmured and rode forward. He wondered if the captains knew it was his first battle as well. The other skirmishes he'd supervised from the safety of the camp or behind the walls of a fortress.

Gian Maria was sliding his baselard in and out of its scabbard as he watched the horizon, starting in fright as Tommaso came up unannounced.

"What do you think?" Tommaso asked. "Will he show?"

"He's a man of his word, Father," Gian Maria answered. "You made the challenge. Did you suppose he wouldn't take the bait?"

"I didn't think he would."

"You never told me the terms."

Tommaso motioned for Gian Maria to follow him and they walked their horses away from the front line. "You never told me why you were so willing to fight today," he said to Gian Maria. "Why of a sudden should you want to please me?"

"For the sake of my mother and the souls of my dead brothers. I want to make Mother happy, for she's had little to make her smile for a long while. I want to prove to her that I'm as good as if not better than my brothers," Gian Maria replied. "And so, the terms? What made my cousin Romena agree?"

"Whoever takes the field today takes it all."

Gian Maria shot his father an angry glare. "All? All did you say? If we lose then Romena gets my inheritance? My lands and money? My title?"

"Look around you, boy. Half of the Casentino is with us! Do you think he can defeat us?"

"I think that's an exaggeration, but no. We have a great host here, Father."

They rode back to the vanguard and waited a quarter hour before a Porciano scout burst out of the woods, shouting as he rode, his cries unintelligible, but it was evident what caused his haste. Behind him rode two knights in pursuit and behind them was the Romena army.

Tommaso laughed and then clapped Gian Maria's shoulder in a rare show of affection. "We'll see one another when this is over?"

"We'll raise a cup to victory. Go back to your captains, Father. I'll see this through," Gian Maria said and signaling the vanguard, led them forward. Tommaso watched him go and fought the urge to call Gian Maria back and spare him what was to come, or worse, watch him die in battle. As much as he didn't like the boy, he was the last of his sons and only heir.

On the field, Gian Maria picked up speed and shouted at the men to follow. His heart pounded as much from exertion as fear, and he signaled when they were a league away from the enemy, his knights positioning lances and the footmen drawing swords and pikes, moving closer together with shields locking. When he could distinguish faces in Romena's vanguard, Gian Maria raised his sword and as quickly as he advanced he gave the order for a *volt-face*. The army took no time in drawing up as if to retreat.

"Remember who we fight for," Gian Maria shouted at his men, "and honor him!"

"What's the boy doing?" Tommaso cried, watching the retreat. "They'll be slaughtered to a man!"

"*À Romena!* For God and Romena!" Gian Maria screamed, and he led his men and the Romena army towards Fronzola straight into his father's bewildered troops

❧

NO, TOMMASO HAD not expected this.

In his daydreams, he imagined Francesco da Romena waiting in the great hall of the Palazzo della Signoria in Florence to surrender castles and lands to Porciano and swear fealty; he never dreamed that it would happen this way. He wasn't supposed to lose. He shouldn't be pacing circles under the watchful eyes of Romena knights in the great hall at Castello di Romena. He had never dreamed his only surviving son would betray him.

Or his wife!

Tommaso had been born with many disadvantages, and when life was bleak, he took them into account. A glance in a mirror showed him the greatest of his liabilities. Over the years, people had been generous with the words. Some called him plain, others, distinguished, or noble, but the truth of the matter was, he was downright ugly. None of the legendary beauty of the counts Guidi had been given to him. God gave Tommaso a long, bulbous nose that ended in a mole that sprouted hair, pock-marked skin, fleshy jowls and lank strands of thinning, gray hair that stuck out from under caps and hoods like blades of dead grass. The only attribute to compliment Tommaso other than his sharp gray eyes was his voice. It was low and resonant, similar to that of his nephew Francesco's. He also thought he had a gift for discerning true nature and temperament in his associates and enemies. How wrong he was in that!

God, Tommaso thought, had something else to answer for and that was the place Tommaso occupied in the great Guidi family.

He was the grandson of Drudolo Guidi, a man of so little importance that no one could remember where he was buried. To make matters worse, Tommaso's father Tegrimo was a brigand, the embarrassment of the family, content with a vocation of looting, marauding, and farming pigs. This Tegrimo di Drudolo thought it clever to paint the curtain walls of his castle at Stia with piglets and named the fortress Porciano, hence, the surname Tommaso grudgingly bore.

In order to keep what he thought was his, Tommaso would have to sue for peace. It wasn't as though he had a choice. It had been made for him.

Sue for peace! Ah well, Tommaso thought as he followed the pattern of the flagstones with a booted toe, treaties were as flimsy as the parchment they were written on. A careless brush into the fireplace, florins put in the right pocket or the unexpected death of the notary could change the outcome in his favor and he knew just the people to ask . . .

The slam of oaken doors shocked Tommaso out of his ruminations. He glanced up at the spiraling staircase when he heard the footsteps. A notary, two servants, a clerk, and a priest wound their way down to the hall. At the same time, ten of the Romena household guard came from the bailey and ranged themselves around the room. Tommaso's six armed retainers came to attention, hands moving to hilts, but Tommaso shook his head. He knew he'd be outnumbered here. A table set before the platform where the Romena chair of state stood was prepared for this meeting, with flasks of wine and cups and plates of sweet wafers, bread, cheese, and dried fruit. When the notary and priest moved to take seats at a table at the southern end of the hall, Tommaso followed.

"Here, signor," the notary invited, pulling out a chair at one end of the table. Tommaso offered thanks with a nod of his head and sat down. A servant stepped forward and poured a glass of wine and another placed a tray of dried fruit and wafers before him. The notary and the priest both smiled as they shuffled papers and produced ink wells and pens from satchels, setting all in order. No sooner was this done than Francesco himself entered and quietly sat at the opposite end of the table. The first thing Tommaso noticed was the plain, dark, clothing the younger man wore in compliance with Florence's sumptuary laws. He looked no more a nobleman than the priest or clerk. Whether by purpose or unconscious desire, Tommaso called attention to his brocaded overgown of red velvet by plucking lint from one of the sable-cuffed sleeves.

"I am glad you've come, Uncle," Francesco greeted, large green eyes darting from the expensive tunic and overgown to Tommaso's bland face.

Rather than ask if he had a choice Tommaso shrugged and said, "We're both bound to get something out of this."

"I'm glad you see it that way. So. Let us begin." Francesco raised a hand towards the notary who placed a scroll before Tommaso and unfurled the parchment. The notary shuffled back to his place and sat down. Tommaso made a cursory review of the contract and clenched his fists in his lap.

"In exchange for what is ours, we gift you with the farms and vineyards at Borgo San Lorenzo, that and the hunting lodge in the Mugello, with lands and game, and the right to forest," Francesco continued. "This will include rents, revenues—the license to hold fair, if you'd like, with thirty percent of your annual revenues to me, as rightful lord of these lands and estates. You may keep the shops in Stia, but those in Florence revert to me."

Tommaso had heard enough. He leaped up and leaned against the table for support while he shook in anger but more to keep himself from strangling Francesco. "Those are my shops!" he growled. "I spent every florin I had to make them solvent! I spent eighteen years recovering what your father squandered on the worst of vices, vile things which may not be spoken of!"

The retainers and knights of both parties drew up on sides and waited; the clerk scribbled, the notary looked dismayed that all his work would be for naught. The priest whispered in Francesco's ear and was shrugged off.

"You stole them from my father," Francesco answered softly.

"Lie! A lie!"

"Is it, Tommaso?"

"It is the invention of Durante Giustini! He was always jealous of us!"

"Durante hasn't been in Florence for years,"

"Of course he hasn't! He was exiled for the murder of your father!"

"It was never proved one way or another who killed Alessandro or how he died."

"Everyone in Florence knows what happened, and he deserved his death and the way he died!" Tommaso laughed, hoping others would join, but the room was so silent it might have been possible to hear the winter rain falling outside.

"When you make accusations like that you should have proof to uphold them," answered Francesco, "otherwise men will think you craven, and think you know more than you let on. Or that you're a murderer."

"This is proof, I think!"

Tommaso was on his feet with a baselard out and pointed at Francesco.

"Stand down," Francesco warned both Tommaso and the others. "I said, stand down!" He now rose and crossed the room to where Tommaso stood, took the baselard out of his hand none too gently. "You don't learn lessons well, do you, Tommaso? The farm, the house, the lands, forests, and revenues. It is a generous offer," Francesco said.

"If I was a simple country farmer, perhaps!"

"Of course; but what good would they be to you dead?"

"Signor!" Tommaso barked at the clerk; "Write it down that il Conte di Romena has threatened my life."

"I made no such threat. If we continue this war the only way it will end is with one of our deaths. For my part, I have no intention of dying for years to come. You must admit that it makes sense to end this struggle and live peacefully. What say you?"

"A moment," Tommaso said and summoned two of his captains. They conferred in whispers and then Tommaso cleared his throat. The captains stepped back.

"Castello di Fronzola has always been held by the Romena branch of our family," Tommaso began.

"True, but you held it by force until our last meeting." A few Francesco's men laughed, but he silenced them with a raised hand.

"Let me keep Fronzola," Tommaso said. "You have three castles to secure your eastern marches and Fronzola is of little consequence to your hold on the region."

Everyone seemed to hold their breath as they watched Francesco and waited.

"Agreed," Francesco said after a moment of consideration. He gestured to the clerk. "Write that we gift our uncle of Porciano the castle at Fronzola but on these terms. You will acknowledge me as true and good conte di Romena. There will be no question of my lordship. I will leave you with what has been offered here today, your life, and what's left of your dignity."

"You have purchased my cooperation, but you've forgotten those Guidi who've waited for this day and to take their chances," Tommaso scoffed.

"True. Those who do not agree will come to an understanding."

"You haven't enough money to buy all of them!"

"Regard and loyalty are payment enough for some."

Tommaso laughed. "I dare you to say that to our uncle Battifolle!"

Francesco's fist came thundering down on the table between them. "I have five hundred men ready at my word. I can realize five hundred more if need be. I have the garrisons of Benchiaro, Faenza, Canine and Montemurlo! Sign and admit you were wrong and let there be an end to this."

"Now you want my gratitude for these bread crusts off your table? Shall I kiss your ass?"

"Sign or die!"

When Tommaso hesitated, Francesco moved abruptly and every man in the room was on alert. He snatched the document from the clerk and threw it at Tommaso, the parchment sliding over the polished surface of the table.

"Simone da Battifolle is dead. His son swore fealty to Romena three hours ago. The bishop is dead and left his lands to me. What's your argument now?"

"Where is Gian Maria?"

"I have no idea," Francesco replied.

"You both played me for a fool. "Give me Gian Maria and we'll be done here."

"I can't give you what I don't have. But if I do see him, I'll be sure to send him home. If he wants to go home."

"He has much to answer for!"

"That's not my concern. We've come to terms and there's an end unless you have a good reason why we shouldn't honor what we've accorded."

Tommaso had none. The contract was signed. Tommaso crushed his ring into the soft glob of red wax and wished it was Francesco's face. Tommaso and his men left the hall.

"My thanks," Francesco said to the clerk and priest and gave them each a *soldo* for their work that afternoon. As soon as the hall was empty, Francesco stared at the agreement left in his hands. For the first time in his life, the day was truly his. He ought to have rejoiced in this, the greatest of victories. Instead, he sat heavily in his chair of state. The wood groaned under him and he slowly relaxed. Behind him, a door closed and Gian Maria di Porciano appeared.

"Did you hear any of it?" Francesco asked, turning.

Gian Maria poured two cups of wine and handed one to Francesco. "Most of it. All of it not what I was expecting. Father isn't one to go quietly or back down."

"He'll go back on his word. They always do," Francesco muttered. He gave the boy a sad smile. "Now I suggest you stay out of Florence for a while."

"I can take care of myself. Let me ride with you to Florence; I want to be there when you arrive and claim what is yours."

"Thank you, no. I have business in the Romagna that needs attention first. I'll send word when I arrive."

"As you wish, but let me know."

"I will. Oh, and if there's anything I can do to help your mother?"

"Elisabetta needs no champion, Cousin," said Gian Maria, smiling. "No doubt Father is sore angry with her, for a wife to turn against her husband is against all propriety. She's taken sanctuary at Santa Trinita and won't come out unless Father promises not to hurt her or seek retribution. She was sick of the quarrel, truth be told. Who wasn't?"

"How is it to live with such a man?" Francesco asked.

"One gets used to it. In time, everything he does seems normal."

"Normal? Gian Maria, in a world where the evil that men do is as common as air or rain, or the sun coming up in the morning, Porciano's behavior is unexplainable."

"I guess it's easier trying to understand women."

"No, it isn't."

The two young men laughed.

Francesco reached into the purse at his waist and withdrew a square of parchment, which he gave to Gian Maria. "It isn't much," he apologized, "but I did promise you this. It's the charter for Focognaio. You gave me the sweetest of victories. Let me give you this castle. I hope this is enough reward."

Gian Maria smiled. It was sometimes best not to let words get in the way of true happiness, but he did smile at Francesco and whisper "Thank you!"

CHAPTER 6

FRANCESCO PULLED HIS fur-lined cloak tighter and studied the white landscape stretched out on the dusky horizon for leagues. The only way to discern a hill from a tree was the shape. The sky and ground were a blur of white, one bleeding into the other except where the sun was going down and there was a faint streak of orange and purple. The specks of dark color behind them was the rest of his caravan struggling to keep up.

There was no hope for it. They were lost.

"How is it possible to be lost on my own lands?" Francesco complained to no one in particular.

"If everything wasn't the same color of white," Edmund replied.

"We should go to Benchiaro. It's only a day's ride," said Lorenzo, riding forward.

Francesco shook his head. "No. I want to be in Florence by the feast of Christe's Masse."

"Why?" Edmund asked.

"It doesn't matter why, Edmund. Have someone scout the countryside and find out where we are."

It did matter. Francesco wanted to be in Florence to light candles in the Duomo on the morning of Christe's Masse, which was the anniversary of his father's death, and to have prayers offered for all those who died because of his struggle, especially Gismonda.

"We might have waited a day before leaving," Edmund said. "Even Porciano wouldn't have ventured out into this."

"He left two days ago."

"Two days to undo all we've done."

"The last I heard, I was still conte di Romena. Any other complaints?"

Francesco reached down to break the ice forming on the horse's muzzle and caught sight of Edmund's disapproving scowl. Ever since the accord with Porciano, he'd made no secret of his distaste for the entire matter. Francesco knew he thrived on conflict, but didn't think it would extend to their relationship. The sword-edged silence and the uneasy truce between them warned of a new storm coming. He reached for Edmund's reins and steered him away from the caravan.

"Say what's on your mind, Edmund. We have a long journey ahead of us."

"We've already spoken our minds."

"But not all. There are things left unsaid."

It was a moment before Edmund spoke. "I can't believe you're giving in after all this time, and after all you've lost. To decide to make peace—it doesn't smell like roses. It isn't like you."

"It was my decision to make," Francesco answered. "It is my burden should it not prove advantageous. What I do have I'll make better. I'll be able to keep my promises."

"Do you really think he'll keep any promise made? And his son. That goes beyond belief. How deep should you place your trust?"

"As I said, I am still conte di Romena. If you think you've given your sword to the wrong man, I won't hold it against you if you decided to leave. I'd only ask that you don't betray me as others have."

The wind picked up and snow pattered down in flurries as Francesco waited for Edmund's response.

"Forgive me, monsignore conte."

"Forgiven. I have an idea," Francesco said. "I have unfinished business with the Ordelaffi and it's best to take care of it now while the political climate is favorable. I think you're the only man I could trust with this diplomacy. Go to Rimini and treat with the Ordelaffi concerning the disputed lands near Benchiaro. I'll see you when you return."

Edmund nodded in agreement and managed a smile. Francesco watched with relief as Edmund and his escort disappear into the horizon.

"Letting him cool off, monsignore?" Lorenzo asked when Francesco rejoined the caravan.

"He'll be happier away from me and in Rimini."

"It grows late. Do we make camp here?"

"We'll ride until dark," Francesco answered. He gave the signal and the party braced itself against another onslaught of sleet and wet snow. Facing enemies in battle was preferable to the lash of blinding snow, with skin stinging and burning from cold so oppressive it numbed every sense but the will to survive. The drifts were piling higher. Horses lost footing and plunged headlong into a white abyss, dragged back by grooms who scrambled perilously down frozen embankments to save both horse and rider.

Having watched three men go down, Francesco tugged on the reins and urged his horse towards the left in another direction where the ground looked stable and flat. The horse picked its way through drifts and around what might have been a trail or road until the bed of snow crumbled and gave way to the ridge of a hillock where it shied and went no further. The sudden movement made Francesco lose control of the horse and he was thrown, tumbled into what he thought would be a soft bed of snow only to discover rock. The sharp pain as he hit his head surprised him a little less than the bright red snow underneath him.

"Shouldn't be long now, monsignore!" Lorenzo panted as he climbed through the drifts to reach Francesco. He clutched a handful of snow and pressed it against the gash on Francesco's forehead. "I see lights ahead," Lorenzo said, pointing beyond a coppice.

"I think I know this place," Francesco said. He looked around, clearing snow and ice from his eyes, and nodded. It did look familiar, this countryside. They'd stumbled into the northeastern frontier of the High Casentino. God be praised, these were Romena lands.

An order to halt went down the line when one of the men noticed a cluster of lighted buildings lay ahead. These were the abbey and castle of Montebuoni.

"The castle would be more comfortable, monsignore," said Lorenzo as they approached the abbey gate.

"I don't know what fortifications the castle has, or if the garrison is still mine to command," answered Francesco.

"But it is, ser Francesco!" the abbot said as they dined in his hall later that evening. "A week ago, the magistrates of the town refused Porciano's bid when he approached them and they unanimously swore for Romena."

"He did what? The ink is not yet dry on our accord," Francesco sighed and pushed away his trencher. He signaled Lorenzo for more wine. "We shall have words, and they'll be unpleasant. More wine, Abbate Pietro?"

"...now where is that girl? Her father will be wroth, for I did make a promise," the abbot muttered aloud, looking at the door.

"Abbate? Something amiss?"

The abbot accepted the wine offered, took a sip, and looked at the door again. "I was entrusted with the safe conduct of a friend's daughter through the Casentino to her uncle's house in Florence. The girl has been willfully disobedient and shameful since her arrival this afternoon. I had hoped she would dine with me and hear good counsel," he complained. "And with monsignore's arrival, I thought she would be good company for you—"

At this Francesco guffawed. "A willful, disobedient and shameful girl? What stories have you heard about me?"

"My pardon, signor! It was not as I meant,"

For the rest of the evening, Francesco and the abbot talked, but the girl did not come up in conversation again.

The moon in its fullness lit the abbey close from church to hospice when Francesco left the abbot's lodgings at midnight. Everything was a muted shade of black, blue, gray, or white. Rising up behind the abbey walls was the great hulk of Montebuoni. The three towers against the sky looked like a man raising his arms in surrender, the arched windows like eyes wide in fright as the moonlight streamed through them. Not me, Francesco thought, that's not me. Pausing a moment to study the fortifications, Francesco decided to make a tour of the castle before going on to Florence. There'd be time enough in the morning. He was making plans as he walked carefully over ice-rimed cobblestones and patches of snow to the guest houses when two people ran from the castle and through the porter's gate and straight at him. Not knowing what to expect, Francesco drew his sword and shrank into the protection of the covered walk from the gate-house.

They stopped within an arm's length of Francesco, who all but held his breath to avoid detection.

"This is the very worst of ideas!" said one of them, a girl, laughing breathlessly. She threw herself against the hard stone of the walk's double pillars that separated her from Francesco.

Her companion was a young man of slight build and height, barely taller than the girl; he looked as if he could be snapped in two like a twig or knocked over by a gust of wind. He was strong enough, however, to detain the girl in his arms. She made no effort to escape as his mouth, falling gently on hers, silenced her soft laughter. Francesco could feel his skin burning while listening to their sighs and wet kisses. If only he could slip away unnoticed . . .

The girl broke away, heaving for breath. "Gesu! Haven't you had enough?" she giggled.

"Never," he answered.

"Ow! Your hands are like ice!"

"Perhaps this will keep you warm."

Francesco closed his eyes as their kisses grew hotter and could only imagine what was transpiring.

"Would you have me here and now in the snow?" the girl laughed.

"I'll have you, that's for certain—say where and when. You promised when I returned from France,"

"You must be patient! Haven't I told you before? This prize is yours!" the girl said, and pulled away. When she turned, Francesco found himself face to face with her.

He once read a Provençal troubadour's poem of how time stood still for lovers as they first beheld one another and how the breath quickened and the heart raced but never once mentioned how fickle and inconstant emotion could be. Moments ago, he was thinking of Gismonda, but now he could only see this girl. Francesco felt the heat rise in his face as they stared at one another. The moonlight gave her a pale, ghostly, cast, but he could see round eyes, a perfect mouth, and oval face much like the beauties portrayed as saints and angels in church frescoes throughout Tuscany. Much like Gismonda. It wasn't until he smiled that the girl stepped back and collided with her suitor.

"Oh, leave off!" she hissed at the young man when he tried to resume their lovemaking and pushed him away with such force that he stumbled and fell at Francesco's feet.

"Let me help you, signor; I'll be your sworn champion against this fierce lady," Francesco jested and when he offered a hand to the suitor, he saw the flash of a sword.

"That insult will only serve up hurt!" the fellow hissed.

Francesco was ready for him and drew, meeting the first blow of the contest with ruthless efficiency.

They circled one another like dogs, waiting and then pouncing, blow for blow met unevenly. The icy ground only made it deadlier and Francesco lost his footing several times, rolling out of harm's way just as the blade glimmering above him swung down to find a sheath in powdery snow.

The suitor moved out into the close, trying to avoid Francesco's vigorous blows as best he could. Francesco entrenched himself in a soft bank, spiraling to check his opponent's moves and displayed masterful swordsmanship, going down on one knee and whirling about with an upward thrust, switching hands, using his cloak for a shield—all at once. He would not be proven less than a knight, especially with the girl looking on.

The girl was not impressed, however, and she struggled across the close, spilling to the ground more than once and tripping over the muddy, sodden hems of her velvet surcote and gown to reach them. She finally caught her suitor's arm, screaming, "Enough! No more, Niccolo; put your sword away!"

His sword was pitched into the snow and shuddered on impact. The suitor tried to lean against the girl while he caught his breath, but she cursed at him and again pushed him away. Francesco recognized the bright gold hair and pale eyes, the patrician beauty of the young man. "Niccolo? Niccolo . . . Peruzzi?" Francesco demanded.

"Do you know me?" the suitor asked, incredulous.

"Of you, signor. I know your father and uncles. They are my bankers," said Francesco as he came into the light.

"And you are?"

"Francesco Guidi da Romena."

Niccolo Peruzzi dropped to one knee. "Monsignore! Signore Romena, I beg your pardon!"

"Not mine, but this lady's."

Francesco bent down to pick up his sword and in doing so, glanced at the young girl. He carefully replaced the sword in its scabbard, diverting his gaze. The heat rose in his face again and his hands trembled.

"You have the look of one world-weary," the girl spoke up. "It must be from your chivalrous deeds, for which I am thankful. I am in your debt, signor. Thank you for defending my honor."

Niccolo sputtered and then laughed at this, which won him an icy stare from the girl.

". . . Here she is, Abbate! Signorina! Signorina, come away! What means this?"

The monk's shouts made the girl wince. "Lord, I'm done for!" she whispered.

The Abbot swung about at Niccolo Peruzzi when he saw the girl's muddy clothes. "This will not do! Signor Peruzzi, I had expected better! What am I to think?"

"Think nothing. Believe me, abbate; nothing happened that would cause anyone to worry. We only came here to look at the stars," Niccolo protested.

Francesco laughed and then quickly recovered. "It is as Signor Peruzzi says," he said.

The Abbot bowed to Francesco. "Monsignore, I am glad you were here to ensure the lady's virtue was unassailable."

It was the girl's turn to laugh.

Francesco gave her a sideways glance and a crooked smile before he bade them a good night and left Niccolo to explain their late-night assignation. Once in the guest house, Francesco listened to the activity in the close: Niccolo's half-hearted explanations and the abbot's reprimands, the soft crunch of footsteps in the snow, the closing of doors. Francesco went to the window and opened the shutter. The girl was standing outside the abbot's lodgings and looking directly at him. After a long, curious glance, Francesco replaced the shutter.

CHAPTER 7

HE WOKE THE next morning as the bell for Terce rang. It was odd, staying in bed so late. Francesco moved about sluggishly, responding only as necessary to Lorenzo's inquiries as to the day's business while he dressed and broke fast, counted how many florins he had left and wondered about last night's strange encounter in the close.

". . . never seen Florence in my life, Signor," Lorenzo mentioned as he stropped a new razor on a whetstone. Handing it over to Francesco, he next threw back the shutter to allow light and propped a mirror on the table. "I hear the city streets are paved with marble!"

Francesco grunted and lathered up with soap. "More like the broken backs of wool workers and artisans if you want to know. The newly rich— the wool and silk merchants, the bankers—make certain all know they wield the power in Florence these days. They must be careful in choosing their friends and enemies and making enemies of those who labor on their behalf is more foolish than wise."

"Pardon, signore, but your father had shops in Florence and him a nobleman, and the stories Drogo told while we were at your mother's castle..."

"I'm sure they're true, Lorenzo. Being a member in one of the greater guilds is one way of keeping your enemies close—"

"Hey! Someone stop her! She's taken my horse!"

The shouts gave Francesco such a start he cut himself. He swore and leaned out the window to see what had happened, was astonished to see Peruzzi's young lady astride a restless stallion. She managed to keep the animal under control as it reared up and cantered madly while a groom and Peruzzi tried to take the reins. By the time Francesco reached the yard, the girl fended them off and raced to the abbey gatehouse.

Francesco was after her before the others knew what was happening. He took the horse they were saddling for Peruzzi and gave chase. The girl was far ahead of him, but Francesco pushed the charger he rode until he was able to cut her off at a stream by a coppice. Whenever the girl tried to move, Francesco blocked her and was finally able to take the reins.

"Leave off!" she cried. "You have no right!"

"Your rights are equally at question; you've stolen a horse," Francesco said and blocked her once again as she tried to get around him. He carefully dismounted, making sure she wasn't going to bolt or find himself tangled in their reins for that would make it easy for an escape.

"Go away!"

"If you wanted a morning ride you had only to ask. I would have been glad for the honor."

"Leave me alone!"

"Where are you bound in such a hurry?"

"Florence."

"I'm on the way there, too."

"Alone, Signore!"

Francesco studied her enchanting face now frightfully cold. In the uncompromising daylight, she was more beautiful than he remembered. She did have the same chestnut colored hair, the same dark blue eyes as Gismonda.

"More's the pity; I was growing tired of my servant and men. They only talk of war and killing people. I'm sure you and I would have found something to talk about."

"I can imagine."

"Can you? I hoped you could tell me something of Florence. I was born there but never lived in the town. Your friend Peruzzi, too, he could tell me about it."

"Niccolo?" the girl hissed. "Spare me talk of florins and banks and financial intrigues and how one family wants to ruin another!"

"You would speak of dresses and ornaments, of a ballad, or chivalry."

"What if I did? It's more than the nothing most men talk of. God forfend if they should ever read the books they collect for show," the girl said. She was studying him now and Francesco for the first time was uncomfortable under a woman's gaze. "You've cut yourself shaving," she chided, smiling.

Francesco lost his grip on the reins when he rubbed the stubble of a beard still on his chin and came away with soap and blood. He was relieved when she didn't ride off, but slid out of the saddle and walked the horse to a nearby stream. He followed and washed his face in the stream.

"Better?" he teased, looking at her. She blushed and looked away. "Your escape startled me," he admitted.

"And so you came to play the champion? Again?"

"The burdens of the world were getting tiresome."

He watched as she gathered pebbles from the bank and skipped them over the ice-crusted stream. When she looked over, a rosy blush spread from his neck to brow.

"You're staring," she scolded.

"You look like someone."

"Me, I should think!"

"No, someone else; you have her eyes," Francesco said, coming closer. His path ended before her. "You have her hair, though yours has a reddish cast, pretty . . ."

The girl dropped the pebbles into the snow and stared down, her booted foot tracing the pattern they made. "They look like precious gems with the sunlight sparkling on them," she murmured as if to herself and avoided his gaze. She brushed the hair off her face in a self-conscious, nervous movement and was sure there was something lacking in her appearance the way he continued to stare.

"Here is something more precious," Francesco replied and reached out, letting a finger outline the perfect oval of her face.

He lifted her chin and slid his thumb across the soft, petulant mouth. Leaning down, he kissed her. A warm kiss, chaste, yet abounding with promise, was returned much to his surprise. Rather than take more, Francesco smiled and memorized every aspect of the girl's face. He then knelt and kissed the hems of her surcote and kirtle in true chivalric fashion.

Riders approached and Peruzzi's golden head appeared at the head of a scouting party. Francesco watched the girl's bright face dim when he thundered upon them and made a showy halt, spraying mud and snow in his wake.

"Monsignore! I am indebted to you," Peruzzi greeted breathlessly, and extended a hand to Francesco.

"Let me hope you would have done the same for me," Francesco replied as he wiped the splatters of mud off his clothes, and then gestured toward the girl. "Here she is, safe from harm. Now excuse me, I must be on the road to Florence soon."

Francesco mounted up and wheeled his charger about, resisting the temptation to glance back and take in that lovely girl's face one last time. He kept his eyes on the road and galloped back to the abbey, eager to get as far away from that place as possible. By midday, Francesco and his party were traveling at a breakneck speed to Florence, pausing only at nightfall at the nearest town. They stopped at Borgo Rovinate.

Borgo Rovinate was an outpost on the Aretine frontier consisting of a tavern, a church, and half-dozen cottages and the same number of shops clustered around a market square and cross. All was dark and shuttered for the night save the tavern at the end of the footpath, a large establishment called The Foolish Bride.

The innkeeper was locking up when Francesco's party arrived and immediately summoned his boy to fetch supper when Francesco introduced himself. "It is the eve of Christe's Masse, signore, and truth be told, I didn't expect as many travelers as I now board, so many of them going to Florence," said the taverner as he cleared spaces for Francesco and Lorenzo at the center table in the common room. "It's the new Bishop, you see; he's from these parts and truth be told we're all very proud of him. Sit you down, signore, and have supper. I've sent girls to the new addition next door to prepare your bed. It's a loft room over my cook shop. There's a brazier and there are new oilcloths on the windows. You can get there by the bridge between the buildings. The stairs are behind us, just there. Ah! Here's your supper now and may you enjoy it."

The kitchen boy returned breathlessly with the best wine, a loaf of wastel, three meat pies, and a roast pheasant, bowls of winter fruit and dried figs.

Francesco glanced at the feast set before him and then at the bowls of polenta and stew the others at the table were having. "Let me share what I have," he said to his surprised tablemates, a gentleman dining with his family.

The petty aristocrat was small and wiry of build, with shrewd eyes and aquiline features. His clothes were elegant, befitting a man of high office. The handsome wife sitting beside him had too high an opinion of herself, and the bend of her nose was proof, as was the look she gave Francesco as he passed food around on trenchers. Their pretty daughter looked bewildered. Her brown eyes were as round as her comely yet plump face, and she blushed continually whenever Francesco's eyes slid toward hers.

"No thanks for your charity, signor," the gentleman sniffed and he dug into his bowl of polenta while eyeing the pheasant being carved up for the others.

"Will you not join us, madonna?" the Taverner asked his wife. "Or you, signorina?" he winked at the daughter, who ducked her head and shook her it when her father whispered something. She smiled shyly at Francesco however.

Francesco chose the best of the dried figs from the bowl and took a bite, and then placed to her lips, entreating her to share the fruit with him. She bit down, the sticky meat glistening on her full mouth. The girl licked her lips and whispered thanks before offering the fig. Francesco finished it off, never taking his eyes from his admirer.

"Where are you bound, Madonna?" he asked.

She blushed again and stuttered something, that she was not a great lady as he addressed her, and smiled demurely.

"It's no concern of yours!" the father growled, placing a dagger on the table between his daughter and Francesco. The gentleman fingered the dagger as if bent on using it. On his great finger was the Romena ring of office. Francesco looked at the man, then the ring. He shoved the dagger back at him.

"Just making conversation, signor," he answered, "as we are travelers away from home and look for friends and companions as we dine."

"Look the other way."

And Francesco did for the rest of the evening but caught the girl staring at him more than once while she sat with her father and mother and said not a word to join in conversation with the innkeeper and the others at the table. When Francesco bade a good night to his host and the guests she was still at the table, still blushing.

❧

"MONSIGNORE? . . . MONSIGNORE?"

Francesco was roused out of sleep by the whispers that sounded like a cat hissing. He cursed himself for not having barred the door and reached for his sword, pointing it towards the petty aristocrat standing at the foot of the bed, his disembodied face illuminated in a pale, spectral glow from the lamp above the bolster.

"What do you want?" Francesco barked and then noticed the girl standing back in the shadows. He had an inkling of what the man was up to.

"God save me, I didn't know you were Francesco da Romena!" the man said, coming forward. "I am Fiasella, Monsignore, seneschal of Castello di San Galgano."

"Even if I wasn't that gave you no cause for being rude or assuming the worst of me."

"How was I to know? I mean, we've all heard of you, but not one man jack I can speak of has seen you—"

"Fiasella, it's late. Say what it is you've come for."

"Here's my daughter," the man offered and he gently shoved the girl forward. "I've explained the way of things to her and she'll not refuse what Messer Romena commands. We have served the Romena for over twenty years, and it is our privilege and honor to do so. God give you a sweet rest, monsignore."

Fiasella bowed himself out of the loft room and scrambled down the stairs. The slam of the door and more footsteps on stairs marked his departure. In the silence that followed, Francesco leaned down to rummage through a sack and took out an hour candle, flint, and a stick for kindling. After a few tries, the candle was finally lit. He set it on a stool near the bed and positioned himself against the bolster.

The girl waited pensively. Francesco noticed a basket of figs in her arms and wondered if it was the father or mother who thought of that.

"What's your name?" he asked.

"Beatrice Fiasella, messer."

"I don't really like figs. Put the basket down somewhere." Having done what she was told, the girl began undressing. "No need for that!" he scolded. "Turn around. Let me have some privacy."

Francesco slid out of bed and grabbed his breeches. "Tell me, Beatrice, does he also sell your mother for a florin?"

"I wouldn't know, Monsignore."

"But for twenty years your family has served the Romena, and all things considered, that would mean but one thing."

"There were things he had to do for the Romena,"

"Such as procuring women for them?"

"If it put bread on our table, yes, he did it," Beatrice explained and added defensively, "My father served your father and grandsire and all he wanted was a living, but he was ill-used by them."

"He's not made a very good start with me. You may turn around."

Beatrice prepared herself for an assault and closed her eyes. Any moment now, at any moment he would throw her on the bed and tear at her clothes. . .

"What are you doing? Praying?"

She opened her eyes and was surprised to find him on the bed, one long, muscular leg drawn up to support an elbow while the other dangled over the bedframe and straw mattress.

"Where do you come from?" he now asked gently and while she prattled endlessly about her childhood, Francesco tried his best to look interested. He nodded and smiled and tried not to glance too much at the hour candle burning on the stool. The candle flame cast dancing shadows in the room, especially on Beatrice's milk-white skin. Soon he was staring at her breasts and the full mouth that had endless words to share. How long had it been since he'd taken a woman? Last October? The night before the fall of Raggiolo, it was. His beautiful, seductive, clever Gismonda invited him to the lodge at Ortignano. The memories brought an ache to his groin and Francesco shifted so it wasn't apparent to the girl. Had this been a bordello, he'd not think twice about tumbling Beatrice; she was beguiling and Francesco was tempted to kiss her if only to make her quiet. The idea that Fiasella expected it and expected largesse as the outcome was as good as a knife to the throat to kill desire.

". . . my father married my mother, who was a daughter of ser Provezano of Rovinate, perhaps you would know of them, signor, and they were given the lordship Castello di San Galgano, you see. I was born there."

"Castello—?"

"Your castle, monsignore. Castello di San Galgano."

"Of course," he said shortly. "I know it. Or its legend. One of my forefathers honored the saintly knight Galgano with the gift of that castle, but he would have none of it, saying his reward was in the kingdom of heaven. He charged the Romena to clothe and feed the poor and to house them in the castle. I'm sorry that none of us have done his bidding."

"Truly, Monsignore?" Her eyes could not have grown larger.

"It's probably a nursery tale and not a good one."

"I see,"

"Who has lived in the castle since my father's death? Do you know?"

"No one lives there now, leastwise, none of importance. In the spring, Signor Tommaso often comes to stay. He brings a hunting party and lords and ladies."

"Does he now?" Though the words were spoken gently, the tone was harsh.

She nodded, adding guilelessly, "He gave me a silver penny one night, and asked me to do his bidding."

"Spare me the details, Beatrice,"

"No, Signore! It wasn't like that at all. I ran from the bedchamber when I learned what it was he wanted. I know something of the world; enough to deny Tommaso di Porciano his ease. My father was so wroth! I thought he would die from rage. He said that men's fortunes are made by their daughters' generosity. I lit eight candles for him. Eight silver pennies they cost! But if ever a man needed prayers . . ."

Francesco laughed. "You might have burned down the church for all your effort!"

"I would light a candle for you, signore."

"Don't waste a penny on me."

"If the stories are true, it would not be wasted."

"Why? What have you heard?"

She took a breath and met his gaze head on.

"My mother and her women say that you have suffered all your life to take what is yours from ser Tommaso and that you have nothing left. It must be true, you see, for whenever we go to Florence and it is known we are from Castello San Galgano, people talk about the Conte di Romena. They say it is a fool's quest, like that of Roland, or the search for the holy grail."

Francesco hurled himself from the bed at this, his offense at the gossip very apparent by the hard line of his jaw. As he crossed the room, Beatrice moved away and stumbled into the table, knocking over the basket of figs. She knelt to retrieve them. Francesco was there at her side, silently helping her pick them up.

"I shouldn't have spoken," Beatrice said. "I beg your pardon."

"No; you needn't apologize. It's good to know what is really being said. It's a touchstone for knowing one's friends and enemies," Francesco replied.

"I should think you'd have many friends."

"Only those who think I have pockets lined with florins. They disappear when they find out how little I have." Francesco dug into the purse on his belt and shook out two *soldi* and one *denarii*. "Not enough to purchase friends."

Beatrice nodded and smiled, then slipped a hand into the pocket of her apron. She held out a coin. "Take this signor, for when you next meet someone seeking favor."

Francesco stared at the florin in bewilderment and then burst into laughter. He took the coin when she insisted and settled back against the wall. "I wish I could see things with such clarity and purity, Beatrice."

"My mother says I have an addled head and it will cause me no end of grief."

"There are worse things. Being alone."

"I like being by myself. No one to scold, or give orders, or show you your mistakes. I like to listen to the wind in the trees, and the sheep up in the pasture."

"You and I have a different view of life."

"Because our lives are different. How pleasant it would be as the lady of a great house in a city, or in a castle."

A rat the size of a half-grown tabby lumbered by and Francesco thought it was the best time to get off the floor. "And yet the terrors and inconveniences are the same in both cottage and castle," he said, motioning towards the rat. He reached for Beatrice's hand and pulled her to her feet. They stood facing one another and without provocation, Beatrice kissed him. She savored that kiss, running the tip of her tongue across her lips. When he didn't respond as she hoped, Beatrice tried again.

"Beatrice, I don't think—"

She nodded and gathering up her cloak and basket, brushed past him to the door.

"What about your father?" he asked.

She looked back, frowning. "He'll be angry, I suppose. What's that to you?"

"Stay the night. Sleep by the fire. Let him think what he wants."

It was a moment before she let go of the door latch and when she turned Francesco had taken one of the furs and a blanket off the bed and spread them near the brazier. He also gave Beatrice his cloak. "If you want the bed -?" he asked, pointing behind him.

"Oh no, signore. This will do." She wrapped herself in these coverlets and smiled at Francesco as he got into bed. "Thank you, signore. God give you sweet rest tonight."

He drew the bed curtains and listened as Beatrice settled in and heard her whisper the Jesus Prayer:

"Lord Jesus Christ, son of God, have mercy upon me, a sinner."

Francesco silently took up the prayer and relaxed with each word until he slept at last and woke hours later, roused by the sound of Beatrice pattering about the loft room.

She woke shivering, for the fire in the brazier had gone out. Looking around for kindling and finding none, she poked the coals and blew on them, hoping for a spark. When it was useless, she wrapped the cloak around her and drew open the bed curtains, dragging the fur and blanket with her.

"Signore? Monsignore? The fire's gone out! Signore? The fire's gone and it's too cold. May I get in with you?"

Francesco grunted and shifted, making room in the bed for her. Beatrice happily burrowed and claimed one of the pillows.

"Shall I make you smile?" she whispered.

"What game are you playing at this hour?" he grumbled.

Opening his eyes, he saw that was bending over him and with a finger drew a half-circle from his left cheek to the right. "There. I've made a smile."

He laughed. "That wasn't what I was expecting." When she frowned and looked wounded, he asked, "Are you truly an innocent, Beatrice? Don't you know what happens between a man and woman in bed?"

Again, Beatrice frowned. "I've seen the soldiers of the watch rut against serving girls and whores with their skirts above their bottoms. They go up against trees and doors, sometimes over a table. Panting and groaning. No different than dogs or sheep."

"When there is an attraction, there is a difference."

"How you explain rape?"

"That is something altogether different."

"I've heard the troubadours since of faithful and pure love, of how a man will lie with his sweetheart to show his love," Beatrice answered. She brushed the hair off Francesco's brow and smiled sweetly. "Is that how it is for you and me?"

He could have lied for the stirring up of lust she caused and how desirable she looked now, but Francesco shook his head.

"No. Your father would call it a business transaction and expect payment in full."

"But friends, they do kiss?"

"Of course."

"And are we not friends now?"

"If you wish."

"Shall I kiss you?" Beatrice asked huskily.

Francesco closed his eyes and felt her lips on his brow, surprising him, as he expected something quite different. Beatrice then sat up and unlaced her gown and tossed it aside. The shift she wore was of the finest linen and fell softly against her full breasts, sliding off one shoulder as she nestled against his shoulder and wrapped them in the blanket and fur. "It's my best dress and I wouldn't want to ruin it any more than I have, sleeping on the floor," she explained when Francesco glanced up, puzzled.

"And your mother will be wroth, no doubt?"

"No doubt, signore!"

"Let's go to sleep and forget about your mother and father. We'll be the wiser come morning."

He felt her relax and soon her breathing was slow and even. Again, he was drifting off to sleep.

"I would like to know what it's like, signore," Beatrice whispered in his ear.

"Stop talking," Francesco ordered. A shift in the blankets and a gentle thud made him whisper a prayer of thanks that the girl had turned over. Morning dawned quickly enough, however, and Francesco woke to a kiss. Beatrice was bending over him, smiling. The shift had been discarded and she'd pushed her thick, black, hair to one shoulder so that nothing was obscured. She kissed him again, long and wet, sliding her body against his.

"Is that the kiss you wanted, signore?" she said playfully.

"Stop talking," Francesco said as he decided to take the opportunity she so willing offered and pressed her down into the mattress as he kissed her hard.

❧

"I'M SORRY," FRANCESCO muttered.

Francesco reached for the blankets and watched as Beatrice, naked, stood before the basin and washed. "Let me give you something," Francesco said, continuing a conversation started an hour before—a conversation of stilted, formal exchanges while they lay sweating and unsatisfied on opposite sides of the bed.

"I told you, monsignore, I expect nothing."

"A new gown, perhaps? Something blue? Blue would suit you, or something red, with your hair that color,"

Beatrice turned, frowning. The light fell in purple shafts on the overripe breasts and roundness of her belly. So mature a body for such a young girl. He wanted to take her but knew it would be another wasted effort, another embarrassment.

"Whatever you may think, I am not a whore."

"I never did. I just didn't expect—"

"And I still have my maidenhead, so I will go to my husband stainless, won't I?"

"You're betrothed?"

"No," she answered, turning to smile. "I hope to be. My father thinks of finding a rich man for me."

"Ah," he said, and thought, *a nobleman's cast-off mistress secures a better marriage than most.* "Surely you came here expecting something. Your father's prompting . . ."

"Nothing. Truly, signor. I expected nothing."

"But surely,"

"Again, I tell you—nothing."

Her tone was like ice.

Francesco turned over in bed to observe the sun as it tinted the horizon and threw pinpricks of light between the chinks in the wall. There was no frost and the snow had stopped falling. Perhaps the ride to Florence would be easier now.

The sound of the water pouring in and out the basin and the song Beatrice was humming began to irritate him.

"You're a strange man to trouble yourself over someone like me," Beatrice said now, but not unkindly. "I am nothing, and you are who you are. I don't want anything, especially when I know you offer it as consolation for your lacking. I can look to myself."

The comment stung Francesco more than the melted snow that now dripped through the beamed roof and fell on his naked shoulders.

CHAPTER 8

AS SOON AS Beatrice was dressed and gone, Francesco hurried into his clothes, gathered his belongings and went in search of Lorenzo, who was coming to wake him when they met on the bridge spanning the loft and inn. "Are we ready to go?" Francesco asked.

"Just waiting for you, signore. Will you break fast . . . Signore?" Lorenzo noticed his preoccupation with the activity in the street.

"Not hungry," Francesco answered and motioned for the boy to hurry along. The idea of an encounter with Fiasella and his family in the common room wasn't worth putting food in his belly, no matter how ferociously it growled. In no time, his party was gathering in the street. Fiasella ran out of the common room, still in night shirt and gown, his feet bare as Francesco mounted up and started shouting orders.

"Signore! Signore, a moment!" Fiasella cried.

"Good morning, Fiasella." Francesco tugged gently on the reins to calm his restive horse and avoid trampling the man, who was too close for safety's sake.

"Here are my daughter's favors," Fiasella said and shoved embroidered ribbons at Francesco. "She bids you wear them in the lists."

"When I have the mind to joust," Francesco replied, amused. "Good day, Fiasella. We'll see one another again, I'm sure."

Fiasella didn't move. He was staring at the purse attached to Francesco's cincture. "Kindness, one man to another, monsignore, is often rewarded?" he hinted, his eyes sliding towards the door where Beatrice and her mother watched.

The purse was unloosed and tossed to the ground, coins spilling out into the snow, and snatched up greedily.

"Here now!" Fiasella shouted at a goose that swallowed a florin. "What did you ever do to earn that?"

"Indeed," Francesco said and rode out.

The rest of the journey was quick and blessed by good weather and good spirits.

"Do you hear that?" Lorenzo asked as they crested the hills near Maiano and rode down into the Arno Valley.

"The bells?" Francesco asked. It was impossible not to hear them, even though Florence was still three miles away. By the time they circled the walls of Florence and rode past the customs house through the Porta Rossa, they were deafening. Francesco didn't mind. It was Christmas morning, after all, and he had at last returned to his birthplace. He had come home.

The bells thundered in his ears as he rode over the Ponte Vecchio—sweet tenor voices melded with rich baritones, interrupted by the child-like timbres of neighborhood chantry bells; bells from the abbey church ran musical scales, while the lowering bell of the Palazzo dei Priori, La Vaca, added a bass undertone. Their music was so deafening Francesco could not hear the people in the street as his caravan wound through Florence, but he saw their faces and returned their salutes.

"That's the Conte di Romena!"

"...God bless him, but he's had enough of life's ills!"

"...he finally won the day against his uncle of Porciano! That's the way I heard it, and whether it be true..."

"...only a fool would think he could win all and keep it!"

"D'you talk of Porciano or this Romena?"

"God grant you good fortune, Signore Francesco!"

"God grant his father, evil bastard that he was, rot in hell for all his many crimes!"

"Hush! He looks this way!"

"I think my father's house is down this street," Francesco said over his shoulder to Lorenzo as he led them down a narrow street and into the Piazza del Duomo, the cathedral square, at the end of which was a new cathedral rising over the foundations of the old one.

They entered a square starting to fill with people coming from all corners of Florence to hear mass, and Francesco's arrival was unwelcome and poorly timed, for the new Bishop and his party arrived at the other end of the piazza just then. The square was soon congested with soldiers, wagons, carriages, and clergymen on foot, not to mention worshipers doing their best to get around the obstruction to their entry into the cathedral.

"Make way for the Bishop!" an episcopal herald cried at Romena's party. "Do you not hear? The Bishop comes this way! Move aside!"

"This is the Count of Romena, messer!" Lorenzo shouted back. "He is the last of his name and lord of a great house. Make way for Romena now or you'll suffer!"

"Lord of a bankrupt house! What's that to me? I tell you, the Bishop comes upon us! Move aside!"

"Monsignore, if you please—" Lorenzo was about to ask for Francesco's assistance but saw he was distracted. While everyone argued, two noblewomen and their attendants tried to get past to the cathedral steps.

"I'll meet you inside the cathedral," Francesco told Lorenzo and dismounted, plunging into the crowd. Count Guidi of Romena he may have been, the scion of an ancient, noble, family that claimed their fortunes and titles from the days of Empress Mathilda, to Florentines that Christmas morning he was nothing but a nuisance, a traveler in the way.

Francesco saw the glint of copper-colored hair escaping from under a prim veil and then he saw her face and knew it was the girl from the abbey. He smiled when he noticed her quick glance and then her look back before she and her companion were swallowed up by the human tide pressing from all directions. He'd have been pleased if he knew the two women were talking about him.

"If we go this way we can find places in the choir. My father's chapel is nearby," said the taller of the women, a striking beauty named Violetta Arcangeli, with fashionable blonde hair, dark, sloe eyes, and a lithe, willowy, body. "It will only be more crowded here at the font. See, the *contadini* have already come in and soon the wool workers—ugh, how they smell!"

"It is the Christe Masse, Violetta," said the other. Will you not show charity even today? Remember, their labor made your father wealthy."

"And yours, Serafina Giustini!" Violetta sniffed. She pulled the girl Serafina closer and pointed towards Francesco towering over the crowd. "Do you know him? He looks to be wanting your attention!"

Serafina looked back and felt the blush rising in her cheeks as he tried to get through the constantly moving and surging crowd to reach them. He was smiling and gesturing with his head to another direction, that she should follow.

"I think he means to win your favor," Serafina answered with head bowed to avoid attention. "You, after all, are the acclaimed beauty in Florence. Every man in Florence knows who you are."

"One poet's imaginings," Violetta simpered as she flirted with Francesco. "Let me think; who was it? Andrea Pulci? He tore up the sonnet when I said I could not love him and that my father was seeking a nobleman for me."

"He might have been a nobleman for all you know—wait, where are you going now?"

"He's going towards the choir. Come along! We should find out his name. Serafina, God's life! Will you hurry?"

"Go on; I'll join you shortly."

Serafina had stepped back to where the wool workers and servants of Florence crowded together to one side of the holy water font. She unloosed the velvet cord to her purse and distributed alms. Silver pennies passed from her immaculate hands to hands gnarled, dirty and scab-ridden, hands stained by dyes, hands groping and demanding. The wool workers pressed too close for Serafina's liking. She felt threatened and glanced around for an escape route. There was a tug at her neck and her pearl and ruby necklace was gone; someone groped at her sleeve, trying to remove the costly ornamental buttons of gold filigree. She was shoved against a pillar and stumbled, losing both prayer beads and breviary as she fell.

She felt suffocated by so many bodies closing in. Violetta was right; they did smell horrible, but what fault was it of theirs if they had no soap nor proper clothing because they had no money for the price of purchase? This was a momentary inconvenience for her; theirs was a lifetime.

The money in her purse was gone and now they were looking at her fur-lined cloak and gloves. Glancing up, Serafina thought to receive aid from one elderly man and was greeted by a mouth blackened by rotting teeth. The mouth hissed, raining spittle. And then a cackle—such a horrible, frightening sound she'd never heard in her life. A hand seized her shoulder and wrenched her upwards so that she was dashed against the pillar once more. The stench of garlic and decay was nauseating as he pressed closer.

"Pretty thing; pretty; so pretty! It's not pennies I want, Signorina! Not pennies! Be generous, Signorina!"

Serafina swallowed hard, closing her eyes, imagining abuses of the worst kind to befall her right under God's nose. Before she could call for help, he smothered her with a kiss and tore the empty purse from her girdle. The thief plunged into the crowd, laughing as he escaped.

She was delivered from further horrors when a gentleman scattered the workers and peasants and retrieved her breviary from the pavement.

"Are you hurt?"

Serafina knew the voice. She looked up apprehensively, then stared at the breviary gently placed in her trembling hands by Francesco, Conte di Romena.

"Only a little. My thanks, signor."

"You tremble. Are you certain you're whole?"

"Very much so."

"Shall we?" He pointed towards the northern end of the nave near the transept and close to a pillar without scaffolding. The Conte di Romena walked towards his chosen destination and looked back to see if she was coming. Serafina decided to follow. He knelt and quickly made his devotion, then bounded up easily. Her prayers took longer and when she stood, rising slowly and gracefully as she was taught, she glanced over and saw that he was staring.

Serafina was used to the way men looked at her, though why they should look, she was at a loss. Why would anyone want her? She was nothing like the tall, blonde women of Florence with their swan-like necks and graceful carriage, their high foreheads, and willowy forms. Her cousin Violetta, for example, was the acclaimed beauty of Florence for all these qualities Serafina lacked. They had nothing in common but kinship for when she looked in a glass she saw a diminutive, dark-haired girl with blue eyes so round she looked eternally surprised. As Serafina grew into womanhood, it only became worse for the roundness of childhood became curves that she constantly tried to hide to no avail.

And yet Conte di Romena watched her throughout the Mass, looking away when she glanced over. Their game of 'cat and mouse' ended when the bells rang at the elevation of the Host, and later when people lined up to receive communion. Serafina moved towards the center aisle and paused when she saw he did not follow.

"Will you not receive the Lord?" she asked kindly.

"When I've been to confession," he answered.

"Good day, then." Serafina offered a curtsey before she fell in line. Twice she glanced back and smiled.

When mass was done, Francesco saw the girl with her companion and their ladies as they crossed the nave and headed towards the western door that led out to the Piazza del Duomo. He slipped through the crowd and made a pretense of buckling the scabbard he wore on his belt as he stood by the entrance to the portico. The girl paused to look about several times.

Looking for me, perhaps? Francesco wondered hopefully.

". . . Serafina! We'll be late to supper! Where did you go? I looked all over for you. I blame you!" her beautiful blonde friend snapped and the girl hurried to catch her up.

"What have I done now?" she sighed.

"What do you think? Can you not guess?" the girl scolded as she pulled the other along. "The tall gentleman in traveling clothes. He disappeared into the crowd. Now I will never know who he is!"

The girl called Serafina smiled to herself and followed along.

Serafina.

At least Francesco had a name.

Lorenzo and the Romena caravan waited where Francesco left them. Soldiers and servants looked relieved when he appeared and came to life, mounting horses and carts for the rest of their journey.

"I asked some people about the Palazzo Romena, signore," Lorenzo said as he brought Francesco's horse forward. "It stands in the Borgo Santi Apostoli near the river, or close enough to the river by the old bridge."

Francesco nodded and looked around the square. He counted eleven streets that emptied into the Piazza del Duomo and contemplated which would be the best route. "I think this way," he murmured, turning south.

As they were negotiating their way through the crowd still pouring out of the cathedral, a man wrapped in a cloak stepped in their path. When Francesco moved to find another way out of the square, the man blocked his exit again. Francesco, thinking him a beggar, offered a *soldo* and God's blessing for the holiday. Still, the man wouldn't move. His face obscured by a hood, all that was revealed were cold blue eyes and pock-marked skin across his brow and chin. The eyes were riveting and held Francesco's attention.

"Will you let me pass, messer?" Francesco asked politely.

"I have a message from those who love you well, signor!" the man whispered.

Francesco was about to ask from whom when he saw the flash of a dagger and tried to move out of the way. He thought he'd escaped harm when the sting of the blade was felt in his sword arm as it dug through layers of clothing.

"Death to Romena!" the assassin shouted as he raised the dagger again.

Three of Francesco's soldiers managed to wrestle the would-be assassin to the ground. He kicked and screamed and lashed out with the dagger, keeping the Romena at bay.

"Take it from him!" Lorenzo shouted, watching and trying to shield Francesco. "Look out!"

Francesco managed to draw his sword in defense as the man rushed him, his eyes vacant and mouth gaping and foaming blood. Before he could reach Francesco one of the soldiers skewered his neck with a misericord and pushed him away as he fell.

The crowd around Francesco and his men stepped back as the Captain of the People's men rushed into the Piazza del Duomo and restored order.

"What's happened here?" barked their captain. He noticed Francesco gripping his bloodied arm with an even bloodier hand. "I don't recognize you or your banners, signor. If you've come to Florence for a quarrel our Podesta will set you straight!"

"He was attacked, signor; what will Florence do about it?" replied one of the Romena soldiers.

"Is there anyone besides yourselves that can swear to this?"

The captain glanced around at the crowd, as did Francesco. Francesco saw Serafina and her party on the perimeter and for a moment their eyes met, but the girl looked away and then gestured to one of the serving women in her retinue.

"Of all here, surely there is one who can tell us what happened," the captain said.

"The gentleman was leaving the piazza when he was attacked," spoke up one of Serafina's ladies.

"The lady speaks true. There was a struggle for his knife," Lorenzo added. "He would have done more harm if signore Romena's captain hadn't stopped him."

That was enough for the captain, who now called over one of his men and turning to Francesco said, "The abbey is just there, signor. A holy physic will attend to you. You are—?"

"Francesco Guidi da Romena, count and lord of the same," he replied.

"My apologies for this inconvenience, monsignore. What more may Florence do for you?"

"Escort my man Lorenzo to the house of Tommaso di Porciano. My kinsman has the keys to my house in the Borgo Santi Apostoli," Francesco requested before he went with his soldiers to the Badia, the Abbey of Florence.

ॐ

A LEATHER BAG, with a dozen keys and a book was delivered to Francesco at the Badia that afternoon. Francesco spilled the keys out and placed them side by side on the bed, taking note of the labels someone had taken great care to make and tie to each key. The book was of greater importance, for it was a record of the wool and cloth purchases from the time Alessandro da Romena had opened the first shop in the Via dei Calzaiuoli. He was one of many noblemen who turned to commerce for revenues, especially when inter-family and political quarrels drained bank accounts and emptied purses. Alessandro had saved his fortune and increased it by establishing a trade, only to have his widow lose most of it in her battle with Porciano.

Running a finger down the pages, Francesco discovered that not only was he a mirror image of his father, but their penmanship was identical, too. The fine, neat, italic hand of Alessandro startled Francesco, for the writing was so like his own. And then he smiled when he saw the entry, *three ells of fine linen for the contessa for her lying in.* Of course, Alessandro never saw the child that would be wrapped in the linen swaddling bands. Francesco was born three months after his father's death. There were other things such as new clothes and banners for Alessandro's sons from a first marriage, the finest cloth for dining with the Pope. An entire life was measured in these entries.

The creak and groan of an iron latch raised and the scuffing of feet told Francesco that Lorenzo had come back with his supper and the physic.

"I've faced worse," Francesco grumbled at his physic. "There's no reason to keep me locked up here."

"Another hour or two, to make sure the poultice knits up the wound and there is no chance of infection. As a soldier, you know how quickly cuts fester, and who's to know the blade wasn't poisoned?" the amiable physic chatted as he inspected the dressings and wound.

"Wouldn't I be dead by now?"

"A slow-acting poison. There are some known to take hours in their effect."

"Every day I wait to die," Francesco remarked. He smiled at Lorenzo as a bowl of stew was set before him, a spoon handed over. Fumbling with his left hand, Francesco managed to feed himself. "Any news about the man who tried to kill me?" he asked Lorenzo.

"Nothing, signore."

"There was something familiar about him."

"A brown cloak and hood, the stink of sweat. That could be any cut-throat in Italy," Lorenzo said.

"I'd like to discover that for myself," Francesco said and glanced at the physic. "Will I live?"

"A certainty, monsignore Romena. Be careful not to disturb the wound. Let others do your fighting while you heal," the physic replied. "One night of rest wouldn't be amiss, though."

One night to let the man or men responsible for the attack to take their plot even further, Francesco thought.

CHAPTER 9

NO ONE SEEMED to care that Francesco da Romena had arrived and waited in the doorway of the shop. The activity was quiet and economical, if economic was the word to describe how clerks spoke in hushed tones to clients as they displayed ells and bolts of cloth the Romena companies manufactured in their workrooms in Florence, or purchased at the great fairs of Champagne, Venice, and Constantinople, or how they silently made transactions, or how the weavers quickly worked their looms to create some of the most beautiful fabric Francesco had ever seen. The factors took inventory with economy climbing quietly up and down ladders and marked wax tablets as commerce hummed around them.

Francesco imagined this, the largest of his shops, would look much worse than it did: whitewashed rooms in a three-story building faced with plain Tuscan stone. Unlike the other shops in the street, this shop had large windows facing the Via dei Calzaiuoli that brought in wholesome air and light under which cloth finishers sat, embroidering freshly-dyed cloth, setting gemstones into fabric or brocading patterns on silks and velours. Clerks stood behind immaculate counters and attended to patrons' needs efficiently with a minimum of condescension. Francesco nodded to himself as he stepped past the threshold with Lorenzo at his side. Porciano did know how to run a business.

He was greeted by sterile smiles of acknowledgment and polite nods of the head, silent appraisal by clerks who knew nobility at first sight. No doubt he was to them yet another puffed-up nobleman with nothing on his mind but his own ease.

A watery-eyed clerk shuffled from behind his counter and bobbed like a pigeon. "Good day, signor!" the clerk greeted. "The Arte Romena can offer you the best cloth in all of Florence." He rocked back and forth on his heels, ready to be at Signor's pleasure. The clerk eyed Francesco appreciatively, knowing he could easily wrangle six florins out of this young man's purse for an ell of sarcenet that usually sold for three. He looked just the type– trinkets and cloth to court a stubborn young lady, no doubt the daughter of a good and honest merchant! This nobleman would pay handsomely as long as his purse was full.

"Good day, signor," Francesco said. "I'm surprised to find you open so early in the day. Aren't the shops supposed to open at nine o'clock in the winter months?"

"Oh, well, we had word that the young conte di Romena would pay us twice the wages if we kept longer hours, to see that all is in order when he arrives,"

"Did he?"

"Are you from the guild, signor? Because I have the letter from conte di Romena here, and it states his desires most emphatically." the clerk patted his chest.

"No, no; I am new returned to Florence and surprised to find the shops opened when all else in the street is shuttered. I see this is your good fortune, however, as I am in the mind to purchase the best cloth in Florence."

"What would signor's pleasure be today?" the clerk asked with a condescending smile.

"Something pretty and pleasing. I have my heart set on a lady."

"Ah! A lady of the noble class, perhaps? They're born and bred to expect finery and gentle wooing. Now here's something pretty," the clerk gushed. He took from a shelf behind him a fine ell of lapis lazuli velvet embellished with gold embroidered stars and unfurled it like a banner, snapping it directly in Francesco's face. "Ladies do like this sort of thing. Pretty enough for a bed-gown, eh, signor?"

"Hmm, don't know, really; the ladies I fancy tend to like brighter colors. But this young lady…that rose-colored silk shot with gold. The brocaded one?"

The clerk's face dimmed as he looked where Francesco pointed. "Truly signor, I know this cloth to be the finest. I found it in Venice and got it for practically nothing. I'll let you have it for eight florins, ten denarii."

Francesco offered a dazzling smile as he crooked a finger at Lorenzo, who handed his master a satchel from which Francesco took a book and flipped to a well-worn page. "Did you now? Because when my uncle Porciano found that very cloth in Provence—here it is, here's the entry; do you see?—it was two and six. Signor, allow me to make an introduction; I'm Francesco da Romena."

The shop was suddenly quiet as all eyes turned toward the young man at the counter. Francesco looked around in amusement. Clerks looked around their customers, and customers twisted about to stare. The finishers stopped their needles, waiting. Grains of sand slipped through the hourglass during the uncomfortable silence.

Upstairs a door nearly exploded off its hinges when it was thrown open and a portly man burst out, followed by a clerk.

"What's this? Get back to work now or signor Francesco will warm your backsides with his boot, and if he won't, I will, by God's teeth!" the man bellowed.

Francesco went to the foot of the stairs. "No I won't, and I dare say you wouldn't either. You're Davizzi, the manager of this shop, I take it? I'm Romena, and if you wouldn't mind, I'd like to see for myself what I wrote in that letter."

Davizzi turned gray and then purple in turns as Francesco came upstairs. When Francesco paused before him and waved a hand towards the office door, he hurried to show him the way.

"The letter signor?" Francesco asked, smiling.

"The letter? Ah! Yes, well," Davizzi started to look through documents scattered over a desk already cluttered with ledgers, flasks of wine and the plate of an unfinished meal. "The letter..."

"There isn't one."

"Ah. Yes, that would be correct."

"Using my name to coerce the workers, or rather, bully them into working. Did it work?"

"Oh indeed, Signor! Messer Tommaso said that—"

"That's all I need to hear. Shall we strike a bargain, Signor Davizzi? In exchange for your turning a deaf ear to my uncle's advice, you will keep your position here. That is all for now."

Francesco paused and looked around the office, noting shelves of dusty books and the iron-banded strong boxes on the floor. He bent down and in the middle of Davizzi's protest threw back the lid to discover bags of florins, jewels, plate, and spices.

"There is one thing," Francesco said as he stood and dusted his hands on his cloak. "The lapis lazuli velvet and the rose-colored brocade downstairs. I'll take those. I'll have a man come back for that chest."

Once again Davizzi turned gray and purple as he swallowed his objections and Francesco left the shop.

"Monsignore?" Lorenzo said as he hefted the bolts of cloth on his shoulder and they walked from the Via Calzaiuoli. "May I say something?"

"Of course."

"That was an excellent morning's work."

"I'm sure there'll be more," Francesco replied. "Let us call upon my uncle Porciano. Let's see if we can add to our achievements for one day."

❧

THE SERVANTS LOOKED fearfully and suspiciously at Francesco standing in the courtyard of the Porciano house; more than anything they watched the two soldiers accompanying him as they followed while he paced the courtyard, the flash of the sun on the hilt and pommel of the fine sword in the scabbard at Francesco's hip. Five of them in all, with two staring down from the second floor. When a door slammed and an elegant bald man with the sharp aquiline features of ancient Florentine blood appeared on the third floor landing the servants disappeared. He wore a single chain of office, was dressed in dark robes befitting a cleric or necromancer and came silently and slowly down the staircase, hands folded in fur-trimmed sleeves. All the better to make an impression, Francesco thought.

"You are conte Francesco da Romena?" he asked. The voice matched the appearance precisely and Francesco actually shivered.

"I am. You are?"

"Galeotto. I am the steward of this household. You wish to see ser Gian Maria. He is not here, nor has he been for some time."

"I was told this was his home, at least, his father's home, and he resides here."

"He is not here. Nor has he been. For some time."

"Then I will see his father, my uncle."

"He will not see you. I am to tell you that you have the keys to the house and all that you demanded of him. You need nothing more. Good day, signore."

Galeotto turned and went back upstairs. The soldiers looked to Francesco questioningly who shook his head and motioned towards the door. As they were leaving, a serving girl appeared from a storeroom off the courtyard. Francesco felt her tug on his sleeve and turned.

"There is a cook shop in the Via Santa Elisabetta, signor. Ser Gian Maria often goes there. The sign of the golden fish. They know him in the quarter. See if he isn't there."

"Where do I find this shop?"

"Towards the river, in the Piazza Santa Elisabetta, near the church. Follow the street toward the river. You'll see it."

"My thanks, signorina," Francesco murmured and pressed a florin in her hand before leaving.

He decided to go alone to this cook shop and sent his men back to the Romena tower house. The path from the Via Calzaiuoli south towards the Arno River led him past a jumble of streets, passing dark alleys and corners and finding sunlit piazzas at their ends, walled gardens and courtyards crowded with irregular arches and stairways.

The cook shop stood out from the tower houses in the neighborhood, a squat masonry building crowded at the end of a tiny square, the golden fish sign the only bright thing about it.

No sooner had Francesco arrived than he heard his name shouted in a familiar yet strange voice. He turned in the direction of the shout and saw Gian Maria di Porciano huddled on the steps of a house across the street from the shop. The boy edged back defensively as Francesco approached, fear apparent in his red-rimmed, swollen, eyes.

"So you've come at last," Gian Maria greeted. "You took your time."

"I wasn't aware that you were waiting for me," Francesco answered jovially. He nodded towards the cook shop. "A pretty serving girl at your father's told me you'd be here. I wanted to show you the Torre Romena, but since we're here perhaps you'll dine with me?"

"Sorry, no," Gian Maria answered, taking a drink from the wineskin at his side. "I've got no money. Sold my sword three nights ago to buy wine and a whore. The wine was the better bargain."

"You should have kept your sword. You can always count on it bringing satisfaction," Francesco teased, and then looked more closely, fingering the worn and dirty over gown and tunic Gian Maria was trying to hide with his cloak. So many weeks had passed since the rout of Fronzola and the accord that followed. "Gian Maria, what's happened to you? When we parted at Castello di Romena—"

"Robbers and bad choices. That's all you need to know."

"What of the revenues from Focognaio?" Francesco asked.

"You didn't tell me it had been deserted for twelve years and needed repairs."

"You know I was an absent landlord. Didn't I say it wasn't worth much?"

"It's a little less than that, but I'll make it something worthy when I've enough money," the boy vowed, avoiding Francesco's inquiring gaze. "Oh, all right! I enfeoffed the castle to pay my gambling debts!"

"You've no revenues, then?"

"I have means,"

"But you just told me you couldn't pay for supper,"

"I can get another sword. There's not a man in Florence who can best me."

"At dice?"

It was a moment before the boy's resolve crumbled and his lip gave way to trembling. "Go to hell, Francesco!" he spat. "Spend your righteousness on someone who cares!"

Gian Maria crumpled to his knees and sobbed into his filthy hands. The shadow falling across him made Gian Maria look up and he saw the bright white linen of a pristine cuff, took in the scent of citrus and sandalwood.

"Consider this a loan of two florins. That should buy supper and wine." Francesco offered, his hand extended.

It purchased considerably more for the Golden Fish was a wretched hole in the wall where the quality of the women and the drink was questionable and the patrons looked to be planning their next murder or robbery. Gian Maria didn't care, nor did Francesco as they leaned elbows on a damp plank board table that reeked of stale wine and greasy meat pies and little streams of ale crept into the seams of the wooden planks.

"Why this concern, Cousin?" Gian Maria demanded as he waved over a serving girl. Another pitcher of ale and a hot meat pie were set before him. "In all the weeks since your victory at Fronzola—"

"Our victory. Without your men and strategy, we'd have been slaughtered. You're a fine soldier. I don't know why you make your living as a merchant. The world's in need of decent battle commanders."

"I don't make a living at all."

"You're Tommaso's only surviving son and heir and I know for a fact that he's one of the richest men in Florence with one of the finest homes."

"Yes, you have the truth of it. He's got a home and riches, but I have neither. I can't go home because I haven't got one. I sleep in churches and stay in neighborhoods my father would never dare enter. I look over my shoulder every time I hear a footstep or the sound of metal to make sure it isn't one of Father's condittiore. I've a mind to go to Venice, or Rome when I've got the money. As far away as I can to stay alive," Gian Maria spat. He grabbed the pitcher and poured a cup to overflowing. "You don't know what it's like, Cousin!"

"How do you know?" Francesco demanded softly.

"You're the Conte di Romena! People are lining up to kiss your handsome ass and win a favor or two!"

"I don't see you bending over."

Gian Maria was ready with a bawdy and wicked reply when the cook shop owner suddenly appeared at his shoulder and whispered in his ear. Gian Maria swore and looked around, muttering, "That's right I don't have one!"

"What are you talking about?" Francesco laughed.

"I don't have a sword and now would be the best time to have one. Don't ask questions, just come. Now! The Romena colors gave you away!"

Francesco was ready to demand an explanation when he saw Tommaso di Porciano and three of his servants approaching them.

"I'll have no trouble here, signori!" the cook shop owner barked. "Take your quarrel outside!"

"This is how you repay your father for all I've done for you?" Tommaso growled as he came at Gian Maria, weaving drunkenly and stumbling into people and furniture. "This is thanks?"

"What you've done for me?" Gian Maria exclaimed. "You threatened to kill me in my bed if I didn't leave! What you have done is kill my brothers and would have me dead, too, because we wouldn't play your game! It matters little to you what others suffer as long as your bed is warm and your table plentiful!" Gian Maria spat. "How much longer will you steal from your kinsmen and friends and think it right? Better still, not get caught!"

"The mouse has some courage, does it?" Tommaso sneered. "I guess with wine and the sainted Alessandro's bastard brat to protect you it's easy to say what you like and not worry about the consequences!"

"What's that supposed to mean?" Francesco demanded.

"Alessandro turned my brothers and sister against me after he got them into bed! It doesn't surprise me I've found you here of all places – after all, this was where he made his assignations and raped men and girls alike!"

Tommaso's men and Gian Maria held Francesco back as he reached for his sword.

"Oh, you don't like unkind things said about your father, even if they are the truth?" Tommaso laughed. "Ask anyone who was alive then! He'll tell you more than you want to know and it won't be pretty!"

"It's unfortunate Alessandro didn't kill you when he met you here to do your whoring and drinking all those years ago," Gian Maria spoke up. "You wouldn't have had to worry about sons."

"Sons are no good to me!"

Tommaso went for Gian Maria, who did his best to fend off the attack, but he was overwhelmed by Tommaso's men and dragged out in the street despite the efforts of bystanders and Francesco to intervene, as they were held back by cook shop patrons and followers of Porciano. Alarms rang and people called for the soldiers of the commune when two of the men started to beat Gian Maria until he fell to his knees and tried to fend off the blows. Francesco was able to draw his sword and after a brief skirmish wounded one of the men and chased off the other two.

"Leave off!" Francesco barked at Tommaso when he kicked Gian Maria. He threw Tommaso against a wall and held a knife to his throat. "If you lay a hand to the boy again, I'll kill you!"

It was a moment before Francesco loosened his hold. Tommaso shrugged the younger man off and wiped the sweat from his eyes. "Will you now?" he queried, and his smile mocked. "He's my boy, from my seed. I don't need you to tell me how to teach a wayward traitor of a boy a lesson in manners! There's not a man in this town that wouldn't do the same!"

"What's done is done. Be grateful for the one boy you have left."

"Do you tell me my business?" Tommaso growled.

"I do. Pray I need not do it again!"

Shouting for Lorenzo, Francesco left.

Gian Maria called after him and then ran as fast as he could to catch up. "Where, where...do you go?" Gian Maria panted.

"To my house in the Borgo Santi Apostoli." Francesco helped Gian Maria onto the withers of the horse. "Think of it as sanctuary."

The boy leaned wearily against Francesco and as they rode off to more hospitable quarters, Francesco felt the sobs that racked his cousin's body. With his free arm, Francesco embraced Gian Maria and said everything would be all right.

CHAPTER 10

THE NOISE AND disturbance at the cook shop brought neighbors in the Via Santa Elisabetta to their windows, especially at the Torre Arcangeli, which fronted the shop in its dark little corner. The shabbiest of the noble tower houses in the ancient neighborhood, it was the property of the notary Agnolo Arcangeli, a gentleman of some means but poor choices where it concerned his political allies. What he could salvage of his honor and fortune was here in this tower and in the person of his niece, Serafina Giustini, who had arrived in Florence and had taken up residence with him. One of the greatest heiresses in Tuscany, she had lived outside of the city of her birth for all of her young life and had come to claim her legacy now that fortune's wheel had spun in her family's favor. She was a stranger to everyone, especially the servants crowding the windows for a look to see what was happening.

"Pah! It's only Tommaso the cloth merchant from the Via Calzaiuoli," said one woman to another. "I should have a *soldo* for every time he quarrels with someone."

"Who is it now—ah! It's his boy, ser Gian Maria," said another.

"What's he done now?" asked a third.

"Look, someone's roused the Watch and good thing, too. Who's that with Gian Maria? The tall one with the dark cloak?"

"What's this?" Serafina's nurse Marghareta demanded as she entered the bedchamber and found the maids gawking. "I'm sure you have better things to do than watch a street brawl! Come away!"

"I'm sure they do, but let them have the pastime," Serafina said following her in. She was dressed in a nightshift and bed robe and paused to study the dresses unpacked from trunks and laid out on the bed.

"Fools arguing in the shop across the street," Marghareta grumbled as she sat on a cushioned stool and picked up her needlework. "Ah, my stomach! I shall tell the cook her dishes are too savory for my liking." Marghareta sighed and picked up her embroidery frame. "I'm more accustomed to good, plain, fare such as that in the houses of the Poor Clares and the Cistercian sisters, for which I am thankful." And here the nurse belched so loudly that Serafina's little dog woke from its nap and started yapping.

"Really, Marghareta!" Serafina laughed and turned a deaf ear to the excuses being rattled off each finger, from baked apples to stewed eels.

Marghareta sniffed. "Begging your pardon Madonna, if I were looking for a husband, I wouldn't eat as much as some young ladies did at supper!"

"I'm not looking for a husband. And some of us can afford to eat as much as we like."

"And like as not, some can't. You barely fit into the green sarcenet your father sent from Lucca! Men like their women soft and round, but not as round as a dumpling."

"Men like the dowry brought to their bower and keep their mistresses. They care nothing for their wives. Any man that takes me to wife will have to take me for my soul, not my body," Serafina answered as she held up two dresses with provocative necklines. As expected, Marghareta shook her head and pointed to a gown, a gown, of dark blue wool.

Marghareta glanced at Serafina between stitches. The girl was taking a turn before the looking glass. A body like Serafina's would better suit a taller woman. Those fine, full breasts, round hips, and thighs only made her look plumper than was fashionable. And such a tiny waist in the bargain! It was a curse and blessing, Marghareta thought as she crossed herself, that Serafina looked so much like her mother. There wasn't a man in Florence who'd take the girl for her soul once he'd set eyes on her!

Already she'd had offers to pose for several Florentine painters at work in the new cathedral. Marghareta chuckled quietly when she thought of her young charge posing as a serene Virgin—Our Lady of the Back Stairs Assignations!

Serafina was now spanning her waist with long, tapered fingers, and from the sighs Marghareta heard, she wasn't far off the mark that taking a little less at supper would not have been amiss for the girl.

"I think you are the only person who isn't afraid to speak the truth to me," Serafina said, her voice muffled by the fabric of the gown she was pulling over her head. She waved over a servant to lace up the side seams.

The noise of the quarrel outside the cook shop was rising and the trumpets of the podesta's guard now added to the disturbance.

"Shall it always be like this in Florence?" Serafina wanted to know as she peered out a window.

"If you wanted the quiet of Santa Felicita, you should have told your father you preferred the convent," Marghareta sniffed. "Though what I should do,"

"You'd find another girl to scold and make miserable," Serafina teased.

"And living another two years in the convent would have done some a world of good. Child! Where do you go?"

Serafina had wrapped herself in a cloak and was draping a veil over her head.

"There are things to be done," she replied, placing bundles in a basket.

"I go to see a friend."

"You've got no friend that I – oh!"

It took very little persuasion for Marghareta to fetch her cloak and follow, for the last time her mistress had gone off alone, she'd received a beating.

They crossed into the Oltrarno, the poorest of the neighborhoods outside the walls of Florence, to the Via del Leone and a tenement built up on the river bank so haphazardly it resembled a nightmarish castle. They stopped at one of the better houses, where an elderly woman in twice-turned but immaculate clothes answered Serafina's knocks.

"God give you peace this day, Anna," Serafina greeted.

"Madonna Giustini! We weren't expecting you for weeks!" the woman called Anna exclaimed, and she turned to look behind her, then back at Serafina, her face flushed in scarlet.

"May I come in?"

"We weren't expecting you, you see,"

"Things have changed and my father bade me come sooner." Serafina took a parcel from the basket and handed it to the woman. "Here you are, a new gown cut in the Venetian style, and a new apron embroidered with crimson wool. I had my sarta make them for you."

Anna received the gifts with a prim incline of her chin. "It would have been better to use the money for food and coal," she sniffed as she opened the door wider and brought them inside, glancing out into the street before shutting the door. "There's been nothing to eat for days. I bought a small amount of coal yesterday, but I had to pawn my wedding ring for it!"

"Where's Gemma?" Serafina demanded, glancing around. She didn't see the familiar servant that had been her childhood companion.

Anna sighed as she turned to the hearth where a porridge boiled. "I had to let her go. When I offered to help, madonna, I didn't offer to pay the wages of a girl I can ill afford. I have only so much room and so much food. And you haven't paid for the last five months."

"My father," Serafina stopped, knowing the reaction finishing that sentence would bring. She dug into the purse on her girdle and let the chink of coins hitting one another end further discussion on the matter. When Anna starting whining about a new roof, Serafina gave her a look that warned to tread carefully, then crossed the chamber and drew back mildew-stained curtains from a corner bower, exposing a woman in her sick bed.

"Mother, I've come," Serafina whispered in the woman's ear.

It was some time before the woman opened her eyes. Recognizing Serafina, she brightened and smiled.

"You've grown! Let me look at you. You're a woman," she whispered in rasping, borrowed breaths. "Your father's been charitable to let you come."

"How are feeling these days?"

"Today I woke and felt strength . . . for the first time in weeks. It comes and goes. But I know . . . my time is soon, and I've made my peace with God . . . and a few others. Your father. Is he well?"

Serafina coughed to hide her resentment. Her mother was dying in a tenement and could count her remaining days on one hand, yet she cared only for the man who had abandoned them to save his political soul and neck!

"Well enough," Serafina answered cryptically.

"You say!" Anna laughed. "He's done well for himself, I think! The commune pardoned him. He was exonerated of past crimes!"

"Is this true, Serafina?" the woman asked, her eyes brightening.

"You have the right of it," the girl said dully.

"And did he come with you from Lucca?"

"No; he'll be here soon."

The woman's face clouded in puzzlement and she began to weep. "Of course! I should be a fool . . . to think he'd come . . . for me after . . . these many years!"

Serafina now regretted her hardness and smoothed the woman's hair and kissed her. "Nay, Mother! These many years he has loved you well. I know he holds you in esteem."

Across the room, Anna noisily set upon the porridge bubbling and scorched in the kettle. "He held her hostage these many years!" she groused. "And what about you, madonna Serafina? What esteem has he shown you? He took you in grudgingly – and only because he was forced to! Look 'round yourself, child! What do you see? Not his esteem. Most days there isn't fat for the fire! He might have saved her from this life! And my husband, rest his immortal soul, my husband was your father's partner! He ruined my husband! He's not done right by me, either!"

"Not fair, that!" Serafina protested. "He didn't have a choice. It was Alessandro da Romena; everyone knows it was Romena who ruined us."

"He made his choice by protecting him!"

Serafina rose and took Anna by the wrist, preventing her from stirring the kettle. "Enough! You don't need to remind my mother of all that passed. You forget that my father suffered for what he did. Had he returned to Florence, he would have been put to death once he passed through the gates."

Anna freed herself and waved Serafina's argument away as if it was an insect. She wiped her hands on her apron and started to tidy the chamber. "Oh yes, we all know what he did! All those years she met in secret with him! The shame! So many nights riding to tryst. In ale houses, cow byres, churches even! He never thought that if they were discovered she'd be cast into the street or burned for an adulteress. It never occurred to him! And I was made a party to it! While they made love and whispered honey-sweet words and fell asleep in each other's arms, I was made to stay awake and keep watch, for fear they'd be discovered!"

"Yet you did not complain, nor did my mother."

"How could we? We were promised much and given little. He got her with child in a hurry! What could she do?"

"They loved one another. That rights a wrong."

"And brought more mouths to feed! Oh, child! Do you think he loved anything but his own ease? Life isn't what the *trovatori* sing."

Anna reached out and grasped Serafina's soft white hand in her careworn, leathery, palm. A hand once as beautiful as her own, Serafina thought; a hand once adorned with jewels. Serafina felt a strange heat and strength in the grasp. She did not dare move and was compelled to look in the older woman's eyes. They were bright with fire.

"If you only knew . . . it's a blessing the plague came and took her two sweet boys, else we would have starved," Anna continued. She smiled then and winked. "I took care of you, though. No one thanked me for saving you from the fever. You were only a few months into the world, so small and frail you were . . ."

"My grandmother took me in," Serafina corrected her. Anna had a way of turning life's tragedies into triumphs for herself.

"Your grandmother!" Anna spat, and she turned to stir the porridge. "Your grandmother tried to ignore all that happened and accepted your father's money to stay silent. After all, she had her ladies to think of, her candle shop and spices, her noble customers! Not a man with a title was safe from her! No! No, hear me out! Your father Durante was young and a fool. When he fell upon hard times and the money stopped, she got rid of him easily enough. Your grandmother pressed your mother into service to pay her debts! What your mother gave Durante freely he was now expected to pay for! And your grandmother knew he couldn't and didn't care. He might have taken your mother into exile, but did he? No. And he didn't want to."

"How could he?"

"Ah, after all these years, you champion him?"

"I don't condone what happened, nor what he did, Anna; I am only saying that any man in his circumstance would have had the same obstacles. He did what he could from Lucca."

"Indeed!" Anna laughed. "He paid your grandmother back in kind. He had his kinsmen bribe the Commune to arrest her and try her witchcraft! The candles and spices were used for casting spells, they said. She was sent from Florence to do penance in a convent. She's dead by now, and if she isn't, I pray God that she is and burning in hell! She left your mother with nothing but what you see here. And your father did no better for her!"

"And you were a guardian angel."

Anna banged the spoon against the kettle and then pointed it at Serafina like a weapon. "You have me to thank for saving you from this life!"

"How?"

"One night I took you to your father's kinsman, the notary Arcangeli. He gladly took you in—not as a servant as so many baseborn brats are, but as an heiress. There was no other to follow after Durante Giustini, so he took what was given to him as if he knew things would turn around. And so they did. A little bastard heiress. Your mother never forgave me for that."

"Serafina!"

The cry from the bed was a godsend. Serafina turned and found her mother pointing to a coffer on a shelf.

"Come! There's something . . . you should . . .have," the woman gasped.

Serafina reached for the carved box. Her mother's treasures were revealed when she threw back the lid: pieces of colored glass set in pot metal, ribbons, a baby's tooth, a pressed flower, and wrapped in a square of rubbed velvet was a large amethyst pendant suspended on a silver chain with silver findings.

"How beautiful this is!" Serafina whispered. "Mother, why was it never sold to buy food and clothes?"

"It is dear to me. Your eyes are . . . like this stone, Serafina. So said the gentleman . . . of my eyes, he that . . . gave it."

"Did Father give you this?" Serafina demanded.

"No, poor fellow! He was a nobleman . . . a great . . . ancient . . . house. Once I did . . . love him, but there were ugly . . . rumors. He betrayed me."

Serafina wrapped the pendant in its velvet and was ready to put it back in the box when her mother pressed it into her hands. "Take it! It's yours. I have nothing . . . more to give you,"

"I'll sell it for you,"

"I . . . forbid . . . it! People . . . will know!"

"Know what, Mother?"

The woman began to weep and mutter under her breath until Serafina finally slipped the pendant into her purse. She held out her hand to Serafina, who took and kissed it.

"Surely your . . . father has . . . given you finer things?" she asked.

"Nothing as beautiful as this, or that I could keep. We've sold much of my plate and jewels to pay debts and to rebuild the trade."

"But at least . . . a dowry."

"In truth, no. The lands and title I have make me a worthy prize for many. Father expects my suitors to pay him."

"And the . . . Peruzzi? I thought that Niccolo -?"

"Ah, that. Were they powerful enough to help Father realize his ambitions, I would have been married to old Battista months ago, and not his grandson! My father aims higher."

"Father's . . . ambition put me . . . here. Find . . . a husband . . . I die happy . . . knowing . . . cared for."

"I shall take care of you, Mother. I don't need a husband to do that!"

"Niccolo . . . is a good match – he loves you."

"It shall not be," Serafina answered impatiently.

"But surely," the woman's eyes clouded and she looked away, staring at her left hand, holding it up as if to study the bony fingers and wrinkled skin. "You will promise me . . . good marriage of . . . love."

"Oh, Mother," Serafina sighed. "There's no certainty of that. What is marriage other than a business transaction, to acquire property and titles, make babies and grow old with a stranger that, if fortune smiles, you will eventually learn to love?"

Anna cackled at this, adding, "There's my girl! She's right. Take a look around you. How many houses in Florence are full of married strangers? You see how man and wife grow old together. The world is full of unhappiness, and much of it starts in the marriage bed."

"Then I shall do my very best to change the way of things," Serafina replied.

"You . . . will marry . . . misfortune," her mother whispered and began to weep.

This woman, Ginevra Salvemini, the daughter of an infamous whore, had been the reputed beauty of Florence for many years. Men had loved her, desired her, quarreled to death over her, and her mother had made certain every man in Florence went to sleep at night desiring her. Durante Giustini, vassal to the Conti Guidi and signore of Montebuoni, had claimed her and given Ginevra this girl named Serafina.

"We've said enough, today," Anna said. "Madonna, your mother needs her rest," she hinted.

"Good child; a good child," Ginevra Salvemini whispered, and said she would sleep, for sleep restored all things and made her heart, now failing, stronger for a few hours. Serafina waited and then closed the curtains around the bed, leaving the once beautiful and legendary Ginevra to dream of happier times.

CHAPTER 11

SERAFINA HURRIED HOME by way of the Borgo Santi Apostoli where, in the Torre Romena and its house, Francesco and Gian Maria sat in the solar while servants around them continued a progress of restoration and cleaning that began on the first day Francesco da Romena arrived in Florence and took possession of them.

"Turn to the light, Gian Maria; I can stitch up this cut if I can see what I'm doing," Francesco said as he held a fish hook-like needle and length of silk thread over the gash in his cousin's forehead. Reluctantly, Gian Maria turned towards a window and reached for the wineskin on the table before them.

"I'd sooner have an apothecary do this," Gian Maria said as he took a drink and then winced as the needle dug into bruised and bleeding flesh, the silk burning and tickling as the wound was knit together and closed after torturous minutes.

"There. Now we pray to Saint Luke you'll mend and not die," Francesco said.

Gian Maria examined his bruises and cuts in the reflection of a salver on the table. "I can always say I got this brawling with the Alberti."

"Who?"

"My father's rivals in all things. He hates Andrea a little more than he hates me right now." A moment, then: "I don't suppose there's a room here I could claim for a while?"

"Of course. There are rooms enough."

"Well," Gian Maria sighed, glancing about the solar, "Tommaso will leave you alone. Too many ghosts in this place. Things happened here that may not be spoken of."

Francesco frowned. "Do you also believe the stories about my father?"

"I believe them if they're the truth, Francesco."

"Perhaps when I've been here a while people will forget the evil Alessandro was said to have done and see Romena in a new light."

"So says every son of an infamous man," Gian Maria said as he rose. His movements were slow and rather than show his cousin how painful it was, he put on a brave face and glanced around, smiling. "This will do nicely for a while. Until I'm back on my feet. And now cousin, let's drink to our fathers and their fathers before them and for all the trouble they caused. Let's dine. Our supper was interrupted."

❧

THE THRUM OF harps and drums and the whistling of pipes filled the night air in the Quartiere Santa Croce beyond Florence's walls. The watch had changed hours ago and the gates into the town were closed, but it didn't stop the custom in the bordellos and inns spreading out towards the Lungarno and the southern reaches. Here nobleman and merchant were equals, at least to the girls and their pimps. A florin was a florin, two was even better. In one of the better establishments, Francesco was finished dressing and turning to the pretty red-haired whore curled up in nothing but his violet cloak, placed a few coins on a table by the bed. Some intimate play finally gave Francesco his cloak.

"Stay awhile, signor," the girl purred in his ear while her hand slid inside his shirt.

"As much as that would please me, I can't," Francesco apologized as he gave her a last kiss and pulled the heavy velvet curtain back to step into the corridor lined with tiny rooms expensively furnished like this one. Somewhere among brocaded cushions and featherbeds, in the cloud of incense and candle smoke heavy with the stink of cloying perfume and sweat, Gian Maria was quarreling with someone over the bad throw of the dice. Francesco had already witnessed the trouble his cousin's mouth could raise twice that night and so walked the maze of corridors and rooms until he found Gian Maria in the owner's great parlor nose to nose with a merchant half his size but holding a dagger to the boy's throat.

"I tell you, the throw was good, a six and a two, which is more than your three and one!" the merchant spat. "Now pay!"

"Gian Maria, we must be going," Francesco said as he walked up and took the purse from his belt and counted out florins. "This is more than six, two, three and one. Good night, signor."

"That was the last of my money!" Gian Maria protested as Francesco dragged him off.

"No, it was the last of mine," answered Francesco and as they were leaving the bordello, Gian Maria pulled away and purposefully jostled a young man also leaving.

"God's life! Gian Maria!" the drunken young man bawled when he regained his footing.

Gian Maria squinted in the amber torchlight and grinned, his face macabre and amusing. "God's prick, cousin Azzelino! How opportune to find a man of God in a bordello! And of all places! Come to give absolution to us sinners?"

The two young men fell upon one another with embraces and kisses, the best of friends, then shoved the other away. Both glared. The tall, blond, young man with bloodshot green eyes now assessed Francesco, nodding in greeting. "Who's your friend, Gian Maria?" he wanted to know.

"This is our kinsman, Francesco da Romena," Gian Maria introduced. "He's only just arrived in Florence and has reclaimed the inheritance left to him by his father. Cecco, this is our cousin by a devilish marriage, Azzelino Alberti."

"Signor," Francesco greeted with a cordial nod of his head.

"Conte di Romena? Impossible! I heard you were murdered on Christmas Day!" Azzelino now burst into laughter. "Well, it must be true then. That you're the Son of God, messer Francesco, because here you are! Risen from the dead! Where's the seraphim and cherubim?"

"I sent them home," Francesco said drolly.

Azzelino chuckled at this and draped an arm around Gian Maria's shoulders. "I see our cousin Gian Maria wasted no time in falling in love with you. The Guidi of Porciano have a habit of getting into bed with the Guidi of Romena, but they never learn from their mistakes, do they?"

"I've heard the stories," said Francesco.

"Not all of them by far."

"Let's go," Gian Maria said to Francesco and shoved Azzelino aside.

"Be careful, ser Francesco; you don't want to end up like your father. Make a bedfellow of this one and you'll wind up in a dung heap a feast for wolves and worms!"

Azzelino's comment made Francesco turn. "What do you mean?" he asked.

"No one's told you about your father's death? D'you know it's a pauper rotting in Alessandro's tomb? They had to bury someone! A hundred church bells rang the night they dragged his body out of Signora Salvemini's bordello and tossed it to the wolves outside The Stinche. It's not far from here," Azzelino said and pointed southeast towards the black facade of the notorious prison jutting up into the sky. "There wasn't much left of him, but I heard the wolves died of indigestion!"

Gian Maria saw the sword sliding out of Francesco's scabbard and his hand instinctively went for a scabbard and sword not on his belt, clutching a strip of frayed, soft leather instead. Francesco shook his head and motioned with his chin for Gian Maria to back away.

"What's this?" Azzelino laughed.

"Walk away now," Francesco said. "I have no quarrel with you; walk away."

"Your anger makes it otherwise."

"Take back your insult of my father and walk away."

"Insult? Why, it's the truth. Everyone in Florence knows the story."

"I'm his son and it's the first I've heard it."

"Of course your mother wouldn't have told you what really happened,"

"Francesco, it's best to leave this fool alone," Gian Maria said. "What's done is done. He only apes what his idiot of a father does and says, but it's good enough for the Curia. After all, most of the cardinals are sodomites and pimps. How do you think cousin Azzelino got into holy orders? By sucking the Holy Father's cock and that of anyone else who had money or the Holy Father's ear – or should I say cock?"

Francesco moved just as Azzelino drew his sword in an arc as if wielding an ax and sliced the air. He spun about and paused to get his ground. The next drunken attack was no better but closer and he pushed Gian Maria out of the way as the blow landed on the stone face of a Madonna in a street corner tabernacle, cutting through sandstone and candles, spraying rock and tallow. The even clang of the metal against walls, the ground, and wooden doors as Azzelino tried to hit his mark was like a tolling bell.

Slice after slice was futile as Azzelino swayed and bobbed, the sword heavier in his hand with each attack. Francesco countered each if only to prevent Azzelino from hurting himself. Another blow fell on the pavement and shot sparks into the night sky, but a third would have dug into Francesco's shoulder had Gian Maria not grabbed a sword from Francesco's servant and in his effort to knock the weapon out of Azzelino's hand, stabbed him in the palm, the point digging through flesh and bone to the other side. The sight of the sword sticking out of Azzelino's hand with flesh and tissue dangling from the tip ended the confrontation.

"You'll pay for this! You'll both pay dearly!" Azzelino screamed as he fled with his bleeding hand wrapped in his cloak.

"You started it!" Gian Maria yelled back. "You'll have to explain to your father and the Archbishop just exactly what you were doing in a bordello. It doesn't become a man in holy orders! You were warned once before!"

"Let's go before the Watch comes," Francesco said.

"Best not to go home yet; the podesta's soldiers will know where to find us. I know a place," Gian Maria said, and leading Francesco through back alleys and dark streets to the northern walls of Florence found refuge in the crowded common room of a tavern hidden under the battlements of the Porta alla Croce.

A dark-haired girl came to their table, hips swaying gently and perfume announcing her arrival.

"Gian Maria," she purred.

"Contessina!" Gian Maria greeted, dragging the pretty girl onto his lap. "How long has it been? Do you have time for me?"

The girl had slipped her hand into Gian Maria's tunic and unfastened his cambric shirt, letting her fingernails scrape none too delicately across his chest. "You'll get nothing more from me until you pay your debt!"

Contessina giggled but nevertheless allowed Gian Maria the liberty of unfastening her shirt and pulling it off her shoulders.

"Sweetheart, I'll do whatever you want this time," Gian Maria begged.

"No, I said! You owe me three florins!" Contessina's voice had taken a hard pitch and she now managed to pull her clothing together and slide off Gian Maria's lap. "You know where to find me when you have the money. I'll only wait a quarter hour, and it will cost you plenty!"

The little whore strolled away. She paused, leaned down to adjust the garter on one stocking and made sure Gian Maria could see all that he wanted.

"For the love of Christ, Cecco, give me the loan of seven florins, I only have two!" Gian Maria begged, watching to make sure she didn't find someone else.

"She said you owed her three and how will we pay for this wine?"

This sword of yours will bring four at least!"

Francesco grabbed the weapon and gently pried it out of Gian Maria's hands. "I've only got the one. Judging by our adventures tonight I suppose I'll need it again soon, especially if you can't keep quiet."

"That's sounds as if you think the quarrel was my fault."

"Wasn't it? There's only so much wine a man can drink and so many women to bed. Eventually, you have to make an accounting."

"God help me, but I've saddled my fate to a sacrosanct priest!"

"You're too fond of wine, Gian Maria."

"And you're too fond of looking holy – or finding fault in others!"

"Go to hell."

"Thanks to you, I've been there more than once!" Gian Maria said. "Maybe I have saddled the wrong horse; maybe you're as bad as everyone says you are. I'll lock my bedchamber door just in case."

They stared at one another for a long, painful minute. It was too early for a breach, not when the friendship was young. Gian Maria cursed himself for the wine that made his tongue and thoughts so loose. "Sorry, didn't mean to say that," Gian Maria apologized. "I don't mean to say a lot of things, but they just come out, God help me."

"Leave it."

"You're the last soul on earth I'd want to disappoint. Not because of what you would feel, but what you might do." Gian Maria admitted now.

"Don't make promises you won't keep."

"It's not a promise, but a matter of self-preservation."

"Is it true about my father?" he asked.

"Depends on what you want to know."

"A pauper lies in the tomb?"

"Yes."

"My father's body then, was it thrown to the wolves outside the prison?"

"Yes. All that was left of it—never mind."

Francesco nodded and pulled a flask of wine into his hands, folding them around clay bowl and while his hands shook, drank deep. He was still drinking when Gian Maria slipped quietly away.

PART II – THE PRIZE

CHAPTER 12

"PARDON, SIGNOR . . . THERE'S a gentleman at the gate."

The customs official glared over his cup of ale. "There usually are gentlemen at the gate," he sniffed, "it being the way into Florence."

"Truly, signor, you must come down," the soldier begged. "The men say he is an exile from the days of signore Bardi."

Counting backward, the customs official ciphered twenty years or more since Bardi di Bardo was the podesta, mayor, of Florence. That could only mean...

He glanced at the soldier before draining his cup and snapped his fingers saying, "My chain of office. Give it to me." The heavy gold medallion dangling from an equally heavy chain was hastily fastened around his collar as they went down.

A gaunt gentleman blocked the northern gate into Florence. Behind him waited a caravan of a half-dozen knights, several loaded carts, and a carriage. The horse he sat was tired, looked near to death, but the gentleman carried himself like a nobleman and his clothes certainly touted affluence. In his cap was a fine gold medal, which the customs official recognized as the insignia of the tyrant of Lucca, Castruccio Castracane.

"Letters of safe conduct," the gentleman said before greetings could be exchanged. He pulled out a sealed document from his sleeve and handed it over.

A cursory glance was all that was needed. "Florence welcomes you home, signore Durante," the customs official greeted and bowed to former exile Durante Giustini, signore of Montebuoni and vassal of the Guidi of Romena.

Nodding, Durante accepted his good wishes and gently urged his mount through the gates and past the battlements south into Florence.

What lay before Durante Giustini was nothing more remarkable than a town in the midst of commerce on a market day. Florentines washed down their pavements and tradesmen were raising the awning over their shops, setting their goods out on counters, the aroma of baking bread and meat sizzling on spits covered up the more disgusting but usual smells of humans and animals, the stench of death and decay, of perfume and soap mingling. The sight before him brought tears to his eyes. It had been so very long since he'd been here; so many years since he had been one of the great men of Florence.

He would be so again.

Durante turned to one of his captains and said, "Go the rest of the way to the Via Santa Elisabetta to my brother-in-law's house. Tell ser Agnolo I'll join him shortly." And Durante tugged on the reins so that his palfrey went in a southwesterly direction to the Borgo Santi Apostoli and the Torre Romena and its house.

The shock of seeing Alessandro's house after so many years came as a surprise; in his thoughts and dreams, it hadn't changed. All the houses in the street with their towers of nobility were faced with plain stone and had little ornamentation. Not so with this house. Alessandro da Romena wanted something like a castle. Had Alessandro been any other man, Durante thought, no one would have cared. Certainly not the magistrates of Florence. Instead, this building project was seen as a threat to liberty and peace. Durante stared at the lions' heads mounted on the unfinished façade above the gates, the brass plates illustrating the story of Parsifal mounted on the doors. The morning he was banished the brasses had been new, the marble lions smelled pleasingly of newly cut stone. Today they looked a century old. Even the celebrated glass windowpanes that reflected light and caused everyone to call it the "House of Mirrors" were in disrepair. Workmen were now cleaning the grit off the brasses and mounting standards blazoned in the Romena colors of *murrey* and *or*. There was truth to the rumor that in Florence titles could be purchased cheaply!

A servant washing down the pavement in front of the palace stopped when he saw Durante and nodded curtly. "Is there something you want, signor?" he asked.

"Who is your master?" Durante queried in turn.

"The conte di Romena, signor."

"And do you know he's been dead these twenty-three, almost twenty-four years?"

"I'll tell my master that; since he looked very much alive when he rose from bed this morning." the servant answered.

"Tell your master Durante Giustini wishes him well of that he's taken, though conte di Romena he is not!" and saying this, Durante spurred his horse and was gone in a shower of snow.

Francesco was at a window facing the street when the servant came in.

He turned, asking, "Who was that?"

"A gentleman called Durante Giustini, monsignore. He bade me say to you that he wishes you well of what you've taken, but you are not the conte di Romena."

"There are days when I wish that were true. I'm going to market. Tell Lorenzo to meet me in the courtyard."

Francesco enjoyed market day as much as the fairs of Champagne. Anything the heart could hope for was crowded into the Mercato Vecchio, built, according to legend, over a Roman forum in the heart of Florence. Wagons from the *contado* packed every inch of the square, their brightly painted counters dropped down and laden with everything imaginable, from wine to silk ribbons. From stall to booth and booth to cook shop, Francesco moved amiably among the people he now called his kinsmen, smiling at and greeting those who recognized him, accepting their wishes and prayers for a happy future.

Lorenzo offered to find a wine seller and left Francesco near the spice merchants' stalls. Here pungent sandalwood burned, beckoning the curious to inhale its perfumed smoke. Fragrant spices for cooking were uncovered and prospective buyers were urged to sample the pepper, saffron, ginger, and mint from the Levant and Orient displayed in colorful clay pots. Merchants with gleaming eyes and bright smiles lured young men and girls to their stalls, hinted at spices sworn to enhance a man's sexual passion; spices sure to keep a face soft and white, hair as soft as silk.

Francesco accepted one merchant's invitation to buy sandalwood from the East and while they enjoyed the delightful ritual of bargaining, Francesco caught sight of a young girl alone in the market.

Again, through a cloud of intoxicating, perfumed, smoke, Francesco was mesmerized. Again, he watched as a girl strolled leisurely through the market, tasting winter fruit, laughing at compliments and spurning solicitations from young men.

This time, however, and in this place, it was the young girl from the abbey, not the market in Faenza, not Gismonda Cavalleri.

As if reading his thoughts, the girl turned suddenly and met Francesco's intense gaze with a shy smile and a nod. She was rooted to the ground as he came through the crowd, past fishmongers, and milkmaids, peddlers and troubadours.

She greeted him wordlessly, with a suggestive incline of the chin and a demure sweep of lashes. When he said nothing, she moved away and he followed, through the sea of brightly colored tents and wagons, past the makeshift stalls. She looked at everything, taking particular note of the bargains, but never glanced back to look at him, even though his eyes never wandered from her.

The girl led him back to the spice merchants. "Sandal!" she exclaimed when she saw the brightly painted pots. "And frankincense!"

"Signorina, here." The spice merchant bade her come closer. He crooked a finger and lifted the cover of an iron pot simmering on a fire and released a fragrant steam. Then he scooped golden grains and pearls of resin to the brew. "What do you think? From Jerusalem! It was used in the Temple of Solomon in the Holy of Holies as an offering to the one true God! It is sanctification! Come!"

The girl, laughing, turned to Francesco with raised brows.

"Go on," he coaxed.

She leaned towards the open pot and closed her eyes as steam rose and washed over her face.

"Now this," the spice merchant took a jar from his counter and opened it, showed an ointment made of frankincense. She dipped a finger into the cream and slid it across the back of her hand, the scent pungent and sensual.

"Two *soldi*?" Francesco asked, taking coins from his purse. "And the incense – another *soldo*."

Two jars, one of the ointment and another of the precious resin, were placed in her market basket. She glanced up at him, a look of puzzlement and fear. "I must account for these," the girl protested and started to take them out.

"They are gifts from a friend, nothing more," Francesco said, setting them inside the basket again and covering them with the napkin she carried.

They found themselves at the goldsmiths' stalls next. The girl bypassed the booths occupied by the best artisans in the city and found a cart set apart from the rest, tucked away in a corner. The smith tinkering with a hammered gold clasp looked to be down in his luck. Most of his wares were second hand and of poor quality, if they were of pure gold at all.

"Good morning," she greeted the curious smith when he asked her business. "I was wondering, signor . . . how much?"

She withdrew from her purse a costly gemstone set in silver findings. The smith's eyes popped and he began to sputter. Even Francesco had to gasp at the sight of it. It was an amethyst the size of a robin's egg and it dangled from a heavy, finely-wrought chain as dear as the stone.

"Two – no! Six florins!" the smith gasped.

"Done," she replied and when her purse bulged with coins she said good-bye.

"I think that stone was dear to you," Francesco as they walked on.

"No. The money will pay for food and clothes for the poor children of the Oltrarno," she replied with a shy smile.

"Well, if it's alms you're asking, I could offer twice as much." Francesco tugged at the strap on his purse. "Let me buy it back."

"No!" she protested. "Signor, I do thank you for the kindness, but,"

"I know what it's like to go without."

"If you knew that stone's history, you'd not waste a moment but throw it into the Arno."

Francesco stopped tugging at the purse and looked her straight in the eyes.

Such beautiful eyes.

"Very well."

She paused now to admire the smith's own work displayed on a worn felt cloth.

"What do you think?" she asked, and held up two hair ornaments: a *frenello*, a string of pearls and gold filigree beads to be woven in the hair with silk ribbons, and a garland. The jeweled trinkets sparkled brightly in the morning sunlight. Francesco shrugged and reached for the garland of gold adorned with enameled violets and roses. A perfect choice for her. He turned it over in his hands and shrugged again, smiling, imagining what it would look like in her unbound hair, perhaps with a breeze playing with strands and curls.

"Madonna! Madonna!"

A serving woman running breathlessly through the market was headed towards them. She tripped on a basket of fish and pushed around sacks of grain, her skirts hiked up to reveal fine scarlet stockings beneath the plain black gown, surcote and cloak she wore, leather boots of fine workmanship marred only a bit by the snow and mud on the ground. She jostled and pushed market goers and merchants out of her way as she approached.

The girl was ready to escape when the servant caught her arm. "Pardon, madonna! You must come at once! Monna Violetta bade me find you. Your father's arrived from Lucca!"

She was gone, just like that.

Francesco looked down at the garland in his hands. He turned to the curious and impatient goldsmith waiting and offered four florins.

"Four!" the goldsmith gasped.

"Six, then – and the bauble. How much for that?" Francesco pointed at the amethyst.

"A florin, perhaps? I don't know it's maker,"

"Six for the ornaments and two for the gemstone?"

"I only expected one, monsignore!"

"The lady's worth more than that!" Francesco replied as money exchanged hands and he carried off the precious hair ornament and the amethyst.

CHAPTER 13

MARGHARETA WAITED AT the courtyard gate and watched for a sign of the servant girl she'd sent to fetch Serafina and the wayward girl herself. She wasn't about to submit to ser Agnolo Arcangeli's wrath. Let the girl give her excuses and lies about why she stole out of the house so early! Marghareta couldn't wait to hear what fantastical and outlandish story it would be this time.

Aha!

There she was at the top of the street, running as fast as she was able in so many robes, her cap and veil in her hand so that all the world could see her face—and all the world was looking!

"Where have you been?" Marghareta scolded when she pushed open the gate to let Serafina in. "Great lady and heiress and lady you might be, I've made an end of making excuses for you and taking punishments!"

Serafina collapsed on a bench near the well, recovering from her sprint. She waved Marghareta off while trying to catch her breath and managed a weak "Sorry!" in apology. The servant now ran in and knelt before her, doing what she could to fix Serafina's hair and replace the cap with its ribbons and cording binding up coils and braids of thick, rich chestnut shot with red and gold.

"He wasn't expected until tomorrow!" Serafina gasped.

"Well he's here, Madonna, and in good spirits. He said he brings news that will please you," Marghareta said as Serafina finally rose.

"If it concerns the pardon, I've known about it for weeks. I can't think of anything else that would put my father in a pleasant mood or cause him to smile," Serafina said.

"You'll have to change that dress. He's expecting something befitting a princess."

"Oh no . . ." Serafina whispered as they walked upstairs past the offices and public rooms of the Arcangeli tower, past her uncle Agnolo's private rooms where her father, Durante Giustini, paced the study adjacent to the bedchamber.

Durante surveyed the drab furnishings from the immaculate linen cloth on the tables to the new glass panes in the windows, the polished chairs and cabinets crafted of cedar wood from the Holy Land. Sweet-smelling clean rushes were strewn on the floor, whispering underneath Durante's feet as he scuffed along the wooden planks that met evenly at each joint. Hanging over the mantle was a devotional panel of the Virgin and Child. Arcangeli's wife Pierina, Durante's younger sister, had posed for the work only a month before her death. Durante wondered if the candles lit before it was for the Virgin or his dead sister. Pierina had been a beautiful child, a lovely woman. There, also, on the prie-dieu near the eastern window, were Pierina's prayer book and rosary beads. If he touched them, would a film of dust come off on his finger Durante ventured, and was surprised that they were as clean as if just used.

On the table was a jar full of Pierina's favorite flowers. It was the dead of winter, and there they sat as if cut fresh from the garden. No, they were imitation, made of stiffened silk. He remembered those flowers from years gone by. Pierina used to spend hours making them. Nothing had changed in all the years he'd been gone. It was as if time had stood still.

He closed his eyes and it was no effort to remember his last night here. He could hear the mailed boots on the staircase as soldiers of the Commune came to take him away; the screams of his mother and Pierina when he tried to escape and was beaten into submission. He could inhale the scent of the fireplace as he was dragged away, never to see them alive again . . .

"Welcome home, Brother!"

Agnolo Arcangeli entered and embraced Durante too warmly for his liking.

"You've changed nothing," Durante commented, turning to take a silver cup off the sideboard. "This was where I left it all those years ago. Thank goodness you drank the wine, and the wafers that always sat on this plate were eaten." It was a bitter jest not lost on Arcangeli.

"It's your house, Durante," he said, shrugging. "I was only keeping it for you." Arcangeli snapped his fingers at a servant waiting at the threshold with a tray of cups, wine and wafers. "I trust these will taste better." He studied Durante now, saying, "You look well. But then, you were always one of the most handsome men in Florence, weren't you?"

Durante caught his reflection in a window pane and looked away quickly. He was until years of exile and betrayal had turned his auburn hair to silver and his tanned, unlined face, pale. Only the startling blue eyes hadn't suffered time's unkind hours. Ginevra used to call them her sapphires.

Ah, sweet Ginevra! He would have to see her and make amends for the neglect and indifference, his jealousy . . .

". . . Ghosts are returning to haunt us," Arcangeli chuckled, and when Durante frowned for lack of understanding, he added softly, "Alessandro's boy has won the war against Porciano. He was seen entering the gates on Christmas day."

"Boy? I thought Alessandro's boys were executed after a rebellion."

"No. Albera's son. He was born after you were banished."

"God help us!" Durante whispered, crossing himself.

"Ah no, Durante! It's nothing like before. He's an honorable young man with a just cause." Arcangeli poured wine into Durante's cup and poured a cup for himself, raising it in salute.

Durante swirled the wine and watched the whirlpool. If the boy was indeed one of the Romena, he thought, the matter of honor would be questionable.

"What cause?" he ventured.

"The recovery of what's rightfully his."

"And what exactly is that?" Durante wondered aloud, but before Agnolo could answer, he glanced about and demanded, "Where is Serafina?"

"Here, Father."

Durante looked towards the door and smiled at the sight of his daughter. They'd not seen one another in almost four years, Durante having sent her to the Low Countries when his fortunes and politics were both in danger. Damn her, but she was the image of her mother! Fifteen years, was she? The child was breathtaking; no wonder after her stay in Bruges the troubadours of Flanders wrote love ballads in her honor. Durante also felt a stirring he ought not to have felt, looking at his daughter. She was his flesh and his blood, the flowering of his seed. She was his punishment for an illicit love that never should have been.

Serafina was looking at him now, waiting.

"Come here, sweetheart," Durante beckoned, opening his arms. She came forward and curtseyed before him and submitted to his embrace and kiss.

"You have all you need here?" Durante asked. "My brother-in-law treats you kindly?"

"Of course, Father!" she laughed, turning to smile at her uncle.

"We would be severe with him if he was not," Durante teased, playfully wagging his finger at Agnolo. "We'd force him to listen to you reading Euripides. You know how he hates Greek, and I how much trouble Greek has been for you, though why you should trouble yourself to learn it when it's least of your marriage portion!"

Arcangeli and Durante laughed at this joke, but Serafina lowered her eyes and frowned. Taking a breath, she recited, "Παιδιά παραστρατημένα στις μητέρες τους, και τις αίγες στο κοπάδι, πρόβατα στον ποιμένα, μέσω του λυκόφατος τα φτερά του πουλιού, όλα τα πράγματα που το πρωί έχει διασκορπίσει με τα δάχτυλα του χρυσού, όλα τα πράγματα εσύ ο πιό, βράδυ Ο! επιτέλους στις πτυχές," And then, staring at her hands clasped tightly before her in anger, said:

"*Children astray to their mothers,*
"*and goats to the herd,*
"*sheep to the shepherd,*
"*through twilight the wings of the bird,*
"*all things that morning has scattered*
"*with fingers of gold,*
"*all things thou bringest,*
"*O Evening! at last to the fold.*"

When the men stared at her and each other in puzzlement, she said, "it's a poem from a lyric poet, Sappho. She was a contemporary of Alcaeus of Mitelyne. Perhaps you've heard of her? They discovered fragments of her work in Greece, poems in which she glorifies nature and love."

Durante looked at Arcangeli, who shrugged, and both settled into their chairs. "I shall thank your tutor and the sisters at the convent for your education. Not many girls are given such an opportunity, eh, Agnolo?"

"Money well spent," Arcangeli said.

"Thank you," she replied.

"Perhaps not wasted, either the money or the education," Durante said, drawing her close and reaching out to touch Serafina's cheek. "But perhaps unnecessary, sweetheart." Before Serafina could ask, he winked and said, "I've found a husband for you."

A chill overcame Serafina, the kind that came with bad news. She looked at her father and nodded, bowed her head in submission and folded her hands neatly at her girdle, her fingers rubbing the smooth, round cabochons in their metal findings, waiting.

"Gherardo Ranieri, the conte di Verrucole has spoken for you and I have agreed."

The chill became a shiver down her spine. Again, she nodded.

"Serafina?"

"I know this man," Serafina said quietly. "I saw him in Brugges and in Lucca. He was like a shadow. Wherever I went, he was sure to follow. He even came to the convent."

"And you will see him tomorrow afternoon when we are received by the Commune."

"I am to go with you?" Serafina asked.

"Of course! I would have you with me when I receive the honors denied me for so long and am welcomed back to Florence."

"As you will, Father." Serafina assented. "Is that all?"

"Is it not enough?" Durante chuckled.

"May I have leave to go to my chamber?"

"If by that you mean you will need to think on your husband's qualities and choose a dress and ornaments for tomorrow, you have it."

She withdrew after giving both father and uncle kisses. When the door closed behind her, Durante drank his cup empty.

"She's not pleased," Arcangeli murmured.

"Why must she always make things difficult?" Durante sighed. "It's the Peruzzi boy, I'm sure."

"Oh no, Durante. I've seen that he's stayed away since her arrival—just as you asked."

"But you couldn't keep an eye on him in Lucca or Brugges." Durante rose and placed his cup back on the sideboard. "You're certain she's still a maid?"

"Her woman confirms this though there was a night in Lucca."

"Nothing happened, I take it?"

"It was prevented."

Durante grimaced and then nodded. "Idiot boy! Once we've gotten through tomorrow's ceremonies, I will have to come to terms with young Niccolo."

"His suit precedes that of Ranieri's. The Peruzzi will not be content with a few bags of gold or a farm to pay for your change of heart," Arcangeli warned.

"They will take what I offer them and be glad of it," Durante said and as he walked through the house to his suite of rooms, he passed the little chapel and saw Serafina sitting quietly on a stool with a Bible in her lap. For a moment Durante thought she was reading aloud, but the unmistakable snuffling of sobs proved him wrong. He almost went in to comfort her, but decided against it, choosing to leave her to her grief.

Durante did, however, thank the Lord he had been born a male, and not forced to endure what was thrust on women. What he did not understand was why any woman, especially his daughter, would not be happy with someone who was willing to care for them for the rest of her life. The world was such a dangerous and treacherous place, after all.

❧

"THEY'RE WAITING FOR US!" Durante said impatiently as Serafina hurried downstairs with her women in tow and fell into a deep curtsey before him.

"Such beauty is worth the wait, don't you think, Brother?" Arcangeli said, helping Serafina to her feet.

They went with their servants in procession from the Via Santa Elisabetta to the Palazzo Communale where they were greeted by notaries and magistrates decked in ceremonial robes. When the doors to the council chamber were thrown back a stench of frankincense caught Durante by surprise. He discreetly held a finger to his nose to keep out the pungent smoke. Frankincense reminded him of worse times, of candle shops and garishly appointed bedchambers, of cloying perfumes and a young lover who waited in the darkness behind richly-embroidered bed curtains . . .

"Il Signore de Montebuoni, Durante Giustini and Madonna Serafina, his daughter!" a herald wailed.

Eighty pairs of eyes followed Durante as he approached the dais where the *gonfaloniere de giustizia*, the standard bearer of Florence, Pico della Colle, sat with his councilors. The podesta, mayor, of Florence, Michelino Groppa, sat to Colle's right, while *il capitano di popolo*, the captain of the people, the representative of the citizens of Florence, Matteo Sanseverino, sat at his left. They were an unholy trinity, Durante thought as he knelt. In contrast to the soft whisper of his coarse homespun over gown as it brushed the floor was the irritating jangle of necklaces, chains of office and rosaries striking one another as people moved to get a better look.

Durante's eyes went immediately to Sanseverino when he was given leave to rise. Sanseverino hadn't aged a day, Durante thought bitterly. Did he receive the greater part of the Giustini livings after the sentence had been passed? From the girth of his stomach and richness of his clothes it would seem so.

Gauging Michelino Groppa was more difficult. Durante knew he came from Prato and had served Florence well in the past. Was this his third, or was it his fourth, term of office as mayor?

The gonfaloniere rose and motioned to a clerk, who presented a scroll bound by scarlet ribbons and wax seals. "Messer Durante, we welcome you home. The charges of theft, treason, and murder laid against you could never be proved, and we regret it has taken so long to clear your good name."

"May I ask why it has taken so long?" Durante asked.

"Of course; those who were charged with you, and those alive at the time of the unfortunate events that gave rise to your exile have either come forward with the truth such as is known or they have died."

Durante nodded, swallowing hard. "I have lost much, signor, not only in goods, lands, and revenues, my offices and titles, but in days and years."

"This Florence understands. Though we cannot give you back the time lost, we do offer compensation," the gonfaloniere stated.

Compensation? Durante glanced at Serafina, who was standing with her women at the back of the chamber. She kept her eyes downcast and her hands clenched together in the folds of her dark green gown. When she did look at him, Durante smiled as if to tell her all would be well, that his many sacrifices would not have been in vain.

"All I need is a roof over my head and a cloak to keep me warm at nights. It is what I've gotten used to," Durante jested and waited for the laughter. When none came, he avoided the curious stares of the spectators and gave an obsequious smile to clerk now standing before him. The clerk offered the scroll and backed away.

With hands trembling, Durante broke the seal and unfurled what he hoped would be a golden future. The sigh he expelled told many in the room that he was far from satisfied by the Commune's generosity.

Durante's eyes fixed on the elegant, italic hand of a clerk, the penmanship as artful and beautiful as any painting. The borders were a work of art in vermilion, azure, and purple. Such elegance was not to be believed, as unbelievable as the content of the decree.

"Messer Durante?" the gonfaloniere spoke up. "Is this compensation satisfactory?"

Compensation? This was an insult! Durante thought of his lands and revenues, his castles, all seized by Florence. His family was distinguished and ancient; he had been struck knight by the Archbishop himself. He deserved more than hollow gratitude. When the emissaries from Florence arrived at his house in Lucca to announce the Commune's decision, Durante countered their offer with a demand for the return of all that had been stolen from him. That demand obviously fell on deaf ears.

"It is . . . compensation."

"We now desire to offer you Florence's friendship," the gonfaloniere continued. "As you may see from our proclamation, we reinstate you in the greater guild, the Arte della Lana, and bestow you with offices as befit your high station—there is an allowance of eight florins per annum." He now looked at Serafina, who had raised her eyes and attempted a smile. "For your daughter, Messer Durante, we had hoped to be just as generous, however, the circumstances of her birth and sex . . ."

"Your consideration is welcome, messer gonfalon," Durante interrupted, "but unnecessary. I have procured a good marriage for my daughter. I had hoped to use this opportunity today to take care of such legal matters as the transfer of the lands, goods, and chattel I intend to bestow upon her, those which were in the care of Florence in my absence."

"We will be glad to assist you in this, and we wish Donna Serafina well in this match," said the gonfaloniere. "Tell us, is the fortunate young man a Florentine?"

"Ser Gherardo Ranieri, conte di Verrucole, here, has spoken for her, and has agreed to our terms," said Durante. A murmur of surprise crawled through the chamber as a handsome and an elegantly attired man in his thirties stepped forward.

The conversation in the room mounted like the buzzing of bees around a hive:

"*Conte Gherardo!*"

"*I heard he prefers large dogs and little boys to women!*"

116

"Gesu, one night in her bed would be the cure!"

"Cure you? Didn't you know? She's the Salvemini brat! One night in the girl's bed would kill you!"

"I heard he asked for the hand of a French princess and was turned away outright."

"What do you expect when he's married and buried three rich wives and a mistress?"

"When the purse is empty and the wells go dry, he looks for another heiress and look who he's found, poor girl!"

"Durante doesn't have much to offer in the way of a dowry."

"Doesn't he, though?"

No one paid any attention to the girl, her face frozen in anger as she picked up snatches of the many conversations, all of them insulting. Serafina shuddered. Yes, this was the man who appeared like a shadow when she lived in Lucca and then Brugges. She remembered their encounters all too well. Every time he left her feeling frightened and tainted. She experienced an urge to bathe in a holy water font or confess sins she had never committed.

The stories of his exploits were but tales of cruelty and self-aggrandizement, of treachery. Tales that bespoke evil one could not utter aloud.

Serafina glanced up when she heard her name whispered and saw that Gherardo was standing beside her a hand extended to lead her forward to the dais. His eyes were fixed on her, to her breasts that now rose and fell angrily, to her pouting mouth and downcast eyes, as they made their progress. He stared hungrily as if she was a prize won in a hard-fought contest.

"When shall we celebrate the marriage, signorina?" the podesta asked, smiling at her. He raised his brows at Durante and then winked.

"Not until midsummer, but we bid you come tomorrow when the betrothal will be made," Durante said. He slung an arm around Serafina's shoulders and held tight. She looked angry enough to bolt like an unbroken mare.

"Tomorrow? Did I hear you correctly, signor? But the banns are not read, and the *impalmare*—!" the gonfaloniere laughed.

"All this was done in Lucca, Messer. We are in haste, for the Holy Roman Emperor has called me to Aachen," Gherardo said. His pronouncement brought a wave of astonished whispers. An imperial summons meant great things.

"I think all this was done in contravention of Florence's prescribed statutes!" the podesta spoke up. He turned to Durante. "Now I see why you desire the commune's cooperation in this! You are here among us no less than an hour and you flout the laws and customs of our commune? Perhaps we will reconsider our offer to assist!"

"It is, signor podesta, as Gherardo stated. All shall be done properly, I assure you of that."

"And you, madonna?" the podesta asked Serafina. "Have you anything to say?"

She said nothing.

After a quarter hour of bargaining and reminiscing, the Giustini party was dismissed. With most eyes upon her, Serafina made an elegant reverence and turned before her father and Ranieri. She made another reverence, but ignored the hand extended. As much as she desired to run out, if she fled everyone would know how angry she was. She'd not give them something else to gossip about. Instead, Serafina kept her eyes straight ahead and moved through a parting sea of courtiers and nobility to the courtyard.

Marghareta bobbed a curtsey when she saw Serafina coming, and before she could ask, they were in the gonfaloniere's chapel. Serafina sank to her knees before the crucifix. "Tell me!" Marghareta begged when Serafina refused to respond to her inquiries.

"I am bought and sold," Serafina whispered, her eyes fixed on the feet of the dying Christ, the red stripes of paint winding down the instep and between the carved wooden toes. "What did you expect?"

"He made a promise! He swore before the holy relics of Saint Elizabeth. It is as good as a blood oath," Marghareta protested. "You were promised to Niccolo Peruzzi!"

"He weighed the goods of a banker with that of the vilest man in Tuscany who owns castles and has an army. Promises are nothing to my father. What did you expect? I'd be a fool times ten to think Durante Giustini ever kept a promise and Ranieri can't keep a wife, but he knows how to hold fast to a dowry."

"Serafina, hush! Others will hear . . ."

"Why trouble yourself, Marghareta? Everyone knows how little Serafina Giustini favors me," Gherardo said as he entered the chapel. He knelt beside Serafina and Marghareta shrank back as if he were the Antichrist, even going as far as to cross herself.

"Perhaps when you're not so angry we might discuss why you hate me so much," Gherardo murmured as he kissed Serafina's cheek. Serafina was careful not to flinch or recoil. When she didn't respond he wrenched her face toward his and kissed her full on the mouth. "Don't believe what you hear," Gherardo said when he released her. "I do appreciate a woman's body. And I am gentle when the moment calls for gentleness. I would think you'd be pleased with our betrothal, Serafina. I have the means to make you a countess and give you a comfortable life, yet I have not received even a small gesture of gratitude," Gherardo half-jested.

"If you mean to show me kindness, Signor, then release me from the promise my father made. He did not ask my consent," Serafina replied.

"I didn't think it necessary!" he said with a laugh.

"He swore an oath upon the relics of Saint Elizabeth that I should marry another and one of my liking."

Ranieri pulled a lock of Serafina's hair from under her veil and held it for a moment, then placed it on her breast. His hand lingered longer than Serafina thought necessary and she brushed it away.

"As I said, I didn't think it was necessary. I need a wife to bear sons who will be healthy and strong and inherit Verrucole. Durante needs the lands and castles I can give him and the might of my army for his enterprises. It's a fair exchange, I think."

"Forgive me, signor. I think all that is a lie. Truth be told, I fear you."

"Fear me? Why in heaven would you be afraid of me? Have I not always shown you courtesy?"

"I've heard stories . . ."

"Stories?"

"Of your wives, and there were women you had brought to your castles."

"Ah, that."

"I've heard of your cruelty to women and how their pain brings you pleasure. I wish for what other women pray for: to be held in esteem by their husbands and to be respected, even loved."

Gherardo held her at arm's length then, and when she refused to look at him, made her look as he pressed her face between his hands as if it was an apple and held her captive.

"Let go of me," Serafina said.

"You will hear me out, Serafina."

"I said, let go!"

"You will hear me out! There is a small observatory near my fortress of Castelnuovo. It is dedicated to Saint Anne. There is a statue of the blessed saint by the holy water font and I swear upon a thousand Bibles that the face of that sweet saint is just like yours. When I first saw you in Lucca—do you remember that morning? You were walking in the Piazza del Duomo with your women. When I first beheld you, Bella, you reminded me of my sweet Saint Anne!"

"Will you make me a thing to be worshiped? I would rather have a husband love me."

"And so you will. God forgive me for saying this in such a holy place, but I have no thought but to take your body and teach you how to enjoy the pleasures we can give each other. I swear I'll make you happy; anything your heart desires I will be more than willing to give, for you are precious!"

"Then give me freedom."

Gherardo laughed then, ugly, snorting, braying, animal sounds. Serafina heard those laughs until well into the night and the next morning when, despite Marghareta's pleas to put on a show of goodwill and get out of bed, she feigned sleep as the household prepared for the betrothal ceremony.

"Where is the girl?" Durante snapped at his brother-in-law Arcangeli.

"It wouldn't do to pace another circle in the floor, Durante. Leave her to sleep another half hour; there's still time," Arcangeli replied, looking at the hourglass and then handing him a linen cloth to wipe the sweat off his brow.

"Yes, well, I didn't expect it to go so badly! You swore that everything we did was prescribed by Florentine law! I didn't expect the podesta to question our work!"

"And it was, Durante. Everything has been done according to the law. As for Serafina, well,"

"Willful brat! Make no excuses for her! She gets to live in Florence for most of the year! He'll be gone at Aachen most of the time! Ranieri intends to be generous and kind, he'll give her a castle; I don't know why she is so bent on destroying all I've worked for!"

"Don't you?" Arcangeli whispered, and jerked his head towards the door.

Niccolo Peruzzi had entered the room, accompanied by his old grandfather Battista.

"So, signor Battista! Signor Niccolo! You decided to come after all," Arcangeli greeted the banker and his grandson.

"Only to bring a gift for mona Serafina," Battista sniffed and hobbled on a cane to the nearest bench, easing himself down. "Niccolo, if you would,"

Niccolo waved a servant forward and stepped aside. The boy carried a small casket that Battista attempted to open, but it proved difficult for his palsied hands and Niccolo sprung the catch and threw back the lid to reveal costly jewelry from pearls to diamonds set in gold.

"What's this?" Durante asked.

"Your mother's jewels. Surely you cannot have forgotten you left them with us as security for one of your loans?" Battista said. "Your daughter should have them and so the Peruzzi company returns them to her."

Durante nodded, making sure his face masked his true feelings. No one was hated more in Florence than its prominent bankers, for they were treated like nobility and the nobility feared them. Bankers held the fortunes of great men in their closed fists and were never at pains to remind clients of that power.

"I never went to sleep single night these last twenty-four years without making an account of the florins and *soldi* owed to the Peruzzi," Durante said, forcing a smile.

"We ask you to reconsider this betrothal to Ranieri, signor Durante. In exchange for the marriage of your daughter to my grandson, here, we will forgive your debts."

Niccolo held his breath as he watched Durante. A flicker in those cold blue eyes, how his skin blanched and then went scarlet, then he stared vacantly at Battista, then Niccolo.

"You're too late," Durante said at last. "You're welcome to stay for the ceremony if it pleases you. Now if you will excuse me, there is still much to do before signore Gherardo arrives."

"And not a word of thanks," Battista muttered as Niccolo led him away against the tide of guests arriving, avoiding the curious looks and whispers.

"Grandfather, I'll meet you at home," Niccolo said of a sudden when they reached the courtyard. Before Battista could argue, Niccolo slipped away and up a staircase to the family's private chambers. A door opened and closed as he reached the second floor landing and Serafina appeared.

"I didn't expect to find you here. I asked you not to come."

She was still in a simple dress of plum-colored wool and an apron. She was so damned beautiful! Niccolo wanted nothing more than to make love to her.

"We brought your grandmother's jewels, Grandfather and me," Niccolo stammered. *Good God! Why was he finding it so difficult to talk to her of all people? His childhood friend and first love?* "It's not your fault things haven't gone as planned. My grandfather asked Durante to reconsider."

"I asked you not to come."

He kissed her and was surprised when she failed to respond, to see a darkness in those violet eyes.

"Serafina, if you'd give me some hope," he whispered.

"You must forget, Niccolo!"

"God help us all when a wife loves her husband!" Niccolo replied bitterly.

"What makes you think I love him?"

"There you are!" Marghareta whined as she came upon them. She boxed Niccolo's ear and said, "What on earth do you do here – never mind! It's time to make ready - ah! The notary's arrived. Come on!"

"What makes you think they'll start without me?" Serafina hissed.

"Serafina," Niccolo began.

"Why are you still here? Go!" Marghareta commanded.

❧

THE TIRING WOMEN set upon Serafina, exchanging her domestic garments for a gown of blue wool with slashed and laced sleeves that showed a pale blush-colored shirt underneath and a surcote of blue velvet slashed at the sides and lined in silver tissue. Her hair was let down and brushed until it shone like new silk. Marghareta stepped back and inspected her work.

"You're not as I would have you, but still," the old woman sniffed. She bemoaned the lack of proper toiletries to make Serafina's skin smoother and whiter though Serafina wondered how that could be accomplished. Her complexion was like snow already.

There was a knock on the door.

"Open!" Serafina instructed.

Violetta Arcangeli entered with Serafina's maids of honor and Ranieri's musicians to escort her to the ceremony. After receiving kisses and flowers from her five maidens, she fell in step behind them.

Durante waited downstairs in the great hall. He sat in a chair of state on a platform, the gentlemen of the Arcangeli and Giustini families stood at one side of the hall, the ladies to the other. They bowed in unison when Gherardo Ranieri entered followed by Stefano and Roberto, his illegitimate sons.

The notary entered and took his place at a desk, arranging his papers with overblown ceremony. After greetings were exchanged, the great doors to the courtyard were thrown open and Serafina entered with her women to the happy notes of a ballad.

What would now take place was the last of three ceremonies to occur before the actual marriage, the *messa del congiunto*, which would be celebrated in church after consummation. The first of these, the drafting of the marriage contract and wedding formalities, had been accomplished by legal representatives of the families in scandalous haste and secret. Second, the *impalmare*, the shaking of hands in church over the marriage contract between representatives of the families, was done before Durante left Lucca and until he had announced it before the Commune, it had been another hasty and very secret matter.

Now, this afternoon, the third ritual, the ceremonial presentation of the betrothal ring. This was above board and proper.

The notary read aloud the terms of the marriage contract between Serafina and Gherardo. Reciting in obtuse, formal language, he explained the amount of dowry offered and the *morgengabio* prescribed by the families, this last a gift from husband to wife after the wedding night. In many aspects, what the husband gave his wife the morning after their union would set the course for the marriage. The notary went on to list the gifts of houses and land bestowed upon Serafina by her father in right of her marriage and as his only living heir. Once approval was given by Durante and agents for Ranieri, Gherardo slipped a golden ring on the third finger of Serafina's right hand and kissed her full on the mouth, the kiss signifying that Serafina was "half-deflowered."

The fetid taste he left on Serafina's lips and his stale scent were not as disturbing as the chill of the metal against her burning fingers and its weight. She stared numbly at the bright gold band, a plain, ugly, thing, a shackle.

A cup of wine was offered to the couple. Serafina glanced at Gherardo's angelic face as the cup passed between them and watched at how quickly it turned cold and evil. He glared at his son Stefano who was leering at her, his eyes darting up and down her body. A shake of the head was all Stefano needed to stop. Gherardo then turned to Serafina as he ran his tongue over his lips and nodded with a libidinous smile.

"Will you drink, mona Serafina?" Gherardo murmured, touching the cup to her lips.

She hesitated, catching Stefano's smile again and remembered what she'd heard about brides murdered by their jealous stepchildren.

"Come, it is a loving cup," Gherardo whispered. "Let us be friends if you will not love me. Take it in friendship."

Serafina drank the rich, sweet wine and was careful not spill a drop on her new clothes, for to spill a drop would mean ill fortune for the marriage. It didn't matter. In drinking, she had sealed her fate. Taking the cup was the first communion between a man and wife.

There was one last ritual to the ceremony, all of which prompted bawdy jests and snickering. Durante now led Serafina upstairs to her bedchamber. She went behind a painted screen and disrobed, slipping into a silk shift and a plain woolen robe. She sat down on the bed in the presence of her father, the notary, her women, and Gherardo's witnesses, and removed her slippers. The priest came forward and uttered a hurried prayer, and then instructed Serafina to lie down, closing the curtains around the bed.

Now a door closed. Serafina heard heavy, even footsteps and burrowed deeper into the bed, clutching a pillow against her, as if it would give her shelter from what was to come. Gherardo drew back the curtains, and never taking his eyes from Serafina, sat familiarly on the chest to remove his boots. By tradition, he was supposed to lie beside her and touch her bare leg under her shift with his naked foot. This simple, innocuous act of intimacy validated the marriage. Under the laws of the church and Florence, the union was legal.

Gherardo closed the curtains on the witnesses as they approached.

"Open the curtains, Signor!" Durante protested.

Gherardo threw Serafina onto her back and smothered her with a kiss. His tongue explored her mouth while his hands found their way under the shift. Serafina struggled against him, especially when a hand wandered and began caressing slowly, deliberately, between her legs. He moaned and unlaced his breeches, pushing against her, but Serafina refused to give ground, and shoved him off, making sure her knee struck him in just the right place and with just the right force.

"Bitch!" Gherardo gasped, grabbing himself in pain.

"Is everything all right?" Durante asked.

"Satisfactory, signor!" Serafina replied as she bounded off the bed and reappeared, Gherardo a few moments later. He pulled her to him for a more public kiss that was too long and wet for her liking but brought a happy response from the witnesses, who clapped and cheered. As the couple acknowledged the well wishes and congratulations, Gherardo whispered to Serafina, "I can come back to tonight and we can finish what we started and your response will be entirely different once you've been abed with me!" He then turned to the witnesses and said, "Signor Durante and I agreed that the *messa del congiunto* will be set for the end of July, but I wish it could be this very afternoon as my betrothed pleases me well. Now I bid you all to come with me to raise a cup to this union. My father Durante, will you lead us?"

"Just so, just so, my son!" Durante laughed nervously, avoiding Serafina's angry stare. "We'll dine and let my daughter spend some hours in contemplation and prayer, as is the custom."

No sooner had the last witness departed than Serafina slammed the door shut, the echo reverberating in the gallery. She stripped down and threw the garments at a bewildered servant. "Burn these!" Serafina hissed and put on a familiar, faded robe that lay discarded on a trunk.

"You bleed! Did he–?"

"He tried but didn't succeed," Serafina said. "Get on with your work." She paused by the looking glass to study the girl in the mirror and found a strange person there. The skin on her neck and breasts was flushed from where Gherardo had tried to plant love bites, and there was a bruise rising near her throat. The face was pallid, the eyes dark and old.

The contracts were signed and the ceremony done with. She was as good as married and would now be accorded the rights and privileges of a married woman. Her life was over. There would be no strange new discoveries save those of the marriage bed Gherardo hadn't revealed or Niccolo Peruzzi hadn't tried, and the frightening specter of childbirth from which she might not survive. *I might as well be like you*, Serafina thought, staring at the polychrome wooden statue of the Virgin Mary that stood on a shelf by the bed, a candle melting down at her bare feet.

"Will you take supper, madonna?"

Serafina came out of her reverie and stared at the girl waiting for an answer.

"I'm not hungry," she said at last.

The door creaked open then and the girl giggled, "Now what are you doing here? You know dona Serafina cannot have visitors!"

Serafina took a knife from the jewelry box on the table and spun about, thinking to find Gherardo and frightening her cousin Violetta instead.

"Sweet Gesu!" Serafina gasped. "Announce yourself properly or say something the next time you come in uninvited!"

"I only came in to congratulate you, cousin!" Violetta sniffed. She pointed at the gifts laid out on the window seat across the chamber. "And to see what Gherardo brought."

"More than he should have," Serafina murmured, putting the knife back.

"Venetian brocades and fine linens," Violetta giggled. "And crystal cups! Look at this jeweled girdle! The engraving alone is worth a fortune!"

"Take them. I don't want them."

"You're shivering! What happened to the fur-lined robe your father gave you," Violetta saw the robe on the floor and picked it up. "Ah! And the fine silk shift—oh, now I see!" She patted Serafina's cheek. "Poor Serafina, to get your courses at this time!"

"It isn't that!" Serafina hissed.

"*Ahh!* At least on your wedding night there won't be any surprises and with any luck at all, Gherardo will show you how to give and receive pleasure. It's difficult at first." Violetta and servant shared knowing looks and giggled like two conspirators. "I know. You'd rather it be Niccolo Peruzzi in your bed and I don't blame you!"

"Go away. I didn't ask you here," Serafina grumbled. "Just go."

"You father asked me to—"

"*Go*, I said!"

As soon as Violetta hurried out—surely to report their conversation to Durante—Serafina glared at the serving girl. "Shouldn't you be doing something?"

"I'll lay out your things for the morning. You're to be shrived and churched tomorrow," said the girl. "There'll be no nursemaids and escorts for you after that! You can go where you like and when you like. That's one benefit of marriage, isn't it?"

The girl was right. Serafina went to the window and leaned on the sill—something she couldn't have done an hour before. Let Marghareta scold her now! The street was quiet; only a few people going about their business. A boy was running down the street and stopped a man coming out of the cook shop. By gestures and looks, the boy was seeking the Arcangeli house and was pointed in the right direction. He dodged a hay wain and a knight to cross the street. Moments later there was pounding on the gate as the boy sought entrance.

"Go see what that's about," Serafina told the girl, who nodded and hurried out to the stairwell. While Serafina waited she paced and listened to the laughter and conversation that wove their sound through the stairwell from the rooms across the gallery. Gherardo was praising Serafina's beauty and womanly graces and expounding on his lovemaking skills, which caused one woman to say that his young wife would surely open like a flower, for who could resist what he had to offer? There was more laughter and lewd commentary.

"Serafina! *Serafinahhhh!*"

Marghareta's shouts brought Serafina out to the passageway where Marghareta had crumpled at the top of the stairs and wailed as if her heart was being torn out.

"Christ's blood!" Serafina gasped. "What's happened?"

"It's your mother!"

"Help me dress," Serafina ordered and pulled the woman to her feet. Within the hour, they'd slipped out of the house unnoticed, heading toward the Lungarno.

CHAPTER 14

GINEVRA SALVEMINI'S END came as no surprise. What amazed her neighbors in the Oltrarno was how she cheated death for so long. A few remembered when she was the prize of Florence's courtesans and when she became Durante Giustini's mistress. It was hard to believe that this gaunt, abandoned woman dying in a tenement had been the most desirable woman in Florence, a woman whose very existence caused the most sensational scandal to come along in years.

A Dominican brother arrived at midday and Anna crossed herself when she saw him. "You're not welcome here, Frate!" she spat. "It was a Dominican who denounced my mistress all those years ago!"

"I go where I'm called. The prior ordered me here," the Dominican snapped.

"That's as may be. But I'd sooner have a man of God, not you!"

The Dominican held the white sleeve of his habit to his nostrils as he entered. The unmistakable stench of death rivaled a bean porridge scorching over a fire. He muttered something unflattering and colored when Anna heard it. She banged the spoon against the kettle so that porridge sprayed the Dominican's habit.

"It won't be long; she's been in a fever for hours," Anna remarked, and she shoved aside the curtains in a vestibule, revealing the makeshift bedchamber where Ginevra Salvemini lay in her own waste. "She's called for her daughter and husband."

"Husband? I didn't think she was married."

"She says she was married to the conte di Romena when she was fourteen."

The friar turned a color not unlike the wax tapers he held: a pale, translucent white. "Nonsense!" he said. "It's deathbed fever, that's all."

"Deathbed truth, if you ask me!"

"I didn't. Give me a flint to light these candles. Conte di Romena, you say? Why, he's just into his manhood and this woman is past thirty if she's a day."

"Idiot! Not young Francesco!" Anna sighed. "His father."

"But his father is dead,"

"Aren't you the clever one to figure that out."

"Serafina!"

The friar moved to the bed and knelt, mumbling a prayer. The dying woman opened her eyes when she sensed his presence.

"Serafina?"

The woman's breathing was shallow, rattling. Her chestnut-colored hair lay in greasy, lank strands; the once luminous blue eyes were vacant.

"Do you wish to confess your sins and make peace with God?" the friar asked.

"Forgive me!"

"Do you wish to confess your sins?"

"Forgive! Forgive! My husband!"

"Signora?"

"Alessandro. We married . . . girl . . . fourteen. My mother forbade . . . he was great lord . . . secret marriage. No one . . . except . . . *he* encouraged Alessandro, made promises . . . San Miniato . . ."

The friar pressed her to sleep a while, but she refused. A handkerchief went to her mouth and came away stained with blood, prompting the friar to ask about the sick woman's comfort.

Anna brought a posset of honey and comfrey, saying, "This only prolongs the end, frate. She would make an end soon; she's said so enough times."

". . . used to come . . . in secret. Write this! I would truth . . . be known! Doesn't matter . . . you see . . . Bishop Gandulfo. . . ! *His* fault . . . write it!"

Parchment, a quill, and a jar of ink were fetched from the friar's bag. As soon as he was ready, Ginevra asked to sit up in bed. She pointed to a coffer on a shelf above her, and Anna opened it. Ginevra now pointed to the inside of the painted lid and Anna shook her head. "There's nothing here, signora," she said.

"Secret. . . pull," Ginevra said and touched the brass clasp. Anna tugged gently, once, then twice and the smallest of drawers suddenly slid out and from that she took a gold ring and placed in Ginevra's open palm. For a moment, her face held the radiance of youth. "Here is . . . ring . . . bade me . . . in secret . . . he *promised!* Promise . . . in church but. . . never did . . . noblewoman instead! Serafina, she promised . . .!"

The confession was interrupted by a fit of coughing that left Ginevra exhausted. The friar bade her speak no more, then motioned to Anna.

"Who is Serafina? This noblewoman, perhaps?"

"Her daughter, frate. She's here in Florence. I can send for her,"

"Does she know of this marriage?"

"I think not. In truth, I never heard it until today," Anna replied. When she saw the friar roll his eyes, she snapped, "But it's the truth! She's not one to lie!"

A gust of wind rustled the branches of a fig tree outside the window and now their dancing shadows interlaced macabre patterns on Ginevra's face. She turned to watch them, to spy on a bird hopping from branch to branch in search of food on this winter's day, study the delicate patterns of frost glimmering on the sill and the oilskin shade pulled open. These would be her last human observations. The heat of the candles surrounding the bed, the odor of cheap tallow, the spreading stain of water along the wall. The smell of death.

Serafina! Where was Serafina? Surely her girl would be here to witness a deathbed confession, one that had been promised for years . . . Durante! She would tell him all. To tell Durante . . .

Ginevra slept for an hour and woke in a spasm of coughing. The friar applied pen to paper when she signed she was ready to continue. The words came in painful fits, bits and pieces of a life passing woven together in an incredible tale. The friar wrote slowly, bidding Ginevra take her time, to rest as he strove to capture every word.

". . . begged forgiveness. . . . it was not for love . . . political alliance. He did not love her. . .hated her. . . promised annul . . . I loved . . . Durante then. . . only Durante. . . loved Alessandro. . ."

"Why did you not speak out?"

"to. . .my sorrow. . . he died."

Ginevra's breathing came in uneven spasms now. The rattle in her chest was more pronounced.

The friar set aside his pen and looked at the confession. "This gentleman Durante should know what is written here. A grave injustice was done to him, do you not think?"

Anna nodded. "Give it to me. I'll bring it straight away."

The friar pulled away as Anna reached for the scrap of parchment. "It makes no sense this way. Let me draft something. She will sign it and you will be the witness."

Another scrap of parchment was taken from the friar's bag and after a time, he finished the document, satisfied with his work.

"Do you read?" he asked Anna.

"No. Tell me what it says and I'll make my mark."

The friar cleared his throat and recited an affidavit attesting to the truth of the confession. Anna stood with closed eyes and hands folded at her breast as if praying and listened, nodding. She opened her eyes when he finished and crossed herself, then made a cross on the bottom of the page. The friar took her hand before she left. "Not a word of this! You cannot say a word to anyone!"

Anna nodded and went.

Ginevra opened her eyes at the slam of a door, the scuff of shoes on the cobblestones.

"Where . . . did . . . she . . . go?"

"Signora, can you answer questions for me?" the friar asked, taking Ginevra's hand. Strange, that a woman burning her life away in fever would have hands like ice.

"Anna? Serafina? Where . . .?"

"If you were indeed married to Alessandro da Romena, why did you not come forward?"

Ginevra forced a smile. "Word of . . . nobleman. . . holds more weight! Threatened. . . death. . .me. . .my daughter . . . "

"Did you have a child by the conte? Your daughter, perhaps?"

"Durante's . . . baseborn."

"Who performed the marriage rites?"

"Baseborn. . . . no fault of hers,"

"Who performed the marriage? Is he in Florence? Do you know where he is?"

". . . not be blamed. . ."

"And witnesses? Were there any witnesses? Signora! Were there any witnesses?"

Ginevra was seized with coughing and breathed her last. Her face had taken on a radiance of afterlife, the lines smoothed and her waxy skin pale, yet translucent. A smile curved her lips.

The Dominican leaned over the bed to whisper a last prayer. His eyes lighted on the wedding band. After a glance to appraise its worth, he tossed the wedding band out the window.

"You won't be needing this, madonna contessa!" the Dominican sniggered as he took the little coffer from where it lay on the pillow. His smile broadened when he saw the poor treasures inside the box, thinking they would bring at least a *soldo* if he went to the rag and bone man near the church of Santa Croce. Gathering up his things, the Dominican hummed a tune he'd heard in the market square, and carefully laid the box in his sack.

"Gesu!"

He had turned to draw the curtains around the dead woman and found himself face to face with the most exquisitely beautiful girl he'd ever seen.

"The box is mine, sirrah!" the girl stated.

"She—she's dead," the Dominican stammered. "There wasn't anything I could do. She was nearly gone when I got here. I was taking the box for payment."

The girl turned and ran, her pitiful sobs echoing in the Dominican's ears as he went about the room, putting things in his sack.

❧

"I STILL DON'T believe it." Durante pushed the confession across the table to Arcangeli. "The friar was with her when she died; he heard it, Agnolo. All these years . . . I thought even after . . . What's done is done. Once a thing is done, it's finished."

130

"But it isn't, and you know it," Agnolo said, tapping the document violently with his finger. "Go to conte Francesco. You must tell him what Ginevra said before the wrong people find out. If you want to regain favor with the Guidi, this is the way to do it."

Without responding, Durante took back the neatly folded square of parchment. Deathbed confessions by courtesans were commonplace, as featherbeds held the secrets of great men. But this admission? The young conte di Romena had much to worry about if it was true.

"Durante, shall I send a man to Romena? He needs to know." Arcangeli pressed. Durante looked at his brother-in-law as if he was moonstruck and after a moment shook his head. "Such knowledge is powerful!" Arcangeli cried in exasperation and thumped his fist on the arm of Durante's chair.

"Agnolo, it is not our business."

"I make it my business when a stupid pig farmer stands to gain from another's misfortune and would place everyone we know in danger. Porciano's been looking for a fight and this is the quarrel."

"But it is not my quarrel. It never was. Besides, the Commune has granted me pardon and restored some of my fortune. If I interfered in this, there's no telling what would happen. My chances of regaining everything I lost... no, Agnolo. It's not my quarrel."

"You're a fool then!"

"Fool I may be, anxious for the grave, I am not. You don't understand."

"You're right. I don't understand at all."

"If I must explain . . ." Durante hurled himself out of the chair and left, tossing the confession onto the floor.

❧

THE ROMENA TOWNHOUSE and its tower of nobility looked new from the modifications and restoration being done. The beautiful courtyard with its interplay of architectural angles and light was just as astounding now as it had been when Durante first entered it as a boy of sixteen. He was the landless, titleless, son of minor nobility and taken into the Romena house as a squire and to be apprenticed as a wool merchant. From the moment he set eyes on Guido Guidi, conte di Romena, Durante despised him not for his beauty but his shrewd manner and lack of humanity. Yes, lack of humanity: the man was chiseled of ice that never melted. If anything affected Guido, no one knew. Behind those chilling, pale blue eyes was someone secretive and evil.

But Guido's son Alessandro was a different matter. Durante was overcome by Alessandro's unworldly beauty, swept away by his charm and thought himself blessed that the Archangel Gabriel thought him worthy of notice, so overawed by Alessandro's attention. Friendship soon replaced awe, and Durante and Alessandro were inseparable until Alessandro played him for a fool.

This tower house had too many memories. Any moment he expected Guido to come to the gallery and shout at him to get back to whatever it was he was supposed to be doing while ignoring Alessandro's cajoling and invitation to go drinking and whoring. . .

A servant cleared his throat and Durante ceased to pace a circle around a rusting drain, looked in the direction of the staircase where a moon-faced boy waited.

"Will he see me?" Durante asked sharply.

"Follow me, signor."

The conte di Romena had his back to the door and was bent over a map unfurled on a table.

"Signor Giustini, monsignore," the servant announced and quickly disappeared. The haste in which the boy fled was unnerving. The slam of a door made Durante's teeth rattle. He held his breath and waited.

"How in God's name did he do it?" the conte di Romena said under his breath. The map was tossed to the floor and another replaced it. Durante watched as he traced a path along the lines of the map and it was some time before he summoned the courage and said, "Signor?"

Romena spun about and smiled. "My pardon, signor! Hello, I am Francesco."

Durante gasped and took a step backward, his movements so abrupt that Francesco's brows rose and he smiled again. A chill ran up Durante's spine. Had he not seen Alessandro's mutilated body he would have thought it was the man standing before him now.

"Forgive my preoccupation; I've just returned from Castello di San Galgano," Francesco explained. "Mercenaries were making incursions into my lands and causing no end of trouble. They were my uncle Porciano's men—but I shouldn't trouble you with this." He paused, waiting, and then, "You had something to say to me? Here; you look ill."

He took a cup of wine from a small table overflowing with stacks of scrolls and papers and all but forced it into Durante's hand.

"I am, I am Durante Giustini."

"Yes, I know. My servant Lorenzo so informed me."

Durante looked up at Francesco and just as quickly looked away when their eyes met. It was too uncomfortable. "You don't know who I am?" he asked.

"You were vassal to my father and held the honor of Montebuoni. That much I know."

"I was your father's friend."

"That would make you remarkable indeed, for I've been told that my father had no friends. He was deserted by those who could most help him."

"Monsignore, I have something to say. Some knowledge that has come to me that you should know—it may or may not put your claim to the Romena legacy in jeopardy." Durante blurted. He waited and was relieved when Francesco signed his permission to sit, the table between them. Durante took the nearest chair, a high-backed piece decorated with carved angels and stars. He almost leaped out of it when he realized it was Alessandro's chair. The chair from which Alessandro had ridiculed him on their last night together.

"What is this knowledge?"

Durante steadied his hand and took a drink of wine, savoring the drops on his lips before speaking. He took a breath and said, "Before you were born, there was a political struggle between the bishop of Florence and your father."

"I know of it. Rest their souls."

"Yes, rest their souls—their? The Bishop? Is he—?"

"Dead? Yes. I heard the Bishop ate a dish of bad figs. We should all be careful of what we eat, shouldn't we? Go on."

"I needn't tell you everything about that time. Surely you know of it."

"As much as I want to know for the time being."

"But you will want to know that your father made a contract of marriage with another woman before he married your mother."

Francesco raised his brows at this. "In the catalog of his sins, this is probably the least of them. He was married once before. His first wife died of sickness."

"*After* her, signor, God rest her immortal soul. After the lady Leonora. He made another contract. I'm telling you this because I know your uncle Porciano would make use of it."

"True," Francesco leaned over the table. "But perhaps it is another rumor to discredit me started by Tommaso?"

"I have the confession. It was made by a woman on her deathbed. She swore that she married him."

"Does anyone else know this?"

"Only the friar who heard the confession."

Francesco rose and paced the room. Durante barely turned his head to watch him, looking for something familiar or foreboding and was relieved when nothing came to him. The young man was at the window now, looking down into the street as if something more important than what he'd just heard had caught his attention.

"If it was a confession, messer Durante, then it would be protected under the seal of confession. That you would come to me and share this makes me wonder as to your motive."

"If I wanted to do you ill, I would have come here with soldiers of the

Commune to remove you forcibly from this house. I came alone and that should suffice as to motive," Durante said, his ire rising.

"How did you come by this news?"

"The friar who heard the confession wrote out a statement. I can send word to him. Perhaps you would speak with him?"

Francesco turned and said, "If by that you ask that I silence him in some manner, no, I cannot. I will send him a letter thanking him for his Christian duty to the woman," he said.

Durante nodded and stared at the plain cup in his hand. Something Alessandro would never have owned.

"Was she dear to you, messer?"

Francesco's question made Durante look up sharply. His face washed with bright crimson, he nodded. "She was someone I loved. The mother of my only child."

"I've lost someone more precious to me than life, so I know what you feel."

The moon-faced boy entered interrupted, saying, "A messenger from Faenza, signore Francesco."

Durante rose and set his cup on the table. "I leave it to you to act upon this knowledge. Even if you don't believe the sincerity of my intent. I thought you should know," he said.

"You've done well in your actions and I will consider what is required of me. Let this be a thing known only to us."

"We are agreed and I have nothing else to say on the matter. Good day to you, messer conte."

"You may call me Francesco," he said as he showed Durante out. "I am not my father."

☙

THAT NIGHT AT supper, Francesco recounted his interview with Durante to Gian Maria being careful to leave out the most damning information. Gian Maria swore softly as he speared another slice of venison.

"From what I heard, he was a scapegoat for the bishop. Gandulfo never let anyone interfere with his enterprises. The sentence was for twenty years, and when the bishop tried to get the podesta to extend the banishment for life, he was told to mind his own business. No one could prove one way or another if Durante murdered your father. It's said Alessandro's little whore dug the blade into his chest. But it was Durante's knife all the same. It had been a gift from Alessandro. Still, Durante was sent off more to keep the peace if anything and stay out of Gandulfo's way. Everyone that was privy to the murder is dead now; I suppose that's why they let Durante come home," Gian Maria explained between bites of venison and gulps of ale.

Francesco pushed away the gravy-soaked trencher before him. "How do you know all this?"

"It's been a bedtime tale for years," Gian Maria sighed. "I heard it every night while we dined. Father would tell the story over and over. I've heard it so often that I often wonder what is true and what isn't. Strange to think that the quarrel might have started over a piece of a woman rather than a piece of land. Strange that he should come to you."

"Absolution, perhaps? To let me know that he's not my enemy?"

"You go to a priest for absolution. You go to your enemy's son to take the measure of him."

What if he went to his enemy's son to tell him he was a fraud? That he had no claim?

"What if he came to tell the son to take care?"

"Durante is a dog without teeth. He makes threats, but all he can do is bark. You've nothing to worry about where he's concerned. Now our cousin Azzelino, however,"

"That reminds me," Francesco said and he rose to take a letter closed up in a book on the sideboard. Returning to the table, he poured two cups of ale and shoved one towards Gian Maria and then handed over the letter.

"What's this?" Gian Maria asked, then read, and spat ale across the table as he started to cough, choke and laugh, all at once. "A duel?" Gian Maria gasped. "Easy, easy! That's enough!" he laughed and Francesco stopped pounding his back. "He's called you no true son of Alessandro, a baseborn whelp got off a moon-mad noble slut, and demands satisfaction for your injury to him. In exchange for sparing your life, he will take some lands, a castle, the title of count of Raggiolo. But if you will not agree to this, then he has no choice but to kill you in a duel."

"How many men has he challenged and killed?" Francesco wanted to know.

"I couldn't say. I can tell you how many it is said that he's paid to have killed." Gian Maria reached for the bread to sop up the gravy on his trencher and finished his supper. "Well? Are you going to do something?"

Francesco shrugged. "Words," he said; "They're just words." *But they were only words if they were only just that*, he thought, *and it depended on how much Azzelino Alberti knew.*

CHAPTER 15

PEOPLE IN THE street moved aside for Andrea Alberti and his stepson, Azzelino, as their retinue made its way from the Alberti tower house to the houses of the Cavalcanti near the New Market where the members of the Arte di Calimala, the cloth finishers' guild, met weekly. The wealthiest of merchants belonged to this second-most powerful and influential of the Greater Guilds that controlled commerce in Florence. The cloth trade was the life blood of Florentine economy, whether one wove the cloth from wool imported from England, or purchased cloth in Flanders, England, and France and dyed and embellished the fabric to resell.

"He'll be attending, I'm sure of it; he's a guild member," Azzelino said to Andrea as they went along.

"Yes, yes, I know; why do you keep repeating yourself?" Andrea snapped. "Tell me when there wasn't a time the nobility outside the walls of Florence didn't stick their noses into our business. If Alessandro had listened to the advice of his betters he wouldn't—ah! Now I'm repeating myself. Signor Tommaso, good day!"

Tommaso di Porciano had arrived at precisely that moment with his own sizable retinue and the two adversaries bowed to one another in greeting.

Tommaso nodded in greeting. "Good day to you; what brings you to the Arte di Calimala?"

"We've come to speak with you about the injury Gian Maria did to my stepson Azzelino," Andrea said.

"Is this about the drunken quarrel near Santa Croce?" Tommaso asked, moving past them to get inside the house. He nodded at the porter and kept walking towards the great hall on the street level, motioning to his guards to close in so that there was distance between himself and the Alberti. "I've heard it was Azzelino who started the quarrel. Gian Maria only wished to keep Azzelino from doing injury to Romena or himself. And I also heard that it was ser Francesco that gave the injury, so why come to me? I can't help you and I won't."

"Gian Maria gave insult!"

"I wish you the best of fortune in getting whatever it is you seek from

Gian Maria; you're not bound to get it."

"If I can't exact a price out of your son for this latest insult, I can take it out of you," Azzelino said as he caught up with Tommaso.

"There isn't much to be had these days," Tommaso sighed.

"If I look hard enough, I'm sure I'll find something, Uncle."

Tommaso was going to speak but held his tongue. He had never liked this boy, his sister Marietta's by-blow, gotten off a wool merchant at the fairs of Champagne. Thank God a man like Andrea Alberti, a man usually without scruples, thought enough of Marietta to marry her and take the boy in, raise him as his own blood. Azzelino was as dangerous in his acquisition of titles and political power as any spoiled son of a wealthy family, but his entanglements and intrigues at the Papal Court were proving useful for Tommaso's enterprises.

Tommaso glanced to see where Andrea had gone and gently shoved Azzelino into a chamber off the great hall. "If I hadn't listened to you, Azzelino, matters would be quite different!" he hissed.

"Will you blame me for your raids into the Mugello?" Azzelino demanded.

"I wasn't the one begging for money or whining for a castle. I'll give your stepfather Alberti credit for not giving in to your demands, however it's bled me! If anyone owes, it's your stepfather!"

"You swore that I would have—"

"When you challenge a stronger army what do you think will happen?" Tommaso growled. "No more! If you want retribution, take it yourself! And I wouldn't go up against Romena. Not now while all Florence is in love with him."

Azzelino held up his bandaged hand, the rust-colored stain covering most of the palm. "A castle, a town, a cardinal's red hat, might pay for this!" he hissed. "Someone will have to pay, Uncle."

"Someone always does, but it won't be me. I have no sway over Gian Maria these days. He betrayed me and I have nothing to do with the boy now, and there's the truth of it. Petition the Commune for retribution if you must. Excuse me now."

Tommaso left the room, joining the other guild members for the meeting. As he was taking his seat, a servant approached and said, "Signor Andrea wishes a word with you."

He turned and noticed Andrea standing alone in the passageway and looking uncomfortable and out-of-place.

"What is it you want, signor Andrea?" Tommaso greeted him. "We are about to begin the day's business,"

"What I always want," Andrea said. "Peace between our houses. This latest brawl, well, I don't know what to do."

"Of course you do. That's why you're here. I don't doubt that your stepson planted the seed in your ear."

"Swords were drawn."

"Isn't that always the case?"

"Enough is enough. Someone is going to die. The quarrel always starts with your son's insults and lies. Gian Maria needs to be reined in, watched. If you won't keep him in line, I can do it."

Tommaso shook his head and tried not to laugh. "Forgive me but no solution you've ever had has worked. As I said to Azzelino, I have no control over Gian Maria these days; even so, leave me to take care of my blood. You have worries of your own what with the certain failure of your bank if the English king cannot repay his loans. The Alberti are no longer the great men of Florence, are they?"

"Wait a moment, Tommaso. Stay and listen. A marriage with my daughter Cunizza would bind our houses and make peace."

"Now let's be truthful in our tales, Andrea!" Tommaso chuckled. "What you really want is a house, a farm, a castle, for your daughter and your future grandsons. You want money enough to purchase a cardinal's red hat for Azzelino. Why not just say so?"

"I say so now."

"What do I get?"

"As I said, peace between our families. This alliance will prove beneficial for all our fortunes and desires. You will have our surety for everything," Andrea said.

"Who will give assurance for what you offer me?"

"Friends who would be only too glad to help you reclaim what your Romena nephew's taken from you. Friends who have no love for the Guidi of Romena, but know you for the honest and forthright man of business that you are, and those who would help you find a place in the government of the Commune. Think on it, Tommaso, and let me have your answer."

Tommaso frowned and nodded, watching Andrea hobble away greeting all he encountered with the ease of someone who owned everyone. Throughout the meeting of the guild masters his mind was on the opportunity Andrea laid at his feet and he came to the conclusion that meeting Francesco on the battlefield again would be more agreeable than what was asked of him.

CHAPTER 16

FRANCESCO CROSSED OUT a sentence, then another, in the letter he was writing and then started again. Gian Maria's conversation with the messenger who arrived from the Porciano house interfered with his train of thought. The argument, for that was most definitely what it was after an hour, carried up three floors to his studio.

He was seated at a great oaken table that was a depository for anything and everything Francesco had carried into the chamber. Personal treasures and business ledgers shared the cluttered table, from a Turkish carpet spread over the table top, to the polychrome statue of Saint Michael, to a jasper bowl with silver findings, to piles of documents that Francesco sifted through for a reference. Behind him the oilskins and shutters on the windows were no protection from icy blasts of wind and rain; they yawned and creaked incessantly and an arras thudded softly against the northern wall, making the fire in the wall hearth dance.

When the doors facing the Via delle Terme banged shut, Francesco started, his pen making a jagged arc across the page. Another door slam and the stomping of boots on the staircase was all Francesco could take. He was on his feet and halfway to the door when Gian Maria entered.

"What ails you?" Francesco demanded. "I have magistrates coming to discuss business with me and I'd like to finish my letters and preparations in quiet."

"I've been forced into a contract of marriage with Cunizza Alberti!"

"So?" Francesco asked, going back to his table.

"Alberti's daughter. Azzelino's stepsister. Now do you understand? It's a peace treaty. Or I'm being taken hostage!"

"But you're kinsmen," Francesco remarked, gathering up documents into folios. "A dispensation will have to be procured and that could take months, years. Be at ease." Francesco continued shuffling and organizing papers on the table until Gian Maria took them out of his hands, sending deeds, contracts, and bills of sale flying around the chamber.

"I don't see how taking it out on me is going to change things," Francesco said good-naturedly and bent down to snatch a deed before it sailed into the hearth.

"My father offered me a gift of land and revenues, but I won't get them unless I agree to the marriage!"

"I think your choice is simple and obvious,"

"Francesco, this is just another means of Azzelino getting his hands on more Guidi lands and wealth. My father has always favored him because he has a way of getting what he wants, and he always shares what he steals with Father!" Gian Maria growled as he threw himself onto the window seat. "I should have killed Azzelino that night in the borgo! Now it looks as if I'm the next to die!"

"How?"

"You don't know about the good and pious widow Cunizza, do you?" Gian Maria sneered. "No man that bitch weds lasts a twelvemonth! Everything she inherits by right of her marriage is divided equally between Andrea Alberti and Azzelino. The family of the dead husband is given something for their trouble—a farm, a shop—and thank their saints for the privilege of living another day! I hope Andrea hasn't sold the castle at Rovagno; my mother's always wanted a country home!"

"Well, you'll have to spoil things by outliving us all, won't you?" Francesco replied. "Why not use this as an opportunity to keep this cousin Azzelino in line?" Francesco suggested. "He may have your father in his camp, but you have me." A servant entered and bowed and Francesco handed him a stack of documents. "The podesta and captain of the people have arrived, I take it?"

"They wait downstairs, monsignore."

"I'll be with them shortly," Francesco as he gathered up more documents, a folio, and turning to Gian Maria, added, "if this meeting goes as I hope, you shall enjoy more than Romena behind you, cousin, but Florence."

"MESSER, IT IS a reasonable request," Michelino Groppa said, a nervous smile spreading across corpulent lips to show teeth.

"Yes, monsignore, it's very little we ask, and I speak on behalf of the gonfaloniere, who, as you know, may not leave the Palazzo dei Priori during his term of office," added Matteo Sanseverino. He nodded in agreement with his equally nervous colleague and co-conspirator. "Since the days of the Black Guelphs and the White Guelphs, in the days after Giano della Bella, the nobility who live outside the walls of Florence have used the unrest in Florence to seize power, to take seats in the greater guilds and make their fortunes by commerce," Groppa began.

"Meaning the Guidi," Francesco said.

"Not all of the Guidi, monsignore."

"Surely my father was one of those."

"Of course, of course he was, but he did not interfere with the governance of the Commune," Groppa said.

"Didn't he? I thought that was the reason for his murder." Francesco looked at each in turn.

"Oh no! It was more than that!"

"The Battifolle and the Porciano are our chief concerns now, signor," Sanseverino interrupted and threw Groppa a glare made of daggers, shaking his head.

"The very worst of us," Francesco muttered under his breath, and then aloud, "It's been quiet of late."

"How do you explain the raids into the Mugello and on your lands? Only last week we heard of a battle," Sanseverino spoke up.

"It was a skirmish at Castello di San Galgano. We chased them off. They were household knights with nothing better to do."

"You almost lost your life in the skirmish, so we heard. I should think you'd want peace," Sanseverino reminded him. "Let me be plain. Let us be plain. Florence wants no more of these quarrels. Sooner or later, Florence will be drawn into it. We cannot consider your request for the marcher towns and lands near your borders if you won't sue for peace with your uncle."

"It isn't much. All we ask is a declaration of peace made before the high altar of the Duomo," Groppa added.

Sanseverino offered a scroll to Francesco. "Here are the terms. It really isn't much."

"What you're saying, then," Francesco said as he reviewed the document before him, "is that if I want the towns, lands and the castle on my western frontier that were promised to me by Florence and have yet to be delivered, I must agree to these terms?"

Groppa and Sanseverino nodded as one person.

"No."

Groppa stood so abruptly that his chair went backward. It was not a violent gesture, but one of frustration. "Why not?" he cried.

"Signori, I can count on both hands and feet the number of times I asked Florence for help against Porciano and retrieving my lands and castles from him and the number of times I received excuses for the nothing Florence gave me," Francesco answered. "Where were the men and arms I needed to take Castello di Romena from Porciano? And Castello di San Galgano? Porciano contracted some of the Commune's soldiers for that incursion and I'm still counting my losses. And Raggiolo? Florence was supposed to take Porciano into custody. I paid a dear price for that folly. I received nothing of what I was promised even though on many occasions I have allowed your merchants the use of my roads for trade free of toll. Now the threat is very real to Florence and you make petty conditions. If one reads the carefully worded and collegiate language, these Latin formularies here, Florence considers me nothing more than a soldier for hire rather than the legitimate heir to an ancient title and birthright. You punish me for my father's crimes."

"If Florence were to reconsider," Sanseverino opened.

"Be silent!" Groppa hissed.

"—if Florence should reconsider and offer some towns of consequence to shore up your borders close to ours, would you be willing to align with Florence?"

Francesco studied Sanseverino carefully, never once removing his gaze. Sanseverino's eyes held his, refusing to waver despite Groppa's agitated whispering.

"The bishop of Arezzo is seeking my aid against the conti Berardi, who makes incursions into his episcopacy. I hold that bishopric and entitle the bishop to hold it for me. It is mine by ancient consent and right. Alum mines and forests are only two of its beauties. If you want my cooperation, I could make things easy; I might be able to secure Arezzo's allegiance and give Florence rights to the mines and forests. The garrison at the episcopal castle alone is worth a treaty."

"How?" two hopeful voices spoke up.

"It depends on what you give me."

"Monte San Sepulcro, Lucignano, Bibbiena, Caprese, Pratale," Sanseverino offered.

"Hmm, towns of some consequence, I'll give you that. And what else?"

"The forests of Bibbiena and Caprese."

"It still doesn't protect the bishopric. I can't afford to lose the alum mines to Porciano or his vassals. Anything else?"

"Leonecuoro, perhaps? Bucena?" Sanseverino suggested.

"What do you mean?" Groppa squealed and ignored the boot that jabbed into his shin.

"I know exactly what Matteo means," Francesco said. "Florence holds Bucena and Leonecuoro for the Bishop of Florence. Sign these claims to me and I'll assure you a greater return on fair revenues than what the bishopric gives you now."

"But—!"

Sanseverino nodded. "Done."

"Done," Francesco echoed. "I can place my garrisons at your disposal. I'll have your rights to the alum mines drawn up, as well as the forests."

"This is madness!" Groppa blurted out. "Bibbiena has been a matter of dispute between the bishops of Arezzo and Florence for years! A bid has been made for Leonecuoro!"

"By whom?" demanded Francesco.

"I cannot tell you that."

"My gold's a little brighter,"

"Andrea Alberti, perhaps?" Sanseverino answered and Groppa turned on him with murderous eyes, saying: "We cannot give what is not ours!"

"The bishop of Florence doesn't even know we hold them, Michelino. We could," Sanseverino turned to Francesco now, "say that the conte di Romena was too persuasive?"

"Bibbiena is surrounded by Romena towns and castles. As is Leonecuoro. They'll be mine sooner or later." Francesco replied, pouring fresh cups all around. He drank and settled back into his chair. "My garrisons at Castello di Romena and Castello di San Galgano are yours for the asking. I'll consider enfeoffing Consuma to Florence."

"Consuma?" Sanseverino and Groppa asked. Consuma was an important town at the mountain pass in the Tuscan Alps and was held by Francesco. Through Consuma lay the trade routes to Florence.

"Consuma," Francesco said, amused. "Provided you hold it in my name. If things work to my advantage, I might even give you share of revenues."

"Done!" Sanseverino almost shouted and looked to Groppa for assent.

"This once I'll oblige you provided you return the favor as we have discussed," Francesco replied. He smiled at Groppa and waited.

"You have our word," Sanseverino swore and turned to Groppa. "Michelino, what say you?"

"How shall I explain Bibbiena?" Groppa sniveled. "I cannot go to the priors and say we gave it to him outright; I don't know how I'm going to explain it! And God forbid, Leonecuoro!"

"Tell them I gave you no choice. It's the truth, isn't it?" Francesco suggested.

Groppa was about to open his mouth in protest again and then quickly snapped it shut. "You have my promise," he sighed at last.

"I'd rather have your men if I need them!"

The magistrates agreed and joined Francesco in congratulatory cups of wine and kind words of praise.

"There's one more thing. Never once has Florence acknowledged me conte di Romena," Francesco said. "It was done for my father and his father before him. It makes a good deal of sense to acknowledge me both as the holder of an ancient birthright and your most good, dread, lord."

Francesco's gall made Michelino Groppa nearly apoplectic, and he cried, "*Our* most good lord? How dare you make such a condition! We do not bend to threats! Princes do not govern Florence! We've only just rid ourselves of Charles of Calabria! Florence does not want or need your good lordship!"

"You do, signor. You need to see it. I hold much of the land and castles surrounding Florence; I would think you'd see the wisdom in making an alliance with me. Just see that it is done," Francesco replied icily. "It really isn't much."

"You think too highly of yourself, Signor!"

"No," Francesco answered, smiling. "Only self-preservation."

"How can I explain this to the bishop?" Groppa cried.

"I told you about the bishop..." Sanseverino murmured.

"The *new* bishop! Well, he'll be in a fit! How are we to make this come about?"

"Messer conte, we'll see that all we have agreed upon will come about to your satisfaction. Perhaps a mass in the Duomo to invest you with the rights and titles?" Sanseverino gushed.

"If we're to have a love day, let's be sure it's on Romena land and in a Romena church. I want the advantage." Francesco suggested.

"Even better, I think!"

"Especially if there's blood to be spilled," Groppa muttered. When he saw Francesco looking at him, Groppa smiled insincerely and bowed his way out of the chamber, taking Sanseverino with him.

"Wait! I'll come with you; I have business in the old market," Francesco called. He grabbed his cloak and from a coffer on the desk took the golden and enamel garland purchased several weeks ago, dropping it into a pouch.

Francesco walked with the men as far as the Mercato Vecchio and parted with handshakes and promises to dine. He then followed the perimeter of the square, ignoring the tumblers and gypsies entertaining a crowd, brushing off the crafty merchant shoving holy reliquaries in his face. *Last week the chicken bones were the fingers of Saint Cecilia, today they are of Saint Luke*, Francesco thought, smiling as he walked on.

The sharp morning air was scented with *berlinghozzi*, little dumplings boiled in vegetable broth that were purchased and eaten in one rapid transaction; it was punctuated by the cries of merchants to sample the finest wine in Tuscany or the mellowest, most pungent cheeses to be had north of Rome, to examine the most excellent craftsmanship in leather goods in all of Florence. The shouts of a priest casting proud and avaricious Florentines into Hell for their love of luxury rose above the shouts of children as they chased chickens and geese underfoot, the lament of a troubadour and the cacophony of bartering tradesmen and customers.

Francesco smiled and bade a good morning to a young girl carrying a tray with marzipan animals her father the baker had fashioned just hours before. Prominent among the cats and dogs were little replicas of Marzocco, the lion of Florence. Francesco purchased a half-dozen and ate as he strolled through the market to the stalls of the cloth merchants.

Serafina was there. Every week for a month, she'd been there.

Francesco sidled up and said nothing, then turned to smile a 'hello' and saw her through an exquisite *reta*, a diaphanous, netted cloth woven with gold thread and seed pearls that an anxious merchant was holding up for her inspection. The strands of gold caught sunlight and cast glints of copper in her hair. Francesco surveyed the costly fabrics before them, letting experienced hands wander across the sensuous backs of embroidered velvets, the silk brocades, and *rete*. It was Romena cloth and he knew its worth.

"This color suits you, madonna," he at last spoke. Francesco held up a brilliant violet-hued silk embroidered with silver stars. "It's from Provence." She gave him a fleeting glance of disbelief. "My agent carried it from the Avignon faire himself."

Serafina leaned in to get a better look. Francesco leaned in, too, but more for an excuse to stand closer. She nodded and looked up, smiling. As soon as their eyes met she blushed.

"I have something for you," Francesco murmured, and opening the pouch on his belt, withdrew the garland. He pressed it forward. "For you, Serafina."

"I couldn't!" she gasped, her eyes widening at the sight of the jeweled hair ornament.

"Surely you'd take a name day gift?"

"My name day was a week past, signor," she laughed.

"Well?"

It was some time before she accepted it.

"Thank you," she whispered and glanced around as if to be sure no one watched as it was placed under a cloth in her market basket.

"It's pretty," he replied, "You might wear it for a feast or tournament. I've seen ladies do such a thing."

"I might," she said, adding, "But I am more impressed by a gift of sixteen florins made to the Church of the Carmine on my behalf. The poor children of the district will have new clothes made of good woolen cloth."

Francesco shrugged indifferently, although he was pleased she knew about his gift. "I know what it's like to go without," he said and when looked at him with a curious narrowing of her eyes, added, "Ah . . . you think that because I have a title and some castles,"

"I think," she said, "that you are a good man."

He followed as she went through the market square, silent for most of the time, unusually tongue-tied in her presence. He helped select cheeses and sausages and loaded them into her basket. It gave them an excuse to touch hands, entwine fingers. They were at the spice merchants' stalls now, where they always said goodbye. Francesco purchased a bunch of rosemary and tucked it into the basket. "For remembrance," he whispered. "Perhaps next market day?" Francesco said.

"Perhaps. And perhaps it will be your name day," she teased.

Serafina nodded in farewell and turned to leave when she pulled the crucifix from around her neck and offered it to Francesco at the last moment. He was grinning like a fool as he walked home, the gold and emerald cross clasped safely in his hand.

CHAPTER 17

EDMUND CLIFFORD WAITED in the courtyard of the Torre Romena and amused himself baiting a cat with crumbs of sausage and bread and laughing when it danced on its hind quarters for more. Whenever a door creaked open or slammed shut, Edmund glanced hopefully in the direction of the sound and was disappointed every time. He turned to the servant sweeping the pavement around the well and asked, "Do you know where your master is?"

"He went to the old market as is his custom and usually returns for supper."

"And when is that?" Edmund's tone was argumentative.

"Soon."

"I've been here nearly an hour; I sent the conte di Romena a letter so he'd know I was arriving today,"

"I wouldn't know about a letter, signor."

Edmund shoved off from the pillar he was leaning against and slapped his riding gloves on his thigh, each blow more forceful and angry as he watched the servant go about his work, and as he was forced to wait. "Do you know who I am?" he demanded.

"No, signor."

"I am your master's oldest friend and his second in all things."

"Forgive me."

Now the servant moved his sweeping elsewhere but kept his eye on Edmund.

"Look you, tell your master I was here and tell him I won't be in Florence long! I've got better things to do," Edmund snapped. As he was saying this, voices and laughter coming from the street announced Francesco's arrival home. Francesco came in with Gian Maria and stopped short upon seeing Edmund.

"Edmund! Well met!" Francesco said and strode across the courtyard to greet him. "How long have you been here?"

"Just this morning. I've stabled my horse here if you don't mind,"

"No, not at all. I wish I'd known you were coming."

"I sent a letter."

"Ah well, it didn't arrive. But you're here and we'll talk about your work in Rimini. Come, we'll have some wine before supper. My solar is this way," Francesco waved in the direction of the stairs leading up three floors. The stairs zigzagged at each level, slicing between pillars and beams of striped stone. The afternoon light cast geometric shadows and angles making it seem as though the courtyard and upper storeys were puzzles in wood and stone to be solved. Francesco led the way to his solar, a room divided in two by gilt and painted columns. The bed sat on chests behind curtains at one end, a table and chairs, a wall hearth in the larger half. On the walls was a legend told in fresco panels, of a knight and lady sitting under baldachins of gold lilies on a sky-blue ground.

"A fine house, this," Edmund said. "Reminds me of that little place you kept near the river in Avignon. If I remember correctly, you won the house in a dice game."

"It was that or lose some of my best knights to a margrave from Cologne whose titles and holdings were a little less stable than mine," Francesco said as they sat down.

"Boy," Edmund said to Gian Maria, "bring us wine and wafers."

"Do you take me for a servant, Englishman?" Gian Maria snapped, his hand instinctively going to the dagger on his belt.

"Who are you, that I should care?" Edmund said as he quickly rose and squared off.

"Easily, friends! The fault is mine. I should have made introductions," Francesco interjected. "Edmund, here is my cousin and friend, Gian Maria di Tommaso. Gian Maria, this is Sir Edmund Clifford of Gate Fulford, about whom I've spoken many times. Edmund, my cousin has proved himself a knight fighting with me. And cousin, were it not for Edmund, I should have died a hundred times in my life and I owe him that much."

"No, signore," Edmund laughed; "I remember it was the castle of Focognaio. I'd gladly take hold of it now that the worst of my work for you is done."

Gian Maria frowned and looked first at Edmund, then to Francesco. "Focognaio? But Cecco, you gave it to me."

"You promised Focognaio to me, monsignore. At the chantry after the fall of Castello di Romena," Edmund stated quietly.

"Did I?" Francesco innocently asked, a smile playing on his lips. "God's life, but I don't remember. I gave it to my cousin, Edmund."

"But you made a promise!"

"I tell you, I don't remember. Would you have me take it back? I'll find something more suitable, Edmund. We'll resolve our differences tonight at supper."

Edmund hesitated and then nodded his assent.

Francesco clapped him on the shoulder and then shouted for Lorenzo, who poked his head around the door. "See that our guest is made comfortable and give him whatever he desires." Now he turned to Edmund. "Tonight at supper, then?"

For Francesco the matter was settled.

As far as Edmund was concerned, it wasn't.

He'd hoped to have a private meal with Francesco to discuss his business in Rimini and other matters weighing on him, but Gian Maria di Porciano claimed Francesco's attention and dominated the conversation, from discussions about warfare, to commerce, to women.

"I tell you, Cecco, I saw you with her!" Gian Maria laughed. "Don't deny it."

"I don't know what you're talking about," Francesco said. "I was in the old market to make sure Davizzi isn't robbing customers or stealing my cloth."

"She was beautiful. Why haven't you said anything?"

"Perhaps it isn't your business to know," Edmund said, as he drank his cup empty and poured another.

"That's where you're wrong, Englishman," Gian Maria replied; "we share everything. And I want to know why my cousin hasn't shared the name of his pretty lover!"

"She is not my lover," Francesco laughed. "For all I know she's someone's wife."

"I should hope so, otherwise, it would be a waste. Though I wouldn't find it an impediment. She was fashionably dressed. I suppose she's rich, or nobility? Wonder what kind of dower her father offered?" Gian Maria continued.

"You're wondering about her bower, but that is mine to discover, cousin," Francesco said and Gian Maria raised his glass in tribute while they continued to discuss this mysterious girl from the market square for what seemed like an interminable time for Edmund. He grasped the neck of his goblet so tightly the wine churned in its bowl and spilled onto the sleeve of Francesco's overgown. Francesco merely glanced at the darkening stain on the new black velvet and asked if Edmund was feeling poor.

"Beating a dead horse?" he gibed when Edmund asked about the castle during a moment alone in the solar that evening.

Edmund sighed, or rather, groaned, and said: "I understand why you'd want to gift Gian Maria. It makes perfect sense to reward a man for his loyalty."

"And you think yours hasn't been?"

"I know it has not!"

A child knows when not to beg for sweets, Edmund."

"I've never had to beg from you, Cecco. Don't expect me to start now."

Francesco put aside the documents he was signing and looked at him squarely, saying quietly, "I would not have it so."

149

"Francesco, consider the injury done me,"

Edmund knew he'd blundered when Francesco heaved himself out of his chair approached him, stopping just inches away. "When I've had the time to consider how I've wounded you, and when I've had the time to consider my holdings. I'll make a decision and find something adequate," Francesco said. When Edmund didn't move, he added, "What else?"

"You wanted to talk about Rimini."

"Tell me."

"You have the promise of forty men and horse from the Malatesta, and I have letters from the Ordelaffi—terms for the lands surrounding your mother's castle."

Francesco frowned and stared back at Edmund, whose gaze was steady despite the fact that he opened and closed his hand on the cross guard of the sword at his waist.

"Forty men and horse. That's all? That's not enough to secure my marches."

"It's what Malatesta can afford for now."

"It's not what was promised."

Edmund kept his gaze steady. "Yes, we do know how the great keep their promises."

"You blow hot and cold, Edmund. Should I have cause for concern? Would you turn on me?"

"I would not—I could not. Since Raggiolo, I have wondered—"

"God's life! Let it go. Let it go for now."

"For how long?"

"You shall have your answer soon and hopefully by that time all shall be as it was between us. That is all. If you want to join us at The Rose and The Knight, come then," Francesco answered as he reached for his cloak.

"Us?"

"Gian Maria and I always spend a few hours at The Rose and The Knight. We play dice, there are pretty girls, troubadours, wine, and food. Perhaps it would take your mind off of castles?"

"No, the ride from Rimini—look you, Cecco, I'll be going to bed."

"Very well; good night."

Edmund was rooted to the floor of the solar long after Francesco had gone. He burned with anger, wondering at Francesco's change of heart and more importantly, his change of loyalties.

CHAPTER 18

TRUE TO HIS word, Matteo Sanseverino presented Francesco's terms to the gonfaloniere and the *priori*, the governing body of the Commune, but hours of debate gave Francesco an unexpected result.

"It is as I said," the gonfaloniere explained to Francesco pacing the council chamber floor. "The Commune of Florence has no need of princes and palatinates. We are a democracy. While we welcome the commerce your great name and company give us, it will not be said that we are ruled by you. To make you our lord even only in name will entice others of your class to ask for much more. Then where will we be, signore? We would be here. Watching two great lords and their families quarreling and bringing Florence into that quarrel."

"And yet you would have me open my valleys and roads to Florentine tradesmen on their way to Venice and Genoa and Rome without consideration for the cost to me to defend your wagons and caravans against thieves and your enemies," responded Francesco. Men that should be guarding my borderlands. The lands Florence promised me more than once."

"We hope that would be the case," Sanseverino answered timidly.

"What do I get for this accord? Tell me."

"Peace," Michelino Groppa spoke up. When Francesco merely stared back, added, "Your uncle must place his hands on holy relics and swear to never make war against you or Florence never, ever, again. You will have the men and arms to secure your borderlands outside of Florence's walls in exchange."

"In fair exchange," Sanseverino echoed.

It wasn't, Francesco thought, but what could he do? Another path was traced across the council chamber floor, hands first behind his back, then running through his hair, with boots scuffing and spurs ringing on the pranks, several pairs of eyes watching.

"There will be no punishment for what Porciano's done to me," Francesco stated quietly.

"I would think, messer, that being forced to humiliate himself, to concede defeat, before the great and noble of Florence would be punishment for someone like your uncle," the gonfaloniere responded.

"All those witnesses," Francesco whispered to himself. He stopped pacing and held his hand out to a clerk who brought a document to the gonfaloniere's desk. Francesco read it quickly, then signed his name and pressed his signet into the glob of red wax.

No sooner had the decision been made than the nobility of Florence and her environs found the way to Francesco's doorstep to congratulate him and offer allegiance, if not to secure favor.

The Day of Accord, as it was called was set for the Feast of the Annunciation, Francesco's twenty-fifth birthday, the first day of the New Year in the Florentine Commune. It was a year to settle accounts, to make peace and make things right.

The eve of the feast dawned cold and clear, the coldest morning anyone could remember. It had snowed during the night and the servants grumbled that the weather was a bad omen as they crawled out of warm beds to break the ice on washbasins and light fires in the hearths.

"Signore! Where are you going?" Lorenzo asked when he entered the bedchamber and found Francesco dressed and ready to leave.

"Out. Be easy; I'll be back before we need to leave for the castle," Francesco answered as he wrapped up in his cloak and reached for a pair of fur-lined gloves. On his way out he pointed to the gold brocaded tunic and overgown on the bed chests. "I'll wear that with something blue."

"Aren't your colors dark red and gold?"

"Find something red, too. I won't be long!" Francesco called over his shoulder.

Francesco took a seldom-used door near the garden to leave. He didn't want to be delayed by well-wishers and last-minute questions needing answers. Walking across the *borgo*, Francesco went to the church of Santi Apostoli and slipped into his family's chapel. He was there only a few minutes when the hour bell rang. Then he heard footsteps behind him and smiled. Serafina entered the chapel and genuflected, turned to nod at Francesco.

"Ser," she greeted.

"I hoped you'd come. Please," he gestured towards a bench and she sat down. Serafina kept her eyes down as she sat in silence and when she finally looked up after a while, he was staring at her the way he always did— that look of seriousness and gentleness. He cleared his throat now and pushed himself up, going to the candle stand to light one of the tapers.

"You didn't answer the letter I brought round last week and I thought you were ill or had left Florence," he began. The next came in a flood of word and nerves. "I would like you to come to the castle this afternoon. I suppose you've heard that my uncle and I have an accord and we mean to make peace between us with feasting, hawking, dancing. That's why I asked you to come this morning. So I might ask you in person, or to find out why

. . . it would make the whole affair tolerable if I had a friend among so many Florentines expecting largesse and favors of one kind or another."

Francesco sat on the bench opposite Serafina and waited for her response as he stared at the altar frontal where embroidered angels danced and played musical instruments on the linen fabric embroidered with gold thread and jewels.

"Today?" she ventured. "This afternoon?"

"You're not coming."

"No, I will be happy to attend. Ah but signor, there is something,"

The hour bell struck and a priest carrying a basket of vessels and linen to prepare for mass shuffled into the chapel, stopped short when he saw them.

"We're going now," Francesco said to him and to Serafina, "Tell me at the castle."

"I will need an escort – may I bring my father and cousin?"

"As many cousins as you like. I would be honored to meet your father."

"As you will, but,"

"Signore, madonna, I must prepare for mass," the priest interrupted.

"Of course. Serafina, tell me later. At the castle."

As quickly as Francesco departed the Torre Romena he returned and prepared for the short journey to his castle of San Galgano. Gian Maria was standing at the window taking in the freezing air when Francesco entered the solar. The boy's face was a sickly olive color and he managed a weak smile when Francesco said good morning.

"Lorenzo," Francesco beckoned; "bring the vial. The one in the cupboard above the bed." Lorenzo brought the stoppered bottle and handed it Francesco, who emptied its contents into a cup of water and passed it off to his cousin. "Here. I don't know if this will help— meadowsweet, ginger, dill, and bitter herbs. Some ground eel."

Gian Maria gulped down the concoction and within moments heaved out the window. "I feel better already," he said, wiping his mouth on the towel Lorenzo offered. "Eel does wondrous things." He waved Francesco over with the towel and pointed to the street. "God help us, I see your farce will be played out! My father and mother, Alberti and his daughter have arrived. Hmm. And there's Azzelino."

"He'll be on my land and in my castle," said Francesco as he turned to dress. "Have you reconsidered staying on?"

"As much as I would like it, no. Part of my settlement with Father is that I return to his house and we live at separate ends of it."

"So you'll marry Alberti's daughter?"

"You've seen her haven't you? There are worse things in life. I've done what he's asked and all's forgiven."

"Until he gives you another reason to reconsider the truce."

"He bought me for two hundred florins." Gian Maria handed Francesco the tunic of gold silk. "He had to purchase my loyalty, Francesco. You didn't."

"What about Focognaio?"

"That's not a bribe, it's a punishment!"

Francesco laughed and slipped on the fur-lined overgown sewn of cloth of gold next, belting it so that the gold tunic and his mulberry-colored hose and boots were visible "Perhaps you should give it to Edmund and see what he'll make of it," he said.

"A florin and a cask of wine say that tonight at the feast if I were to offer him the castle he'll turn it down because it came from me," Gian Maria suggested.

"Had I a florin and a wineskin I'd take those odds," Lorenzo quipped as he crowned Francesco with a blue hood made of the softest wool felt. Francesco pushed back the hood so that it fell in ripples of folds on his shoulders.

"As much as I would agree to it, it seems a bit unfair," Francesco said.

"Showing him humility wouldn't be. You'd think he was the conte di Romena the way he goes on," said Gian Maria.

"Would you like him better if he was Tuscan?"

"That wouldn't change his degree of self-love and self-importance," Gian Maria answered as they headed to the stairwell. "But it would make him easier to kill if the need arose. Most Englishmen I've met I like and I can't say that of signor Edmund."

"I'll make sure that never happens," Francesco said and gave Gian Maria a frown that made the boy swallow his next insult.

A messenger waited for Francesco on the landing and bowed, handing him a letter. Gian Maria assumed it was bad news by the look on Francesco's face and knew the day's entertainment would be postponed.

"Will there be a reply, monsignore?" the messenger asked.

Francesco shook his head and shoved the letter into a pocket.

"Everything all right, Cecco?" Gian Maria asked.

"Nothing important," Francesco answered, and clapped him on the shoulder. "Shall we go? We have a celebration ahead of us."

Yet another messenger waited in the courtyard and was talking to Edmund when Francesco and his party came downstairs. Assuming more bad news, Francesco called him forward.

"Messer Agnolo, his daughter, Messer Durante and his daughter have accepted your invitation and will come to Castello di San Galgano. They'll join you on the road to San Galgano, by the chantry of Santa Maddalena," the second messenger reported.

Francesco's face lit and his mood instantly improved.

The cavalcade began to take form in the courtyard. Francesco's favorite gray charger, Justinian, was barded in the Romena colors of mulberry and gold to match the magnificent cloak Gian Maria had presented for the occasion. Francesco's personal device, the silver falcon enchained, was embroidered in silver thread on the left breast, the round eye blinking with a great emerald. The same bird blazoned the quartered banners carried by his heralds and knights. Once Francesco was mounted, others in his party followed suit and the cavalcade snaked out of the courtyard past the gate and into the street where the Romena colors and device hung from every window. Neighbors cheered, waving kerchiefs and shouting praise, cheering more loudly as prominent guests joined the parade along the route: retainers, friends, and business associates, and the *magnati* and politicians of Florence. The party continued to swell in numbers when the papal legate, Guillaume de Longis, and the bishop of Arezzo with their sizable entourages met Francesco in the Piazza del Duomo. With a blast of trumpets heralding it the Romena cavalcade set out for Panicaglia, which lay in the Mugello Valley some fourteen miles northeast of Florence, and was dominated by the Romena fortress of Castello di San Galgano. The broad valley was a lovely yet isolated place surrounded by hills that gave way to the Benedictine Alps and the frontier of the High Casentino.

"A fine day, monsignore Francesco!" Andrea Alberti greeted as he rode up.

"It is, isn't it?" Francesco said cordially.

"A day your father would be proud. To finally have peace in the family. Mind, I didn't hold your father in high regard, but his son is a different matter. Let there be an accord between us as well?"

Francesco took the hand offered and said, "It shall be so, as long as need be."

"Signore?"

"We shall remain civil towards one another, friends even, as long we both respect one another's lands and properties and know where our loyalties lie."

"Let it be so, then."

They rode in silence paying no particular attention to anything until they arrived at the chantry of Santa Maddalena where a carriage joined the cavalcade with its own escort. Francesco immediately noticed the tall, elegant figure of Durante Giustini as he urged his milk-white stallion in line with the rest of the Romena knights and asked Alberti, "What do you know of this gentleman?"

"Honorable, but one who has different faces, like the pagan God Janus. He changes like the weather. You have to watch him carefully. He was abused by the Commune and looks to settle scores now that he is free to do as he wants. It may be as small a slight as coughing in his presence, or accusing him of murder. One wonders if that's all he did in his exile from Florence, but keep an account of who did what to him and how they'll pay."

"I know his grievance. I don't know him at all. Should I make an ally of him?"

"No."

The tone of voice was enough to tell Francesco there was something unspoken.

Andrea offered his courtesy and rode ahead to join his daughter, who was riding with Gian Maria and now called to him. For someone who hated the very idea of being married to Cunizza Alberti, Francesco thought with amusement, Gian Maria seemed content to keep her company and was making her laugh but who wouldn't laugh and be glad on a day like this? The afternoon was as clear as glass though biting in its cold. Spring was making a bold appearance in the valley with flowering mulberry and pomegranate trees lining both sides of the northeastern road. Tufts of new grass sprang from drifts of late snow, as did lilies and jonquils. Closer to Castello di San Galgano the vineyards and farms were better tended and villages beehives of activity. Villagers paused in their daily business to cheer them on and wave the Romena colors. A little girl ran out to give Francesco ribbons of gold and mulberry embroidered with his name. The progress slowed as more and more people in the villages they passed came out to greet their lord Francesco. Soon Francesco had Justinian at barely a canter in order to receive gifts and well wishes and make the villagers' acquaintance and that delay proved fortunate for it gave him an opportunity to greet the ladies in the carriage: Serafina's pretty blonde companion, Serafina, and two serving women. Serafina was reading and didn't look up when he tapped on the carriage roof to get their attention. The others simpered and giggled when they saw who it was.

"Ladies, you improve the afternoon," Francesco greeted.

Now Serafina glanced up and flushed, then tucked the book under the furs on her lap.

"What do you read?" he asked her.

"Nothing; nothing, important," she stammered.

"Serafina was entertaining us with the sonnets of Dante," the blonde girl spoke up, batting her lashes. "I am Violetta Arcangeli d'Agnolo, signor."

"Madonna, indeed you are; the first flower in the meadow," Francesco replied, doffing his hood in an affected, chivalrous manner all the while looking at Serafina.

"I know those words," Serafina said. "You know the work of Guido Cavalcanti?" She sounded skeptical but was smiling.

"This virtue of love, that has undone me
"Came from your heavenly eyes:
"It threw an arrow into my side.
"So straight was the first blow

156

"That the soul, quivering, reverberated,

"seeing the heart on the left was dead," Francesco recited and added. "and the poet Dante Alighieri. He was given shelter by my father and grandfather at Castello di Romena. Would you share with us your favorite of his sonnets, madonna?"

"It's nothing someone like you would be interested in," Serafina said quietly, burrowing deeper into the furs as if to hide.

"You'd be surprised,"

"Perhaps messer conte finds educated women to his liking?" Violetta giggled. "How different from ser Gherardo, who likes his women in other wise! "

"Violetta!" Serafina hissed. "Please excuse my cousin, signor."

"I'm sorry if I offended you, or made you uncomfortable," Francesco apologized. "Perhaps we may talk of poetry and what I may or may not find interesting another time?"

Serafina's reply was interrupted by the joyful shouts in the cavalcade. Straight ahead the walls of Panicaglia were crowded with townspeople waving the Romena colors and outside the gates, a pageant was being played out: Saint Michael in combat with Satan. The resemblance of the archangel to Francesco wasn't missed by the guests, nor was the resemblance between Satan and Tommaso di Porciano. A choir of children dressed like angels sang the praises of Francesco while girls danced to pipe and drum.

Francesco thanked the townspeople for their entertainment and accepted the fealty of Panicaglia's magistrates, then led the cavalcade up to the great castle and forebuildings clustered before them on the promontory of a mountain.

The castle itself was a half-mile from the village, above the parish church of San Giovanni Maggiore. It was just one of three hundred castles the conti Guidi owned in the territory surrounding Florence, a trapezoidal structure embellished in the Guelf style with swallowtail battlements. Within the greater ward was a fortified barbican, matriculated donjon with eight rectangular towers and a round tower. One approached the outer curtain from the town walls, riding up a steep incline to a barbican that stretched over a gorge. The embrasures and parapets were teeming with castle folk cheering as Francesco rode through the barbican, over the drawbridge, and into the ward.

Francesco dismounted in the greater ward, heralds pronouncing him. Fiasella was the first to kneel at his feet, offering the keys. Next, the retainers and servants welcomed Francesco to Castello di San Galgano, and as they knelt before him one by one, Francesco glanced over their bowed heads to see little Beatrice Fiasella standing with her mother.

She curtsied, her new silk gown and surcote crackling as she bent the knee. She was very proud of her appearance and smoothed the cloth delicately as she stood again. He nodded in greeting, which wasn't lost on her father.

"Once again the Fiasella of Castello di San Galgano rejoice in Romena's favor," Fiasella gushed as he pushed his way through the household knights and servants to scurry after Francesco as he walked into the donjon, a little rat in the rushes. "The steward's quarters are made ready for Signor Clifford, monsignore. I think him an admirable choice. If it be known, I was weary of the task."

Francesco cut him off with a perturbed look. "Never satisfied you, did it? Twenty gold florins per annum, is that all it is?"

The question was ignored. "I'm not one to complain, messer, but I was struck knight in honorable fashion. I come from the *magnati*, served under your kinsman Battifolle, as a knight, of course. When Battifolle died, I brought my own banner to battle for Romena."

"That's not what I heard."

"A soldier's only as good as his captain, or knows which side is the more victorious—but that's not to say you would never achieve—I now stand for Romena!" was the impertinent yet flustered reply.

"Do you? I've learned in my battles that it's best to keep the enemy close to the skin. I wonder if I will have a need to keep you close?"

The two men exchanged glances. Fiasella looked away first, turning crimson. If it were possible for a man to read another's thoughts, he was sure Romena had just done so.

And then at the entrance of the donjon, Francesco turned, holding the keys aloft, a symbol of his authority. One fellow shouted, "God grant you a long life, Francesco!" to which the assembly added their own praise. He glanced down at Fiasella who was still staring at his boots.

❧

TOWARD DUSK THE remainder of guests began to arrive for the first of three banquets. They were met by folk from the *contado* of Panicaglia who gathered outside the walls to receive alms from the banquet tables or perhaps greet Francesco. Two fountains were built on either side of the barbican. Wine poured from elaborate cisterns and anyone could drink freely.

The household bustled with activity it had not seen in years. Francesco toured the grounds accompanied by Edmund, Gian Maria, and Elisabetta. He was amazed by the industry around him, swearing that if the countryside was arraying for war it could not have been busier. Baking house, granary, cow byre, piggery, stables, chapel, and cottages in the greater ward were scrubbed clean and made fresh with herbs; at the entrance of the forebuilding stood a tabernacle and dovecote where smitten, giggling adolescent girls waited for Francesco. When he appeared, they offered him sheaths of evergreen boughs and simpered when Francesco thanked them with pretty compliments. He was next greeted by women of the household outside the chapel. "Monsignore Romena would not have you bend the knee," Gian Maria teased, bringing each of the ladies from their curtsey. "You'll only spoil your new clothes—for which your fathers no doubt paid fortunes."

Beatrice Fiasella came to the front of the small crowd, smiling bravely, and hoping for acknowledgment. She looked as if she would die of joy when Francesco smiled at her and stopped.

"Friends, here is Beatrice Fiasella," Francesco said. "Signorina Fiasella, our cousin and good friend Gian Maria Guidi di Porciano, his mother my aunt Elisabetta Porciano da Romena, and our counselor and friend Edmund Clifford of Gate Fulford in York, England."

She curtseyed, proud that she should be singled out. Let the others think she boasted fantasies now!

"What a pretty color of blue," Elisabetta commented, fingering the girl's silk gown. "This must be Romena cloth."

"A gift from ser Francesco," Beatrice said proudly and smiled at him.

"She must be quite amusing to earn a gown," Gian Maria quipped. "What magic do you perform that others do not, eh, Beatrice?"

Francesco was visibly annoyed. "The child is none of our concern. Let's go in."

Edmund turned to smile at the pretty Beatrice. "Lady, that color suits you," he said in passing.

"I am no light-o-love, signor. I am not like the others," Beatrice spoke up bravely.

He stopped, smiling. "It would be any man's fortune to discover that. I hope the honor will be mine."

The women began to gossip when Francesco was out of earshot.

"We'll have a *Castellana* before the summer's out," Signora Fiasella commented wistfully. "Did you see the way conte Francesco looked at the girls?"

"So many of the reputed beauties of Florence are here!" another sighed and set the women to laughter by imitating one girl in particular.

"The young conte has his choice and he looks like one who'd never waste time deciding. He looks like he enjoys plucking roses!" the cook's wife sniffed.

Signora Fiasella glanced at her daughter watching Francesco intently. "Beatrice! Surely you don't think Romena - !" she laughed, and the others joined in.

Beatrice shrank from them and touched her blue silk. If the conte di Romena were so free with cloth for a dress, would he not be just as free with his heart?

CHAPTER 19

THE GREAT HALL blazed with torchlight and the gilded leather paneled walls finished only that afternoon reflected rainbows of light dancing off the *magnati's* jewels. *Jewels enough to ransom the pope*, Francesco thought wryly of these people dining with him that night. These were lords and ladies whose only purpose in life was to adorn frescoes such as those in his great hall; once in a great while they would make alliances if it was expedient or convenient. Their presence would prove one or the other by morning. On the wall behind Francesco's great chair of state were more gilt leather panels and a cycle of frescoes illustrating the tale of *La Chatelaine de Vergy.* Above the dais a banner proclaimed his *raison: Honor Above All.* Tapestries on the northern wall depicted the glorious deeds of Romena's ancestors in Richard Coeur de Leon's Crusade. It was all very pretty, but if Francesco was forced to sit through another hour of minstrels and mummers, listen to accolades accorded by complete strangers, he knew he'd go mad. This wasn't what he had in mind when he sought to claim his legacy.

He glanced down the table to where Gian Maria wooed Cunizza Alberti. Their heads were close and Gian Maria at last succeeded in winning a kiss. In less than an hour they'd be trysting in some bedchamber; hopefully not his, Francesco thought in amusement. The girl's laughter was irritating and Francesco was glad when she made excuses to leave the hall, gliding across the floor with hips and buttocks swaying in steps obviously practiced and purposeful. Several cups were raised to Gian Maria's victory, for it was proclaimed that Madonna Alberti was a prize to be had. Andrea Alberti was looking mightily pleased with himself.

Beyond Gian Maria sat Giordano, now abbot of the Imperial Abbey, with Groppa and Sanseverino. God knew what they talked about; their heads were bent close together like crones discussing remedies for catarrh. When they noticed Francesco's interest, they hailed wishes of good fortune. Further down the table below the salt cellar was Azzelino Alberti dressed in expensive clerical vestments and looking piqued. Francesco could have invited him to sit closer as his station dictated, but he thought, why bother? Azzelino was no one in his greater plan.

"Francesco!"

Startled, Francesco looked in the direction of the happy shout and smiled. "Edmund! Sit with me."

"Eminence, if you wouldn't mind?" Edmund begged the bishop of Arezzo's indulgence and squeezed himself in between the bishop and Francesco, weaving and swaying to settle himself. "My lord bishop, will you hear my confession?"

"If you mean to confess that you're drunk, we are all certain of that. *Absolvo te*," the Bishop teased as he made the sign of the cross over Edmund.

"This is the Lord's doing and it is marvelous in our eyes," replied Edmund and knocked his goblet against the bishop's and emptied it in one gulp.

"Where've you been all evening?" Francesco asked. "I've been stuck here looking noble and holy."

"Trying to seduce that pretty girl in the blue dress. Beatrice. She's giving me a chase. But I see that Gian Maria has all the luck," Edmund said, pointing to the dancers in the hall. Gian Maria was now dancing and flirting with Serafina's cousin Violetta.

"That's not a conversation I want to be in the middle of," Francesco added, gesturing with his cup towards Cunizza Alberti, who'd returned to the hall and now stood to one side, quietly fuming as she watched Gian Maria with Violetta. "Our bad luck with women aside, we shall do well here, Edmund."

"Do you think so?"

"Look around us. Every man in this room has one reason or another to claim my colors. All but one. Eventually we will have even Porciano."

"By giving away another castle, signor?"

Francesco let his eyes slide around the rim of the cup he held and glared. "That was unkind and uncalled for. You must be patient, Edmund. I have a solution."

"Solutions are not what was promised."

"What say you to the lordship of Giampereta?"

"Has it a castle?"

"No."

Edmund grimaced and between clenched teeth and in a voice as controlled as he could manage said, "Francesco, you did promise a castle with a garrison, not only a town. I am a soldier and have always been a soldier."

"Be satisfied for now, Edmund. I cannot afford to gift another castle at this time. I have enemies enough,"

"And why is that? Do you forget promises so easily? What of all these Romena liege men so anxious to claim your colors?"

"You've chosen the wrong day and the wrong time to find a quarrel,"

Francesco hissed.

"Now's as good as any a time to pick a fight."

"You're drunk, Edmund . . ."

"In wine there is courage to say what you think. I think I've made myself clear."

"Be content with what I offer now!"

"You've never gone back on your word before,"

"Be content, I say."

"But—"

Francesco went brusquely to his feet. "*Be content!*"

Dancing and music stopped. The sudden outburst brought curious and embarrassed glances in their direction. Edmund stepped around the toppled benches and plates of food and bowed away, saying, "I shall try."

Francesco summoned the musicians to play. Rather than sit again, he leaned against the wall and studied the assembly, making note of personages and snatches of conversation. Things that might prove useful.

"Don't make an enemy of him, Cecco," Gian Maria murmured, sidling up and offering his cup.

"Did you offer him Focognaio?"

"No, but where it concerns that promise you did him a great wrong and know it. And I know it. Which one of us do you least want to offend? Give him the damn castle. I don't want or need it. I'm sick of hearing about it. You do need to keep Edmund Clifford in your good grace."

Francesco stared at him, amazed. "That's excellent advice coming from you," he laughed.

"I'm drunk. I do my best thinking and arguing when I'm deep in my cups. Unlike some men." Gian Maria said and went off to reclaim Violetta's attention.

That *was* excellent advice, Francesco said to himself and went off in search of Edmund to set things right with him. He found the greater bailey deserted, but there was light in the chapel set into the curtain. No doubt Edmund had gone there to sleep it off and as Francesco approached, a woman ran from the chapel, a man swift in pursuit. The man caught up with her, and after an angry exchange of words, he attacked, struggling with the woman until they were both on the ground. When Francesco heard the ripping of cloth and the woman's frightened pleas turn to furious protests, he drew his sword.

"Step away from the lady!" he shouted, his sword leveled at the attacker. The couple moved as ordered and Francesco recognized the sweep of copper hair when it caught the torchlight, the large eyes and perfect face of Serafina Giustini.

"My cousin Romena," the man said as he stepped into the light. Azzelino Alberti made an obsequious bow and then grabbed Serafina's hand, pulling her roughly to him. "How good it is to know that not all of the Romena are whoring bastards, but look after the honor of others."

"Leave her alone. No one takes advantage of a woman in any circumstance, especially in my house."

"This lady promised me a kiss."

"We were children then!" Serafina protested. "You cannot hold me to it!"

"Leave her alone, Azzelino."

"You have no business to interfere—"

"It's my castle, my bailey. My guest. I may do what I like."

Azzelino let go of Serafina and swaggered forward. "But for how long?"

"Don't threaten me,"

"You're interfering in a private quarrel, Francesco. Mind your own business."

"I said, leave her alone."

"Or what?" Azzelino laughed. "Summon your archangels to battle with me? Tell me, do you really believe you have so much power that I'd do as you order, especially when what I do doesn't concern you? I don't bow to pretty little boys. I'm not Alessandro. Come, Fina. Let's end our conversation in better company." When he started to lead her away, Francesco's sword separated them.

"Leave the lady here. You may go."

For a moment, Azzelino was ready to respond but thought better of it. He smiled, shaking his head and walked away. Only a fool would have stayed to argue. Azzelino was a fool, but he had enough presence of mind to take Francesco's suggestion.

"Are you alright?" Francesco asked Serafina. She had moved into the shadows of the walnut trees to repair her clothes and appearance. Enough damage had been done that Francesco offered his overgown for modesty's sake and she slipped it on.

"Once again I've saved you from an unwanted suitor," he jested bitterly.

"I do assure you, this time I had no liking for him!"

"By my count, that's three times I've defended your honor. A charitable lady would offer something in return. Perhaps a token of regard?" The jest was not received kindly, for Serafina's eyes blazed, more in fright than offense and Francesco regretted his false step. "That was unkind; I apologize," he said.

"No need. I am the subject of cruel gossip; that much I am used to. It will be said this quarrel was expected."

"Let me escort you to your women."

"No. I'd sooner stay here for a while."

Francesco shrugged. "God give you a safer night, then."

He was halfway to the donjon when he turned and looked at the girl standing alone under the walnut trees. She didn't look like one who wished for solitude.

"I can't leave you alone here. Shall I keep you company?" he asked.

"No, I mean, if you'd like. I'll be alright in a moment."

When he came within arm's length of Serafina she backed away, the overgown clutched around her. She trembled violently.

"You're cold; let's go inside." Francesco motioned toward the chapel and pushed open the door. He stepped inside, not knowing whether the girl followed, then lit the great altar candles and planted himself on the sanctuary steps. Serafina remained by the door.

Francesco read the trepidation in her stance and said: "It's too cold to stand outside. You need not fear me. No one will touch you in this chapel."

That brought her closer, almost to the steps. Francesco played with his baselard, noting how the mirror-like steel caught flashes of candlelight and reflected in Serafina's hair.

"How do you come to know Azzelino Alberti?" he asked.

"We were pledged to one another as children. Nothing came of it, no *impalmare*, nor solemn oath because his father Alberti sent Azzelino to the church."

"For that may we truly be thankful!"

When she did not reply he looked up and smiled, seeing that she had come yet another step closer. She was near enough that he could tell the weave of her blush-colored gown, catch a scent of perfume.

"Serafina. An unusual name," he remarked as he stretched himself out on the steps and leaned back on his elbows. "Do you know the legend of the girl saint of San Gimignano? How yellow violets sprang forth in the dead of winter on every tower and hillside of the town the moment she died? How the bells rang? She is called Santa Fina. She was pious, devout, dutiful to her family, and very beautiful."

Their eyes met. *But the little saint's beauty was nothing compared to yours*, he thought.

Serafina laughed softly, and strolled around the chapel, her hems whispering on the flagstones. He noticed that she'd relaxed and let go of the overgown so that it fell open like a cape around her shoulders. She glanced back at him and smiled every so often and finally paused near the altar. His ancestor's tombs in the chancel caught his attention when Serafina's shadow moved over them and Francesco gestured with a hand at the thick pillars and rounded arched ceilings, heavy and plain with window embrasures just as thick and heavy and plain.

"Not the most pleasant place, is it?" he said, sitting upright now.

"My mother once said it was not the stones and ornaments that made a church, but the hearts of believers."

"That's not the opinion of my family, as you can see. Their persons and not their deeds are left to memory. My father is over there, I think, I'm not really sure—I was told that he was devoured by wolves the night he was murdered; if it's him, he's over there with his sons, my stepbrothers. And there, my grandparents, and there, I don't know—Gesù! It's newer than the others. I hope it's not for me! Let's see . . . I never met any of those kinsmen. This is an ugly place. My wife is buried in an ugly chapel like this at my castle of Benchiaro."

"I'm sorry,"

"Don't be. If you knew my history you'd agree she's better off." When he sensed her disquiet, Francesco shrugged and was suddenly blunt. "It was a marriage of necessity. That is all you need know."

"All marriages are of necessity."

"They need not be."

"You wouldn't think that if you were led before prospective suitors as if lamb to market," Serafina replied as she crossed her arms defensively and now followed the outline of mosaic tiles on the floor; "inspected and talked of and bartered about as if you weren't even present, or have a pretty jewel dangled before your eyes with the hope that the suitor dangling it is as desirable as the gift. And all the while you are told to smile and be grateful."

"You have the right of it; it's certainly worse than being seen as pastures, vineyards, and castles."

"I've seen how it is. Fathers start telling their daughters to stand up straight and smile when the noble Francesco da Romena crossed the market square." They laughed together. "Poor us!" Serafina giggled and started a new path along the flagstones. "Life will never be like that in troubadours' songs."

"The sins of envy and pride,"

"What?" she asked and paused on the sanctuary steps so that Francesco stood below her and they were eye to eye. Serafina's thick, glossy hair spilled across her neck and shoulders and now tickled his face. He caught the heady scent of perfume as she lifted a hand to brush the hair aside and took the hand.

"We envy those who can choose who they will marry and bed. Yet we are too proud to change convention because it sets us apart from others."

"What would you do?" she asked.

He pulled her close for a kiss that was long and passionate. "I would take you to my bed tonight!" Francesco whispered when she broke away and then moved in again for another kiss. "Say yes."

Footsteps at the entrance made them turn. Azzelino was back; how long he'd been there Francesco didn't know. He kissed Serafina and she slipped away, hurrying as fast as she could to the donjon.

"Didn't I ask you to leave?" Francesco wanted to know as he brushed past him.

"The lady is not for you," Azzelino warned.

"Meaning what?"

"Just what I said."

Francesco took the crucifix Azzelino wore around his neck and let his thumb glide over the relief of the suffering Christ. "You're in holy orders?" he asked.

"Yes."

"That's what happens to younger sons and bastards, isn't it? I suppose if my brothers had lived, I would be living in Rome now, serving the Holy Father and not God. But I wouldn't make poor attempts at seduction; there are very few women who agree to rape."

The force of Azzelino's blow amazed Francesco more than the taste of blood and then bile in his throat. His lip had been split in two and he didn't know if his nose had been broken. He couldn't feel anything around his mouth. The swelling came immediately.

Swords were drawn and they squared off, but Gian Maria came upon them in time to prevent one cousin from murdering the other. "What's this? A scuffle over a bad toss of the dice?" he asked, looking first at Azzelino then Francesco.

"Just that, nothing more," Francesco gasped.

"Nasty cut there," Azzelino said, sheathing his sword. He patted Francesco's mouth none too gently. "I don't think you'll be seducing anyone tonight; not that you could. I've heard stories."

When Francesco lunged at Azzelino Gian Maria pulled them apart and shoved Azzelino up against a tree, saying, "I don't know what prompted this, but it would be in your very best interest to not anger those who might be of help in future! And for once in your life at least make a show of being a priest if you're not going to take holy orders seriously!"

"He is, Gian Maria; acting like a priest that is," Francesco mumbled through swollen lips.

It was Azzelino's turn to pounce and once more Gian Maria was the arbiter. He waved off the household guards responding to the scuffle and shoved Azzelino towards the great hall. "You do know how to pick your enemies, Cecco," he said as followed Azzelino.

Francesco picked up his sword and watched the cousins' retreat. In his present mood, there was only one solution this new dilemma.

He would wait to take his revenge.

CHAPTER 20

FRANCESCO KNELT AT the altar and listened as prayers were offered for unity and an end to war. Cardinal de Longis came forward with a circlet of hammered gold and rubies and held it aloft, proclaiming Francesco to be conte di Romena, true and good, signore of the High Casentino and Mugello, by right of birth and inheritance. Francesco was deathly still as the circlet was pressed onto his head, sure that blood would be drawn when the finding on a ruby grazed his scalp.

Francesco swore in a clear voice free of emotion to uphold the rights of his vassals and promised to be Florence's chief ally in all matters temporal. Trumpets sounded as he took his place before the choir screen and accepted oaths of fealty from his vassals. While a *Te Deum* was sung, Tommaso approached with his vassals and exchanged the peace with Francesco, though their gestures and looks were anything but lovesome.

So much power in the grasp of one man—an extremely young and virile man—gave Tommaso chest pains. A man with Francesco's appetite would get more sons and live long though he'd have to look over his shoulder at every step. A glance round the church proved there was much the upstart had to worry about.

The *magnati* of Florence were crowded into the church of San Giovanni Maggiore to witness this, the first spectacle to come along in months. Pity the Commune's lot if some catastrophe were to befall the church; or, depending on how one viewed the existing political climate, how convenient. Tommaso nodded cordially to the witnesses to this solemn occasion as he returned to his seat. Durante Giustini was present, no doubt curious about Alessandro's brat. And there was Alberti, God forbid! That old fool would purchase a seat at his mother's execution. Well, his days were numbered with Gian Maria's marriage to Cunizza. It wouldn't be long before the Alberti fortune was in the Porciano coffers.

Prayers for the repose of Alessandro da Romena's soul were now offered. Gian Maria parroted responses while he leaned against a pillar and wished for once he hadn't drunk so much the night before. He wanted to be anywhere but where he was, and more particularly with the girl. Gian Maria could not remember her name but there she stood beside the red-haired girl Francesco lusted after. Simonetta? Bianca? Rosalina? Violetta?

Violetta was it? *Yes!* She had been so agreeable once he promised marriage. He learned by experience it was the best way to get a virgin to yield, and what a compliant little piece Violetta had been! Landed women of gentle society sometimes proved more adventurous in bed than the ladies who plied the same trade in back rooms of alehouses, candle maker's shops, and in alleys.

Gian Maria yawned rudely when Tommaso passed by. Oh, to bed to sleep! Violetta had worn him out, and no woman thus far had done that. He fixed his gaze to her, down to the breasts under the fine silk velvet of her gown, to her taut belly and narrow hips, the shapely legs. When this comedy was done, he'd take her. He was sweating for her now. The little harlot was smoothing the velvet of her dress in such a way that not only Gian Maria was roused, but every man in the church that stared at her. He caught Violetta's attention and they exchanged smiles until her father noticed. The two men nodded cordially. Gian Maria knew that ser Agnolo had an idea of what had transpired the night before and would want to speak with him, but how to explain the marriage contract with Cunizza— better still, how to get out of it? Now Cunizza was staring knives into him. Gian Maria blew her a kiss and then placed his hand over his heart, but the only one who seemed to care was old Alberti, who bobbed in greeting and smiled back. Gian Maria let his eyes slide to the roundness of Violetta's high, white, breasts and prayed God for a way to get out of the Alberti marriage. . .

Francesco stared out into the nave as his mind wandered from the Eucharistic prayer Cardinal de Longis offered, to the scuffs on his new boots, to the frescoes in the vault above him, to the problem of arming a garrison. He now glanced over the nobility and wondered who had spent a year's revenues on their clothing for the occasion. That was easy enough: Tommaso di Porciano. No one could stand up under the weight of his jewel-embedded robes, but Tommaso was managing quite nicely. If he coughed or sneezed, however, he'd fall over like a pine tree.

Now his interest fell to the ladies standing together in a corner of the church; a strange custom that forced the women to huddle like brightly-colored sheep at one side of the nave apart from the men. Yet there they all stood, and somewhere amidst the sea of ruched velvets and silks, the constellations of glittering, gaudy gems, was Serafina. He could still feel the touch of her lips and taste them, and in his mind's eye, saw her lovely smile and those large, beguiling eyes. . .

Someone touched Francesco's shoulder and he started. Cardinal de Longis whispered that he should kneel to receive the Lord. After taking the sacrament, he sat and watched as people came up to kneel at the rails to take communion: dignitaries, merchants, fathers with their marriageable daughters nodded in greeting as they passed him. He watched and waited, but Serafina remained behind. He wondered about that while the post-communion prayer and blessing were offered and when the altar party arranged itself around him and escorted Francesco out of the church. He paused halfway through the nave and nodded in greeting to Durante Giustini, who bowed and met Francesco's glance for glance and then with a smile. That moment caught the attention of many and started tongues wagging, especially when Francesco sought out Serafina for the walk back to the castle. He greeted the little groups clustered outside the church and worked his way to Serafina. She was wearing the garland and the morning sun caught the gemstones and gold and made little rainbows and fireflies of color dance around her hair and face when she moved; the veil over her coiled braids washed with soft hues.

"Madonna Serafina, will you walk with me to the castle?" Francesco said. The women and men around her all knelt when he approached and he signed them to stand, but for the most part ignored them as Serafina held all of his attention.

"Monsignore, you do me honor," she said quietly with an incline of her chin.

"I trust you are well," he said.

"Well enough."

"Do you return to Florence today?"

Serafina glanced over to the church steps where her father and Margareta were standing, looking about for her, and unfortunately for Serafina, found her and pointed so that Durante glared over the heads of people coming out of the church.

"Tomorrow," Serafina answered Francesco as she moved out of her father's sight.

"Please reconsider; stay a while longer," he said low.

"My father has business to attend in the town and thinks it unseemly for me to stay here without an escort."

Francesco looked at the men in their circle, which grew with every minute that passed. "Where is he? Let me persuade him to stay."

Now they were surrounded by fashionable ladies and their servants. Before Serafina had a chance to respond, Violetta glided through the crowd and paused expectantly. Serafina gestured towards her and asked, "Do you remember my cousin, signor? Violetta?"

"Ah, the flower in the meadow," he responded and brushed her extended hand with his lips.

"I have heard such wonderful stories about the castle, signore Francesco," Violetta said. "Is it true that your grandfather and uncle fought for the hand of a lady in a tournament there?"

"When my grandfather drew his last breath in the holy physic's tent, it was to proclaim his love for that lady," said Francesco.

"And was she uncommonly beautiful? Why else would a graybeard and a young knight quarrel for her favor?"

"If you knew the history of my family you wouldn't think it the stuff troubadours put in their love songs."

"But still, she had to be one of the acknowledged beauties of Florence. Serafina's mother was an acclaimed beauty and the queen of many tournaments; will you take part in the tournament?" Violetta purred.

"He can't," Gian Maria spoke up as he joined them. "My cousin will judge the competition. I will ride in his stead. Now, shall we be on? There's feasting and dancing to be had."

"Will you walk with us?" Violetta said, looping her arm through Francesco's.

"I've promised dona Serafina that we'd discuss Dante' sonnets," he answered.

"Let me escort you, signorina," Gian Maria offered.

For that interception Francesco was grateful and smiled as Gian Maria steered her away towards the young lords and ladies waiting to process to the castle.

"And you, madonna? Do you enjoy the tourney?" Francesco asked Serafina.

"I've never seen a tournament," she said.

"I shall wear your favor one day; what do you think?"

"I think," Serafina said, smiling, "Violetta will be quite disappointed if you did."

They led the guests across the meadow to the castle, a bright, animated ribbon threading through carpets of new grass and budding flowers. The sun had come from behind threatening rain clouds and brought farmers and villagers alike out to watch the pageant.

"Which of the sonnets is your favorite?" Francesco asked suddenly after they had walked silently for a time. Serafina glanced up, puzzled, and he said, "The poet Dante. You were reading his sonnets to the ladies when we came from Florence."

"Ah . . . that. I hardly know—I've just started reading it. My father," Serafina paused. "My father believes the Psalms are better poems for a lady to read."

"*Surely thou wilt slay the wicked, O God: depart from me therefore, ye bloody men. For they speak against thee wickedly, and thine enemies take thy name in vain!*" Francesco recited. "I suppose if one looked for love in that verse it would be the love of murdering one's enemies."

"Many of the psalms are poems of love to God," she mused. "I find much love and beauty in them."

"Is this not more loving: *I met a gathering of damozels, she that came first, as one doth who excels, had love with her, bearing her company: a flame burned forward through her steadfast eye. As when in living fire a spirit dwells: so, gazing with the boldness which prevails o'er doubt, I knew an angel visibly."*

Francesco then plucked a lone jonquil from the path and handed it to Serafina. As he was doing so, he noticed Durante Giustini's frown. "What a weathercock that Giustini is," he mused. "I've offended him somehow. He was friendly enough in church, but now his looks are poison."

"Something always offends my father, and of late he's been most concerned with my friendships," Serafina said, glancing back at him. "My father has made promises to the Ranieri of Verrucole and your attention to me is worrisome, I think."

"Durante Giustini is your father?" Francesco asked, looking from Serafina to Durante. "He's your father?"

"Yes. Did you not know, signore? I thought that was why you invited him."

"I would I knew sooner before his promises were made," Francesco replied as if to himself, but Serafina heard the comment.

And I, too, Serafina thought as they walked the rest of the way in silence.

❧

THE NEXT MORNING heralded the much-anticipated tournament that would conclude the festivities. Serafina woke to the sound of laborers building the lists and stands. She peered out through the bed curtains and saw the chamber was empty. They let her sleep in and just as well, for yesterday evening had been long and memorable.

Serafina rolled over in bed and clutched the bolster, smiling. How many times had Francesco danced with her? Did he not sit with her father and talk and share cups of wine? Did Francesco not single her out for conversation, and did his eyes not follow her throughout the evening, even when he danced with her cousin and other ladies or when she danced with other gentlemen? Did the guests not smile and whisper as she glided by with Francesco? The sweetest memory was at the end of the evening when Francesco escorted her to her chamber and gave her a book no larger than the palm of her hand, a volume of sonnets. And then he lingered over her hand with a kiss and a smoldering look.

" . . . a florin against Francesco's merlin!"

Voices rose from the courtyard followed by laughter and the pleasant tinkling of bells.

"What do you take me for? Merlins are for ladies and elderly knights. I have the best peregrines from England. Lorenzo, bring Isolde here. Place your wager on this beauty!"

There were whistles and praise. Serafina threw off the covers, wrapped herself in a robe and went to the window.

Seven men including Francesco and his cousin Gian Maria were standing around a coal brazier warming themselves against the chill of the early spring morning as a hawking party assembled. On Francesco's gauntlet was a magnificent peregrine that sat quietly as Francesco petted her and showed her to his companions.

"She's pretty enough, your bird; but I do find it strange you're not with that beauty you hunted last night," Gian Maria said. "You went after her with such determination. Perhaps little Isolde here will help you find your quarry."

Men's laughter followed the jibe and Francesco's response was lost in the teasing that brought more laughter.

Laughing herself, Serafina threw open chests in search of clothes. The dark green wool kirtle with the mulberry sleeves, the pale blush surcote, where was her cloak with the fur-lined hood? And her boots of doeskin.

She didn't hear the door open at first, but Serafina heard the plodding footsteps while struggling with her laces. "Ah, Marghareta! Help me with this dress. I want to go with the hawking party; ser Francesco is—Father! I thought you were one of the maids." Serafina sank in a curtsey and when she stood again she continued to pull at the laces of her bodice and watched while Durante paced the chamber, the footsteps heavier and slower.

"I prefer that you stay behind this morning, Serafina," Durante said, smiling weakly.

"Why may I not go?"

"Have you forgotten your betrothal to Gherardo?"

"Even if I wanted to, you'd make certain I did not," Serafina muttered.

"What?"

"Of course I haven't, Father. May I not enjoy my time here at San Galgano with our friends?"

"But not in the company of Romena. He made you the subject of ridicule last night. How long before the gossip and whispering start? I don't doubt it's already started. It shows a lack of character and chivalry to pursue a lady promised to another," Durante said. "Heed this, Daughter."

Durante was leaving when she said, "How do you know Gherardo isn't lying to us about his wealth?"

"He has no reason to lie."

"I've heard he has empty castles. We know that's not true of Romena."

"Do you not listen? Our future is secure with Ranieri. We do not know as to the other."

"Other? His name is Francesco," Serafina laughed and then gasped when her father struck her across the face.

"Be advised. Stay away from him! Do not ruin our chance of returning to favor."

"But—!"

"I mean what I say!"

Durante was gone.

CHAPTER 21

WHERE WAS SHE?
The tournament was into its second hour and no champion yet in sight. So far the contests had been exciting but there was no clear winner for as soon as the victor of the last contest met his next opponent, he was quickly replaced, that is until Gian Maria entered the yard and surprised everyone with his martial ability and unhorsed several knights. People were calling for Francesco to don armor and take up the joust, but he laughed and protested. Who would be craven enough to unhorse the host of the festivities? Not his own cousin! As judge, he was content to watch.

Sitting with his aunt Elisabetta, Francesco applauded and cheered with everyone else, but kept his eyes on the pavilion where young women and girls held the 'Court of Love.' The winner of the tournament would crown one of the ladies the 'Queen of Love' and she would sit with the champion and Francesco at the final banquet that evening, presiding over the festivities.

Where was Serafina Giustini?
"Oh, my!" Elisabetta gasped as Gian Maria's next challenger rode into the tournament grounds and approached the yard. The crowd was on its feet to cheer Edmund Clifford. "My son's luck has run out," she said to Francesco, "Unless they want to play at dice rather than cross swords!"

"Those two are beginning to wear me thin," Francesco said in half-jest. "They quarrel over everything. They're like two bitches in a farm yard, growling and baring teeth whenever they meet. Whomsoever wins this contest is still the loser."

"More to the truth, Nephew, they quarrel over you as if you were a precious jewel or sweetmeat," Elisabetta teased.

At least it wasn't women, Francesco thought as he watched both men receive favors from different ladies. Gian Maria had wisely chosen Cunizza Alberti's golden ribbon over Violetta Arcangeli's blue while Edmund watched as Beatrice Fiasella tied a silver ribbon of lace and pearls on his *greve.*

Circling, Gian Maria and Edmund paused at the pavilion where Francesco sat and offered their courtesy and then rode to opposite ends of the yard. As soon as they were in place Francesco gave the signal and lances were couched for the first engagement, spurs dug in and combatants bent low in the saddle as horses gained speed.

"A miss!" called out the herald when they passed one another. The crowd at the barricade jumped out of the way when Gian Maria lost control of his lance and it flew like a javelin, bouncing and rolling at the feet of squires when it finally landing.

"Are you certain you don't want to compete? We'd be out of this cold and home to supper by now," said Andrea Alberti to Francesco and they laughed together.

A blast of the trumpets saw Edmund and Gian Maria ready for their next meeting. "A *soldo* on Porciano," shouted one knight to another.

"Only if they choose flagons of wine as their weapons!" the other shouted back and started laughter all around.

"I'm English. I can drink him under as many tables as you like," Edmund jested loud enough for all to hear. "Let's finish our work here so we can go find out."

"You'll eat your words," Gian Maria growled and wheeled about to gallop to the end of the yard. He slammed the visor down on his helmet and jabbed spurs at the horse's flanks so that it reared up and screamed, losing Gian Maria precious minutes. Edmund was ready for him. This time, Gian Maria's lance was shattered, but he managed to keep his seat. He saluted both Francesco and Edmund as he made a round of the yard and took a new lance from one of the squires. Trumpets called for attention and Francesco once again gave the signal. If it was possible that so many people could hold their breath at once, it seemed to be the case. The aim was good and the timing perfect when Gian Maria struck Edmund's breastplate with his lance. Edmund somersaulted over his horse and landed on his back. Gian Maria vaulted out of the saddle as Edmund got to his feet and drew a sword. His own sword was out when they met, the crash of blades ringing over the shouts of the spectators. For each of Edmund's attacks, Gian Maria returned as good as he received and gave back. Twice now Gian Maria fended off what might have been a deadly glance or strike but his shield took the brunt of it and the painted pine rectangle was soon hacked and splintered.

"Stop this," Elisabetta begged Francesco. "This is no game!"

"Why did you think it otherwise, Aunt?" Francesco answered. "I can't stop them,"

"Surely you will!"

"They'll find occasion to take their quarrel where there are no rules of chivalry. Let it be."

Edmund now raised his sword as if to swing it down on Gian Maria's head, but he turned too quickly and fell. Gian Maria was standing over him with the sword point leveled at his throat.

"I yield!" Edmund gasped.

The tournament at last had a winner, and it was Gian Maria di Porciano.

"*Now* we may go home to supper!" laughed Francesco. He took purses from Elisabetta and tossed them to Gian Maria and Edmund. Then Elisabetta crowned her son with a garland of golden laurels. "Gian Maria di Porciano, our good cousin and friend, we name you champion and invite you to sit with us this evening with your Queen of Love," Francesco said. He motioned towards the ladies and the crowd went silent as Gian Maria rode over to the pavilion. Without hesitation, he saluted Cunizza Alberti and handed back her favor after kissing the silk.

Francesco next presented Edmund with a magnificent dagger topped by an emerald in the pommel. "Edmund Clifford, you are second to none and we honor you for your strength and courage," he said, and while the crowd cheered the champion and his second, Francesco noticed the look of cold indifference on Edmund's face, and grew concerned when his mood hadn't improved when they left the yard.

"Be of cheer, Clifford," Francesco said, clapping his friend on the shoulder. "It was Gian Maria's luck more than prowess. The best knights were worn to the bone from the earlier contests."

"Luck you say? Was it luck that gave him what is owed to me?" Edmund replied and walked away. Francesco was of a mind to go after him when Gian Maria sauntered up.

"He nearly killed me! It was supposed to be friendly," Gian Maria, but Francesco stopped him with a raised hand.

"Not now. Not today. For God's sake, I don't have an infant to carve into halves!" Francesco answered and left for the castle.

He arrived before everyone else and was glad for the quiet. He'd have some wine and rest before the banquet, which was sure to be as great a battle as the competition between Edmund and Gian Maria. Francesco entered the solar shouting for Lorenzo and was surprised to find Serafina standing in the middle of the room dressed in a traveling cloak and boots. She turned when he came in and dipped into a graceful bow, pure beauty to watch.

"Serafina! You were missed today," Francesco greeted.

"My father thought it best that I not attend," she answered. "So as not to dishonor our name. Last night, you see,"

"Yet you are here."

"I wanted to say goodbye. My father has already left and expects me to follow," she answered. "I came to give you this."

A letter was in her gloved hand. Rather than take the letter, Francesco chose the hand and drew her near enough to kiss but kept her at a distance.

"Why not tell me yourself rather than have me read it when you've gone?"

"I hoped that you'd still be in the yard; I have no courage some days,"

"I know that you are promised to Ranieri and it was a secretive, hasty, thing. If that's what's in your letter. Or is it something else?"

"You must understand my father's concern. It is more than that." Her voice was tremulous, almost a whisper. He noticed the tears immediately.

"I'm not concerned about Durante. I have concern for you and I believe you have a great deal of courage."

"Forgive me, Francesco. I must be going."

Serafina held out the letter again and when he did not take it, she moved away and tossed the letter into the flames of the wall hearth, watched the parchment singe brown on its edges, then curl and turn to ash. As she turned to go, she said in passing, "It wasn't my decision to make. That is what I wrote in the letter."

"Let me speak to Durante. Surely my suit would agree with him as I would hope it agrees with you."

She was in his arms. They exchanged kisses and Serafina buried her face into the soft fabric of his tunic so that she could hear his heart hammering in his chest and smell his scent.

"Stay with me?" he whispered. She nodded and pressed closer. "I'll speak to your father when I return to Florence. But this afternoon," Francesco slipped away after kissing her and whispering, "Only a moment, my love."

Francesco had gone to the other side of the room to lock the door and partially shutter the windows. While he did this Serafina glanced around. She'd never been in a solar as luxurious as this, yet the fine tapestries and carpets, the personal effects, and the evocative sandalwood steaming in braziers failed to make an impression. All that Serafina saw was the great bed upon its chests and the fine curtains surrounding it, the soft amber glow of the lamp hanging from the headboard, the soft, wavering light of the hearth fire.

And then she could only see him.

Francesco returned with a cup of wine. The cup passed between them slowly until it was empty, hands trembling as fingers brushed accidentally.

He drew her close. His hands gently caressed the small of her back, gliding from the waist to the nape of her neck as they kissed. Serafina was rooted to the floor. She expected to feel nothing; and more than that, she was afraid Francesco would soon concede defeat and send her away or threaten rape, as Ranieri had done so many times. Her virginity was unassailable; surely he would remember Niccolo's abysmal failure that night at the abbey. Now, however, a pleasant sensation unlike anything she'd experienced overwhelmed her. She was relaxed and at the same time aware of a tension that begged for release.

Francesco gently parted her lips with his tongue, while his hands gently explored the curves of her hips and bottom and moved slowly up to her breasts, where they lingered.

When he stopped kissing her, she was disappointed, but dared not move—not because of what he might do, but what he might not do.

"Come to bed?" he whispered.

"Signore, you must know something. I am not what you think."

He laughed gently. "Shall we tell truths and make confession?"

"At the abbey, you see. I know what you saw. My mother was a whore, and it is assumed that—I can assure you, I do not—I mean to say, I am not a harlot, and I do not know what it is like—that is, to lie with a man. There it is. If you want me to go, I will, and we may part as friends. At least, I would hope so."

"If you were to go, I would follow, and I would count you the most precious of friends. But I would rather you stay, for I flatter myself in thinking that you do like me, and not just a little."

"Here's the truth of that," she said and kissed him.

☙

SERAFINA WOKE FIRST when the shepherds of Castello di San Galgano were returning from the high pasture, when night was ready to set upon the Tuscan countryside. She slid her hand across Francesco's naked chest playfully, but he did not stir. Pulling up the coverlet, she lay quietly against him and wanted to sleep again, to dream of their afternoon together in this bed.

"I am yours," he said to her before they made love. Francesco drew her close and then placing her hand on his heart said, "I am yours."

In that darkened solar with just slivers of sunlight breaking through the shutters, apprehension turned to wonder as layers of wool and silk were slowly stripped away, until nothing but cool afternoon air touched her skin and then the downy softness of the fur coverlet beneath her. His skin was smooth and warm and rough against her. Hands as keen as a sculptor's took the measure of her body, moving purposefully; they sought to learn and gain trust. She was soon eased from fear to relaxation by his gentle caresses and kisses that were at first tender, then deep and more and more sensual, marveling in the physical sensation that overwhelmed and swept over her, and then his response, tender and yet violent until he lay sweating in her arms, whispering, "I want no other but you; I am yours."

She smiled, remembering, and was content to stay in Francesco's arms until she heard the knocks on the door. "Signor? Monsignore?" a servant called. "They call for you downstairs. Signorina Giustini has gone missing."

She would have to return to her apartments before a search party was released into the countryside. And there was the problem of Marghareta. She had eyes and ears in every corner and was probably gossiping in the kitchens already if she hadn't sent word to Durante by now! Serafina slipped out of bed and retrieved her shift from the floor, pulling it over her head as she tiptoed to the wall hearth and stood by the fire as she struggled into her clothes, the laces giving her trouble as she tried to dress swiftly before Francesco woke . . .

"Let me," Francesco said.

He'd risen and thrown on a robe and now pulled the silk cording through their eyelets, closing the seams. "You're trembling. Is it cold or fear? Did I hurt you, Serafina?" he now asked, wrapping her in her fur-lined cloak and hood.

"He'll know," she said. "I'll go to my wedding bed a fraud."

"Not to my bed," Francesco whispered and gently kissed her. "Your father will take my suit and we will be married. I promise."

"When will you speak with him?"

"I'll send word."

Serafina reached up and brushed the curls off his face, which made Francesco smile and kiss the palm of her hand.

"Shall I see you on market day?" she asked.

"Of course."

"Goodbye for now,"

Serafina was at the door and was ready to throw the bolt when she turned and went back to him, was caught in his arms.

"Not yet!" she whispered huskily.

GUESTS WERE ASSEMBLED in the great hall and waited for Romena to arrive. Forty nobles and their wives and retainers sat uncomfortably in stiff holiday robes and stared at the food growing colder by the minute.

Azzelino noted Serafina's absence first, and then his eyes darted to the great chair standing empty at the high table. He leaned toward Tommaso, whispering. Tommaso now glared accusingly at Gian Maria, who shrugged. They couldn't blame this on him. For once it wasn't his fault. Not even he knew where Francesco had gone.

Gian Maria looked across the empty chair to Edmund, who was conversing with Elisabetta. "Where is he?" Gian Maria whispered rather loudly.

"I thought you knew. Didn't he go with the others this morning?"

"No; he said he had to meet with the Bishop of Arezzo."

"The Bishop left at dawn. You're saying he didn't go out with the falcons?"

"I thought he was with you all day," Gian Maria said, and then raised his brows at his mother. "Well? Do you know something we don't?"

"I thought you two were the keeper of Francesco's secrets," Elisabetta answered. "You haven't asked Cunizza yet and there are a few more at the table who might have a clue. Patience, have done. He'll come when he comes."

Gian Maria slumped back in his chair and took another drink of wine. A door opened, and everyone turned, but it was one of the servants bringing trays of fresh, warm, bread. It was then Gian Maria looked around the hall and noted that Serafina Giustini was also missing. "Gesu, where's the girl? Where's Durante's girl?"

Edmund frowned and looked towards the ladies' pavilion, making a tally of the women with his eyes. "Lord, that's all we need!" he sighed, taking a pull from his cup. "Shall I go upstairs, or will you?"

"Neither. Better to say nothing. It's none of our business, anyway," Gian Maria said.

"For once we're in agreement about something. Well, we'd better not let the food and drink go to waste. He wouldn't want that." Edmund stood and cleared his throat. The guests turned and stared quizzically. "My lords and ladies, it has come to our attention that Signore Francesco is worn out from so much good will and revelling that he has taken to his bed with milady."

A wave of laughter and snickering went round the hall.

"Do you know what you said?" Gian Maria hissed, but Edmund waved him off.

"I'm sure Francesco would have you raise a cup in his honor and take to the table and to dancing as he has to his bed. Play, musicians!"

Sitting down, Edmund ignored Gian Maria and raised a cup towards Beatrice Fiasella, sitting with the other women of the household.

"Your slip of the tongue hasn't been lost on many," Gian Maria growled.

No, it hadn't, Edmund thought; *especially on Azzelino Alberti.*

❧

GIAN MARIA STAGGERED up the donjon's circular staircase to the parapet and took in a deep breath of cold night air when he reached the top. Setting his flask of wine on the stones, he leaned over and wretched into the inner bailey below. The people in the torch-lit bailey at that late hour paid no attention as they were hastily packing trunks onto a wagon. Gian Maria leaned his head on his hands and watched the activity, and wondering what was going on, especially when a carriage rolled up.

"Come back to bed, sweeting,"

Violetta Arcangeli was standing beside him, draped in nothing but a silk robe that was whipped about by the wind and outlined her voluptuous curves.

"In a moment," Gian Maria murmured, taking a drink of wine. He spat then, Violetta sliding out of the way.

"I know what will cure a headache," she said, letting a shoulder of the robe drop.

"Cunizza will wonder where I've gone. I told her I'd be gone only a moment," Gian Maria said as he nuzzled first her neck and then a breast. Violetta shuddered with delight and pulled him closer. "Adventurous, aren't you?" Gian Maria pushed her up against the parapet and was fumbling with the laces on his breeches when he saw torchlight wavering and then a figure moving in the shadows, the glint of a blade.

"Gesù! It can't be!"

"What is it?" Violetta asked. She pulled away and tiptoed to see over the parapet. "Ah, signor Romena! Well, I guess the rumors of his being a monk aren't true at all, for there he is with his lover—by my saints! Is that my cousin Serafina?"

Just so, Francesco and Serafina came from the donjon and Francesco escorted her to the waiting carriage. They stood close for the longest time, kissing, and held hands even after Serafina boarded the carriage and it slowly rolled out of the castle. Francesco watched the carriage leave, unaware of what was happening behind him, the little drama being played out that had caught Gian Maria's attention.

"You're tormenting me!" Violetta whined. "Let's go back to bed."

The watch called the hour, answered by the bleating of sheep in the high pasture beyond the castle. A wind was gathering from the east and blew the cresset flames into a frenetic dance. Gian Maria cursed the freezing wind for its bite, cursed himself for not wearing a cloak, and cursed himself for having seen what he had seen.

"Gian Maria,"

"I heard you!" he snapped.

"Whatever is the matter?" she demanded.

Gian Maria pulled her to him for a kiss. "I'm sorry, *Bella*. It's just, I must speak to Francesco,"

"Now? His life is his own and none of your concern."

"No, not that."

"Well, can't it wait until morning? If I were Francesco, I wouldn't want to talk politics or business at this hour."

"I suppose you're right," Gian Maria conceded and followed Violetta down. They passed Francesco on the wooden foot bridge between the great tower and donjon.

"Cousin, you should be abed," Francesco teased in passing; "Take your lady somewhere warm!"

Gian Maria spun about and called to him, but it was too late. Francesco had taken the staircase to his apartments in the tower.

☙

FRANCESCO SENT LORENZO away and got into bed, drifting off just as the watch called three. At that hour, only one guest was still awake.

He moved by stealth to the solar. The guards usually standing watch were conspicuously absent, proving that when a coin exchanged hands, so did loyalties. It would be too easy, he thought, and let himself in, carefully sliding the bolt into the lock so that it made no noise. Candles gutting on the table were extinguished one by one. The windows were shuttered and only ribbons of moonlight streamed down into the chamber. Good. The dark would make it easier.

The bed curtains were open. Francesco was stretched out on his stomach, snoring. He didn't realize until then how big a man Francesco was. And if he woke, it would be no contest.

Why this hesitation? He had killed before . . . better to get it over with and worry about the consequences later.

Francesco heard the door open and didn't bother getting up, thinking it might be Lorenzo forgetting something yet again. He rolled over to close the bed curtains and felt the burn of a knife as it dug into his left forearm.

The assassin flung himself upon Francesco and the blade gouged his left shoulder now. The blade was lower now and towards the chest when Francesco managed to wrestle free, searching for the sword absent from its customary place at the right side of the bed. The assassin pounced again.

The noise of the struggle brought Lorenzo, squires, and knights to the solar. "Help me with this door!" Lorenzo screamed. They took weapons and whatever they could use to break down the doors, hacking and pounding until the heavy oak doors finally gave way.

They stumbled into a pitch-black room and tripped over broken furniture, falling in every direction, scrambling over one another to get to Francesco, who was sprawled on the bed chests, clutching a sheet to his shoulder to stanch the bleeding, the only calm man in the midst of hysteria. The doorway was suddenly crammed with soldiers and curious guests. The confusion made it easy for the assassin to escape.

"Close the gates! One of you raise the watch!" Lorenzo ordered.

"Did you see who it was?" Lorenzo asked.

"In this dark?" scoffed Francesco. To a bewildered squire who was wrapping a second bed sheet around his shoulder he snapped, "Find the physician, and bring some light, damn you!"

"Francesco, I heard—what in Christ—?" Edmund had entered the room with sword in hand and stared in disbelief at the scene before him.

"Where's Gian Maria?" Francesco demanded. "Someone find my cousin and make sure he's safe!"

"Here!" Gian Maria answered as he pushed past spectators into the room.

"Did you see anyone on the stairs?" Francesco asked.

"No, it was pitch black in the stairwell. Someone's taken the cresset lamps."

"Well, this was neatly planned!"

"I'll order a search," Edmund said on his way out. He hurried alone across the wooden bridge separating tower and donjon but bypassed the staircase leading to the gatehouse and stables and took the staircase leading back into the donjon. Tommaso Porciano came out of the shadows as Edmund hit the landing and watched disinterestedly as he bounded down the stairs, two at a time.

CHAPTER 22

THE SKY WAS still dark when Serafina and Marghareta hurried into the old market. Farmers and merchants offered greetings and went about their business. No time for conversation on market day. The wealth of Tuscany waited to be unpacked and displayed for all of Florence and beyond.

The town was swathed in a soft, silvery fog, people wandering in and out of it like spirits to be swallowed up. Cornerstones and chimneys of buildings were sometimes visible, oftentimes not, but mostly resembled mythical creatures, the kind that tormented Serafina when she was a girl. What might have been a bridge over a narrow lane connecting one building to another became the neck of a dragon, windows, and candlelight its eyes and fiery breath; the smaller buildings were its scales and body, sometimes the smaller shops resembled gargoyles and wolves. Only in those dreams, a knight whose armor was decorated with silver and gold roses would ride out of the fog and vanquish her demons and save her.

But not this morning.

The market square was distinguishable only by canopied stalls that were the same color as everything else that morning: gray. From somewhere in the forest of stalls and booths came a plaintive song of gypsies accompanied by flute, drum, and shawm. A housewife screamed at them to clear off and emptied a chamber pot to make sure they left. The ladies were fortunate to have ducked the shower and wound through the market square to the spice merchants' stalls.

Not this morning.

"It's been almost a fortnight and no word of him. It is as I said," Marghareta chided.

"I don't believe you," Serafina answered.

"Perhaps now you'll hasten your marriage to Ranieri for there's no other way out of it. Come with me; I know an apothecary."

"I don't believe you!" Serafina protested as she was dragged to the other end of the old market to a dark and dank shop that smelled of mold and herbs. The crone behind the makeshift counter nodded at the women and resumed her measuring of powders into a bowl.

"Love potion for the young lady? Or something else? Such a beauty, this one! She's given her maidenhead. I can tell by the flush in her cheeks. Tincture of meadowsweet and mandragora, then?" the crone asked.

Marghareta barely nodded and pushed three coins across the counter. The crone turned and rummaged on the shelf behind her, then showed a small vial stopped with wax. She reached out and patted Serafina's cheek, and turned her towards the dim light. "Such beauty! Such beauty to be sure. A shame to kill the seed unless the attention was forced."

"I assure you it was not!" Serafina answered hotly and slapping away the crone's hand, fled from the shop.

"Madonna! For shame!" Marghareta cried and followed, leaving the vial and the coins. She chased Serafina back to the house in the Via Santa Elisabetta and caught up with her on the staircase to her apartments.

"Leave me alone!" Serafina growled and as she shoved the woman away a door slammed below and a discussion between her father and another man distracted her.

Francesco was in the house! She recognized his voice and went to the landing where she could see. He was handed his cap and cloak by a servant as Durante escorted him to the courtyard gate. When he turned to shake Durante's hand Serafina ducked out of sight.

"What may I do for you? How can I make you understand that what I propose is for the benefit of both our houses?" Francesco was asking.

"I have given you my reasons. Foremost of those is your attention to my daughter despite her betrothal. It has been the subject of gossip."

"I will do nothing to dishonor the lady, for she is dear to me. We would both benefit from this marriage, do you not think so?"

"To break the contract with Ranieri would mean an incalculable loss. You must understand ser Francesco that the years have not been kind to me and I will not gamble away my daughter's future and that of her sons if God is to grant her any," Durante said kindly, but Serafina recognized the edge to his voice and the steel-like, controlled tone.

"You know my situation. It would be no gamble. Any sons Serafina gives me would be heirs to the Romena title and all the lands, revenues and appurtenances. I hope to regain all that my father lost and my mother squandered. I intend to regain all by my thirtieth name day," Francesco countered.

"I cannot, signor. I will not."

"Let me sit down with Ranieri and reason with him. Perhaps he'll take a gift of land in exchange for your contract."

"He has land enough. He is determined to have my daughter."

"And I shall not give up so easily. We'll talk of this again, and soon. You are welcome to dine at the Torre Romena whenever you like."

"My daughter will not attend if that's what you were hoping."

"Whenever you like," Francesco said, smiling and left.

Twice more he called upon Durante and went away empty-handed. Each time Serafina watched from a safe distance and after the last disappointing encounter, she had her woman give Francesco a message. *Market day in the old market.*

She left the house unattended and wrapped in an old cloak and hood borrowed from one of the servants. No one paid attention to the girl hurrying along the narrow streets on a blustery spring morning that threatened rain. It was market day after all; serving girls and wives of tradesmen and merchants would be on their way to the old market for a day's custom.

The square was already crowded by the time Serafina arrived. Good! With so many people about no one would think twice about a girl and her lover. Serafina went to the spice merchants' stalls and as she hoped, he was there. His back was to her, but the unmistakable height and curling hair, the form, were his. Serafina reached up and tapped his shoulder lightly.

Francesco whirled about. "Hello."

Relief overwhelmed her when he smiled and touched her cheek. Serafina took a step forward. He held out a hand and she marveled at how it trembled when she clasped it. Francesco enveloped them in his cloak as they kissed.

"Come with me!" Francesco whispered and taking her hand, walked swiftly to the Torre Romena. Once alone in the great bedchamber, Serafina saw how he relaxed, his jawline softening and smiles coming easier. He called for food and wine and while they waited, he built a fire in the wall hearth and cleared a space on the table for them. His domesticity was endearing and she couldn't help but smile with him as he moved codices, scrolls, maps and weapons to a corner of the room, threw discarded clothing into a clothes press and chased a hound out. Once their meal was brought from the kitchen Francesco dismissed the servants and leaned down to kiss Serafina.

"I've missed you!" he murmured huskily. "I planned to call upon your father this afternoon when I received the note and wondered what my lovely Fina could be about. Seeing how it's fallen into place, I couldn't be happier."

"I've come to you because I thought perhaps together we might convince my father to accept your suit."

"Not because you love me?" he teased.

Serafina blushed and took a sip of wine. Her hand trembled in doing so and his was there, warm and steady, to take the cup. "He will not see the truth of it—what mistake he's made in trusting the wrong people and seeing Gherardo Ranieri as our savior. He will not bend. I know you've made efforts to convince him otherwise, and I've heard his angry diatribes late in the evening. He believes that you seek vengeance for your father's death in my bed, by dishonoring me as your father dishonored and ruined my mother."

Francesco nodded solemnly and pushed away from the table to tend the hearth fire. The morning was cold, but not so cold that a larger fire was needed. The way he stabbed at the glowing embers with a poker and stirred the ash was an indication of his anger and frustration.

"How long before the marriage?" he asked after a time.

"I don't know. Ranieri's gone to Lucca."

"When did he leave?"

"Two days ago. The roads through the mountains were finally safe."

"We have time."

Francesco rose from the hearth and poured a cup of wine, drinking quickly, and nodding. "Tomorrow we'll plight our troth at Santi Apostoli and then we'll go to Castello da Romena and be married in the chapel. You can't marry Gherardo Ranieri if you're married to me."

"Truly?" she asked, hopefully.

"Are you surprised, Fina?" Francesco asked, embracing her.

"Not so much surprised as relieved, for I do know you'll bring this about. What other works of magic have you in store?"

The first was as she had hoped. This time, however, the sunlight streamed into the bedchamber and a wealth of perfume filled the air when she unlaced her gown and slid from it; the sunlight cast golden showers on her naked skin when she tossed aside kirtles and underpinnings, unbound her hair and let it fall like a silk cloak over her shoulders and down to her knees. There was no shyness as Francesco tumbled her onto the bed. She eagerly responded to Francesco's lovemaking.

"Why must we go to Castello di Romena, Francesco? Why not your church of Santi Apostoli?" Serafina asked much later. She raised her head from his breast when he didn't answer and smiled, for he'd fallen asleep. Contented, she curled up in his arms and began to doze when he said, "No one will touch us."

They slept until the pounding on the bedchamber door started several hours later. Francesco kissed Serafina and put a finger to his lips, then pulled the curtains around the bed. He threw on breeches and a shirt and unbolted the door to find Lorenzo and one of the household guards.

"What's this?" he asked.

"Pardon, monsignore; the Englishman is on his way," Lorenzo answered. "They've got the man who tried to kill you. He's being brought here."

"How soon will he arrive?"

"By nightfall."

"No. Florence will want an accounting. We can't deal with him here." Francesco turned to the guard. "Ride out and meet Clifford and tell him to go to Castello di San Galgano. I'll be there as soon as I am able."

Closing the door, Francesco turned and saw Serafina peering out from the bed curtains as she dressed. She looked frightened and forced a smile.

"Now you understand why it's best to be at one of my castles," he said softly.

❧

THE ATMOSPHERE, AZZELINO Alberti mused, had probably been the same when Christ was brought before Pilate. Everyone was out for blood. They had not bound him nor beaten him into submission. He could look at that as some show of grace. Well, Romena was known for his republican ideals. Azzelino felt secure knowing he'd be treated fairly by his judge, who sat in silence in his great chair. He glanced about and ciphered ten, perhaps twelve men crowded into the castle solar. The room itself was large, almost as large as the great hall and divided into two chambers by screens and tapestries. The high, beamed ceiling was a prison for the smoke that hung over them in a blue haze. In spite of the spaciousness of his surroundings, Azzelino felt as confined as if in an oubliette or the darkest, smallest, dungeon cell.

Francesco sat absently twisting a small sapphire ring round his little finger. The ring Azzelino recognized. He'd seen it on Serafina's hand and didn't wonder how it came into Francesco's possession. He'd ridden hard from Florence, it was said. There was no reason to speculate on what his business had been there. Francesco studied the faces of his soldiers and retainers as if looking for someone in particular and then motioned to the captain of his garrison to come forward with two guards. It came to Azzelino suddenly, fear bringing out a cold sweat when he realized what was about to happen.

Gian Maria leaned towards Lorenzo and whispered, "You owe me a silver penny!" He might have teased the boy into paying, but Francesco had looked his way and shamed him to silence with the coldest glance Gian Maria ever received.

"You were a fool not to go back to Avignon," Francesco opened. "You could have gotten away with it if you'd kept running. Attempted murder is still against the law."

"Murder?" Azzelino sputtered. "Is that what this is about? D'you think I—" Azzelino started to laugh now. "Cousin, as much as it would please me to have you dead, I care too much for my future to ruin it by murdering kinsmen!"

Francesco unwound his legs and crossed them again. He took a baselard from the table and began cleaning under his immaculate nails with its deadly point. "But if not you, surely one of your men."

"You can't prove that!"

"It cannot be proved otherwise."

187

"I wouldn't have wasted a man on the deed. I'd have done it myself if it meant that much!"

"Be careful what you say. Words are as powerful in their intent as deeds."

"They're words, nothing more! How many times have you—"

"You've reason enough to have me dead and you've admitted that nothing would please you more—"

"Words spoken in anger."

"Tell me who it was."

"I can tell you nothing because I don't know! Damn you! This is against all laws of the commune!"

"But we're not in the Florentine Commune, are we? It is my law here."

Azzelino swore softly. Every man in the room stood for Romena; even that prick Edmund Clifford, who had no reason whatsoever to love the man, stood at Francesco's right arm.

"You provoked our cousin Gian Maria into brawling," Francesco said coolly. "You came to blows with me, twice, for no good cause, and you offended and abused a woman—"

"Ah, now I see! It's the girl! You want the girl and you know you can't have her!"

"You're poorly served. Though it is none of your concern, it looks as though I've got a chance."

"You won't win,"

"It's not about winning, but who's better at the game."

"Try me."

"I'll wager I'm better at any game you can think of. Try me." Francesco leveled the baselard toward him.

Azzelino now began to sweat in earnest.

"You know the rules of the game, Azzelino. We've each made our move, and now, by ancient rite, I do the honorable thing—I give you some lands, a castle, to purchase your cooperation. You will take what I offer and go away quietly."

Laughter interrupted Francesco and he gestured for silence. He continued, saying, "If I give you Castel San Niccolo, will that make an end to this foolishness?"

"With so little offered, I'd rather stay a priest or a scribe for the Holy Father."

"One or the other, that or a dead man, if you cross me again. Persist, and I swear in faith you'll wish you were a village baker!"

Francesco now stood and walked slowly toward Azzelino, who started to show his fear. He dared to look up and saw Romena's green eyes burning into him.

"Listen to me." The voice was calm, deadly. "My vassals have orders to cut you down if you trespass again. Stay out and stay away. Leave me alone. Most importantly, leave her alone!"

Azzelino spat into his face. Without taking his eyes from Azzelino, Francesco wiped his cheek. *Not yet*, he thought to himself, *not yet*. Revenge was sweeter when it came unexpectedly. He did, however, touch the point of his baselard to Azzelino's bull neck and press gently. Gasps came from around the room. Romena would never shed blood in his own house, he heard one of the soldiers swear. He removed the point and saw a minuscule drop of blood centered on the throat. Just enough to be reminded.

"Accept this gift," Francesco motioned to a clerk standing at his elbow, "and leave us in quiet. Be content."

He presented Azzelino with a charter that was studied and then dropped on the floor to be crumpled by a boot.

"I'll take what I want, not what you're willing to give me."

"Then I give you nothing."

"I say string him up from the curtain walls!" Gian Maria proffered, and there came a murmur of agreement.

"No. We should be worse than he, resorting to such drastic measures."

"The man tried to kill you!"

"Edmund, what say you?"

"It is as you say. Leniency has its benefits and rewards," he spoke. "If it is known you gave him the courtesy of his life, what man would gainsay that? And what man would be foolish enough to not take such an offer?"

A murmur of approval circulated through the solar. Only Gian Maria remained steadfast in his position. "You only give him the opportunity to strike again," Gian Maria argued, and turned to Azzelino. "He'll do that. He's got the worst of the Guidi blood in him."

"And so do you," Edmund spoke up.

The unexpected remark brought silence to the room and Azzelino smiled, realizing the most stupid of his cousins had made matters easy for him. He watched gleefully as Edmund placed a hand on the back of Francesco's chair as if to proclaim where his loyalty lie and Gian Maria tried to keep his temper. Francesco was frowning and watching both. Surely he didn't know what to do! And what he didn't need at that moment was divided loyalties.

"I am as much Romena as Porciano!" Gian Maria hissed.

Edmund placed a hand on his sword. "Bought and paid for, Gian Maria. Doesn't that make you a harlot?"

When it looked as though the tension between them would erupt into a blood feud, Francesco pitched his knife into the floor between them.

"Leniency does have its greater rewards," Francesco replied curtly, staring at Azzelino. He motioned to his captain and guards. "Escort him to the frontier and see him safely back to Florence or wherever else he wants to go. I have nothing more to do with him. And see that he arrives without incident. It will not be said I provoked trouble or caused him harm."

Francesco motioned that the night's entertainment was concluded, but called to Gian Maria as he was following the rest out. "Christ's blood! What was that all about?" he demanded when they were alone.

"I don't trust Clifford," came the excuse.

"He's been my friend for years," Francesco snapped. He signed for Lorenzo to bring wine.

"Friends are known to turn—"

"And so are kinsmen."

Gian Maria's hand was trembling so hard that he could barely contain the wine in its silver hanaper. A pretty thing, this English silver cup, inlaid with purple and yellow stones. Studying it gave him a reason not to meet Francesco's gaze. When he could stand it no longer, Gian Maria exclaimed, "Gesu, Cecco! Do you really think that I would?"

"No," was the simple but laconic reply. Francesco filled his cup again. "Here. I prefer you drunk, for then our conversations are never serious. I've had enough seriousness for one day."

"Do you think—"

"No. We are all we have."

He now gestured to the chess game set up on the table. They'd started it weeks ago. Gian Maria took his place beside the bed while Francesco sat with his back to the hearth. It was soon apparent that Francesco's mind was not on the game, for he had removed the small sapphire ring from his finger and was holding it against a candle flame so that sparks of deep color shot across the board.

"Why don't you go back to Florence? I can see to things here with Edmund's help."

"I'd come back and find you with your teeth in each other," Francesco quipped. "Though I do like being fought over!"

Gian Maria laughed at this, but when he saw how quickly Francesco sobered, he reached for his cup and found Francesco's hand there instead.

"You are all I have!" Francesco whispered. There was sadness, a choking in his voice.

"I would never betray you," Gian Maria swore passionately.

"God help you, I knew it from the first. Keep safe from my quarrels; promise me that!"

"You have my word; you know you do, Cecco."

He was satisfied for the moment, but Francesco still had misgivings. Love had its price, and Francesco knew this all too well.

Rather than delve into unknown waters and realize disappointment, he handed Gian Maria the wine flask and told him to make his move. He then looked at the hourglass and ciphered that the courier he'd sent upon his arrival at Castello di San Galgano would have reached Florence by now.

CHAPTER 23

DURANTE GIUSTINI STOOD at the window of his bedchamber and through the sheets of rain splashing relentlessly on mullioned window panes watched Romena's messenger gallop away. It was close to midnight; by the time the fellow had returned to Castello di San Galgano, it would be close to dawn. And if the weather let up, Serafina would be on the road to Lucca by then.

Damned weather! There was no chance of it. This was confirmed by the bolt of lightning that sliced the sky over Florence and bounced off of weather vanes and crosses, finally exploding brick into the street.

Durante moved away as another bolt shook the sky, lighting the street from the Via del Corso to the Piazza del Cimatori, showing grotesque silhouettes of houses, spires, and churches, frightening horses in the stable across the way. Storms like this were always a bad omen.

For the better part of an hour, Durante had controlled his rage and wondered how he would deal with this predicament. He'd thought Romena an honorable man, virtuous and decent and had hoped they would become friends. What friendship could he have with a man who seduced an innocent, taking advantage of her? What friend would repeat his father's mistakes and history? It was as he'd feared.

As for Serafina, Durante was appalled and felt betrayed. For so many months he'd kept Niccolo Peruzzi and even Ranieri at a distance, making sure they took no pleasure from her so that Serafina would go to her husband stainless, uncorrupted. And in so short a time she allowed herself to be seduced by a handsome face and sensual voice.

Durante was beside himself. Another man would have beaten his child and thrown her into the streets. The only other place for disobedient daughters was the church. There they could pay with the rest of their miserable lives for whatever sin they committed. Some fathers had even drowned their daughters; it was commonplace enough.

God's teeth and blood! If only he had not gone to the Torre Romena thinking to make amends with the man. He would never have seen his daughter and Francesco sharing a kiss and an embrace in the courtyard. He wouldn't have watched her cloak herself and hurry off to return home and pretend that nothing had happened!

He'd have her sent away—no, better to send away that slovenly cow of a nursemaid! He paid Marghareta three florins a month and for what? The bitch had delighted in recounting Serafina's coupling with Romena at Castello di San Galgano and Torre Romena and with very little persuasion. One would think she'd been in bed with them.

Perhaps, he thought as he wound his way through the house to Serafina's rooms, perhaps his daughter had indeed found a better match than the scoundrel Ranieri.

But perhaps she had learned her mother's ways.

She was bent over an embroidery frame when he found her; something unusual, for Serafina preferred the company of books and learned old men to womanly tasks. Yet here she was meticulously picking out golden threads that had been wrongly placed.

"What? Not abed?" he asked.

"The storm. I couldn't sleep."

"Nor could I. Serafina . . . "

She looked up and smiled. She looked refreshed, and there were roses in her cheeks. Durante swallowed gall, knowing it was Romena's doing. The girl was in love and had freely given herself.

"I thought you were going to Lucca this night," she said.

"The weather's taken a turn for the worse. Only a fool would go out in this," Durante opened, gesturing towards the windows where the rain battered, sloshed, and dripped under the sills and made puddles under the expensive arras, soaked the rushes and made everything stink like mildew.

He eased himself onto the bed where she sat curled up against the bolster, watching her pull glistening strands from the embroidered linen. It was a scarf for a buskin. An illuminated initial 'F' was in its infancy. She smiled and continued drawing the errant threads, turned her lovely face to his, waiting.

"All is well with you, Daughter?"

The needle suddenly stopped and the ruby set in a ring she wore next to her betrothal ring caught a reflection of lightning that crackled out of the sulfur-colored sky.

"Marvelously well, Signor."

No doubt!

"You lack for naught?"

"You see how I am!" she laughed. "I am well contented, Father."

"Then why," he growled in low, short, tones, "do you dishonor me?"

"Dishonor you? What have I done to—"

"Don't pretend innocence! Your perverse behavior has been our undoing!"

Serafina said quietly, "It was not meant to happen, but it did. And it was not perverse."

Durante stroked the burnished hair that reminded him so much of her mother. He then took a rope of it in his hands and pulled slowly but deliberately so that she screamed, and yanking tautly, he lifted her from the bed.

"And now you are no better than the woman who brought you into this world!" Durante hissed, his breath stinging her ear as he continued to pull until she was on the floor and clutching blindly at him. "What should I do with you, eh? Should I pretend that it never happened? Should I turn a blind eye and let you ruin every chance we have of regaining respectability?"

"Please, no!"

"You give yourself like a jade to that man whose father ruined our lives! It was because of Romena we lost all!" Durante ranted. "Just like his father! He knows how to seduce and win hearts with a honeyed word, a smile! He got revenge for his father's death in your bed!"

He relaxed his grip and Serafina managed to escape for only a moment, only long enough to scream for her servants. Durante blocked her exit and slammed the door shut, sliding the bolt, the grinding of metal against metal her death sentence. Moments later the servants were battering on the door, begging to enter and screaming for mercy on behalf of their mistress. Serafina blindly ran toward their voices, stumbling on the uneven stone tiles of the floor and feeling their coolness against her cheek as she struck them, then the sharpness of the clothes press as she threw herself against it in an effort to get out of Durante's way.

Durante's handsome face was variously purple and scarlet now, his deep-set blue eyes glowing like sapphires as he continued to shout obscenities and slurs. His finely trimmed beard was rhimed with froth.

Again, Serafina tried to escape and found her opportunity when she saw the dagger poking out from under the featherbed. It was enough to purchase time and get to the door and unbolt it . . .

Durante knocked the baselard from her hand and grabbed her roughly.

"Let me go! Have mercy on me!" Serafina screamed while he struck and shook her, while she struggled to gain freedom. "Have I not always done your bidding? He is an honorable man and worth ten of Ranieri! I beg of you, Father, accept his suit and let us be married!"

"Honorable! He is using you as his father used your mother—to get to me! To ruin me! You're a whore! A jade!"

Durante grabbed for the costly fabric of her gown when he lost his hold. She was vain enough, he thought; she'd never let her best gown be ruined. How wrong he was, for Serafina continued to struggle and claw her way free until the shoulders of her gown gave way and Durante held flesh beneath his fingers.

His words were lost. He was shouting and uttering profanities, hammering blows and mindless of where they landed. When Serafina screamed, he woke from the catalepsy and stared in horror at what he had done.

Before him stood his daughter, half-naked, the right side of her face was swollen; ugly purple bruises were already forming on the cheek, the stripe of a scratch ran from her neck down to her right breast, her skin torn and bleeding where his fingers had dug and clutched. Her copper curls were matted and tangled about her face. But more than anything, he saw the eyes. They were undamaged, but what had just happened would be reflected in them for years.

Serafina turned away to cover herself and ignored his pleas and weeping. Without looking at her father, she said, "I will do what is expected of me. Do not ask for more. Fortunately, you hold no sway over my heart or soul. I do not regret a moment of it. And were it mine to do again, I'd change nothing."

❧

MARGHARETA WATCHED AS Serafina continually daubed at the bruises on her face, studied her injuries in a pier glass mirror and said nothing. Said absolutely nothing. It had been thus for days.

"Your father's gone," Marghareta said one evening. "I don't know where but I hope he rots there!" She turned and clucked her tongue. "Child, it's been a week, almost two! You might change your bed gown!"

"Is there anything to eat?" Serafina asked.

"Shall I fetch something for you?" Marghareta asked hopefully.

Serafina motioned her assent and continued her inspection at the mirror. She enjoyed the momentary solitude, listening to the activity in the Via Santa Elisabetta. The rains had finally stopped and people were going out to survey the damage. The storm had finally run its course.

Where it concerned the weather.

Below she heard a quarrel between two merchants over whose tree it was that destroyed a stable, the wheels of a cart being pushed, and the exclamation of those whose lives had been inestimably altered by the savage storm.

And then the pounding of hooves.

At first it was distant, but soon the entire street shuddered under the cadence of armed horse and men.

Serafina dared not hope. She stood by the hearth and prayed silently, continued to pray as she heard the shouting below, the footsteps, the opening of doors and the angry protests as footsteps grew closer until the bedchamber door exploded with a groan of metal hinges giving way.

"My God, oh my God! What has he done to you?" Francesco whispered as they kissed.

❧

THE SHADOW OF a cat in the moonlight as it ambled from tree limb to tree limb and then pounce upon a shuddering new leaf caught Serafina's attention. She was like that leaf, being batted about and molested for no purpose other than her father's political advancement.

Somewhere in the night, the Gabriel bell rang and the watch cried the hour. Soon, very soon, she thought. When the watch changed . . .

Francesco perceived Serafina's anxiety and eased her for a moment with a hand upon her neck, kneading gently, experimentally, her body still wholly new and unknown to him, hoping to allay her fears. "I feared you would not come; that you would not receive word in time," Serafina said at last.

"Soon, beloved," he whispered, and kissed the neck he'd just caressed. Rather than melt into him, Serafina stood rigidly by the window. Francesco, too, had no desire at that moment and settled nervously onto her bed, mindful of his clay-caked boots and the rigid, uncomfortable brigandine he wore beneath his cut-velvet tunic.

"However much I hate him now, I shall never be able to see him again," Serafina murmured.

"For the present, yes."

"If I decided not to go—"

"Don't say that. It will only be worse with Ranieri. Young wives make old widowers. There's always someone in the family who hates the child bride."

She remained by the window until the moon slipped behind the buildings crowding the Piazza dei Cimatori. When the bell for lauds rang, she moved away and sat beside him.

"You're sure?" he whispered into her hair.

"Yes. I'm quite sure." Turning, she wiped the tears from her face and offered a brave smile.

"Then we should leave now."

Francesco took Serafina's hand and the saddle bag she'd prepared and led the way through the house as quietly as possible. They were on the landing to the ground floor when Marghareta came from a bedchamber with a candle in hand, her robe askew, a nightcap falling on her brow.

"Who's there? What's your business at this hour?" she hissed.

Francesco's foot hit a loose plank that creaked and Marghareta swung the light in his direction.

"Monsignore!" she gasped, and then, "Madonna! What are you about at this hour?"

"Put the light away!" Serafina hissed as they sped down the stairs, waking the hounds asleep in the great hall and set them to barking.

"Help, help! Signor Arcangeli! Signorina Violetta! Stop her! Stop them!" Marghareta shouted as she chased after them, but it was too late. By the time the household was roused and they ran out into the street, Serafina and Francesco had ridden past the church of Santi Apostoli and over the

Ponte Vecchio.

"Where do we go?" Serafina asked once they cleared the city gates and circled around, traveling eastward. She rode pillion and to stop her shivering from cold and fright, Serafina leaned into Francesco and wrapped herself in his cloak. He kissed the top of her hair but said nothing. She felt his muscles constrict as he kicked the horse with spurs and they sped faster through the Tuscan countryside. When they heard riders approaching, Francesco turned the horse north and galloped across fields and hills, staying off the main roads. The last of the moon hung on the horizon by the time they reached Castello di Vincigliata near Fiesole, northeast of Florence.

"There's a village near the castle. It has a large inn with a tower," Francesco said. "They know me here, and we'll be safe." True to his words, a stable hand and the innkeeper were waiting for them as Francesco rode into the courtyard.

"Welcome, monsignore," the innkeeper greeted. He waved his cresset towards the stone buildings behind him. "All is ready. Come with me. Madonna, you are most welcome."

"Any travelers on the road, Simone?" Francesco asked the innkeeper.

"Only yourself and your good lady, signore," the innkeeper replied as he led the way into a vacant common room and up two flights of stairs to the tower, where he gave Francesco a key and bade them a good night.

Serafina fell wearily upon the plump feather bed once Francesco locked the door. He pulled her into his arms for a kiss. "We're close to my lands, but we have another day's ride to Castello di Romena," he said.

"I am content," she answered and they fell asleep. She woke hours later to find Francesco smiling down at her.

"Shall we say good morning properly?" he whispered, kissing her neck.

"I'm to be the wife of the conte di Romena," she sighed happily.

"The contessa da Romena, the fair lady of the Casentino. Fairest lady in all of Tuscany," he said, gently pulling the cloak off her shoulders and tossing it to the floor. As they kissed articles of clothing fell away. She laughed softly when his night beard tickled her throat and cheeks. "Do you think songs will be written about me, how ser Francesco stole his lover from a bower and took her to a castle and made love to her?"

"I have no doubt," Francesco whispered as he planted kisses on her neck and breasts as he unlaced her bodice and pulled the shirt from her shoulders and slid it down until she was naked to the waist. Gentle love play became urgency and need and petal soft kisses turned to love bites. Francesco was ready to take her and Serafina all too willing when the door the chamber broke open and soldiers came into the room and pulled Francesco out of bed. Serafina hurried to cover herself and was ready to demand an explanation when Marghareta entered, followed by Durante, then Azzelino, whose eyes immediately fell on Serafina. He turned to Durante and laughed, "Messer, did I not tell you? It is all as I said it would be. Serafina's woman has redeemed herself."

"I hate you! I'll kill you!" Serafina screamed at Azzelino, and would have attacked him had Marghareta not pulled her away.

Francesco made an effort to reach Serafina, but Durante raised a hand and the guards tightened their grip. "Stay, Romena! You don't want to make things worse."

"Release him!" Serafina sobbed. "He's done nothing!"

"Nothing, you say? Did you hear yourself?" Durante laughed. It was a cruel, guttural sound—an animal's snarl.

"Release him!"

"I could have him imprisoned for breach of contract and adultery!"

"Release me and we may talk as friends," Francesco spoke up. His tone of voice and composure were cool enough, but inwardly he was in torment.

"Release him! Let him go!" Serafina demanded. "We're outnumbered! What harm could he do?"

Durante nodded at his men and they unloosed their hold on Francesco, who stepped a safe distance from both them and Serafina. "What would you say to me as a friend, Romena?" he asked.

"You came to me and gave me information,"

"The ramblings of a man deep in his cups."

"You were as sober as a man could be!" Francesco protested.

"I have a fondness for too much wine and you know how it is when men drink to excess. They tend to speak what is in their thoughts without regard for the truth."

"Liar! You came to me and gave me information, you sought to help me!"

"Why should I do that? I have the backing of Ranieri of Verrucole."

"He is nothing. He has nothing. Reconsider Durante, before it's too late and you've been used again. I won't go back on my word!"

And then something happened Francesco would always regret.

Out of the corner of his eye, he saw Serafina break away from Marghareta and reach for Francesco's dagger partially hidden underneath her cloak. She tossed it to Francesco and he managed to break free and catch it, was ready to skewer one of his captors when he heard the scream.

"Romena!" Durante hissed. "Here's your alternative."

Francesco turned and saw that Durante had Serafina by the neck, a knife against her throat. It should have been enough to make Francesco give up the dagger, but he did not, and waited. Strained breathing and the girl's sobs filled the silence.

"Leave now without further incident and we shall dismiss this night as a bad dream," he said. "Stay and claim what you think is your right, and you need not speculate as to what will happen. The choice is yours."

Francesco's eyes slid from Durante to Serafina, to Azzelino, who smiled in triumph, and back to Durante. He assessed the man's dispassionate blue eyes mocking him. Serafina was barely breathing, afraid to move. No one in the room moved until Francesco's dagger clattered onto the wooden planks and lay untouched.

"Fina? What say you?"

The voice was not his. It was raw, choked with emotion, husky.

"Go," she said at last. "I have no choice. And neither do you."

"We cannot allow this!"

Durante pressed the knife closer. "Listen to her. For once she's done as she's been told!"

"Go," she begged. "Please go!"

Francesco didn't remember leaving the house, but he soon found himself on the road out back to Florence, riding for his life.

CHAPTER 24

GIAN MARIA WAS concerned.

Not that anything but vice mattered in his insular world; he was quite willing to forego propriety, to let matters run their natural course, to let others worry about the setting and rising of the sun when it mattered if it did matter.

So when moon-faced Lorenzo appeared one evening at the Porciano house and said that Francesco da Romena had taken a turn, Gian Maria immediately assumed the worst and sobered up enough to go to the Borgo Santi Apostoli. Gian Maria had few friends. He didn't relish the thought of losing the only one he truly had, the only one he loved; therefore, he was somewhat annoyed to find Francesco only drunk.

He'd been drunk for days, almost weeks.

"Since—you know," Lorenzo responded cryptically to the inquiry as to how long.

"If I knew I wouldn't have to ask," Gian Maria snapped.

"I thought everyone in Florence knew about his quarrel with Messer Durante!"

"I've just returned from Arezzo. What's happened?"

Lorenzo recounted the events of a month past. The tale rattled Gian Maria, who now attended the man snoring in his wine-sodden pillow.

Hard to believe that women found this attractive: hair matted and lank, the prickly beard, the stench, and the bloated face. God love him, Gian Maria thought as he struck Francesco soundly across the face, but he was normal. Apollo had come down from Mount Olympus at last.

"Francesco! Francesco, you idiot! Can you hear me?" Gian Maria shouted. He continued to slap Francesco until his own hand stung from the repeated blows and Francesco's face was bright and raw. Ordering Lorenzo to bring a bucket of cold water, he plunged Francesco's head into it. An hour later Gian Maria had Francesco seated before a fire, and drinking broth.

"Do you want to talk?" Gian Maria asked gently. He received the response he hoped for, a sign that Francesco was on the mend. Francesco regarded him with dark, circumspect eyes and a shake of the head.

"Go to hell," Francesco muttered.

"When you've got legs to stand, let's take supper elsewhere. I'm sure the servants would like nothing better than to clear out this chamber and burn everything in it. The stench alone is pestilent!"

For that Francesco offered a smile.

The tavern was quiet that evening. Only Gian Maria, Francesco, and a pair of merchants sat in the common room. It was reminiscent of Christmas when Francesco watched as Gian Maria devoured everything in sight. Now it was Francesco's turn to gorge himself, for it truly had been days since he'd eaten anything, and when it looked as if he would be sick, Gian Maria offered cool water instead of wine.

"Any word from her?"

Gian Maria figured he'd go at it in small draughts, just enough to hear what he wanted, to allow Francesco time. It occurred to him that warfare was easier to manage than this.

Francesco's tawny hair was all Gian Maria could see over the rim of his bowl. He took particular interest in the water and savored it like the best of Tuscan wines.

"No," he murmured, "nor do I expect to. Ever."

"It takes a woman to forget a woman," Gian Maria said and shouted for a torchbearer.

"For you, perhaps. Leave me to wallow in my misfortunes. It's what I do best," Francesco protested.

They were soon prowling the dimly lit streets of Florence, avoiding the night watch by following the Borgo Santi Apostoli east along the Roman walls past the Via Castellano, the Via de Leoni, to the inns of the Borgo Santa Croce. In the Corso de' Tintori they stayed at the house of Signor Bonfiglio until a bad toss of the dice and an attempt at cheating got Gian Maria into trouble. By then Francesco was sober enough to drag his cousin out before knives were drawn.

"Wait a moment! I need to piss," Gian Maria shouted as they came to the Palazzo dei Priori. Francesco groaned and signed his men to stay while Gian Maria unhitched his calzone and went into an alley to relieve himself against the wall of the municipal palace.

"I've assured myself of a place in hell," Francesco grumbled.

"Praise be to God, Francesco! You're healing fast. I wondered when you'd start complaining—"

"Romena!"

Gian Maria stopped in mid-stream and turned in the direction of the voice. Two men, then six, blocked their exit. "By Saint John's prick!" he cursed and struggled to lace up his points.

Francesco prevented Gian Maria from charging them. He knew the odds were terrible, worse because of Gian Maria's drunkenness. Still, they would have to put up a fight.

Shadows formed on the rough-hewn walls of the palace, dark, menacing stripes that formed into even more menacing shapes as they approached. Francesco grabbed a torch burning in the sconce behind him and waved it, spewing oily, rank pitch and smoke until it made a sufficient screen against the first of his assailants. Disembodied eyes the color of earth blazed before Francesco and then he saw the glint of a sword point as it was raised and came through the protective barrier of smoke and flame. Instinctively he thrust outward and up, heard a scream when he felt the sword dig deep into flesh and lodge there.

Behind him, he could hear the chime of metal as weapons met, the strained breathing and screams of men. Bells were ringing, for someone had raised the Watch.

Two men now lay dead. Francesco couldn't see due to the blinding light of the torch, and when he heard Gian Maria cry out, he jabbed the torch at his next opponent and got out of the way as the man fell, screaming in pain as his flesh burned.

Gian Maria was putting up a good fight until he was cornered against the western wall of the Palazzo dei Priori. Francesco made a flank attack, preoccupying the assailants long enough to find an opening to the street. He found a low wall and scaled it, scrambling up to the roofs of Florence. Gian Maria followed and together they fled from their assailants across the rooftops, treading blindly over tiles slippery with mist and rain, groping window sashes and shutters for support, using clotheslines for anchorage as they swung like tumblers from building to building in their haste for freedom.

Francesco was tiring rapidly, knew he was dead if he couldn't make it to the Borgo Santi Apostoli. One of the assailants fell from the Imperial Abbey, his body broken on the cobbled pavement of the cloister. Gian Maria was rescued from a similar fate, Francesco pulling him off the ledge of the refectory. The assailants fled into the night when they realized the quarrel was lost—but not before Francesco recognized Azzelino's livery on their backs.

It became a quarrel over lands, titles, and the possession of a woman's body. Azzelino's supporters terrorized anyone who wore Romena's colors or spoke favorably of him. Property and life were of no consequence. A poem deriding Francesco's prowess in both political and personal matters was nailed to the doors of the Torre Romena. Each stanza ended with the phrase, *Donna Giustini is not for you.*

Francesco ignored it for the most part though his supporters and friends pressed the urgency to respond. He was at the fortress of Castello di Romena overseeing repairs and renovations when the first news came.

"This will run its course," Francesco commented as he quickly scanned the letter sent by Michelino Groppa and returned it to the messenger.

"Will you favor the podesta with a reply?"

"No reply," he answered and turned his attention to the glazers setting thick, round discs of glass into the window panes of the solar.

"No reply," he said when a messenger brought word that an effigy of Francesco was burned outside the church of Santi Apostoli and he was being called a craven rapist.

"It's no one's damned business," he said when the Romena shops were looted by men identified as Azzelino's servants.

"I told you," Francesco panted the afternoon another messenger arrived at the castle while he was at tourney practice in the yard, swinging at the quintain with his broadsword, "it's . . . no . . .one's . . .damned . . .business! Shit!"

The quintain swung about wildly with Francesco's last blow and knocked him squarely in the chest, propelling him onto the straw. No one moved though Gian Maria's jaw was straining to hold still. Any moment now he'd burst into laughter. Lorenzo was prepared to run to his aid, but Edmund arrived with Beatrice and other girls from the household and strode over to set Francesco on his feet.

"Aim a little lower," Edmund suggested and winked at Beatrice.

"Signorina Fiasella, ladies, you've seen me at my worst," Francesco joked.

"We would have you challenge ser Edmund," Beatrice replied, linking her arm through Edmund's and smiling prettily at both men. The men in the yard applauded and urged Francesco on, but he laughed them off.

"Another time, Beatrice, and we'll name you queen of love so that you may crown the winner and give him a kiss."

"Or something more?"

"Another time," Edmund laughed now, but the sound was forced and he threw a less-than-cordial glance at Francesco.

"I'm glad you've joined us, Edmund," Francesco said, taking up the lance and shield he'd thrown. "No doubt you heard the latest news."

"The effigy at Santi Apostoli? Yes. What will you do about it?"

"Nothing. He wants me to respond. Besides, it's no one's business."

"Perhaps you should make it our business," Gian Maria said as he hoisted himself into Francesco's saddle. "Edmund's and mine. Hand me a lance," he commanded Lorenzo.

"How would that help me?" Francesco snapped. "I'd be responsible for the deaths of my friends if it came to that. I don't need that keeping me awake at night!"

"We can be your emissaries. He'll have to treat with us, not you," Gian Maria responded.

"I agree with Francesco," Edmund spoke up. "If it's our concern, it becomes the concern of Romena's enemies, Gian Maria. We're fair game for any man who wants a fight to the death. And your father is at the top of that list."

"That's my father, not me!" Gian Maria answered, and took a jab at the quintain, knocking it so hard that it spun wildly and Edmund had to duck to avoid a blow to the head.

"Did I say anything about you?" Edmund sniped. He turned to Francesco. "If you need someone to treat with him, with Azzelino, that is, I could manage it," Edmund spoke up.

"D'you think he'll listen to you?" Gian Maria laughed.

"Watch your back!" Francesco called and winced as the quintain struck Gian Maria from behind. Gian Maria adjusted his hold on the lance and couched low in the saddle, waiting for the next pass.

"Why not? I'm no kinsman of the blood. I'm removed from your quarrel. He'll listen to me," Edmund responded quietly though he'd have liked nothing better than to break Gian Maria's handsome, perfect, nose, especially now that Beatrice Fiasella and her companions were flirting with him and cheering him on.

"For your service you'll want a castle," Gian Maria sniped as he made another pass.

"That wasn't necessary, Gian Maria," Francesco said.

"Let him speak. I know ser Tommaso will listen to me, and I'll be sober," Edmund replied.

"Do that," Francesco ordered, and picked up one of the gauntlets Edmund dropped. In doing so, he noticed the ring prominently displayed on Edmund's forefinger. It looked familiar. He studied it a moment longer before meeting Edmund's eyes and saying quietly, "I'll leave you to the arrangements. You have our charge and our trust. I depend on you as no other, Edmund."

Francesco turned now watched as Gian Maria spurred his mount, charged at them and stopped a hair's length from Edmund. "Gian Maria," Francesco said with a laugh; "no matter your feelings, I need him very much alive!"

"As you need me, Cousin!" Gian Maria replied, grinning. He pitched his lance into the dirt at Edmund's feet and then slid easily out of the saddle to land directly before Francesco. "And I should think the choice is obvious."

"I don't need another little war on my hands." Francesco murmured as Edmund approached, and then, "The good men of Pratovecchio are coming to dine this evening to discuss who owns what and through whom; who wants to join me in what may prove to be a most boring supper? Lorenzo, I'll need a bath and some fresh clothes,"

"Monsignore!" One of the sentries at the western gate pointed towards the east. "A rider approaches!"

"Who is it? Can you read the banner?" Francesco called.

The sentry leaned over the parapet too far for Francesco's liking. "I see scales quartered in blue and silver with a bar sinister," he shouted back.

Francesco knew the banner said to Gian Maria, "See to it. Go on." He picked up the pace and headed back to the donjon. Today was not a day for intrigues.

❧

"YOU'VE RETURNED SO quickly," Serafina said to the messenger when she met him in the courtyard. "Do you have a reply?"

"None, madonna."

"Perhaps you should have made a request—no, the fault's mine. Here's something for your pains."

Serafina offered a coin and watched the messenger leave, locking the gate to the Via Santa Elisabetta behind him. She nearly died of fright when, turning to go back upstairs, she ran headlong into Violetta.

"God's lady! Must you follow me like a shadow? Did my father press you into service to keep watch on me?" Serafina snapped.

"Easily! I have more important things to do than spy for Durante. I thought the messenger was from a friend," Violetta countered.

"He wasn't wearing the Porciano colors if that's what you mean," Serafina said as she started upstairs.

"Oh that messenger's already been here," Violetta giggled. "I've been invited to Gian Maria's wedding, and so have you. Tommaso has invited all the great and noble families of Florence to attend."

"I hope to be dead by then,"

"What? I didn't quite understand."

"I have no say in the matter; it is for my father to decide, as well as my betrothed."

"How easily you gave up the fight," Violetta sniffed. "You, of all people – ow! Let go of my arm!"

"You'd have done the same if you had a knife to your throat!" Serafina hissed. "Stupid cow!"

Shoving Violetta out of the way, Serafina ran to her bedchamber and locked the door. The thump of the bolt brought Marghareta out of her nap beside the window. Snorting and muttering, the old nursemaid frowned and reached for a cup of wine. "What is it now, Madonna of the Tragedies?" she grumbled.

"I'm leaving."

"To Lucca?"

"To a sanctuary house at San Marco."

"Let me come with you."

"No! You betrayed me once before. How do I know you're not in my father or Ranieri's pay?!" Serafina said as she started to gather up her belongings.

"I told you, Madonna, I had no choice! Ser Durante threatened me and said he'd throw me into the street if I didn't tell him—"

"I told you nothing, old woman! You had your spies to be sure."

"How can you trust Romena? The stories of his family alone,"

"Stories. They are only stories," Serafina countered. "Strange that you of all people should ask me that when you know how evil Ranieri is."

"Please, Serafina!" Marghareta came forward to embrace her, but Serafina turned on her holding a dagger. The old woman began sobbing and fell to her knees, clutching at Serafina's hems as if she was a small child. "Forgive me! I had no choice! Your father!"

"He is why I am leaving. Let go," Serafina hissed and pushed her aside.

"He'll kill me for certain if I stay, he's said as much. If you take me with you I will be faithful. You'll have no truer servant."

"Why should I believe you?"

"I swear it on the souls of my dead children, on the soul of my husband."

Serafina frowned and stared at the distraught woman for a moment and then she went to a cupboard and took out a small gold coffer inlaid with enameled decorations. She opened it and set it before Marghareta on a table. In the coffer was something that looked like a withered finger with a ribbon crisscrossing the leathery flesh and fossilized bone.

"Here is the finger of Saint Agatha. Swear upon it, swear upon your very life that you will never betray me again," Serafina said. She pushed the box at Marghareta, who winced when she saw the relic and after a moment she touched it and then kissed the lid of the coffer, saying, "I swear upon my life, madonna!"

"Very well. See that you keep that oath, for to break an oath sworn on a holy relic is a grievous sin. You wouldn't want to suffer as Saint Agatha did, would you?" Serafina said. "*She* had her breasts torn off!"

Hours later, Serafina and Marghareta hurried along silent streets slick with the last of a rain shower, skidded dangerously on cobblestones, and trod through the mud until they reached the church and monastery of San Marco.

Serafina pulled the cord to the sanctuary bell herself. A moment passed, and she yanked the cord harder so that the bell danced frantically as it rang. A brother of the order at last answered and slid the door's shutter to one side.

"What do you seek?" he asked.

"I claim the right of sanctuary and the Lord's protection from my enemies and those who mean me harm," Serafina replied.

The brother leaned into the grill to better see the frightened women, but his decision was made when Marghareta shoved a coin through the grillwork. The door was opened and as Serafina passed through she handed over a purse weighty with coins. That money would secure food and the best of the sanctuary houses.

The morning brought hope. Serafina rose early and lit a fire in the hearth, made porridge out of the barley and acorn flour the brothers sold to her, and together with salted beef and fruit, and laid a table. Marghareta praised her industry and Serafina basked in the accolades until she was gently reminded that it wouldn't last forever—what would they do if Francesco did not steal her away from sanctuary? What would they do when the money ran out?

It was a sobering thought. That Francesco could not, or worse, would not, take her into his loving, protective, custody, never occurred to her. It was unimaginable. And when Francesco's whereabouts were undiscovered, when her letters were returned unanswered, she began to despair.

And then, a month later, it all came crashing down like the fantastical houses she built of *tarrocchi* cards, dissolved before her eyes like a soap bubble gliding on air.

She went with Marghareta to the chapter house to hear Low Mass. There was nothing unusual about her slipping in behind the rows of monks, a string of beads clicking between her fingers as she sang the responses. There was nothing extraordinary about her presence until shouts and the alien ring of mailed boots and harness echoed through the cloister. The brothers singing the office didn't miss a syllable, but wary eyes slid toward the outer doors, back to Brother Prior, and then to the frightened girl bent over her missal, her face obscured by a translucent veil.

The doors of the chapter house fell off their hinges as the soldiers stormed through.

❧

"I CLAIMED THE right of sanctuary!" Serafina screamed at Gherardo Ranieri. "You will bring me to a convent at once! You had no right at all to take me from San Marco and bring me to this place! No right at all!"

Gherardo leaned over Serafina and smiled, his eyes dark and reflecting the fire crackling in the hearth. He nuzzled her cheek with his lips, murmuring, "I do have a right. I claimed you for my wife, to be my contessa. My claim has precedence over a trumped-up lordling, don't you think?"

"Some might call it abduction!"

Gherardo laughed softly and moved away to pour a drink. "You know I'm right. The contracts were signed and words spoken. We are legally bound to one another. I warned your father when he came to me with his misgivings about our marriage that if he tried to dismiss my claim, he would be ruined and that I would strike at him with the most painful of blows."

"Release me. Take my dower if it's money you crave."

"No."

"The church will never sanction or bless our union," Serafina argued. "I gave myself to another. That makes me an adulteress. You may turn me over to the church authorities for their verdict."

"You're not for burning, Serafina," Gherardo laughed. He handed the cup of wine to her and gestured towards a cushioned, high-backed, bench next to the wall hearth and she sat. "Let us have an accord between us," he said, sitting too close for her liking. "To start, this castle shall be your court. I know you prefer towns and cities, but we have much to be proud of here at Soraggio. Kings and princes come to hunt in my forests, to dine at my table. Look at this solar—have you been in anything more comfortable or rich?"

Yes, she thought, *and one that she could remember from timber to tapestry!*

"I have no care for such things. You're mistaken if you think I don't know your purpose; this place is high above the roads where no one can find it. It's my prison."

"I wanted you to have time alone with me. To show you I am the flower of courtesy and as courtly and as honorable as any knight that has ever caught your fancy. Does this not bespeak chivalry and courtly love?" He gestured towards the windows where the moon was starting to glow through the pine trees of the Garfagnana forests surrounding the castle hidden high in a northwestern corner of Tuscany. The silvery light made the distant villages speckling the mountains glow like new coins. *Yes,* Serafina thought, *it is beautiful, but I will never admit that to you!*

Gherardo gave her a gentle kiss and rested a hand on her breast. Serafina knew better than to slap it away; that would only rouse anger in him and some men were known to use anger to find their pleasure. Knowing this anyway, she said softly, "And so you will make love to an unwilling lady? A captive?"

"My wife and contessa. We'll be married as soon as your father arrives."

"No!" Serafina tried to rise, but Gherardo shoved her back down on the bench, pinning her against the cushion while he smothered her with a kiss.

"There's no reason why we cannot celebrate the marriage now," he said as he started to unlace her gown. "You let that boy take what was rightfully mine. Now let's see if you learned anything useful from him!"

Serafina continued to struggle until Gherardo struck her with his fist again and again, his lust rising. "And you will never, *ever*, disobey me again!" he said as he claimed what was his by right.

CHAPTER 25

CUPS OF WINE circulated down the bridal table for the third time and Gian Maria stood and raised his goblet in tribute to Cunizza, who nodded with an appropriate show of modesty, took sips from her cup and held it aloft for Gian Maria, which brought applause and cheers.

Tommaso now stood and drank to the health of the newlyweds and the families of Alberti and Guidi, joined irrevocably. His inability to pronounce 'irrevocably' and how obscene the word sounded rolling off his tongue brought shouts of laughter and prompted Gian Maria to call for the musicians to strike a tune. Tommaso staggered over to the women seated in their pavilion and grabbed Violetta Arcangeli, whom he groped and kissed during the dance.

Francesco watched quietly from his end of the table, picking at the food on his trencher and politely refusing anything else to drink. From time to time he felt in his pocket for a square of parchment, a letter that had been delivered only that evening. His fingers slid over the smooth lump of red sealing wax, and down the folded edge in a continuous motion until Gian Maria threw himself down next to Francesco and offered a drunken, brotherly kiss.

"Marriage agrees with you." Francesco wiped his cheek and handed Gian Maria a cup.

"So far," Gian Maria sniggered. "Though tonight won't have many surprises. Once she knew I was hers, Cunizza showed her gratitude so many, many ways. Some I didn't think possible. Look at her; she's putting on a good show of modesty and decorum, isn't she?" Gian Maria blew a kiss at Cunizza and then blew a kiss at Violetta when she danced by with his father.

Francesco shrugged and pulled the letter from his pocket, setting it on the table.

"God's lady, you're still carrying that?" Gian Maria scoffed. "How many weeks ago was it?"

"This is new. It came today," Francesco answered.

Gian Maria glanced at the handwriting and raised his brows.

"Go on."

Expecting an outpouring of sweet, childish sentiments and promises of undying and yielding love, Gian Maria frowned when he read the brief message from Serafina to Francesco, and turned the letter over in hands, read the message a second time. He folded it carefully and gave it back.

"I suppose you expected this," Gian Maria murmured.

"Yet another turn of fortune's wheel against me," said Francesco as he rose and left the hall. Any other time Gian Maria would have ignored him and returned to drinking and whoring, but tonight he sought Francesco out and found him sitting alone in the loggia on the roof.

"If you truly love this lady, end her misery and yours," Gian Maria said as he approached. He grabbed Francesco's arm to prevent him from bolting, which he knew Francesco would try. Francesco wrestled free and glared at him, but stayed, nevertheless. Gian Maria continued. "Once you have her in your protection, conceal her in a convent until such a time as is both convenient and safe for you both. God knows you love her well enough. I expect you to do no less."

Francesco looked up at him, wiping the tears from his cheeks. "Why would you think that?"

"Because you'd expect the same of me," Gian Maria replied with a shrug of his shoulders. "And it's what I would do. It's what you must do."

FRANCESCO SENT HIS household in a frenzy to prepare for the journey. He got as far as Castiglione, which was not far enough, for the Garfagnana countryside in early spring was treacherous. Snow still clung to the crags and sheer rock and streams overflowed to wash out roads, making mud of forest paths. A week's journey in such conditions would take two, perhaps three weeks. By the time Francesco entered the town gates, his horse was blown and lame from its exertions, dropping dead before Castiglione's amused sentries. Francesco found a new horse soon after his arrival, and set out again, but it was too late. A messenger bearing a letter from Gian Maria caught him at Naggio:

> *"When I heard that you were stranded in Castiglione, I took it upon myself to play the pander and came to Soraggio, where I write this.*
>
> *"I sent word to Serafina and we met in secret. Your lady bade me give up the mission for your sake, but as you may realize by now, I have not — and would not.*
>
> *"It comes to this: Gherardo Ranieri summoned his vassals and assembled them at his castle to witness his marriage to Serafina. I also went as a witness at her insistence that you should know it was not of her doing.*
>
> *"The rites took place in the dead of night in a locked chapel.*
>
> *"What a sight it was, the bridegroom waiting at the sanctuary steps while Serafina was dragged in protest to the altar! She*

screamed and begged for death and fell twice before the altar of the blessed Virgin, crying for intervention. Durante and one of Gherardo's bastard sons pulled Serafina to her feet and held her by force at the altar.

Our cousin, Azzelino, performed the marriage rite. We thought Durante would expire in the midst of the ceremony, for he suddenly turned gray and opened his mouth like a fish, gaping for air. Azzelino solemnized the marriage so quickly it might have been some cattle faire. Once the rites were concluded, Monna Serafina was secreted away to the bridal chamber.

"One would think it was a funeral for the absence of merriment. There was no bridal supper. As soon the incense smoke faded, Gherardo dismissed his men. Taking his command, we found our supper elsewhere. We did not see him for a day, but when he did join us at Mass, he looked cheerful and swaggered like a boy after having his first milkmaid or whore. Serafina came to church at vespers and looked as if she were near death. She was veiled of course, but it was easy to see that her face was discolored and swollen with bruises. She held a cape against her but when it slipped, I saw the welts and cuts of a beating on her neck and breasts. Francesco, I do not wish to speculate what happened on their wedding night, nor would I wish to tell you if I learn the truth. Serafina's woman says nothing when importuned, but shakes her head and weeps and begs you to deliver them.

"She was very pale and beautiful, this Serafina, one look at her explained why you love her so completely, so foolishly.

"Gherardo Ranieri keeps a mistress, a Florentine gentlewoman named Isotta, who was married to one of the Ildebrandi sons. Gherardo got rid of him, and the lady Isotta never returned to Florence after her husband's death and since then has lived in noble estate in this castle of Soraggio. She was present at the wedding, as were Gherardo's bastard sons by her. I heard a foul story that she forced Serafina to submit to Gherardo and watched as the marriage was consummated.

"Durante looked worse than the bridegroom. He asked Serafina's forgiveness when all was said and done. She said nothing for her part, only glanced at him. God help me, I should never want to be looked at like that!

"Serafina begged your forgiveness as we left the chapel, saying, 'Tell Francesco to hope beyond hope,' whatever that means.

"No more to impart except my sympathies. I would not have written this but for your insistence that you should know of all that passed. Commend me to my wife.

211

"With great affection and love, your truest friend and cousin,
Gian Maria di Tommaso."

Francesco folded the letter carefully and placed it between the leaves of his breviary. He put the book down and reached for the wine flask and drank deep, then flung the bottle into the fireplace, watching it explode.

❧

"WHEN DID YOU return?"

Gian Maria glanced up from his writing and barely acknowledged his wife. Cunizza Alberti stood in the doorway of his bedchamber and waited for a response, glancing around as if expecting something or someone. Gian Maria was grateful for his man's quick thinking: sweet rushes on the floor and cypress wood burning in the hearth masked the chambermaid's cloying perfume still lingering hours after leaving Gian Maria's bed, a bed he'd made up himself. Cunizza actually looked disappointed that she hadn't caught him. She was always asking for a quarrel. He knew she had axes to grind. After all, didn't she remind him every day that she'd come to this marriage expecting the rights and privileges of a noblewoman and found herself nothing more than another mouth to feed in a burgeoning household? Her exquisite beauty, Cunizza pointed out time and again, the beauty that was idolized in poems and ballads, was nothing to him. Her last words before sleeping every night were, "You should think yourself fortunate. Others would die or kill for me!"

Ah, Gian Maria thought, studying the last sentence he'd written, *give me a sword now* . . .

"When did you return?" she repeated the question.

"Two, three, hours ago."

"Ah."

Cunizza swept in with her skirts scattering Gian Maria's cats that clamored for attention and her scowl chasing away his servant. She made an exasperated sound and knelt at the hearth. "Gian Maria, if I've told you once . . ." she sighed and shoved his muddy riding boots and soiled cloak away from the grating to avoid a fire. "I suppose it would be my fault if something were to go up in flames!"

"Sweetheart, you know that's not true," Gian Maria laughed.

"Everything seems to be my fault!" Cunizza snapped as she paced from doorway to bed. "The dowry and name I've brought to this family are insignificant. The way your parents carry on, one would think the marriage had been their sacrifice and not mine! And you!"

"What have I done now?"

"Need I say? I asked you not to go. Whatever your cousin Romena's problems, they are not our concern."

"I disagree."

"When haven't you?"

"Francesco is my friend and my kinsman,"

"Did you prevent the marriage?"

"Unfortunately, no. Proof positive we are all destined to unhappy alliances made for the convenience of our aging and greedy parents."

Gian Maria's eyes immediately rested on Cunizza's face when he reached for the wine bottle. She was fair, lovesome even, but cold as a winter's storm. If half the lovesick men in Florence knew how badly he fared in her bed, they'd find other ladies to waste their poetry on.

What surprised him were the tears misting her eyes. Did she really expect him to pity her, or to beg forgiveness?

He shifted uneasily on his bench and stabbed his pen nib into the inkwell. He wanted to be away from her, to lie in Violetta Arcangeli's arms. Violetta would have given him a homecoming of the most delightful kind, which was what he needed after the unpleasant task in the Garfagnana. That little temptress had almost cured him of the whores of Santa Croce. Yes, Violetta pleased him mightily and now he was itching for her. God forbid, he even loved her!

"To whom do you write?" Cunizza was at his shoulder now and had placed a hand gently at his neck. Was she trying to be tender? Gian Maria shifted again.

"My cousin Romena."

"Ah."

Gian Maria waited, expecting more since the tone was argumentative. Cunizza never ended a conversation easily or quickly.

"What is it, Cunizza?" he asked. *Why wait for the inevitable?*

"It isn't that I dislike your cousin Romena, only his self-love. His manner of superiority."

"That is Father's invention. Francesco would never call himself better than another man. Take care finding fault in others, though; the book's overflowing with your sins."

She made ready to answer but instead let a clenched fist fall softly on his shoulder. Perhaps in jest, perhaps not.

"I'd like to finish this letter in private."

"Ah."

❧

HITCHING A CLOAK around his shoulders, Gian Maria threw the heavy iron bolt across the doors leading out into the Via Calimala. The groan of dry metal against wood brought Elisabetta to the gallery overlooking the courtyard. "Gian Maria? The watch has changed and the curfew bell's rung," she cautioned.

"I'll only be a moment, Mamma. A favor promised to Francesco."

"Has he returned?"

Gian Maria paused. "Just an hour ago. His man came to fetch me. Go

213

to bed. I'll only be a moment."

"Will you? Be careful, Son."

Blowing a kiss, Gian Maria said good night and followed his servant out into the street, eyes downcast, watching the watery, wavering reflection of the torchlight on the moonlit paving stones.

God forgive me for the lie I just told, he thought as picked up speed and headed away from the Borgo Santi Apostoli towards the Via Santa Elisabetta. To his servant Gian Maria called, "Are you certain she's there?"

"Certain enough. I saw her man myself."

Gian Maria began to relax once past the church of Orsanmichele and the orchards that gave it its name. He was edgy and nervous, why, he didn't know. Something wasn't right this evening. He felt as if he was being watched.

"The lantern's out, messer," the servant advised pointing down the Via Santa Elisabetta to the tower house at the end of the lane. "Just as she promised."

Three knocks, then a pause, and two more. Gian Maria stepped back as the doors opened a bit and then laughed softly when Violetta flew into his arms, smothering him with kisses.

"I knew you'd come back!" she giggled and brought her lover inside.

THE SERVANT DOZED on his feet and snapped to attention when the torch sputtered and sparks singed his hair. Yowling in pain and cursing his young master, he scratched his scalp where locks smoldered and stank. Looking at the sky, he marked unhappily that it was nearly dawn. No sense in wondering when the boy would come down. There'd been many nights like this before, and there'd be a *soldo* in it for keeping watch. Gian Maria was a man of his word when he had the money. Thanks to Romena, Gian Maria's purse was kept full these days. Reassuring himself of this, the servant yawned, squatted on a parapet and glanced about, sensing a change.

Strange . . . there was movement in the Piazza Santa Elisabetta. Too large to be dogs or even a stray horse. The servant rubbed his eyes and peered at the gray shapes at the end of the lane now. Before he could drop the torch and reach for his sword, the servant felt a blade at his neck . . .

CUNIZZA GLANCED TOWARDS the door when she heard the knock, nodding as her footman entered and bowed. She finished her ablutions and sent the maid away, then knelt at her prayer desk. Turning pages in the open Bible, she studied the bright illuminations and out of the corner of her eye saw how uneasy the footman was. Sighing, she slammed the Bible shut and looked at the man squarely.

"So?"

The man nodded, and Cunizza took a purse from the desk, handing it over. She noticed a stain still lingered on her fingers and called for more water and fresh towels. As she washed her hands again, she jerked her head towards the door, saying to her man, "You'd best be gone, before mona Elisabetta wakes and hears the news."

As the man bowed low, a scream shook the house, followed by angry shouts, and slamming of doors, and the rumble of footsteps on floorboards upstairs. Cunizza sighed and made one more ablution, then dried her hands carefully on a fine linen towel embroidered with her husband's crest.

"It's too late, I fear," she murmured. "They know their son is dead."

CHAPTER 26

GIAN MARIA WAS buried in the Porciano chapel at Santa Croce on a crystalline afternoon, one of those days too perfect to be true, one to be cataloged in the memory, a day Gian Maria would have spent drunk. As a final jest between friends, Francesco tucked a bottle of wine into the sepulchre before it was sealed. To ease the crossing, he whispered to Elisabetta. He stood as chief mourner and remained at the tomb long after the candles melted down to their brass plates and the smell of wax died, the last of friends and family gone home to supper.

"I think that of all who loved him, you shall miss him most," Elisabetta whispered as she came up beside Francesco and linked an arm in his.

"You're his mother, that's a special love."

"He was my son, my last son and youngest child. But you were a brother to him in spite of everything and that is marked in God's accounting, don't you think, Cecco?" Elisabetta mused, smiling sadly. "I shall never be able to repay you for that kindness."

Francesco squeezed her hand and murmured, "Gian Maria said marriage would be the death of him, of us."

"Quietly, Cecco; Cunizza looks this way."

He nodded curtly at Gian Maria's beautiful widow surrounded like a queen by adoring suitors and sympathetic ladies-in-waiting.

"She's not concerned about what I think or say; she's measuring me for her bed."

"Come, take me home."

"A moment longer."

"What's *he* doing here?"

Azzelino had entered the chapel with Alberti and was being fawned over by his kinsmen and their supporters. Francesco stormed out of the chapel with his escort, leaving Elisabetta to make apologies. He walked aimlessly through the streets of Florence, his mind shadowed by memories and regret. Knowing he could have prevented Gian Maria's death somehow. How many more would die because of his inaction?

He found himself at The Rose and the Knight and paused at the door before going in. Perhaps, if he closed his eyes, when he opened them Gian Maria would be sitting at their table near the hearth. Pretty, buxom

Contessina would be on his lap. Gian Maria would be happy and drunk.

Francesco went in and was welcomed with silence.

The innkeeper was not surprised when he looked up and saw Francesco filling the doorway. Contessina burst into tears and ran upstairs when Francesco sat down and asked for wine.

"She'll not be consoled," the innkeeper muttered, trying hard to find an apology.

Francesco understood all too well. Gian Maria had been a favorite patron and the pall of his sudden, shocking, death hung over the common room like the greasy smoke always in the air. "It's my fault," Francesco admitted. "I should have kept him out of my troubles."

The flask of Tuscan red wine stood untouched for the longest time. The pretty young girl he'd bedded several times, Simonetta, a flame-haired beauty with seductive eyes and sweet disposition, brought a pot of his favorite English ale and a trencher laden with meat, cheese, and fruit. She sat on his lap and started dividing the food into two equal portions.

"You have to eat," she purred, tearing off a crust of bread and feeding it to him. "Gian Maria would not have liked you to mourn."

"I never loved anyone better," Francesco said.

"Not even the little Giustini girl?"

"Simonetta, you tread on uneasy ground."

"Come with me and I'll help you forget them both."

It was too much. Francesco threw a handful of coins on the table and despite her pleading, shoved her off his lap and stormed out, returning to the family chapel in Santa Croce, now as bright as day with a thousand candles burning around Gian Maria's tomb. In the midst of the soft, wavering light was a shrouded figure—a lump that quivered and made ugly, retching sounds. Francesco took one of the torches and held it closer, saw that it was Tommaso.

"Come Tommaso, there's nothing more either of us can do," Francesco whispered, offering a hand.

Tommaso started violently and backed away, fearful, cowering beside one of the carved angels guarding his son's tomb. The old man continued to snivel and wipe his runny nose on the sleeve of his gown, the velvet already matted from overuse.

"We both should take the blame for this. I make an end here and now of our quarrel. I bid you do the same."

Tommaso glanced up, frowning. "Go to Hell!" he spat.

"Gian Maria would expect no less from us."

"Now's not the time!" Tommaso growled and pushed his way past Francesco to the door.

Francesco knelt before the tomb and reached out to touch the cool marble, letting a hand caress the letters of Gian Maria's name.

"Feeling lost—or guilty?"

Francesco went cold at the sound of Azzelino's mellow voice and he turned with sword unsheathed, ready.

"Put away the sword," Azzelino chuckled as he came from the chapel entrance. "And do not summon your men; though we are outside the walls, we are still in the Florentine commune. We're not on your ground, are we?"

"He's dead. Your quarrel is gone," Francesco murmured, sliding back into a choir stall. They were far enough away from each other for comfort and safety's sake, but Francesco nevertheless slipped a hand around the reassuring hilt of his sword.

"I heard your plea to Porciano. I'm in agreement with you," Azzelino said after a time. "I think now is the best time to resolve our differences."

"There's nothing we could ever hope to agree upon."

"But you offered to make peace with Tommaso,"

"With Tommaso."

"I'm not here by choice. My father Alberti wants peace between us."

Francesco chuckled. "Does he?"

"He is in earnest. I swear it."

"Ask him in a week what he thinks of peace on earth and goodwill toward men, and you'll get another answer. Unless of course it means gaining another town or castle from yet another unfortunate bridegroom pressed into service for that whore you call a sister. How many would that be? Seven, or eight?"

"Easily, there; she's done no harm to you,"

"But she would, if given a chance."

Azzelino sighed. "Still, Cousin, what you propose and what my father proposes, make sense."

"No, Cousin, not really. You've given me no reason whatsoever to trust your word."

"There's no reason why we couldn't make an effort." Azzelino's voice was turning anxious, impatient.

"Our past meetings have been less than felicitous and I'm not one to hope for Hell freezing over or pigs flying from the treetops in the Casentino," Francesco said.

"It would be a tribute to Gian Maria."

"Don't pretend that you loved him!" Francesco snapped. "Your only care is how to keep what little of the Porciano fortune Gian Maria held. Don't look to me for a solution. Whatever you, Alberti and Tommaso decide upon, I want no part of it, and it will never come to pass. And you know why!"

"Can't mention her name? The wound is deep, eh, Cousin?"

The scrape of boots on the pavement and the groan of wood as

Francesco shifted were an indication that Azzelino had opened the wound.

"Give me the lands and castles you bestowed on Gian Maria as wedding gifts and I will see that the peace is kept."

"No."

"Only a fool would turn away—"

"Leave me alone."

"You know what I'm capable of; you've seen what I've done! Are you that foolish, Francesco?"

"Now is not the time."

"I can do far worse than you can imagine! Are you willing to risk everything? Now *is* the time!"

"I'm not speaking of peace treaties, but of the moment when I crush you."

"You will not reconsider?"

"No."

Angry, clipped footsteps confirmed Azzelino's departure, giving Francesco what he wanted most of all at that time—solitude. He ignored the letters Azzelino sent the next day and during the intervening weeks; relying on promises from that quarter would be like trying to grow roses in the deserts of the Holy Land.

And then another little war sprang up.

"What's this?"

Edmund glanced absently at the petitions Francesco held. They had lain on the table for weeks without notice, and now he'd at last discovered them. Avoiding the subject would serve no good purpose. Edmund swallowed hard, saying, "These are petitions for the purchase of alum rights and license for faire, monsignore. Here is a letter from the gonfaloniere of Florence entreating you to grant the right to enfeoff the—"

"This much I can see. What town?"

"Consuma."

Francesco raised his brows and then set them heavily. "Whom does the commune wish to enfeoff? I know of no one who's asked. This was not part of our accord."

Edmund puffed out the name with a labored sigh. "Azzelino Alberti."

"No. That is all you need to say." Francesco dropped the petitions on the floor, moving on.

Edmund had tired of this silly war. Azzelino was more foolish than clever, the type who would crawl away quietly with a crust of bread to content him if the crust was substantial.

"If you were to assent to this grant," Edmund gambled.

"I just gave you my answer."

"By showing generosity to one man—"

Francesco reached behind him to a shelf piled with documents and scrolls and took a map, unfurling it over the petitions and books already littering the table. Pointing to a position almost parallel to Florence, he said, "Here is Consuma. I granted it to the commune of Florence. Here is the pass at Consuma leading into the Casentino. Here, here, and here are Romena castles and towns! The alum rights notwithstanding, for we need alum to make dye for our wool, the town of Consuma and the license to hold faire are too valuable. Edmund, the key to the Casentino and the entirety of my lands is the pass at Consuma. Whosoever holds the pass holds the Casentino. Now do you know why Azzelino is so hell bent on acquiring it!"

"It is one town of many—"

"Your argument would lead another man to suspect your loyalty."

Francesco returned to his reading and then suddenly flung the papers aside, reaching for a pen and new parchment.

"Why not Romena?" he said with a chuckle. To Edmund he said, "If Florence wants to enfeoff Consuma, let him. It makes perfect sense. Send a man to the gonfaloniere with this letter of intent and a promise of eighty florins as a surety against my word."

"You, Monsignore?"

"It makes sense, doesn't it?"

❧

"YOU HAD NO right to do it!" Azzelino hissed when he stood before the gonfaloniere of Florence a week later. "Why should all be given to Romena? What is one town of so many?"

"Four of my castles surround Consuma," Francesco responded. "That's the best argument I can think of."

"Gonfalon, he doesn't need more!"

"Consuma lies within the borders of Romena lands, and it is his. He gave us the keeping of it and if he desires to take it back it is his decision. It would be imprudent of the Commune to ignore his petition," the gonfaloniere countered. "The agreement stands, signor Azzelino. Florence will give you title and lordship of Poggiola if that will content you."

"It does not! My petition has precedence!"

"It isn't a matter of who offered first,"

"Messer gonfalon, you know there is a quarrel between Romena and me. I would gladly reconsider my petition if my cousin Romena would countenance this—a town and a castle of his choosing. It's a very small price to pay for peace. An inconsequential town, a castle in need of repairs. That's all I ask."

"Were I to give him that much, gonfalon, who's to say he wouldn't stop reaching for more?" Francesco demanded.

The gonfaloniere's eyes slid from Francesco to Azzelino, and back to Francesco.

"Is it so much to ask?" the gonfaloniere wondered aloud.

"Gonfalon, you don't have to ask the question to know the answer!"

"Easily, monsignore! I'm not asking any more of you than I would another man. Consider it."

"I already have, and you and Azzelino have my answer."

The gonfaloniere leaned forward and offered his most charming smile, the one reserved for sycophants and small boys. "It is only a town."

"It has a castle with a strong garrison; it is a town whose gates lie without the pass to the Benedictine mountains; it is a town known for its loyalty to Romena. I will not dishonor the people whose livelihood is my responsibility and whose lives are entrusted to me. I will not give up a stone or a blade of grass to placate a man who desires my good lordship only as a means to destroy me!" Francesco spoke, impassioned.

The gonfaloniere waited a moment before speaking. "It is a sound argument."

"I will not go without compensation!" Azzelino shouted.

"Compensation? For what?" Francesco laughed.

Azzelino held up his scarred hand missing part of a thumb. "Injuries are usually paid for!"

"Not out of my revenues," Francesco replied quietly. "Not out of my life or livelihood!"

"I will take it out of your belly, your heart, or whatever is left of you when you're dead on a battlefield, Romena!"

The gonfaloniere thumped his fist on the table. "Enough! The agreement stands."

"But—!" Azzelino started.

"It stands!" With that pronouncement, the gonfaloniere ended the audience.

Romena had the town, but he had yet to win the war for in November, Edmund's scouts brought disturbing news that Azzelino had employed four companies, those of the Whyte Hart, the Eagle, the Ring, and the Grail, and taken up position around Consuma dangerously close to the Romena fiefs of Montemignaio and Campolombardo. Even the worse, the towns of Bibbiena and Corsalone declared for Azzelino and mustered their militia to join with him.

"Tell Azzelino to move his troops, withdraw to Florence or whatever hellspawn town he thinks he owns, and there will be no unpleasantness from this quarter," Francesco quietly advised Azzelino's herald pursuivant.

"They are in no way a threat to Romena," the herald replied.

"They are less than a day's march from here! Move the troops."

"He will not, monsignore."

"If he wants a war, he has one. Tell him that."

"I'm sure he's aware of it."

"I'm sure that's why he's doing it! I have neither the men nor the desire to quarrel over something as clear as this. Tell him to move the troops."

Azzelino held firm. He was emboldened by an offer of support from the conti Ordelaffi of Rimini and positioned his armies for a long stay in the Casentino. Francesco and Azzelino stood toe to toe at the line and neither budged. The situation escalated toward a dangerous confrontation every day that Azzelino sent his herald to Castello di Romena.

"My master asks you to consider this—in exchange for Consuma, the alum rights, and the right to forest, he will give you San Pietro all'Monte, its abbey and castle."

"They're not his to give; they are endowed to Porciano."

"I think you understand my message, signore."

"Indeed? Instruct me if I do not."

"Canon Azzelino,"

"*Canon* Azzelino?" Francesco laughed. "Good God! Has he purchased more holy orders?"

"Canon Azzelino would persuade Porciano he would gain much from the sacrifice of a castle and abbey and an equal share in whatever he may take from you if you do not honor his request."

"Which, eventually, would be my life. Move the troops."

A week later: "Canon Azzelino considers his proposal most generous."

Francesco bestowed a dazzling smile and placed a hand on the herald's shoulder, clapping it with familiarity. "Tell your master I'll think about it if he would agree to give me Cunizza's hand in marriage. After all, he has to give up something of value."

When the herald swallowed his astonishment and departed to convey the offer, Edmund poured two cups of ale and offered one to Francesco. "You're not serious!" he exclaimed.

"Of course not. Azzelino wants me in his family's bosom as eagerly as the plague. He wouldn't be able to use me the way he used Gian Maria or any of Cunizza's many, belated, husbands, rest their souls."

As expected, Azzelino soundly rejected the offer and reiterated his demands, adding that he expected no less.

"Move the troops," Francesco instructed the herald. "He can move the troops or he can die when I move them. Move the troops."

And still, a week later: "Since you will not agree to these reasonable demands the canon makes, he is willing to take a hundred florins in lieu of them."

"Move the troops off of my land and out of the Casentino!"

"One hundred florins, Consuma, and the alum rights and right to forest in the Casentino."

Francesco glanced at his captains amusedly and then answered the herald with a laugh. He wasn't laughing three days later when word came that the Romena towns of Caiano and Tartiglia had been sacked and Azzelino's army was marching on Consuma. With his own garrison hastily arrayed, Francesco set out to join battle.

CHAPTER 27

A YEAR TO the day had passed since Francesco rode through the Casentino to claim what was rightfully his. Now he came to defend it.

The Romena army followed the banks of the Arno River in a snowfall so dense it was impossible to see forty *bracchi* ahead. This was the worst: marching into nowhere, marching into an ambush. Chasing an enemy that had so far eluded them. As it was, the contest was against all laws of chivalry. Battles weren't fought in the winter; any true man of arms knew that and lived by that, but then, Azzelino wasn't a man of arms. Francesco knew what kind of man Azzelino was—the very worst kind, and Francesco knew he had to accept the challenge thrown down at his feet.

"Azzelino's been here," one of the foragers announced as he sidled up to Francesco. "You can see his tracks. The snow hasn't covered them yet."

"He's a priest, not a soldier," Francesco scoffed, now scanning the gray and white horizon. "It shouldn't be too difficult to follow where he leads— Christ!"

Three horses had gone down in a snow bank, up to the withers. Several grooms and Edmund clamored to the rescue, but they were soon floundering. It would take an hour to dig them out of the powder and slush. An hour lost in their pursuit. An hour would give Azzelino enough time to seize a castle.

In spite of the miserable cold Francesco burned with fever, sweat dripped from his forehead into his eyes and down his nose. A clammy chill overtook him whenever an ice-wrought breeze cut through his visor. Every muscle ached from sleeping in the saddle the night before. Shifting slightly, he leaned down to soothe his destrier with a kind word and caress. The poor beast was weary from anticipation. At the last moment he had decided on a pale horse rather than his customary gray, a good choice, this creamy white mount, given the damned weather.

One of the squires lost his footing on the icy ground and dropped a shield and battle-ax, startling the warhorse. It took Francesco and three grooms to calm the destrier that, while it reared and shied, trampled another squire to death under its powerful hooves. The soldiers in Francesco's vanguard, quarrelsome and anxious before, were startled into silence. Edmund cantered over once the body was removed.

"See that a purse of twenty florins is delivered to the boy's mother. He was her only son," Francesco directed impersonally.

Someone gesturing wildly, silently, towards a clearing interrupted his further instructions. Francesco squinted where directed and saw a scouting party ahead, just coming out of the wood, unaware of the army watching it.

"Monsignore, do we attack?" Edmund queried.

"No. We wait."

"What happens if the army is at their backs? Or hidden within the wood? We'll be slaughtered, sitting here,"

"Out in the open we have a chance. I'll not risk an ambush."

"But, Francesco, think—"

"There's nothing to think about. The last time I took your advice, Edmund, we wound up hacking our way out of ravine with no army behind us!"

"Are you questioning my abilities?"

"Your judgment, perhaps."

Edmund moved his horse away from Francesco's when the beast nudged his stallion and sought blood.

"If you've got a quarrel with me, speak directly." Francesco hissed.

"Only your motives. Nothing else."

Francesco moved closer and firmly laid a mailed glove on Edmund's arm, saying, "When you swore fealty to me, you agreed to fight for any cause of mine!"

"As I will." This said quietly, with forced respect.

Francesco watched him closely for a moment, unable to read his expression. Now was not the time to discover betrayal.

They pressed on. Four miles from Stia the pulse of a marching army shook the ground. From a vantage on the crest of a hill, Francesco called a halt and silently waited. The horses cantered back and forth restlessly in anticipation and the tree branches shimmered as the pulse grew stronger, the sound of the approaching force grew louder.

"There!" one of the heralds shouted, pointing ahead. Two thousand of the best mercenaries and their banners lay on the horizon. Francesco swore softly. He wouldn't have a chance, not with these odds.

Summoning his captains, Francesco rode out to survey the ground. A conference was unnecessary. Everyone was in agreement once they memorized the lay of the land. It would be as good a place as any to engage the enemy: the meadow was bordered on the north by woods, to the west by hillocks, to the south, a tributary of the Arno. Drive them onto the meadow and surround them for the kill.

That night two camps were pitched on opposite sides of the meadow, and throughout the long hours of waiting, the sound of armorers at work echoed and danced back and forth.

"He's plagued by a woman," Edmund said while huddled over a campfire that night. His drinking companion was a Florentine nobleman called Roberto da Quintavale. Roberto was only a few months in service and awed as were most by the Romena presence. He liked Francesco, however, and was put off by Edmund's disrespectful tone and told him as much. His opinion was answered with a bitter laugh.

"We've fought together more times than I can count on both hands and this is the first quarrel I've no heart for," Edmund grumbled, draining his cup. "What is one town to him? He's never thought about it before, this town! If it were me, I'd give it all to the damn priest and reap the rewards later! Even priests fall down stairwells or off of horses!"

"Alberti positioned his men on Romena land. That's asking for a quarrel," Roberto answered, staring into his empty cup.

"We stand to lose our lives over a woman!" Edmund spat. "Azzelino and Francesco lust after the same girl! Don't think it's for honorable causes such as birthright or lands and castles!"

"You've fought for less honorable causes, and, pardon my saying so, but I've always thought the love of a woman was a most honorable thing."

Edmund glared at him with drunken, bloodshot eyes. "You love him. I love him, too. You've fallen under his spell," he whispered sadly. "Just like so many before. Just like I did!"

"You speak like one torn by a choice he doesn't want to make," Roberto commented. He was glad when Edmund, having no taste for the company, excused himself and took his flask to the perimeter of the camp. There Edmund sat, happy to drink quietly and alone.

"Edmund Clifford!"

The whisper startled Edmund and drunk though he was he had the presence of mind to draw his sword.

"Friend or foe?" Edmund growled.

"That depends."

Edmund hesitated, coming closer. He thought he recognized the man hiding among the trees, but the hood obscured his face. It couldn't be . . .

"Get on before I raise the watch!"

"I come to treat."

"Romena will treat tomorrow on the field!"

"I come to speak with you, Messer."

Edmund laughed. "You're a fool then!"

"If you weren't inclined to stay and listen, you'd have slit my throat ere now."

"Speak your mind and then get on before the watch changes."

"There's time enough to change your mind before morning comes. Azzelino's promise comes backed by lands and revenues."

"Romena promised me that."

"But what have you to show for that promise?"

The bracken rustled behind them. Edmund turned anxiously and saw Francesco. How long he had stood there, Edmund didn't want to guess. Before he could explain himself or concoct a bold lie, Francesco was gone.

❧

WHEN DAWN BROKE, Roberto da Quintavale left the campfire and went uninvited to Romena's tent, prompted by curiosity. He called softly, and when no one responded went in. Francesco was sitting up on his cot, rubbing his eyes with closed fists like a small child. He held a *cuirass* and *greave* in his lap. The squires were somewhere else.

"Here; let me help you prepare, monsignore," Roberto offered.

Francesco handed over the cuirass, smiling. "There's something new. A captain with humility enough to play the squire. Thank you. My squires went to hear mass and be shrived." After a moment, he stood and yawned, then pointed at Roberto, saying, "Roberto da Quintavale, isn't it?"

"Yes."

"Didn't your grandfather serve with mine on the last Crusade?"

"I believe he did."

"And you had an uncle? Tullio, I think?"

Roberto swallowed hard before speaking. "I think you knew him."

"Well enough."

"And your father?"

"Manfredo da Quintavale."

"I know him too well! So you're the son he offered as a hostage."

"You're the first man to call it what it is," Roberto said. "If Simone da Battifolle had offered me lands and titles in exchange for betrayal, rather than my father, I wouldn't have agreed to it."

"I heard my late uncle of Battifolle was making some pretty offers," Francesco replied and seeing how the boy trembled, offered his cup. Roberto drank uneasily and then passed it back. He attended to arming quietly, preferring silence to stripping away vulnerabilities and fears.

"What's the mood this morning?" asked Francesco now.

"The men are quiet."

"That's to be expected. Is this your first battle, Roberto?"

Roberto shook his head, paying close attention to the leather bindings on the gorget, afraid to meet Francesco's eyes. "I won my spurs in Pavia. Today I'm given the right wing to command, signore."

"What you do today will decide the battle. In an hour, perhaps two, the fear won't matter. It's always worse, the waiting, letting your mind and heart play games. Letting your men see your fear." Then he said softly, "Where is Edmund?"

"By now he should be ready,"

"Roberto, you shouldn't listen to his rambling," Francesco said matter-of-factly as if answering an unasked question. "You want to know how I know? He always gets drunk the night before a battle. I could tell you stories . . . his headache is so terrible the next morning that it makes killing easier."

"Some things he said,"

"Nonsense, most of it, disloyal, to be sure, but no threat to me. Edmund cannot afford to betray me. And as it stands, I cannot afford his betrayal." Francesco turned and smiled. "Watch him and learn, both what you should do and what you should not."

Roberto nodded and pulled the fittings on the *pauldrons*. His fingers trembled as they worked quickly to dress Francesco. How could they go into battle with so much bad blood between them? God would indeed have to be on their side to win this day.

He glanced out past the tent flap and whistled low. "Look at this!"

"Gesu! I've never seen a snowfall so blinding!" Francesco muttered. "To whom does God give this day's battle?"

"Francesco!"

Edmund's voice brought Francesco back to the tent flap. A herald was riding through the camp.

"What message?" Francesco queried when the rider was close enough for speech.

"That you accept the terms offered before—Signor Azzelino will exchange your good lordship and promise of lands and castles for the withdrawal of his troops from the Casentino. He would then swear fealty to Romena and do you no harm."

"I'd as lief trust the word of our uncle Porciano. I want nothing from him. He will remove himself to Florence, to Avignon, to the pope's bed, I don't really care, whatever pleases him! But I want him gone. Those are my terms."

The herald offered his courtesy and rode off.

By eight of the clock that morning, Romena was in battle array on a hillock overlooking the wood and meadow. For two hours the armies held their lines and waited in the freezing cold to see who would blink first. Finally, two of Azzelino's captains broke rank and rode out to *parle*. Francesco and Edmund met them.

"What are the terms?" Francesco asked.

"Grant Consuma to Azzelino and accept his former offer. In return, Azzelino will grant you title to all Alberti castles south of Florence."

"Consuma will stay in Romena's hands. Tell Azzelino that."

"Lands and castles, signore—"

"Tell him there's nothing more I want than to see his vitals on a spit."

"Lands, castles, titles."

"I'll see your master in hell!"

The second captain dropped his lance then, a moment of clumsiness, but it was in fact a signal to Azzelino's archers. A downpour of arrows arched across the field, aimed straight at Romena.

"Holy 'vangels!" Francesco swore and spurred his mount to get out of the way while Edmund sped off in another direction.

The ride was less than a quarter mile but seemed an eternity. Francesco dodged the arrows showering down, holding his shield above him. His herald pursuivant died in the second volley, an arrow piercing his eye to the back of the skull.

The Romena army waited, perplexed, for direction. Roberto searched the horizon for Edmund and found nothing. *What had the fool done?* Raising his sword and sweeping it down so that the wash blew his horse's mane, Roberto gave the order to charge.

❧

IT WAS A SIGHT not to be forgotten. Azzelino kept his eyes westward as he cleaved a path toward Romena's vanguard, watching the apparition come from the clouds of blinding snow, armor dulled to a patina, mist clinging to it like cobwebs. Francesco da Romena had materialized out of the snow astride his warhorse, his bloody sword the focus of all who watched. The men forging their way on either side of Azzelino urged him to retreat, save himself before Romena got any closer. Azzelino refused, shrugging off the hands. It truly was mesmerizing to watch Francesco's lethal approach, as entertaining and frightening as a tournament.

"Monsignore, save yourself!"

He felt the tug of hands and then Azzelino found himself on a horse and riding for his life, catching a glimpse of Romena's sword as it found its sheath between the shoulder blades of a knight. Azzelino was never as glad as at that moment to get away.

Francesco dug in his spurs and followed hotly, his chase brought to a halt when a boy grabbed the reins of his destrier and slit its underbelly. The boy's dreams of ransom and personal glory at capturing Romena were for nothing when he impaled himself on an ax pole trying to get out of the way as the beast fell.

Francesco managed to kick himself free of the stirrups and tumble out of immediate danger, rolling under bracken to stay clear of knights advancing for the kill.

Edmund watched grimly from his observation point. It was hard to tell who would achieve the day. One of the squires grabbed his arm and pointed to the melee. "Romena's lost his helmet. Look at him! He's fair game—somebody give him a helmet! Gesu Maria!"

True enough, the warrior towering above all others was unmistakably Romena and cries went up from both sides as both made for him.

Francesco's standard was soon gone from the horizon and Azzelino's men had suddenly converged where the pennon had been moments before. The last of Romena had been the tawny hair lashing about as he swung at every man in his path.

Roberto da Quintavale's squire now joined them, falling to his knees before Edmund, convulsing in spasms while choking and sputtering for air.

"Messer Quintavale . . . Messer Quintavale . . . bids me . . . come . . . and . . . ask . . . why you . . . why you . . . do not . . . commit . . . your . . . reserves! . . . He begs you,"

"Romena has not called for them."

"But monsignore Romena—" Edmund's squire protested and held his tongue when Edmund shot him a glance that commanded silence.

"Romena has not called for them."

"Christ! Do you . . . not hear? Romena's down!" his squire cried. "We'll all be dead if you don't do something now!"

On the field, Francesco screamed for reinforcements until his shrieks were rasping and no more distinguishable from the death rattles of those falling around him. He gutted men as if they were fish. Thrusts and blows were clean and mechanical, rhythmic in their execution. Francesco knew, however, he could only hold out a short while longer, as the enemy was closing in. The mulberry and gold of Romena had been replaced by the scarlet and black of Alberti.

Francesco was attacked several times in this assault, and knew he was wounded, but could not think where. The cold made him numb and impervious to pain. Blood seeped through every chink in his mail. Every time he dragged his hand across his eyes, he saw the enemy through a pink haze. His sword arm burned with pain and his sight was dimmed by sweat and blood. Around him was a dissonance of noise: shouts, screams, the cursing of soldiers, thundering hooves as they chopped up the ground and knights under them. He saw one of his squires lying on the ground and bellowed at him to get up. When the boy didn't move, Francesco grabbed his arm and it gave way, a stump of flesh and sinews. The boy was dead.

Several of his household guard at last appeared out of the *melee* and dragged him from a would-be grave, blazing a path of fallen bodies. They were still with Francesco as he was forced down into a gully. The ground was like glass, slippery and fragile, giving way under the mailed boots that pounded it. Francesco tripped over a body and slid buttocks first down into the gully, his harness making deep ruts in the snow. Were it not for his own men sliding behind and over him, a German mercenary would have taken his head from his shoulders. Francesco managed to crawl out and hack his way up to where Edmund waited.

"I did ask you to commit the reserves! How long did you expect me to wait?" Francesco growled none too quietly, mindless of the soldiers and squires gathering.

"Till you required me to come but I expected you would manage all by yourself as you usually do, monsignore. Is there anything else you require? Maybe a helmet?" Edmund's reply was snide. His eyes flickered, waiting for the outburst.

"We understand each other; there's no reason to dance about!" Francesco hissed and shoved his sword at Edmund. "Why prolong the inevitable? End it here and now!"

Edmund stared at the weapon offered. He had gone cold and the only sound in his ears was his heart pounding. The men waited, as did Francesco. God's life! They really thought he'd do it! Trembling, Edmund took the sword and swung it heavily into the air. The men around them had gone quiet, waiting.

"Why do you wait?" Francesco hissed.

Edmund had no recourse, no alternative. His hands shaking uncontrollably, he swept Francesco's sword over Francesco's head and then brought hard to earth.

"Send word to Roberto da Quintavale that the hour is now," Francesco ordered. "*Now*, if you please!"

War again became the business at hand. Battles were engaged anew and with a vigorous and alarming ferocity. On both sides, no quarter was given. Francesco stopped hacking his way through a column of infantry to cheer on Roberto's flank as it charged onto the meadow. Edmund, having already charged the field and pulled back, now rallied his troops and joined Francesco in pursuit of the fleeing Alberti army. The chase led them to the walls of Castello di Romena. The road and surrounding fields outside of Pratovecchio were swarming with men either in combat, pursuit, or flight. The town's governor had prudently closed the town gates and barred entrance to both factions despite Francesco's threats. By nightfall the Alberti army was decimated. The bloodbath that ensued repulsed even a seasoned knight like Francesco.

His shoulder and leg now throbbed incessantly, his armor slimy with his own blood and the blood of others. Francesco tossed his sword to the squire following him away from the walls of Pratovecchio. As far as he was concerned, the battle and the war were over.

Lorenzo was in the greater bailey when Francesco arrived with his captains. Never had he seen his master so battle-weary and frightening. He looked near to death. Lorenzo began stripping Francesco of his armor the moment he slid from the saddle and slumped down onto the stairs. Francesco leaned back as Lorenzo struggled with the harness, gasping in pain as the *cuirass* was removed none-too-gently. It was greased with a thin film of blood. Lorenzo took one of the heralds' pennons and shoved it up against the coat of mail in an effort to stop the bleeding.

Edmund finally arrived at the rear of the household guard. His overdue appearance and lack of concern did not go unnoticed by the men who formed a protective ring around Francesco.

"Edmund, we must talk," Francesco said when Lorenzo and Roberto hoisted him for the journey upstairs.

"Tomorrow, if you're still alive," Edmund replied.

Francesco grumbled in protest, but he allowed the men to help him to the solar. His eyes met Edmund's in that moment and a lot could be inferred in that silent glance.

❧

ROBERTO DIDN'T KNOW what to think. Two hours before, Francesco and Edmund were behind the solar doors screaming at one another, throwing accusations back and forth and opening up old wounds without a thought as to who might hear. The servants crouching around the oaken doors scattered whenever one of Romena's captains appeared at the top of the stairs and they clustered round again as soon as it was clear. Roberto had decided not to go inside when summoned, preferring the safety of the passageway and entered only when Edmund had cleared the landing and stormed out of the donjon. This drama had been played out several times over the course of a fortnight.

Now it seemed as if all had been forgotten, a bad dream. Peace returned by the end of the third week, only to dissolve as soon as the messenger arrived from Florence with a letter. Roberto saw the man's ashen face as he fled the solar with Francesco's curses following him.

"It's a trap," Francesco said to Roberto, who held the summons from the Collegium of the Priorate. Resplendent with seals, it was dropped on the bed where it lay while Francesco, Roberto, and Edmund stared at it.

Francesco scratched his head. "They must think me a fool. What do you think?"

The question had been directed at Edmund, who shrugged, saying, "It's worth discovering, monsignore. The Collegium—"

"This isn't the work of the Collegium. Don't you see? Azzelino Alberti is seeking revenge for Campolombardo!" Roberto interrupted. "He's had enough time to plant lies in the gonfalon's ear and purchase a death warrant. If Signor Romena goes to Florence he won't come back alive."

"I don't have time for this foolishness," Francesco muttered, making his way to the garderobe. The physician hurried forward, clucking his tongue. "Oh, get out of my way, damn you!" Francesco groused. "I didn't break anything! See?" And Francesco spun around and kept going towards the garderobe to prove he was on the mend.

"I'd agree with the physician if I knew you weren't going to hit me," Roberto commented when Francesco reappeared and with Lorenzo's help prodded Francesco back to bed. Edmund watched jealously. They had become fast friends in the last three weeks, ever since Roberto proved himself at Campolombardo with a recklessness that helped Francesco win the day. Why was it that Francesco relied heavily on new acquaintances rather than those tried and true?

". . . I've got to do something," Francesco muttered and attacked a pillow until it was molded into a shape he could be comfortable with. Both Roberto and Edmund chafed with inactivity. Watching Francesco ruin a fine pillow would not solve the immediate problem.

"Shall I send for reinforcements?" Edmund offered.

"They wouldn't arrive in time. I think this will be the end to the foolishness."

Roberto glanced at Edmund out of the corner of his eye. The Englishman was bristling.

"We lost so many at Campolombardo," Edmund continued to argue. "At least, Francesco, if we are prepared for any eventuality,"

"Edmund, how shall I array enough men and arms in so short a time?"

"You play into his hands. You'll have your answer by nightfall."

"And how would you know?"

Edmund hedged, let his explanation die unspoken.

Francesco eyed him cautiously. "I'm not concerned. You shouldn't be. Roberto, see that a message is returned to Florence. Tell the priors we will not be moved by their entreaty, for it is clearly not theirs. If they want me, they know where to find me."

"It will be slaughter—to be so unprepared!" Edmund protested.

"How do you know? It could be a feint. Why respond at all if it is nothing?"

"And if it is? If it' something to worry about?"

"I am not concerned—damn! These medicines confound my stomach! Damn all physicians!"

With that, Francesco stumbled out of bed and disappeared back into the garderobe, a flurry of paper in his wake. Roberto and Edmund knelt as one to gather the documents.

"I know what you're thinking," Roberto murmured.

"Don't flatter yourself with prophecy, Quintavale. You may have Romena blinded by your devotion, but I know an opportunist when I see one!" Edmund fired back.

"You should know. You speak from experience."

"Francesco knows my worth, both as a man and a soldier. He would never think otherwise. I would be surprised if he did not think so."

"That is your own worst fear. I have no doubt about my loyalty. What of yours?"

Roberto's words, spoken in a whisper, fell like ice. Edmund shrugged indifferently and shouted for Lorenzo to bring candles. It was getting dark.

❧

FRANCESCO HAD HIS answer in two days.

When Edmund heard the foragers' reports, he went up on the battlements to see for himself and went sick at the sight along the horizon.

"Someone find Quintavale and then muster every able body you can find!" he shouted at a sentry. "Where is Romena?"

The sentry pointed towards the greater bailey and the stables. Edmund all but slid down the casement from donjon to bailey and skirted past the pigs rutting about in midden, twice overstepping puddles of questionable matter in his haste to reach the stables. Not even the pretty maid Beatrice caught his attention though were this any other day, he'd resume his attempts to seduce her. By the time he reached the chapel, Edmund was sprinting, struggling for breath. He sped around the corner and under the wooden bridge that connected donjon to the north tower. Soon the stables were in sight.

"Where's Romena?" Edmund screamed as he entered the yard. "You!" he shouted at a stable boy, "Where's Romena?"

The boy jumped out of the way as Edmund charged the stable doors. From within he heard the soft nickering of horses anticipating his approach, the bells of falcon gyves. He also heard Francesco's low, soothing voice as he calmed his precious birds. Inside it was black, with only orange shafts of molten light pouring in from between the rough-hewn planking of the stable walls to illuminate the path from door to hayloft. Edmund paused at the threshold to catch his breath. The pungency of new hay, horse sweat, and dung, usually welcome and familiar, now drew nausea.

"Francesco!"

"What news?" Francesco demanded, not bothering to turn. He was comforting his peregrine and seemed uninterested in Edmund's discomfort.

"There's an army at Pratovecchio. I saw the advance troops. We'll be set upon by nightfall if we don't act quickly."

"So much for diplomacy," Francesco answered. The birds in their cages, he bade Edmund follow him to the chapel.

"Sit down, Edmund," Francesco directed, closing the doors behind them.

"We've called for reinforcements; I should be with the garrison."

"Sit down."

The voice was to be obeyed.

Francesco paced the chapel, pausing more than once at new stained-glass windows over the sanctuary, studying them. At one particular window, depicting the legend of Santa Fina of San Gimignano, he paused inordinately and sighed.

"I know I'm the cause of your discontent, Edmund. I've not been able to please anyone of late."

"That isn't it, Cecco—Gesù! They're coming for you! Now isn't the time to make reparations or offer apologies!"

"Isn't it? I've made promises I've been unable to keep. You came to Florence with hopes, and I've let you down."

"Not so much as disappointed. Must we talk about this now?"

"Understand me, Edmund. I had to secure Gian Maria's men and his trust. That is how we won Fronzola. And that was the beginning of my restoration, such as it is. I mean to keep all that I have, no matter how difficult, be it politics or men that confound my efforts."

"True, but now Gian Maria is dead," Edmund responded, at last willing to open old wounds. "Focognaio is now in the hands of Porciano. Forgive me, but I think that gifting of the castle was the truest measure of poor judgment."

"I'll respect your opinion. Don't turn on me, Edmund. Don't betray me. I don't need your tutelage in statecraft or in the darker side of men. I've suffered it and I've practiced it. Heed this, and remember."

"I would not have betrayed you. The man came to me," Edmund volunteered, though why, he didn't know.

"In days to come, I shall have need of a man I can trust. Should that man be you?"

"It always has been."

Francesco sat heavily on a bale and ran his hands through his hair. Edmund noted how his hands shook and the sweat dripped from his brow and chin though the day was cool. "How many lessons do I have to learn?" he muttered low, as if to himself.

"Cecco, what's—"

Francesco had thrown himself off the bale and heaved into the straw, nothing but bile and blood coming up. "It's nothing. It's the medicines . . . I'm sure it's that," Francesco apologized, and then, "Go and find the others."

"You're not going anywhere but to bed! I think we can manage alone."

"Just do as I say!" Francesco gasped.

Edmund nodded but refused to make a move until Francesco limped out of the stable and grabbed one of the boys as a crutch to help him to the donjon.

❧

THE FORCE OF the solar door being thrown roused Francesco. He couldn't be certain if he was still asleep; the shouts of men, coming in and out of his senses like waves upon a shore, were part of a dream. His hands groped drunkenly for the blankets, unsure of their proximity. Somewhere in the tangle of linen and soft wool lay his sword. The voices continued to come to him in waves of shouts and curses. He smelled meat roasting on spits.

Movement came with difficulty. How was the simplest task now impossible?

Francesco tried to stand and fell headlong into a wave of blackness. When he came to, the enclosure of the bed was pitch-colored. He couldn't see his hand in front of his face.

The lamp above the bolster had been extinguished.

Why?

Wrenching open the bed curtains he saw nothing amiss. There by the dying fire was his favorite alaunt bitch. His clothes still lay in a heap on the floor, and under his pillow he found Serafina's dainty sapphire ring. He made several attempts to slip it on the small finger of his left hand and finally succeeded. The blue-grey light of dawn was creeping in through space in the arras. But then he turned in bed and saw Edmund, who had entered unannounced and armed. Lorenzo came running after him. From below came the shouting of men and the unmistakable sound of metal meeting metal in combat, the pounding of missiles against the gates of the inner bailey.

"We're besieged!" Lorenzo cried.

Francesco struggled out of bed. Even dressing himself was a Herculean effort. Lorenzo, frightened and trembling, was fortunately there to assist. Francesco noted his anxiety and ruffled the boy's hair affectionately, managing a smile for him.

"How many armed are we?" he now asked Edmund.

"One hundred and fifty, at most. Reinforcements have yet to arrive from Poppi."

"Damn me for a fool," Francesco swore and pulled the arras back from the window to see for himself. "They've penetrated the first wall and outer bailey. How could that be?" Francesco swung toward Edmund, an accusatory scowl on his face.

Why wasn't he surprised by Edmund's unwonted silence? Alarmed by his cool indifference? An innocent man would protest such a charge. Yet Edmund avoided his glance, choosing to pace the chamber like a trapped wolf.

"Set the women on the roof with the pots, arm them with crossbows. And find Roberto,"

A man had been dispatched though Francesco could not remember his leaving, but there he stood again, shouting at him and gesturing frantically toward the door.

"Jesus wept! Francesco!"

Roberto had at last entered and his cry alerted Edmund, who turned and saw Francesco slumped like an overladen sack against the bed. Lorenzo was trying his best to hold the giant on his feet, but the task was too onerous, and they both crumpled on the chests surrounding the bed. Roberto wrenched Francesco to his feet and shook him, and then struck him so hard Lorenzo cried out and threw himself between the men to stop what he thought was abuse.

This wasn't supposed to happen.

That Francesco might die never occurred to Edmund. It wasn't too late and surely when he explained all, Francesco would understand. Edmund shoved Roberto and Lorenzo aside and took Francesco in his arms, shaking him as easily as if he were crammed with straw and rags.

"Francesco! Can you hear me? Francesco!"

"Some wine," Lorenzo offered.

"That would as quickly kill as cure, boy!" Edmund barked, and turning, pointed at the table. "There! The water ewer."

The ice-strafed water doused on his face and the pounding on the door brought Francesco out of his stupor. He had the presence of mind to know the danger they were in and tried reaching for his broadsword. Edmund took it from him, saying, "You'd do more injury to yourself than anyone on the other side of the door. Can you stand, Cecco?"

"I don't know. What's happened?"

Edmund left Francesco with Lorenzo and grabbed a pike and threw Francesco's broadsword at Roberto. Leveling the pike, he motioned Francesco and Lorenzo behind him. By way of eye contact and hand signals, he told them what was afoot. Roberto unbolted the door and stood out of the way as Lorenzo opened it. As Alberti's soldiers tried to gain access, Edmund skewered them against a wall.

"There's another way," Lorenzo said, and he pointed the way through the garderobe to a hidden stairwell, the safest route they could take.

They had to fight their way out of the donjon, engaging the enemy at every turn, almost dragging Francesco as he struggled to come out of his stupor. Down into the hall, through the bailey, they stepped over bodies and broken furniture in their haste, dodged fires threatening to consume the entire donjon. They finally reached the gatehouse, where they tried to lower the gates and prevent the rest of Alberti's army from overrunning the castle. Showers of hot, sticky oil fell upon the invading soldiers as they came under the murder holes, and then flaming arrows cascading from the parapets lighted the oil. Missiles were projected from tension engines and trebuchets, but the Alberti army surged over the walls.

"Someone let the bastards in!" Roberto shouted when they reached the gatehouse.

"Escape while you can," Edmund shouted at Francesco while Roberto, Lorenzo and he tugged and pulled at the gate ropes.

"I'll stay with my men."

"We can manage ourselves. Azzelino wants you and doesn't care about the rest. Escape while you have the chance!" Roberto said.

"And what will happen if you die?"

"We die—but you'll be alive to deal with them, and I don't envy them that."

Francesco wiped the sweat from his eyes and blinked until Edmund came into focus. "And you? What would you have me do?"

"Go."

"God help you if you betray me at the last—"

"Go, damn you!"

Francesco shook his head and stood guard as the other three assaulted the ropes again. They worked the unyielding cords until their hands bled and their backs ached from exertion, swung from perilous heights over a nest of Alberti's archers and dodged arrows. Finally, the groan of metal gave assurance that their labor had been worth the risk. The gate started to move.

Francesco slid precariously down the gate cords and scrambled after a mare charging out of the stables, using what little strength he had left to drag himself up into the saddle. Head down, he galloped out of the bailey and toward the east. By nightfall, he and the castle were safely out of his enemies' grasp, for Castello di Romena withstood the siege against frightening odds.

CHAPTER 28

A HOT, BUTTER-COLORED sun woke Edmund. Lorenzo hadn't bothered to draw the arras across the windows the night before, as the past week had been the warmest in April that anyone could remember. Now dazzling light burned into the solar and made Edmund particularly cross. He reached for the wine and found the flask empty. Lorenzo didn't answer the shouts and Edmund cursed him for a whoreson. Since Azzelino's aborted attempt at taking Castello di Romena three months ago, the boy had been sulking like a lovesick girl over the loss of a sweetheart.

The door finally creaked open a notch when Edmund shouted again and Beatrice Fiasella poked her head in.

"What's this? Come in, girl!" Edmund greeted, his temper greatly improved. He was genuinely pleased to see her and he was just in the mood; mornings were always the best time for seductions.

The girl brought a tray laden with food and drink, setting it among Francesco's personal effects still cluttering his table. She paused there as if it were a holy shrine, touching his favorite cloak, the violet one, feeling the luxuriousness of the fine wool. *Most probably it would still have his scent and she'd partake of that pleasure too*, Edmund thought jealously.

"Where's the boy? Where's Lorenzo?"

Beatrice startled at the sound of his voice. No doubt she expected to hear his voice. Something lower and pleasing, more sensual.

"Gone to Pratovecchio with the others—it's market day," she answered.

"You've brought enough for two. Why don't you join me?" he offered. "Bring it here."

She carried the tray to the bed and set it uneasily on the coverlet and stepped back, eyes downcast.

"You've roses in your cheeks, Beatrice; were you hoping to find Lorenzo here?"

"No, signor! I, I,"

"Could it be you fancy yourself in love? Lucky man. You're very pretty. I told Francesco that when we first came to Castello di San Galgano."

Beatrice glanced up and saw how attentive he was. She couldn't take her eyes off his naked chest, the great expanse of muscle carpeted by auburn hair. He was goodly to look at, but Romena's body was more perfect, and as she remembered it, more like Adonis than this Hercules.

"Come, girl. Come and eat."

"As you will, signor."

Edmund watched her as she picked at the food as a bird might forage for grain. He chose one of the darkest, reddest apples and bit in, the juice traveling in rivulets down his beard, sparkling across his lips. Wordlessly he offered her the apple and she partook, biting where he had, the act almost sensual, for the juice spilled onto her throat and wandered in between the round breasts just topping her thin summer gown, leaving a glistening trail that beckoned exploration. The apple passed back and forth until the core was thrown to Francesco's suspicious alaunt.

"Now let's see how you taste," he whispered, leaning across the tray between them.

Their lips met awkwardly, at first, Edmund excited by how her body responded in just one brief touch. She tasted sweet, and when he ventured a deeper, more sensual kiss, Beatrice innocently rested a hand against his chest and pressed closer, wrapping her arms around his neck. There was no indifference in her response.

"Your kisses are witchcraft, Beatrice," he purred.

"Surely not, signor! I am a Godly daughter!" she protested and he tried not to laugh at her naivety.

"What I meant to say is that I want to taste more."

She nodded and offered her lips again.

"I'll not force you, lass, but surely you're willing. There's no one to stop you," he said gently.

She looked at him from beneath the silky coal-black lashes spilling onto her cheeks. "Do you love me?"

Edmund smiled and enclosed the delicate hand still resting on his chest with his own. Why was it they all wanted to hear that? Still, if it made a difference . . .

"Do you?" she asked again. "I hope that you might, you see, because you pay court and my father thinks you are a goodly man worth ten of Signor Romena, and Signor Romena never . . ."

His hand dropped to the coverlet. *Romena again!* Edmund studied her earnest face—sweet, all too naive—and decided he'd had enough of Francesco. Well, there were some things he was better at than his handsome and charming friend, and he wanted nothing more than to prove it. He'd see to it that she left the solar wanting no one else.

"Did he?" Edmund ventured.

She looked forlorn and shook her head. "No. But I had hoped."

"Well Beatrice, you needn't hope for nothing. If I say I love you I want nothing more than to show you how much!"

Beatrice smiled as Edmund drew her down beside him. She closed her eyes when they kissed and remembered that night in the loft room at Borgo Rovinate. It wasn't Francesco in this bed, but it was Francesco's bed.

☙

ROBERTO CLIMBED THE solar stairs two at a time and waited for Edmund to answer his calls and knocks. Lorenzo was gone from his pallet in the antechamber, as was the great alaunt bitch. The servants were gone, too. He heard voices, though, and drew his sword just in case. Roberto now tried the latch, surprised to find it free. He was more surprised when he entered the solar and saw the bed curtains open, stopped short upon seeing the couple on the bed, the tangle of arms, legs, the seductive curves, the rhythmic movement. Roberto decided he'd seen enough and tried to back out quietly. He misstepped and knocked over a basin of water. The couple turned and Beatrice shrieked, covering herself. Edmund fell back on the bed and swore softly.

"What is it, Roberto?" he demanded. He was not so much angry as amused, delighted that Francesco's lap dog stared jealously at them. He knew Roberto lusted after Beatrice, recognized the smoldering glances and charming banter that came from his quarter whenever she happened to be around.

"They've found men outside the castle walls. Miners more than like. They were found at the eastern culvert with shovels, but they were caught in the midst of their work. They're below."

Edmund climbed out of bed and while he dressed listened disinterestedly to Roberto's report. "Why couldn't you see to it?" Edmund grabbed the wine flask and took a long drink, passing it to Roberto, who shook his head.

"I have no authority to pass judgment," Roberto said and then leaned closer to say, "I heard a rumor; I heard Fiasella was privy to Azzelino's attack and he means to betray Francesco." He glanced at the bed where Beatrice cowered under the blankets. "Is it true?" he asked her.

"No! All that we have we owe to the Romena!" Beatrice protested, pulling the blankets and sheets around her so that Roberto would stop staring.

"Where do you hear these things?" Edmund laughed. He grabbed his sword and belt on the way out and nudged Roberto towards the stairs. Roberto refused to move and swung round to face him. "Well? What are we waiting for?" Edmund demanded.

"You have your own apartments. In Francesco's bed?"

"Take ease," Edmund laughed. "She's not his property. She's not his Serafina."

☙

EIGHT OF AZZELINO'S men had been put to the sword after a hastily convened council passed sentence. Roberto saw that the executions were carried out and was soon arguing with Edmund about reporting the incident to Francesco.

"If we knew where he was we could tell him, but we don't, so we can't. Let that be the end. We have more important matters to deal with."

"Judas was less obvious than you, Clifford," Roberto snapped.

"There was a report of raiders near Pratovecchio. Do Francesco a favor by taking some men to find out what that's all about?"

"...Clifford!"

They turned at the sound of the shout. A rider was fast approaching and carried a white banner.

"Azzelino!" Roberto hissed. "What's he doing here?"

"I invited him to treat," Edmund shrugged. "This war can't go on forever."

"Does Francesco know about this?"

"He'll thank me for it. Send ser Azzelino to the solar. I'll meet him there. Then see about those raiders." Feeling pleased with himself, Edmund returned to the solar and sat before Francesco's table to look industrious when Azzelino arrived. He had barely enough time to shuffle documents when Azzelino pushed his way in past the sentry.

"Are you out of your mind?" Azzelino growled.

"I should ask that of you, coming here," Edmund remarked. "We have an agreement—"

"And I've got half a mind to go back on it!"

"Then you'll be just like Romena, and I'll be back to where I started. I don't like the idea of destroying cousins, but if I must, I will."

"It's hard enough getting men without having you murder them! Gesu, the number you killed when Francesco escaped!"

"And what should I have done? Nothing? To spare your adversaries in war looks suspicious. If getting what I want is going to be jeopardized because of the more stupid of cousins—"

"Easily, Clifford! One thing Francesco da Romena hates is a traitor."

"Because of your stupidity, Francesco already suspects the worst of me."

"And why is that, especially if you give the man reason to suspect you?"

Their quarrel was interrupted by Fiasella, who entered and threw a bundle of dispatches on the table.

"Why you let him into our confidence . . ." Edmund murmured, and ignored the evil glance Azzelino threw at him.

"Well?" Azzelino rasped, grabbing the wine flask before Fiasella could empty it.

"Those were found on a Romena messenger. Had to kill him for it."

Azzelino hungrily tore at the letters and, making a disgusted sound, tossed them into the fireplace. "What good are bills of sale for cloth? You're an idiot! How much money do I have to spend on men I can trust?"

"To do your dirty work or to warm your sheets at night?" Edmund sniped.

"I ordered you to find him and you bring back parchment," said Azzelino.

"Can't be helped. No one knows where he's gone. No one would say if they did," said Fiasella as he reclaimed the flask.

"A man as obvious as Romena doesn't fall off the earth!" Azzelino sneered, and Fiasella got out of the way of his boot.

Edmund took a turn at the wine flask and drank deeply before saying, "Well, did anyone go to the Garfagnana? She's locked up in a castle there; that's what I've heard."

"The Garfagnana?" asked Fiasella innocently, "Who's 'she'? Who's locked up in a castle?"

Azzelino began to laugh and told Edmund he was quite right, but Francesco was smarter than to play into his enemies' hands. Azzelino knew for certain that Gherardo was keeping Serafina Giustini a prisoner in one of his castles, and Gherardo knew Francesco would try to rescue her if he discovered her whereabouts. There were rumors of an attempt.

"There's another who may know of Romena's whereabouts," Azzelino said of a sudden.

Edmund shrugged. "Gentlemen, it must be seen that I'm still Romena's second. Will you take your conversation and plotting elsewhere and let me see to the business of the castle?" He relaxed when they left the solar deep in intrigue, leaving him to make plans of his own. He pulled the map of Romena's lands out from under a pile of ledgers. Of late he found great pleasure in it, wondering how many of the fortresses would end up in his lap. Treachery was an ugly, uncomfortable fact of life but look where it got you if you knew how to play the game. Too bad Francesco hadn't learned that by now . . .

"If you want privacy to meet with Francesco's enemies, you ought to lock the door."

Beatrice had pulled open the bed curtains and stepped down to the floor, arms folded across her breasts so that the low-cut gown draped provocatively. By the dark cast of her eye and sharp voice, she was in no mood for another seduction and Edmund let the notion go as quickly as it came to him.

"There's no need for privacy; the conte di Romena's household is one of trust and freedom."

"Perhaps once. Does he know you betray him?"

Edmund avoided the question by organizing the documents and books on the table.

"It must be true if you cannot answer me."

"It is none of your concern."

"When Francesco discovers this treason it will be your end."

"I did nothing but look to myself!" Edmund hissed and turned on her. "Go about your business, girl!"

Nodding, Beatrice curtseyed and smiled up at him. "Indeed I will, signor." That gave Edmund pause. Was the girl going to hold it over him, and for what purpose? Edmund followed her out, trying to explain himself. Beatrice refused to listen, saying, "I shall pray for you!" She noted carefully how the hands trembled and how pale his face had become. He would need her prayers.

That night when Edmund called her to his bed, Beatrice wore the blue silk gown Romena had given her, wore her mother's best jewels and looked the part of a noblewoman.

"Well now, here is a great lady!" Edmund teased as he rose to meet her with a kiss. Beatrice turned her cheek towards his lips and moved away.

"It becomes one who has decided to be great," Beatrice replied.

"Just like that?" Edmund snapped his fingers.

"And why not? You managed it for yourself. Imagine Signor Romena's surprise when he returns and finds us both well above our stations."

"What are you playing at?" he said suspiciously.

"I am doing openly what you've done by stealth. Marry me and I'll keep your secrets safe."

He was surprised, rather, shocked, that his complaisant little bedmate had suddenly found a spine. Edmund wondered if Beatrice's clever mouse of a mother had planted that seed.

"I am a soldier for hire, Beatrice. Surely your father would be happier with a merchant or notary for you. Respectable in every way."

"Will you go back on the words and promises you made to me last night?"

"What promises?"

"That you loved me and found delight in me, that I am the most pleasant of bedmates."

"And so you are, and so I did make those promises. I told you the truth. Now, why don't you take off that precious gown so that I can show you again how high I hold you in regard?"

Edmund patted the bed and pulled back the covers to make room for her.

"Not until you swear," the girl replied coolly, but she undressed anyway, making it a show. Movements were slow and sensual, even while removing slippers. She pulled the shift over her head and dropped it on the bed, standing naked before him and out of his reach. The sight of her in the moonlight roused and angered him.

"So be it. You'll have your way, Beatrice. I swear! I swear to marry you."

Beatrice took a crucifix from the wall and held it before him. "Now swear again."

It was a prelude to the most disturbing night of Edmund's life, made worse when Beatrice cried out Francesco's name, and not his.

CHAPTER 29

NICCOLO PERUZZI WATCHED as Romena goods came into his grandfather's banking house and were locked up in vaults. He quietly seethed while German and Milanese harness, silver and gold plate, fine cloth, jewels, and coffers of florins were tallied by the clerks. For an entire week carts arrived from the Casentino full of spoils and their contents assessed and cataloged. Niccolo kept to his work and feigned indifference until the afternoon Azzelino Alberti called at the Peruzzi banking house. "Welcome back to Florence," Niccolo greeted when he was shown into a private chamber on the third floor.

"And you. You've just returned from Avignon, I hear."

"Would that I had stayed. I'd still be in ignorance about your dealings."

"You disapprove!" Azzelino laughed. "Of all the men in Florence, I thought you'd be the most pleased."

"I have no time for your political intrigues, and when you ruin a man you ruin my family because that man won't be able to pay his debt to us."

"I'm taking what has been promised to me," insisted Azzelino. "The gamble was well worth the effort."

"Do you sleep easy now that you've got revenge?"

"If you want something in this world you must take it, whether by force or no."

"Spoken like a true man of holy orders."

"Where do you think I've learned statecraft?"

Niccolo rose from his desk to consider the ledgers brought to him by a clerk. Waving the clerk out, he shut the door again and affected interest in one of the entries. "Do what you think you must do. I suppose I should be thankful for Romena's sake that Serafina is out of your reach."

"All in time!"

"He's not one to be stopped when he wants something, Azzelino. You know that."

"Have you entered Francesco's camp?" Azzelino demanded.

Niccolo glared at him. "I've entered no one's camp."

"As if I'm supposed to believe that! You sound more and more like Francesco da Romena and his supporters every day!"

"I only speak of what I know," Niccolo explained himself quietly.

"You know very little, then!"

"I said I wouldn't help you. If you're finished, please leave; I have much to do before returning to Avignon."

"We're not finished," Azzelino said as he rose to leave. "You'll come around. You have before. This isn't any different. Good day."

"Azzelino! The best way to make a grave for yourself is to take from Romena—whether it be a castle or a woman—and I hear Francesco da Romena is the best of grave diggers."

᜕

THE BENEDICTINE BROTHER scowled at Niccolo and told him to wait where he stood, it being the greatest imposition and outrage that a usurer, the absolute worst of sinners, should request an audience with one of the community. Niccolo sat resolutely on a bench in the guesthouse and did what he was told. Wait. Wait for two hours. No one at the imperial abbey of Florence knew why he had come, only that he wished to speak with Fra Giorgio.

"But he is contagious! A skin deformity," the brother protested when the request was first made and bent lower, whispering, "a leper! They say he was a Knight Hospitaller in the Holy Land."

"I shall take my chances, Brother. Here's something for the abbey." Niccolo handed over three new gold florins and smiled, jerked his chin towards the dormitory.

The brother stared at the coins in his hands. "Abbate Giordano would never countenance this."

"Do as you're bid."

The brother went out, muttering a prayer.

Another hour passed before the door creaked open and the Benedictine returned with a companion. "Here is Fra Giorgio, Signor."

"Thank you. You may leave us." Niccolo said, and digging further into his purse, pressed another coin into the brother's palm.

As soon as the friar was gone, Fra Giorgio straightened his crooked back and threw off the napkins and cowl obscuring his face. "I hope that wasn't the last of my fortune you gave away, Niccolo," Francesco da Romena greeted.

"What's left of it is safe for the most part, Monsignore. A leper from the holy land?"

"Who would be despised more than a mongrel, baseborn son of a Crusader and one with leprosy? It worked. No one's bothered me a day. Did you speak with the Cavalcanti about my loan?"

"I've heard nothing. They move at their leisure."

"I've been three months in this abbey! Another day will be too late!"

"You're safe here. Who would have thought to look for you right under their noses?"

"One can only take so much piety and bad food," Francesco remarked and then smiled. He extended a hand in thanks, and Niccolo accepted it. "I've found a friend where I did not expect to find one, Niccolo."

"I take no sides in any quarrel. That's how a banker must survive."

There was a knock on the door and Francesco hurried as best he could back into his disguise. Abbate Giordano entered then and nodded at Peruzzi.

"My business with Fra Giorgio is ended, Abbate," Niccolo greeted.

"You may call him Francesco in my company," Giordano replied, smiling. He reached up and unwrapped Francesco's face gently. "Do you know, Signor Niccolo, that I held this man as a baby in my arms? See what he's become."

"Desperate and angry," Francesco answered.

"I shall do my best to convince the Cavalcanti, Monsignore." Niccolo promised, and smiling, departed.

"And now you must wait some more," Abbate Giordano sighed. "The news is not at all good. He has had Porciano proclaimed conte di Romena and him, Porciano's heir. His atrocities—"

"I blame this on you!" Francesco shouted angrily.

"On me? What have I ever done against the Romena?"

"You asked me to be patient, to let Porciano's greed run its course; to expect that Azzelino would content himself with a post at the Avignon court; that he'd soon tire and make peace! I see none of that! I stand to lose all because I listened to you!"

"And you would be dead if had you not listened."

"Death would be better than this!"

In the silence that followed, Abbate Giordano crossed himself. "I shall do what I can to help you. Obviously, it won't be enough!" the abbot whispered as he left.

Later in the day, Francesco hobbled about the abbey from baking houses to gardens in his disguise, looking for Giordano. The day had grown intolerably hot, and the flies buzzing about the stagnant pools of water and the horse dung in the orchards only made it worse. He batted away the insects as he hitched and faltered on his cane, cursing aloud such as a holy brother never would. The brothers tending the fields nodded in greeting, but kept their distance, whispering prayers as he passed. Little did they know how much Francesco truly needed them.

He hobbled into the chapel and thanked God for the gray coolness that met him when he opened the door; he heard Abbate Giordano's voice, low, as if in private conversation. Sure enough, there was the abbot with his confessor. Francesco waited a respectful distance and took a place deep among the stalls to wait. He sat unnoticed while Abbate Giordano finished his confession, one that Francesco was sorry to have heard.

❧

NICCOLO RETURNED TO the abbey three days later and did not wait for permission to speak to Fra Giorgio. He found Francesco in the chapter house with the rest of the community and slipped into the stall beside him.

". . .*tibi, propter magnum gloriam tu am* . . . the Cavalcanti will not grant you the loan," Niccolo whispered.

"*Domine fili uni genite* . . . what?!!" Francesco exploded.

The choir went silent at the outburst and the rest of the community stared in horror while the crippled and diseased leper Fra Giorgio strode out of the chapter house quite healed and quite incensed. The choir burst into alleluias.

"Lappo Cavalcanti is at Siena for the faire," explained Niccolo, trying to match Francesco's strides. "If he won't come to you, perhaps you should go to him."

"My thoughts exactly, Niccolo!"

"It's not something I'd look forward to if I were Lappo."

It was an ugly confrontation, but Francesco had the result he expected. From Siena, he went to Avignon, where he had a score to settle. Fortune's Wheel, which had spun past him so many times looked as if it would finally stop on his marker. Then he decided to go to Avignon, where he had a score to settle.

PART III – THE LEGACY

CHAPTER 30

A LARGE COMMUNITY of Florentines lived in Avignon, lured to Provence by the faire of Beaucaire and a lucrative trade with the papal court. Italians regardless of the city of their birth were called 'Lombards' for the first of the bankers and merchants to arrive in France originated in Lombardy. The streets populated by the Lombards were islands of familiarity and homey comfort for the banker and merchant who traveled between the Italian city-states and the kingdom of France. Familiar tongues, customs, and food were balms for a lonely traveler unless you were Francesco da Romena.

Francesco arrived in the late summer and took rooms in the Place du Chevalier. He was a conspicuous Florentine, spending too much time by himself and dining at seedy alehouses frequented by knights and merchants. As a nobleman, he had every right to take one of the finest houses in the city and hold court but chose not to. His proclivity for solitude more than anything became the fodder for gossip.

At dawn he would rise and walk to the church of St. Michel to hear mass and then break fast at a cook shop nearby. The rest of his morning would be spent calling upon Lombards and Avignonnais to repay debts. Afternoons were spent lurking at the papal court to learn news about Azzelino Alberti and to curry favor with such men as could prove useful if a need arose. In the evenings, he went far from the Lombard community to a brothel called 'The Sinner.'

Madame Eloise looked up from her game of dice with a Sienese cloth merchant when Francesco entered the common room and took his usual booth under the loft.

"God grant you peace, Monseigneur Francois," Madame greeted.

"As much as He decides, Madame."

"We have a new girl from England; her name is Brandgoene. And a pretty Egyptian, if you like them dark," Madame entreated as she motioned to two strikingly beautiful and strikingly different girls posturing for customers. Neither sparked Francesco's interest. The brothel keeper now signed to a girl and she immediately brought a pot of ale and a bowl. Madame made sure the pot was full and large, knowing Francesco da Romena had a habit of drinking to excess those days. Besides, after a pot or two, men were always biddable.

"I heard the news, Monseigneur. You're quite the hero among the Lombards. Congratulations on your success."

"Thank you, but you didn't hear all."

"I hear what I want to hear—that a man of noble birth finally conquered his enemies on the field and has reclaimed his name and fortune. It was all I wanted to hear."

Francesco grinned into the tankard Madame had just filled and upended it, wiping his mouth on his sleeve and holding out the tankard for more. "Yes, I suppose that's how it is, isn't it?" he said between gulps. "We tend to cloud the truth and our stories are remembered for heroic deeds and the truth is somewhere lost in the retelling."

"What does it matter? You went to battle. Your enemies made peace with you. You destroyed your cousin Alberti. Your uncle sued for peace. And as for that cousin of yours, all of Avignon gave thanks to God for his downfall! Azzelino Alberti has made few friends where he wanders!"

"That's how it'll be remembered, but in truth, he escaped. I had him, Madame! He was in my gaol, under my guard and he managed to escape. I shouldn't have trusted him."

"Who? Your cousin? Everyone knows he can't be trusted as far as a man can spit."

"Yes. And there was another."

Francesco extended the tankard and smiled as Madame Eloise filled it yet again.

"Meat and bread, perhaps?" she asked.

"Fresh?"

"You have my word," Madame said, winking.

A plate of bread and venison were placed before Francesco, who ate with little relish. And then he drank. In future, he would regret how much he drank that night.

"Monsieur Romena?"

A pretty harlot dressed in an immaculate but out-of-fashion gown slid onto the bench opposite Francesco and poured out a fresh cup of ale. He thanked her and she asked if he would share some of the bread. The trencher was shoved towards her. Francesco could not place her, but knew he'd seen her once before. He knew he'd never bedded her. Francesco remembered now that she often accompanied the older girls. Rarely did he see her with a customer. She was like their lady-in-waiting, a silent observer.

A pretty, pleasant observer. Isabeau.

"Where are your sisters tonight?" Francesco asked in French, dipping a slice of bread into the pomegranate sauce and feeding it to Isabeau.

"There is a banquet at the house of the English ambassador."

"Were you not invited?"

Isabeau lowered her eyes and blushing, whispered, "No. They wanted fully-bloomed flowers."

It was a moment and then Francesco understood, saying, "Ah. Not those beauties whose buds have yet to ripen?"

"Just so, Monseigneur." The girl leaned over the table to wipe the sauce from Francesco's lips and kept her finger on his mouth. "Again you are sad. Shall I keep you company?"

Francesco studied the girl's exquisite face in the candlelit booth. She was flaxen-haired and possessed white skin that was unadorned by cosmetics. Her eyes, though, were almost black, so black he could see his reflection in them. She had rouged her breasts and hung jewels around her neck so that the gems rested in the hollow between those breasts. Francesco crooked a finger round one of the chains and slowly withdrew an amethyst that was warm and scented from her skin. The act was simple yet provocative, the fine gold chain scraped gently against her, and Isabeau sighed.

"I love your smile," she purred; "Why will you not smile at me? Why are you so sad?"

"I loved a woman and she was taken from me. Rather, I let her go."

"Shall I help you forget?"

Francesco smiled sadly. "You won't help me forget, Isabeau. Here," he said, placing a coin on the table. "Buy something to make you smile." He kissed her then and sent the girl on her way. If she was disappointed Isabeau didn't reveal it for she smiled back at him as she went to Madame Eloise and opened her palm. Madame nodded in approval and whispered to the girl, who ran back to Francesco.

"For your courtesy, Madame says I'm to return your money."

"I'll have none of that," Francesco laughed. "It is my gift to you. Tell Madame I'll claim my prize when the time is right."

She leaned down and gave him a sultry, deep, kiss that had Francesco changing his mind, his invitation to go upstairs lost in the noise of the door as it almost exploded off its hinges when a party of men entered. Isabeau was now on his lap, a hand resting lightly inside his open shirt. There was a commotion at the door and several merchants scattered like leaves. Francesco ignored the activity, being more interested in Isabeau's alluring curves and the taste of her lips. He was ready to find a private place with her when a shadow was thrown over the table.

"For a moment I thought I was in hell."

Francesco glanced up and frowned. Standing above him was Azzelino

Alberti, attired in the scarlet robes of a cardinal. He had enough servants in tow to populate a village. Without taking his eyes from Azzelino, Francesco whispered to Isabeau and sent her away.

"Well, I know for certain I am. Am I required to kiss something, Azzelino?" Francesco greeted.

Azzelino thrust a scarlet-gloved hand in his face. Francesco ignored it and poured more wine.

"How long have you been in Avignon?" Azzelino demanded.

"A few days."

"Liar. I was told that you've been here for months."

"Then there's no need to ask me. Keep your spies on a leash, Alberti."

"Azzelino, Cardinal Alberti, to you!"

"And I am the conte di Romena. You are what, a cardinal now? Aren't you tired of spending so much money on titles and offices instead of earning it by faith and good work? Tired of being on your knees for matters other than prayer? My God, they must be building snowmen in hell, or pigs are flying over St. Peter's!"

"Say another word, Francesco . . ."

"On your way; I have supper to finish." Knife in hand, Francesco made ready to skewer the venison and stopped inches from Azzelino's hand poised over the trencher. "The bread's not worth consecrating," Francesco quipped, and then said softly, "Leave me in peace, Azzelino. You don't want to make matters between us worse."

"In the blink of an eye I could have you dead or in gaol! Do you want that?" Azzelino said.

"Right where I had you? I've got more friends than you. I could be out as quickly as you were. I've done nothing but express contempt. That doesn't warrant an arrest."

"We're not in the Casentino."

When Francesco tried to reach for the knife again, Azzelino gripped his wrist so firmly that his movement overturned the wine. The ruby stain was lost in Azzelino's scarlet vestments.

"I have every reason in the world to kill you, and I'm not concerned about your monkeys and puppets here, so do not test my patience!" Francesco hissed.

"Touch me and the whole of the papal guard will be here."

"Is that a challenge?"

Before Azzelino could respond, Francesco had kicked away the bench beneath him and held a sword to Azzelino's chest. The servants in his retinue drew their swords, but Azzelino waved them off. This was his fight. He took a sword from one of the henchmen and came at Francesco.

Francesco ducked the first assault, throwing his overturned bench at the cardinal, who had no trouble moving in his heavy garb. It was easy to see he was used to this. He kept his eyes on the deadly point of the sword, moving adroitly and out of reach whenever Azzelino lunged. He threw obstacles in the cardinal's path, but Azzelino was light of foot in spite of his heavy frame and stayed clear of any real danger. They battled for a good quarter hour and nothing in the tavern was spared, from table to spoon. The floor was littered with broken pottery and furniture as they fought, meeting parry for parry, matching blow for blow. Most of the patrons had wisely fled and left these two madmen to settle their quarrel.

Azzelino cornered Francesco under the stairs, and for a moment Madame Eloise thought her friend a dead man. The remaining spectators fell silent, waiting for the end. Francesco managed to hold Azzelino off until he lunged and parried the thrust so violently it found its scabbard in oak and broke his sword in two. Madame Eloise threw Francesco a broadsword and got out of the way.

Letting loose a guttural cry, Francesco wielded the heavy weapon and grunted when it plunged into a table, wrenching it free and swinging it at Azzelino, who spun about and managed to tackle him to the floor. Francesco tried to break away but felt fingers at his throat, a knife perilously close to his eyes. He rolled, Azzelino tumbling wildly over him. Within his line of sight, Francesco saw the knife sail out of Azzelino's hand and land close by. If he could reach it . . .

The explosion of a fist on his cheek, then the burst of light and the taste of blood made Francesco pull back and hurl himself against the wall. He scooted on his back, watching Azzelino as he kept moving. The knife was there under Azzelino's foot. Francesco threw a punch and managed to catch Azzelino off guard for a second. It was enough time to grab the knife.

With one quick movement, Francesco thrust the knife up, feeling cloth and flesh part under the blade. Azzelino staggered back, clutching at his chest.

Francesco dropped the knife and ran and didn't bother to look back as the papal guard arrived to apprehend the felon who had done injury to a cardinal, a man of God.

CHAPTER 31

"...AND YOU KNOW this for a fact?"

Andrea Alberti reached for his cup and drank quickly, never taking his eyes off the Venetian merchant. He gestured abruptly, the merchant settling noisily on a bench at Andrea's table in The Rose and Knight.

"Messer, I was there. It was never an even match; the conte di Romena might have killed him. Well, it's easy to see which of the two is under God's protection!"

"And the cardinal?"

"He'll live, that's what I heard the next day."

"What of the conte?"

"He's somewhere in Provence last I heard."

"Impossible! Why was he not arrested? Why was it allowed?" Alberti protested. "Now you see what's become of our holy mother church since the pope moved to Avignon! Corrupt, full of vice, simony,"

"That was the case before," the merchant scoffed. "Romena was provoked. There were plenty of witnesses other than myself. The Holy Father had no choice but to drop the matter. There are too many Florentines in Avignon who would have taken Romena's side in the quarrel. It would have been bad for business."

Andrea finishing his cup and poured another. "Pope John cannot afford to offend us, what with his problems with the French King. Still, something should have been done. Where is he now? Francesco da Romena?"

"No one knows for sure."

"Well," Andrea sighed, throwing coins on the table and reaching for his cloak. "We know for certain he'll be coming home. There's nothing preventing that. Good night, signor. Thanks for the news. There's something for your supper and another pot of ale. Drink to Francesco da Romena's health. Everyone else will."

Walking home in the autumn twilight, Andrea had to admit he was a little disappointed Azzelino had survived. Too bad he couldn't have had a man like Romena for a son; Romena had a way of making life interesting. And life had been quite interesting of late. There was a change in the air. He could smell it, like the overripe fruit in his orchard, and like the scent of rain from the gathering clouds over the Arno Valley.

An impasse settled on Florence in that year. Life became dull, predictable, and quite ordinary. The economy was poor, owing to a third bad harvest. The people of Florence were content so long as there was enough grain to make bread, but it was anyone's guess how long the staple would last.

Fortune was smiling on Alberti in those lean days. His old worries were gone. And he lived in state, reaping the rewards of a wise decision to stay clear of foolhardy schemes.

"Good evening, Bernardo," Andrea greeted the steward when he arrived home. "Be certain the wool shipments from England are brought inside tonight; there's sure to be a storm." Looking across the hall at his daughter's quiet face, Alberti didn't doubt it.

"Hello, Father," she said, returning to her reading.

"Be of cheer, Cunizza," he said jovially.

"Why do you say that?"

"Life is good."

"For some," she snapped.

"I know what ails you. And take heart, we'll find another husband for you," he said, a nervous smile crossing his lips.

The cold, fair beauty of this legendary widow was particularly chilly that evening. Cunizza closed the breviary she held and folded her long, exquisitely tapered fingers over it.

"What makes you think I want a husband?" The words fell as icicles melting under a new sun.

"Isn't that what every woman wants? A husband?"

"What every woman wants is to have her own way."

"Humph! You've gotten your way more times than I can remember. And by the by, the podesta's agents were sniffing 'round again."

"I've said everything that needs to be said." Cunizza's eyes were like steel and her face as cold and uninviting as the stone Madonnas littering Florence.

"Obviously, it isn't enough! Porciano and his wife seek retribution and mark me, they will have it. Make up something, for God's sake! Tell them Gian Maria tried to strangle you."

Andrea was about tell his daughter of his conversation at The Rose and Knight when they were interrupted by a servant who looked as if he'd been to supper with the devil. "Well? What is it?" Alberti demanded when he could stand no more of the boy's sputtering.

"It's all over Florence, Messer!"

"What? Out with it!"

"Francesco da Romena has come home!"

Outside there was a flash of lightning, followed by the sound of rain breaking on the oilcloth panes.

❧

TOMMASO DA PORCIANO watched the rain and ignored his wife's entreaties to come and finish supper before it went cold.

"I hope the Lord our God has answered Francesco's prayers. Now that you and Francesco have made peace, it's time that he lived his life in quiet. That we all do." Elisabetta said, voicing her thoughts aloud. "In these hard times, one can only hope for boon companions. I've heard it said, husband, that you are being praised in the great houses for making peace with Francesco."

Tommaso glared at her. "I didn't think I had a choice, wife!"

"Think what you like about Francesco, but you know it was the way of things, and it had to be." Elisabetta paused and set her knife down. "There is another matter and one that has been troubling. I know you gave money to Azzelino to support his enterprises."

Rather than answer, Tommaso turned to the window again, reaching out to let errant raindrops sting his fingers and wishing they were the florins he'd squandered on Azzelino's futile stand against Francesco. "The rain's let up; weather's taken a turn for the better," Tommaso murmured, watching a brilliant rainbow arc across the sky and end somewhere in the Borgo Santi Apostoli. *Impossible!* Even God wouldn't play that cruel a joke on him.

No, the joke came a month later, and it was one that made him take stock in his life's ambitions and come to the conclusion that some things and some people were better left alone, that a thing once of the greatest import had no importance at all.

It began as a head cold for Francesco da Romena and then grew into something much worse for everyone concerned.

❧

"MONSIGNORE, ABBATE GIORDANO is outside."

Having repeated this sentence twice now, Lorenzo waited, countering Francesco's scowl with a nervous smile.

"What does he want?" Francesco asked and then sneezed so loudly it woke up his alaunt.

Lorenzo backed away, keeping his eyes on the large man dwarfed by the larger bed. Black circles still hung round Francesco's eyes, his nose red and raw, evidence of an illness that refused to give way.

"He won't speak to anyone but you, monsignore."

"Does he know I've been in bed for three days with a fever and God knows what else? Give me something to wipe my nose!"

"He won't leave until you've granted him an audience."

"I'm not at all well."

"He's been here all afternoon. If you would?"

Francesco groaned and pulled the bolster over his head. "Send for him," came the muffled reply.

Giordano entered the solar moments later.

"Abbate Giordano, we greet you. Now command us," Francesco grumbled from under his pillow. "I have this day granted petitions, charters, and rights, all from my deathbed. I know the imperial abbey of Florence will not ask for more than it requires or I am able."

"Deathbed, signore?"

"His nose drips and his head pounds," Lorenzo grumbled. "It's more a nuisance than fatal."

Francesco came up for air and sneezed into the napkin Lorenzo produced before Francesco could wipe his nose on the bed linens. "What does the imperial abbey want of me, Giordano?" Francesco asked.

"I come to do service for you, messer conte."

Giordano produced from his sleeve a document, sliding it across the fur skins towards Francesco and saying, "This is something you should have. Ask how I came upon that letter and I will not remember." Francesco turned it over in hands, brow raised. "I beg you read it, and soon. Good day, monsignore."

Francesco ran his fingers over the blood-red gobs of wax imprinted with the imperial seal. A diplomatic entreaty, perhaps. He tossed it aside, in no mood for imperial diatribes. God knew what he'd done this time to offend the emperor. It wasn't until that evening when he returned to his bed he remembered the mysterious document and broke the seals one at a time.

What he read first came as no surprise, but as his eyes darted through the many paragraphs, rage boiled up and the emperor's warnings to take caution were lost.

Giordano was apprehensive, when, after Compline on Thursday of that week, a brother of the order announced Francesco da Romena.

There was no need for formality or cordiality. By the look of him, Francesco had indeed read the letter and knew.

Francesco spoke first, and, much to Giordano's surprise, quietly. "There isn't much else in this world to amaze me."

Giordano stared at the letter thrust towards him. "It's all true, but I suppose you've guessed as much." For one who had dealt a fatal blow, Giordano seemed not to care, as if the letter contained news of a merchant's travels to The Levant.

"Does Azzelino know I have this knowledge?"

"His spies are better than the emperor's if he does."

"All these years, and you never said a word!"

"Monsignore, I promised your mother—"

"She murdered my father! You could have prevented it!"

"I couldn't help Alessandro. He was past help. He didn't want it anyway.

I tried to warn him."

"How did you come upon this confession?"

"I told you,"

"I have a right to know."

"An advantage to serving as an imperial secretary is having access to certain things," Giordano said. "The deathbed confession was given to the woman's lover, and he, in turn, gave it to me. I sent word to the emperor and he made his own inquiries since his interests were being threatened. I told all to the emperor and gave the confession to him. For safekeeping. When we heard of Cardinal Alberti's latest intrigues the emperor thought if the confession was made known, the cardinal would use it for his own advantage against you and Florence."

"The cardinal I can deal with, but this other matter . . . is it true about the bishop of Florence?"

"Yes."

"And you? What of your part?" When Giordano didn't answer, Francesco started to pace. "Don't play me for a fool, Giordano. What good is a confession if you don't learn from it?" Again, Giordano remained silent. Francesco paused before him. "I stumbled upon your confession the afternoon Niccolo Peruzzi came to see me at the abbey. I have no desire to ruin you. I only want to know why you kept it secret and kept it from me."

The abbot sighed, and then shrugged. He smiled faintly. "It is a great relief that someone else should know the truth."

"You might have said something before."

"Would you have listened? I think not. You know what you want to know about your father whether it is the truth or not."

"Why did you condone his murder?"

"An eye for an eye!" Abbate Giordano said softly, and then more passionately, "A life for a life! I held no weapon against him, but my part was just as heinous and sinful. I planned our course of action. But you must understand why I did it. When I refused to cede abbey lands to Romena he took vengeance by raping and murdering my sister and her daughters. The oldest, she was a child! She was twelve if that at all! And the infant—she was barely out of swaddling bands—he was evil!" Giordano whispered a prayer and crossed himself. Francesco saw tears drop on the hands folded in his lap, how the shoulders slumped and shuddered as Giordano tried to compose himself. Francesco was ready to tell him to go no further when Giordano rose and pivoted as if to leave, then turned back. "That was not all. He seized land held by the Bishop of Florence for the emperor. A monastery and a convent. He burned everything and everyone. *Everyone!* He took the chalices and linens, the vestments, the holy relics, the *relics* I tell you! And sold everything to purchase arms and men. Nothing has grown on the land for years because of the desecration. You can see it for yourself; it's only a league from Castello da Romena. He was plotting revenge and for what, we did not know. We were all glad when he died!"

This news notwithstanding, Francesco remained cool, though at any moment thought he would be sick to his stomach. Edmund had once said it was a normal course in life, to suffer and witness the horrors of suffering, that women and children because of their weakness would always be the victims of the most barbaric cruelty. He counseled Francesco to harden himself to the atrocities of war and accept them. Francesco never did, and at that moment knew he could not.

"Albera, my mother, then. She was the one who did it?" Francesco asked when he found his voice again.

Giordano nodded.

"If my father was guilty of all the sins pronounced against him by you and others, then death was what he deserved. But Albera had other reasons."

"How can you—"

"My father's crimes were only an excuse to her. She didn't give a damn about your sister and nieces, the imperial lands, the insult to the Holy Roman Emperor; she only wanted my father's money and lands so she could share them with her brothers and lover." And then, quietly, after a time, "What you did makes me the usurper, not Tommaso, and all the quarreling for naught."

"No one alive knew he'd put aside the girl he married to plight-troth with your mother. No one has to know the truth. The girl is dead, Alessandro is dead. Tommaso di Porciano never knew that secret, leastwise, not that I know of. I don't think there's anyone else."

"There's you and me," Francesco said, and frowning, asked, "Who was Ginevra Salvemini?"

Giordano looked at him in bewilderment. "Don't you know? She was Serafina Giustini's mother!"

Francesco felt a jolt akin to being struck by lightning at the sound of her name. It had been almost two years since he'd heard the name spoken aloud, only hours since he'd thought of her. The mist of a foggy morning, the fragrant scent and the touch of velvety skin under the sheets, the soft laughter and luminous eyes in the darkness of the bedchamber . . .

And then he remembered the afternoon Durante Giustini came to call and told him of the plight-troth.

Was it any wonder that Durante wanted nothing to do with him now? Why would he want his daughter married to a landless, titleless bastard? Who was more dangerous now?

"What will you do about the grant of lands, to Cardinal Alberti, monsignore? And this matter of Edmund Clifford? He's gone too far, and with Azzelino's backing, he is the greater threat."

"No, I'll do nothing yet. This other matter, though,"

"Don't stand idly by and do nothing, I beg of you."

"One thing at a time, Giordano."

❧

TOMMASO WOKE NEAR DAWN to the clatter of horses' hooves and the jingle of harness. A felon being apprehended, he surmised and turned over to settle down to sleep. Good; there'd been robbers in the neighborhood. Strange though, the horses were coming closer and then they were in the street.

Someone pounded on the doors. Before Tommaso could climb out of bed, Elisabetta was there with one of her women.

"What's this?" Tommaso demanded.

"Men at arms are in the courtyard. They forced the gates. Tommaso what have you done? What have you—"

Elisabetta screamed when soldiers of the Commune appeared in the doorway. They stepped aside and allowed Roberto da Quintavale entrance to the bedchamber.

"You've no right to come unannounced and uninvited! I'll have you before the podesta, signor!" Tommaso hissed.

"Then come below; his second waits," Roberto answered.

"Below?" Tommaso laughed. "The town had better be in flames for such a disruption! Else he better tell me what I've done!"

"As you will, messer Tommaso."

They were led to the main hall off the courtyard on the ground floor. The lack of torches unnerved Tommaso. Only a moon piercing the narrow windows and sliding in and out of clouds racing across the sky illuminated the long chamber. Tommaso could see dark shapes at one end of the hall, saw them moving like specters in a nightmare. They were moving quietly and deliberately toward him. Elisabetta clutched at the sleeve of his bed robe as they came closer.

A light flickered from the courtyard and then Francesco stepped from the shadows.

"Was this how it was for my father?" he asked softly. "Was he taken from his lover's bed to confront his murderer?"

"God's holy blood! What do you want? The hour is late!" Tommaso whined.

"After this night, I'll trouble you no further. I've come for answers."

"You might have come at a reasonable hour!"

"Would you have admitted me?"

"We've made our peace."

"Have we? Some would think otherwise."

Francesco pulled out a chair and took a seat uneasily. He motioned to

261

his soldiers and they started to light the torches. Elisabetta immediately summoned her women to find food and drink.

"What do you want? What are you about?" asked Tommaso.

Francesco studied the fine Venetian cup a frightened servant brought and thanked her with a coin as if Tommaso's hall was the common room of an inn. When Tommaso repeated his demands, Francesco, never once taking his glance from the exquisite workmanship of the ruby-colored glass, asked, "Why did you take the blame for my mother? Why did you let everyone believe that Durante Giustini killed my father? Why did you lead everyone, including me, to believe you covered up your part in his death when it was a bold-faced lie?"

"Tommaso, is this true?" Elisabetta spun about, her hair stinging Tommaso's neck and face as she turned rapidly. Though the light was dim, Tommaso could see the high color in her cheeks, the trembling lips.

"Do you see, Tommaso? Even your wife believed the worst of you."

"Francesco, I don't see how this makes a difference in the accord between us," Tommaso replied, avoiding his wife's stricken eyes.

"You allowed your business partner to go into exile for years while you and my mother play out a farce that nearly destroyed our family. Tell me more of the truth, or do I already know?" Francesco voice and face were still soft, but world-weary. "Knowing my mother as you did, did you truly believe Albera would keep any promises she made to you? Is there a child of your union?"

Now Tommaso found himself looking straight at Francesco. He nodded. "A son. Near in age to you, a year older. I don't know what became of him. Albera sent him away to be fostered by country folk. A landowner, actually, in the Casentino. I've never seen him. He may be dead for all I know."

Something in Tommaso's eyes told Francesco it was a lie. Tommaso knew exactly where the boy was.

After Elisabetta had excused herself tearfully, Francesco quietly summoned his men and made ready to leave. He had heard all that he wanted.

"You turn this household upside down without so much as an apology!" Tommaso hissed.

"If anyone is owed an apology, it is your wife. And the apology must come from you."

"What do you want, Romena?" Tommaso growled, his nasty temper finally coming to the surface.

"I told you. I have what I came for."

"I can give you—"

"You don't need to buy my silence. It's not something I wish made public knowledge," Francesco answered flatly as he pulled on his riding gloves. "But least it explains a lot of things. Why men are enemies, for example. Why I had to suffer as a child, why I was brought up to believe my father was a saint and died a martyr's death. I suppose that good Christian end is for you. Why we two kinsmen lived as enemies for no reason. And all because you had a dirty little secret. And why we still cannot make peace!"

Francesco suddenly ripped off a glove and stretched out the naked hand. "Here it is, Tommaso. All you need to do is take the hand and we can be allies, if not friends. Though friendship would be a bitter posset to take, I am willing to make a new beginning. Here."

The room was silent as Francesco waited. Tommaso's hand flinched. The fingers extended and arched, were shoved back into a pocket. Francesco replaced the glove. "I do hope you change your mind. Good night, Tommaso. And thank you."

The rest of Tommaso's night was wasted on argument. Thinking to appease Elisabetta, he went to her room to talk and instead listened to his wife's shrieks and promises of vengeance for all the wrong he'd done, and when at last she fell to sleep, he called for his man and a torchbearer. The sun would be up soon. He'd take a walk to clear his head.

On mornings such as these twenty-seven years ago, he'd leave the Torre Romena reluctantly. Albera's hot kisses were burned into his memory even now, and it seemed only days before that they claimed each other's body whenever Alessandro was away—thank God that had been often!

The promises they made, such grand desires and ambitions. The child coming only made it worse. Lovers soon turned to enemies.

Before she fell to sleep, Elisabetta demanded to know who and where the boy was. Would he cause more trouble if he knew who his parents were? Couldn't she guess, Tommaso laughed? Surely Francesco da Romena had figured it all out.

Surely Francesco had at last realized why, of all his enemies, Azzelino Alberti had always been the deadliest.

CHAPTER 32

EDMUND KNEW SOMETHING was wrong. A day didn't pass that Francesco failed to visit the seneschal's quarters and hear the daily reports. That morning, however, Francesco was absent. No doubt he was delayed in Florence. Edmund watched the eastern horizon an hour past supper and was relieved when Francesco's standard was at last spotted.

"He's coming," Fiasella grumbled, joining Edmund on the wall.

Edmund leaned forward to get a better look as the party rode over the drawbridge. I don't recognize them to a man."

"Does it bother you?"

The tone of voice was mocking. Had it been any other time, Edmund would have shoved the little man up against a wall and skewered him like a chestnut or thrown him over the parapet. Today, however, he merely pushed him out of the way and went down.

True enough, as Francesco rode into the bailey of Castello di Romena, the only man Edmund recognized was Roberto da Quintavale.

Francesco dismounted and dismissed his escort, avoiding the barking dogs circling and clamoring for attention as he walked towards the donjon steps where Edmund waited.

"Monsignore, welcome home."

Francesco glanced at him, brushed past, and turned just as abruptly at the door. "Edmund, come with me. Roberto, I'll need you, also." His mood was off, the cordiality forced.

Once Francesco was made comfortable in the solar he motioned to Lorenzo to leave and close the doors behind him. The three men, Francesco, Roberto, and Edmund, sat at a table with bread and wine between them. The camaraderie of past days was gone. Days when the conversation came easily, when jests about red-haired women flowed as freely as the wine.

"The repairs are coming along," Edmund remarked after a time.

"At least I know I can count on you for that."

The comment was unmistakable in its sarcasm. Edmund, however, chose to ignore it and stretched around in his chair to point to the western wall, where, high above the enormous bed surrounded by expensive, brocaded curtains, was a magnificent oriel window. "If you look at the oriel,

I saw to it that the glaziers and artisans placed your arms there, the silver falcon and chains. And there, where the glass is unfinished, I thought in future the arms of, well, your contessa,"

Francesco thumped his goblet on the table noisily and looked sideways at Roberto. One of those glances that spoke volumes and should have given Edmund cause to shut his mouth.

"What are you implying?" Francesco snapped.

"Nothing. Nothing, at all, Monsignore! I'm pleased with the way things are going here. It's a credit to your industry."

"Give credit where it is due, Edmund. A *soldo* apiece for each man that has spent time from his family rebuilding my castle. You know where to give the greatest rewards."

Edmund waited expectantly, hoping that Francesco would add a jest about his industriousness and reward him for his labor. When nothing came, he took a drink and said, "Monsignore, I was thinking about Focognaio."

"Why?"

"Well, for one, Gian Maria is dead, and you have no one to hold it for you."

"Roberto will hold it for me until God gives me a son."

Edmund laughed. "Knowing you, Cecco, and knowing your history, that may never come to pass!"

The jibe was lost on the other two. Roberto touched Edmund's arm as if to warn or console. Either way, it was unwelcome and Edmund shoved him off, saying tersely, "Ah, let me guess. You've found a bastard somewhere."

"Even if I had, this isn't England. A bastard can inherit his father's lands. Closer to the truth is that there've been encroachments on Romena land near Arezzo. I wasn't in a position to think otherwise. Roberto has already proven himself."

"Had I known . . . "

"It's done. We'll all learn to live with it."

"Am I not a man sworn to Romena?"

"Are you?"

Rather than respond, Edmund drank and now played with his sword, sliding the weapon in and out of its scabbard until it made an irritating and rasping sound.

"If you've something to say, man, say it!"

"I want to take a wife and Focognaio would have suited us fine," Edmund replied, smiling nervously. He was alarmed that Francesco still scowled.

"Marriage? To whom?"

"With your permission, to Monna Beatrice. It is an appropriate match,"

Edmund gushed like a dazed schoolboy.

"You'd take the daughter of a traitor, eh, Edmund? Why not plan a seduction and be done with her?" The tone of voice was uncharacteristic, mocking.

"Because it would be unnecessary, that's why," Roberto spoke out. His eyes went to Francesco first, and then back to the cup of wine he held.

"Tread easily, Quintavale; I'll kill you before you utter another word," Edmund hissed, gripping his sword more purposefully now.

Francesco studied each man's face in turn.

"Roberto? I take it you're against this match?"

"You need only ask Clifford why."

"By the Holy Cross, Quintavale, I'll kill you here and now,"

"Why not tell Francesco that you seduced her in his bed and played at bed sport for most of the day while an army marched on Castello di Romena? An army you knew about."

Roberto and Edmund were on their feet with swords drawn. Francesco parted them by striking the swords with his own. "Is this true?" he demanded.

"The girl came willingly," admitted Edmund, and he laughed, adding, "Just ask Quintavale how willingly she came! He didn't hasten away when he walked into the chamber and discovered us! Thank you by the way for seasoning her, Cecco. It made the pleasure all the more for both of us."

The allusion brought the first profane oath Francesco had ever heard Roberto swear. Roberto reached across the table and grabbed at Edmund's throat, and again Francesco had to tear them apart.

"Enough! Both of you!" Francesco shouted, and shoved both down into their chairs. "Learn from my example, Edmund, and see where love for a woman gets you! As for Focognaio, I'll have to think about it."

Edmund's patience was gone then. "Think about it? What's there to think about? The castle lies empty with no garrison! If you know about the incursions, then you know someone's bound to take it!"

"No one will go near Focognaio."

"I have accepted all that you have done, and all that you have given to me, or not, or promised, or not. This is such a small thing to ask."

"You're desperate. Is the girl with child?"

"No! I made a solemn promise to her that you would consent happily as you did promise her. To give her a titled man for a husband," Edmund argued.

"You go behind my back and do what you please? Perhaps I placed my trust wrongly!"

"No doubt you trusted Gian Maria, and more than once his father tried to kill you, and Gian Maria had a hand in it."

Francesco rose to his feet slowly and glared down at him. He was trembling and hot with anger. "I'll forgive that!"

"I've been as loyal as any man could be, Francesco; I've been your most obedient servant, and ask little in return. All I ask for now is a girl's hand in marriage and the castle you promised me."

"Don't talk to me of your loyalty! How many times in the last twelve months have you gone against me? We have been friends, brothers even! And you do this to me!"

Edmund threw his sword down on the table. "Go to Hell. I renounce my fealty!"

"I'm sorry for that."

"I cannot believe it's come to this! We fought for good and just causes before, but never have you been so willing to risk all for a woman! Yet you deny me one small thing. And what's worse is that you still don't have her!" Edmund shouted.

"You've said quite enough, Edmund,"

"All I ask for is your leavings, for the girl's just that!"

"God's blood! Did you not hear? I said, enough!"

"Do you crawl into her bed whenever the desire for Serafina comes on late at night, when it's too much to bear?"

Francesco picked up the sword and leveled it at Edmund. "I said, enough!"

"By your leave," Edmund whispered, and backed away, bowing toward the door.

Francesco watched, tears smarting. It would end like this, the years of companionship, the love between them.

"Edmund!" Francesco called after him, and he paused reluctantly, glancing at Roberto. "You ask too much! Especially when I know the truth."

Edmund turned. "About what?"

"Do you have to ask? You're the best soldier I know. You must have had a bout with your guardian angel to botch my murder. Think, Edmund; if you'd succeeded, we wouldn't have to go through this unpleasantness. But you wouldn't be sleeping easily at night, even with Beatrice warming your bed. You'd have to keep an eye on Azzelino."

"What did you expect me to do—" Edmund stopped and knew there'd be no defense of his actions.

There it was. The confession Francesco dreaded yet hoped for.

"You hold too much store by promises, Edmund. I speak of promises made to others, promises you made to deliver me to my enemies. And all for a pile of stone and brick! Is that all I am worth to you? A castle? Here's payment in full!"

The room was suddenly filled with soldiers and Edmund blanched when they came at him. Foolishly, he grabbed his sword and would have sliced Francesco's throat if Robert's quick defense had not prevented it. Throwing down the sword, Edmund began to weep. He had written his own death sentence.

Francesco, his face the color of parchment, trembled as he stared down at the man cowering at the feet of two sentries. Without further incident, Edmund was taken into custody and led away.

Was it the most politically expedient action to take? Francesco pondered his actions well into the night. The brightness of the full moon only made him more irritable, and the snoring of the men asleep on their pallets across the room was like the growling of so many dogs that he shouted at them for silence, and called them whoresons when they woke demanding to know what they'd done wrong. Francesco ignored Lorenzo's questioning eyes and went out.

Roberto had taken the second watch and moved out of the shadows to greet him. "Can't sleep," Francesco said.

"May I walk with you?" Roberto asked, falling in step. Francesco shrugged. Roberto knew where he was going and summoned one of the guards to follow along to the gate tower where Edmund Clifford was being kept.

"You don't seem heartbroken about what's happened," Francesco spoke up at last.

"There's not a man in your command who doesn't hate Clifford for what he's done."

"Should I sleep with a knife under my pillow?"

The silvery moonlight made the roundness of Roberto's eyes apparent. "I thought you already did!"

The rest of the way was silent. As soon as they climbed the gate tower stairs and walked down to the passageway to the dungeons, Roberto noticed something different and silently motioned to the guard with them. Francesco noticed it too and pulled Roberto and the guard into the shadows.

A man and a woman were at the door of Edmund's cell, talking in excited, angry whispers. The sentries were standing watch, but for a different reason. After much noise and argument the prison door was open and Edmund came into the woman's welcome arms. As they kissed, the other man growled at Edmund to get a move on. Roberto knew the girl, as did Francesco. It was then Francesco came forward.

"I've run out of pieces of silver," Francesco greeted the startled trio quietly. "Perhaps now is the time to offer a kiss?"

"You always did think yourself greater than the Lord God!" hissed the man and drew his sword. It was Fiasella championing Edmund.

"Go!" Edmund shouted at Beatrice. She hesitated and then threw herself in his arms for a last kiss. When she was gone, he shouted at the sentries to choose their loyalties and attack. The skirmish was heated, fueled more by hatred than by each man's will to survive. Edmund was dismayed when Francesco's numbers swelled, and rather than die there in the cold, damp passageway, ran for his life with Fiasella at his heels.

They were chased out into the bailey and barely skidded under the barbican to freedom as it lumbered down. Roberto watched Francesco's face relax when Edmund was out of reach, out of sight.

"He'll only cause more trouble," Roberto dared to say. His response was a shrug. Francesco continued to watch the horizon.

"I'd rather kill him on a battlefield," he said at last. "That would be more honorable."

CHAPTER 33

A MONTH PASSED uneventfully, then two, allowing Francesco with peace of mind to return to Florence. He was met with deference and courtesy in the streets and shops of the town, took his place in governing council as was his honor when called to serve, and as in Avignon, his quiet existence was only a temporary lull before the next storm. Abbate Giordano's warning came uncomfortably true for Francesco and Edmund's betrayal was a festering wound. Edmund Clifford had sworn fealty to the tyrants of Marciano, the Rolandi, most particularly, Rolandino and his evil son Gibello. For his change in loyalties, Edmund had been gifted with six castles and their towns, castles and towns that lay on the marches of the Romena patrimony and were separated from it by Alberti's fiefs. The rest of the honor was given to Azzelino.

Was it any wonder that Andrea Alberti was at first surprised, and then apprehensive, by the invitation to dine at the Torre Romena?

Francesco's smile was genuine when Alberti entered the hall and offered his greetings. "No doubt you wonder at my summons and the measure of your safety here," he opened.

"Would any man be less concerned?" laughed Alberti. Nevertheless, he turned to make sure the doors were left open and glanced to see if there were any tapestries hanging along the walls, places where assassins could hide. He'd employed that tactic himself several times and knew what a damper it could be to a quiet supper.

A door opened and closed and Alberti started, then relaxed when musicians entered the hall and set up at one end. More servants came and went bringing supper and knights started to appear in doorways and upstairs in the second floor gallery. Francesco watched Alberti jump like a squirrel every time someone passed by or made a sudden noise.

"To prove my honesty in what I am about to do and say, here is my sword." Francesco drew the magnificent weapon from its scabbard at his waist and offered it to Alberti, who only marveled at the beauty of the workmanship in the hilt. "Come and sit. Dine with me," was the next proposal.

A simple meal of broth, bread, cheese, and fruit was laid and the two men dined quietly. Francesco pushed away his trencher and bowl, saying,

"I'm sure you know of Edmund Clifford's gift from the Rolandi."

"I would I had his luck, Messer Conte. Your father and his, Rolandino's, quarreled over the same lands and castles, and to my memory, it was the only quarrel Alessandro lost."

You have lands bordering mine in the south and east, do you not?"

Alberti frowned, ciphering, and then nodded in affirmation.

"Is your daughter still unmarried, Signor?"

"Still,"

"You are no doubt seeking a husband?"

"Still," Alberti repeated himself.

"Look no further."

The news shook Alberti to his boots. His felt a crushing pain in his chest and coughed, hoping it would relieve the air that seemed to settle there. Perhaps some wine. Francesco saw his discomfort and offered a cup.

"Do you mean to say, Messer," Alberti gasped. "Why all of a sudden do you—never mind! It's quite plain! At least, I think,"

"With Edmund the puppet of Rolandino and Gibello, and he a stone's throw from my palatinate, you can appreciate my need for your castles. You have five great fortresses that can protect my land."

Alberti swallowed hard. He nodded. "So what you're offering, what you'd like, Messer, is to have my castles and lands on the Casentino frontier?"

"You wouldn't forfeit them for nothing. I have plenty to go around."

"They would, of course, come as part of my daughter's dowry."

"Of course."

"And do you have something to offer in return? What may I expect for my generosity?"

"The castle of Montemurlo, the rights to faire in its *contado*, the rights to farm. I'm told the land is good for olives and grapes. At least six hundred florins. More, if the Peruzzi will loan it."

"Six? Six hundred, did you say? Can you afford it?"

"I cannot afford not to make this alliance. My other reason is simple enough. I must be certain that there's no trouble from your stepson. Clifford's sworn his sword to Azzelino and together they are a danger. My marriage to your daughter would place me in the bosom of your family, where Azzelino's less apt to cause trouble. I want your word on paper that I shall not meet the fate of your daughter's late husbands and that whatever is mine at the time of my marriage is mine."

"How soon can this come about?"

"As soon as the law permits."

Andrea savored the marzipan-shaped fruits a servant now offered, watched with interest as Francesco played with a crucifix around his neck and stared absently into the fire dying in the hearth.

"My stepson Azzelino is rarely in Tuscany these days," Andrea spoke up.

"We can pay for silence," Francesco said, "but word will find its way to Avignon. We'll have to be ready for any eventuality. Given that it's Azzelino, that could be anything."

"He doesn't have to know. We can wait until all is said and done. And when he does learn, it will be too late for reprisals."

"If done properly, all will be settled before any word gets to Avignon."

Andrea sighed and poured himself a cup. "Ah no, there's too much to be done. It can't happen so quickly, monsignore. I need to speak to Cunizza. I did promise her, you see."

"If you'd like, I can speak with her."

"You? Yes, I'm sure she'll swallow any argument."

"Is she close to her stepbrother?"

"Hates him!"

Francesco nodded. "Your assurances content me. I'll take Cunizza on the conditions we've set forth, and this: if, when all is said and done, after the contracts are drawn and executed, Azzelino just once tries to interfere in any way or tries to do harm either to my person or to my lands, then the contract is worthless from that moment."

"You have my word."

Francesco nodded silently and motioned to Lorenzo, who summoned the clerk. While the contract was being drafted, Andrea continued to watch Francesco carefully, unbelieving both of his good fortune and of Romena's motives.

"Are you certain about this enterprise, Messer?"

"What in life is certain?"

A week later Francesco stood in Alberti's house listening dispassionately as a notary read the terms of the marriage agreement aloud. It was clearly to Francesco's advantage. By this marriage, three-quarters of the land bordering his own vast holdings in the Casentino and Mugello would be his. Francesco da Romena would be the greatest landowner outside of Florence's walls.

He slipped a dainty gold band on the third finger of Cunizza's right hand and kissed her with as much passion as he would a great-aunt with a hairy chin, avoiding her tearful smile of happiness. While the bedchamber exploded into applause and cheers, Francesco stood beside his bride-to-be graciously and accepted the congratulations of those in the room, watching out the window into the garden where a cat ambled from branch to branch of a pomegranate tree. Francesco remembered the last time he'd witnessed a vignette like this. Only then, it was a cold night full of sorrow and rain, and the girl beside him had been torn from his arms . . .

෴

IN A CASTLE high in the mountainous landscape of the Garfagnana northwest of Florence, a separate drama was being played out.

One hundred tapers burned at the bier of Gherardo Ranieri. For three days his widow stood in silent vigil without rest, the perfect example of a dutiful wife.

While she stood at the bier, Serafina thought only of Francesco. Five hundred and seventy-three days had passed since their violent separation. Yes, she'd kept a tally in the margins of her Book of Hours. She counted them like the rain drops spattered on the oilcloth window panes in her bedchamber, the grains of barley in her soup, the stitches taken in a shirt sewn for Gherardo, the beads that slipped through her fingers while she prayed, the hours shut up in the castle tower. In that time came angry, passionate letters from Francesco that went unanswered because to respond would have meant death. Then came miserable silence. Not a day passed when she did not wake in the morning and long for Francesco's arms around her, finding instead that she was alone and her body bruised and broken, just as her spirit.

Now she was free to leave the prison Gherardo made for her. She would go in spite of what Ranieri's family wanted, even if they tried to keep her by force. She would give up everything to go a free woman to Francesco. Of course they would let her go! Nothing would please them more.

Serafina decided she would go to Florence.

CHAPTER 34

THE ARRIVAL OF a young widow in Florence went unnoticed on a dreary Lammas Day. She came on a dusky afternoon with only a canopied wagon, a top-heavy cart, and pack mule in her caravan, unimportant to the faithful country folk leaving Florence with their loaves of bread, freshly baked and freshly blessed. It had rained for three days and the roads were like a thick soup, making it impossible to travel. The wagon was stuck in muddy ruts so many times that the young widow jested to her companion it might be wiser to pitch camp until spring. Hands reached into the wagon for alms, and without a thought to her safety, the young widow gave what she could in spite of warnings from her companion. Before going to her new home on the hill behind San Miniato al' Monte, Serafina Ranieri de Giustini stopped at a neighborhood tabernacle to light a candle in thanksgiving for her deliverance.

"I can just see the tower, Madonna," Marghareta said when Serafina climbed into the wagon again, and they rode over through the Porta San Giorgio and into the neighborhood of the Valdarno. She pointed through the trees at a slate-grey pile of stones above them and off in the distance. "It's such a long way from Florence, though."

"Not that far," Serafina remarked.

"Far enough away from prying eyes, I don't wonder?"

"I've grown used to being alone."

Marghareta leaned over and straightened the severe linen coif Serafina wore, a bright stripe against the girl's black mourning clothes. "Madonna, I've never asked this, and you can say it's none of concern, but it was strange that a man of Ranieri's vigor should die so suddenly, and in his sleep."

"God takes us when He chooses and yes, it is none of your concern."

"Ah, here's the castle! You can see it better from here; it's beautiful! Yes, you did well to buy it, but when you said a country home, I imagined a farmhouse or a hunting lodge. It's too large for us. God's life, will we have enough furnishings for the private quarters?"

"In time; we have enough for now, and more will come later."

"I don't like the thought of your having to beg for what is rightfully yours," Marghareta grumbled. "What a lady brings to a marriage is still the lady's!"

"Unless one is the wife of Ranieri of Verrucole."

"Did you get back your mother's garnet ring?"

"Here," Serafina answered, patting a little velvet bag hanging from her waist. "And the other ring."

Marghareta nodded silently and watched the scenery jostle by as they wound up the hill.

Serafina sighed then, quietly saying, "How difficult freedom will be. I've never been my own mistress!"

The reality of her present situation came to Serafina as sharply as the chill autumn wind that blew over the Valdarno, and it was not unfavorable, nor unwelcome. When the wagon at last rolled into the courtyard of the inner bailey, the sight of her servants, six good men and women dressed in the azure and argent, the blue and silver, of the Giustini, and the blue and silver pennants struck on each of the four towers, made Serafina weep.

"Child, you have your life!" Marghareta comforted.

"I am delivered!" Serafina laughed amidst her tears.

Serafina used the sleeve of her gown to wipe her eyes and said she would go alone into the castle. She disembarked from the wagon and in a regal manner greeted each of the servants before going inside. Marghareta clapped her hands at the gawking servants and had the wagon and cart unpacked in no time, leaving Serafina to explore her new home. By vespers, the living quarters were in order for there was little to fill the large chambers.

"Where is dona Serafina?" Marghareta asked the cook late in the evening as they were finally going up to bed.

"No one's seen her for most of the night," came the reply. "She didn't eat the supper I laid for her in the great hall."

Marghareta stopped in her tracks and buffeted the old woman. "Most of the night?" she exclaimed. "And no one's bothered to look for her? You old fool! She might have fallen out a window! Wake the others! She's not in her right mind these days! *Most of the night!*"

Torches and servants were fetched, and immediately light sailed through the dark corridors and staircases of the castle like fireflies as the household searched from buttery to the topmost tower.

"She's here! Signorina Marghareta! I've found her!" one of the stable hands shouted down the stairwell of the southern tower.

Grumbling and muttering all the way, Marghareta went to see for herself. She whispered a prayer of thanksgiving when she discovered Serafina asleep on a pile of furs and blankets in the great, sparse chamber at the top of the southern tower, a chamber that appeared as if out of nowhere at the end of the spiraling casement from the donjon. Moonlight streamed through the enormous windows and every star imaginable twinkled above in the touchable sky. The entire contado was visible, soft and gray in the night. The flute of a shepherd in a distant pasture was like a cradle song.

"No wonder she ended up here," Marghareta whispered to the cook. "It's a magical place."

The chamber became Serafina's favorite in the castle. Every day Marghareta could be certain to find her mistress there. She knew the carts that pulled up at the postern gate every morning came from the shops and market square of Florence. Servants went up and down the stairs carrying parcels and chests; artisans were employed, and when they weren't decorating the tower chamber, they were eating whatever the cook could manage to find in the larders. One week passed, then two, and finally the activity began to subside.

Marghareta decided she would go see for herself. Thinking Serafina had gone to Florence, she made the corkscrew journey up the stairs and drew her breath at the opulent, sensual apartment created from nothing.

Serafina stood in the center of the room, instructing adoring servants to unpack trunks and barrels. Clothing, books, coffers and bolts of cloth littered the room. Her little spaniel yapped at heels that came and went, sniffed about for something to eat, and at last curled up on Serafina's wedding gown, which had been discarded in a corner. Two of the younger girls were hanging fine curtains of brocaded silk around her bed while another pair were struggling with fine gauze linen hangings for the great windows, windows so broad and tall it was as if they did not exist and the chamber was a garden loggia. The sun shone down in great washes of light and made it unbearably warm, an inconvenience after climbing all those stairs.

"What do you think?" Serafina asked, turning to Marghareta.

"I think it would be better used for a storeroom, a guardhouse, not a bedchamber for a proper lady!"

"It's what I shall make of it and I make it my bedchamber."

"The sun is too warm and bright here. Hang some oilcloths! Those curtains hide nothing! Will you lie in bed for all the world to see?"

Serafina turned from straightening one of the bed curtains and said, "It would be nothing I haven't done before, but now I shall have a say in who shares my bed."

Marghareta realized her blunder and began immediately to apologize. Serafina waved a hand to dismiss the remark and then sent the girls out to find supper. "How many mornings did you enter my dark chamber and find me cowering by the hearth while one of Ranieri's vassals was just buckling on his sword or pulling up his boots?" Serafina asked, folding linens and placing them in one of the bed chests.

Yes, Marghareta knew all too well. She saw that Serafina absently rubbed her wrists where the scars of leather bindings were still visible. On the girl's neck there were other traces of the marriage—scars and bruises. And there were some scars no one would ever see, those on the heart and soul.

"You've never said anything until now."

"Nor will I again," Serafina replied, and Marghareta knew her words to be true. Since the mysterious death of Ranieri, Serafina had been guarded, less apt to share her secrets. Serafina found delight in quiet days spent reading books and tending her herb gardens; hours spent working an embroidery frame or watching the nuns at the nearby convent work looms. It seemed as though her streak of wildness had burned out. In one respect it was a shame, to have lost that girl whose very pleasure in life was to seize it, challenge it, and make what she could of it. Marghareta only wondered when the wounds caused by this evil marriage would be healed and Serafina would be whole again.

"It will be cold here in the winter, and what happens when it rains?" Marghareta chided. "Come; there's a fine solar below. You can see all the way to Pisa from the north windows."

"I like it here. I can watch the moonrise and the dawn break from my bed. It would be like sleeping with no walls about me. Now go find someone else to bother."

"Humph! It reminds me of the loft room I had to suffer when my husband, rest his soul, was a factor for the Davizzi wool merchants." Marghareta grumbled. "We slept with bales of wool and all the vermin that went with them! Over the shop, mind you! How I ever . . ."

"It wouldn't be such a bad thing, would it? To be a shopkeeper?"

"Shopkeeper?" Marghareta squealed in horror. "Oh, no! You're a noble lady!"

"A penniless gentlewoman. I shall have to pay the servants somehow. Honest labor is how I shall do it. It was how my mother managed all those years," Serafina countered and got the response she wanted from Marghareta: a face greener than the apples she now arranged in a wooden bowl.

"Holy Virgin! You're going to—"

"Weave and spin for our bread!" laughed Serafina.

How she was going to do it, Serafina did not know. She had no artisans to rely upon. Widows who took up shop keeping usually inherited a storehouse full of workers and tools.

When Marghareta asked how she would accomplish this monumental enterprise, Serafina shrugged.

"Gherardo Ranieri may have broken my body with his perverse games, but he held no sway over my spirit. In time we shall accomplish all."

Proof of Serafina's resolve in this enterprise came at week's end from

Florence. Marghareta stood with mutton chop arms folded neatly across her ample breasts and watched as a floor loom was erected under the southern windows of the solar. By midday, Serafina was already at work and the lub-dub-lub-dub was like a mother's soothing heartbeat.

"Will you take time from your labor to greet a guest, Madonna?" Marghareta shouted over the clapping of the heddles. "A gentleman's come from Florence!"

It could have meant only one person. The only person Serafina had desired to see for months.

Serafina glanced at her reflection in a looking glass and caught sight of a stranger staring back. A stranger wearing a widow's black mourning cloth and white linen barbette. Tossing the glass and her work aside, she ran upstairs and removed the severe garments she had worn for weeks. Soon she was stripped to her shift and underpinnings. One of the younger girls pulled from an open chest a woolen kirtle the color of a robin's egg and another of russet silk. It took only a moment for Serafina to decide. Blue was one of his favorite colors. When the girl offered a small, jeweled coif, Serafina shook her head. Her hair fell to her hips, a great coppery wealth that caught fire in the late afternoon sunlight. He had always preferred her hair unbound.

"You look like you're going to your wedding bed," Marghareta groused when Serafina skipped past her on the stairs.

Niccolo Peruzzi turned when he heard Serafina's familiar footsteps on the stairs and came up to the landing to greet her with a kiss. He'd not soon forget how her bright face dimmed when she saw him.

"I'd hoped to surprise you," he said, bestowing a kiss on her brow.

"And so you did!"

"But you weren't expecting me."

Serafina shook her head and blushed. Niccolo was always perceptive, always able to read her like a book. He remarked about the loom and the bright azure ribbon of woolen cloth starting to form across the warping threads. When she said that she wanted to make and sell cloth, he offered to see if money could be found to assist her.

"Thank you, Niccolo," Serafina replied, leaving a kiss on his cheek. "I returned to Florence not knowing what to find."

"A friend, perhaps?"

"Certainly that."

Serafina brightened then and offered to show Niccolo the tower chamber. His reaction was much the same as Marghareta's, for his conventional belief was that a lady slept with her secrets in luxury and behind a closed door.

"I'll hang a curtain across the stairway, and here along the wall. That should offer some privacy though why I should need it . . ."

"It will look like a harem!" Niccolo laughed.

"I thought it already did!" Serafina said, and threw open a trunk and pulled from it lengths of expensive cloth. "Help me make it more decadent!"

Niccolo couldn't resist once she smiled. Soon brightly colored silks and velvets hung along the walls and covered the windows, separated the chamber into several smaller chambers that beckoned intrigues and trysts. Pillows covered in gold-embroidered damask were thrown on the window seat and made a comfortable bed. A fur skin was tossed before the wall hearth. The chests supporting the feather bed were spread with more pillows and jewel-colored cloth. All that was missing, Niccolo remarked, was a bare-chested eunuch to wait on his lady's pleasure.

"This is where I expect to always find you," Niccolo invited, and Serafina joined him on the luxurious pillows, leaning her chin on her arm to watch the sun die in the west, her eyes reflecting the light and casting a light of their own.

"God knows how I've missed you!" Niccolo whispered now, tracing a strand of hair as it fell across her cheek.

She reached out to play with the silver aiguillette of the lacing cord to his sleeve, noticed that Niccolo's eyes were riveted to the white stripe on her finger where a wedding band had once encircled it. Self-consciously, she drew her hands one over the other.

"Have you come to save me, Niccolo?" she whispered softly. "Am I in such in need of protection, that no sooner do I enter the town walls, you come to keep me free of harm? To keep me away from him?"

"Serafina, you are my dearest friend. Why should I not care?" Niccolo protested, his face red and his smile insincere and weak.

How easy was he to read!

"I fear your care more than anything or anyone."

Those words echoed in his ears when he left after vespers. They were not as painful as Serafina's request of him.

"Should you have any dealings with the conte di Romena, please convey my greetings."

Niccolo tossed and turned that night, was still awake when the sky turned gray and a pink ribbon of sunlight spread across the Arno valley. His mood was not improved by the arrival of the conte di Romena at the Peruzzi company offices that morning. While the handsome conte bantered familiarly about politics and commerce, Niccolo wondered if he should say anything.

"Monsignore?"

Francesco turned, his hand poised on the door latch. He smiled, brows raised, waiting.

"Nothing. I've forgotten what I did mean to say."

"Come round when you've remembered it, Niccolo. Good day."

"Good day."

Niccolo regretted his recalcitrance the moment he saw Serafina's expectant smile when he arrived to take supper with her several days later. Again she was dressed provocatively, this time in a low-cut rose-pink kirtle with a dark green surcote open at the sides. Her beautiful hair was bound in ribbons, however. Each coil and braid struggled within its bindings and the disarray was breathtaking.

During supper, she spoke excitedly of her weaving. She'd completed the first length of woolen cloth and meant to bring it to the Arte Calimala merchants with the hope they'd purchase it to finish. She begged for gossip. Was the widow Cunizza looking for a husband again? Was it true that one of the most devout wives of Florence, Esmerelda Cavalcanti, was found naked in her married lover's arms in a garden near the church of Santa Croce? Did any persons of great import come to do business that day?

When Niccolo answered the first two questions and shrugged and shook his head as to the last, Serafina became despondent. He did his best to cheer her with stories of the newly acclaimed beauties of Florence, of the jongleurs who had come from France to sing in the halls of the noble houses, the new frescoes in the church of Santa Croce, the new fashions that would look best on her. Not once did he mention that which she would have given her soul to hear.

Again he left with her entreaty to seek out Francesco da Romena and bid him well.

"I've heard that the conte di Romena is making additions to his castle at Panicaglia," Serafina remarked after supper one evening. She was seated at the window in the tower, watching an autumn rain gently shower Florence. Niccolo sat at a small table before the hearth, playing with chess pieces, moving them about with no particular interest or purpose.

"How did you know?" Niccolo asked. He was Romena's banker, and not even he knew this.

"I brought cloth to the palace of the Arte Calimala. I heard the talk. The conte di Romena is more famous than I imagined."

"I suppose with no one left to challenge him, he can afford to make his life comfortable with borrowed money," Niccolo commented.

"Castello di San Galgano is said to be the most beautiful of his castles. I remember that it was."

"Will you hazard a game?"

Serafina glanced over her shoulder to see the chessboard set for a game, and she nodded, sitting opposite him. They played quietly, with the patter of rain and the crackle of logs in the hearth their music. When Serafina closed her hand around the white queen she met Niccolo's gaze.

"I wonder," she asked, "am I the white queen?"

"The queen is the most dangerous."

"And often taken captive."

"No man holds sway over you now!" he swore, reaching for her hand.

"No man but you."

The hand was released and Niccolo sat back in his chair. "I'll not deny what I feel. You knew from the first when you returned last month."

"Do not force me, Niccolo."

Serafina rose and walked to the window seat, picking up the embroidery frame. The afternoon rain had splattered on the brightly colored silk threads, and she now tried to blot the dampness with her sleeve. The colors were bleeding one into the other, making blotches of soft color and ruining the buskin scarf she'd started more than a year ago. It was to be a gift for Francesco.

Niccolo was at her shoulder. She felt his hand, warm and gentle on her neck, as he brushed aside the curls that had managed to escape from her coif.

"Tell me how I should forget," he implored and then kissed her neck. His hand caressed one of her breasts and lingered there as his kisses became more passionate and he pulled her closer, turning her so that his mouth could claim hers. Serafina went rigid and backed away, shoving him gently with a hand against his chest.

"You are a free woman now; you can choose your husband. Did we not promise one another?" Niccolo murmured.

"No."

"I want you. I will have you."

"No you will not!" she spat. Go now before I take a knife to my throat. You know it would be a folly to love me."

It was enough to thwart his desire.

CHAPTER 35

NICCOLO HAD NO choice but to speak with Francesco and once he had, regretted the decision.

"There is something you should know," Niccolo said as Francesco signed the documents a clerk set before him.

"I know that your banking house charges interest a pirate would envy," Francesco jested. He frowned when he saw how grave Niccolo appeared. "Am I to suppose your news will do me harm, Niccolo?"

"Serafina has returned," Niccolo said bluntly and was surprised how easily it came. "She is widowed."

Francesco laid aside the quill as if the writing instrument were a dangerous thing and studied the papers he'd signed, turning them over and over.

"Here are the notes," he said. "Good day to you."

"I know she comes to Florence on market day."

"What's that to me?" The words were sharp and charged full of emotion.

"Tomorrow is market day."

Curiosity made Francesco go to the market square. Despite better judgment, despite honor, he went. A wealth of pleasant memories hung in the air with pungent, sensual aromas as Francesco walked through the old market to the spice merchants' stalls. When he turned the corner he was not amazed at all to see her there but by how he felt. Indifference was replaced by heartache.

"Welcome home," he said after an awkward silence during which they stared through one another, and memories both painful and sweet washed over them like a warm tide and in Serafina's case, leaving hope in its wake.

Serafina turned to the jars of frankincense and delicately touched the resinous matter within, letting it crumble between her fingers and come away fragrant. "You gave me a jar of frankincense."

"You never answered my letters," Francesco said.

"It was impossible and I was afraid. But more afraid there was nothing to say."

"Let's go in here," Francesco suggested, nodding towards a chapel at the end of the square. He glanced around to make sure no one watched or followed, then turned to Lorenzo. "Stay here. Let me know if someone comes."

The chapel was a neighborhood chantry where one could slip in at any hour to light a candle or offer a prayer, or listen to the office chanted. Dark and musky, the light of the tapers in the stands gave off just enough light to see the tiny altar and crucifix on the wall behind it. An old woman was bent over a communion rail muttering verses of a psalm when Francesco and Serafina entered and went to a corner away from the door.

"All is well with you, Francesco?" Serafina asked.

"All considering. It's been difficult. And you? When did you return?"

"A month past."

Francesco nodded towards the stands of tapers. "Will you offer a prayer for your dead husband?"

"For my soul, not his, because I'm glad he's dead and burning in Hell."

"Then I will light one for you. For your safe return." He took one of the candles and used its light to ignite a newer, unused one. Then he dropped a coin in the poor box. "I never gave up hope after that night."

"Neither did I and now no man holds me in bondage," Serafina pronounced and she was sufficiently strong of spirit to look up at him directly and smile. She might have leaned in close and offered her lips, but he stepped back. She was unprepared for his dolorous shake of the head.

"I am pledged to another woman."

Serafina felt as if the wind had been knocked from her lungs. Not another word was spent before she was gone.

THROUGHOUT SUPPER WITH the Alberti, Francesco reenacted the scene in the market square and each time the ending had been different. It ended in his mind with Serafina in his bed, sometimes draped in nothing but a fur-lined cloak that whispered as she dropped it to the floor, sometimes clad in the noonday sun and nothing else, sometimes glistening with sweat as she arched her back and sighed with pleasure and each vision dissolved like smoke whenever someone spoke to him or laughter went up in the room. During two intolerable hours of sumptuous dishes and entertainment, he could only think of the girl's stricken eyes and how she fled from him.

"Where do you go, my son?" Andrea laughed, clapping Francesco on the shoulders as he started to rise. "We have a troubadour from Normandy who will entertain us with ballads and stories. I hear one is about you and the siege of Fronzola!" He leaned over to fill the younger man's cup, but Francesco's hand covered the bowl and he shook his head.

"A month mind," Francesco said cryptically.

"Stay a while longer! The dead always have our prayers!"

"Even so," murmured Francesco, and offered his host courtesy and his bride-to-be a kiss on the brow before taking leave.

"See what he's about!" Andrea snapped at two of his nephews.

Francesco walked to Santi Apostoli. It was past vespers and there were only a few worshipers still lingering after mass. He said good evening to a priest removing vessels and linen and walked past the choir and through the ambulatory, to the small chapel dedicated to his Guidi kinsmen.

The flowers before the statue of the Virgin and Child were faded and dry as if made of parchment. It had been weeks since anyone had come here, evidenced by the dust topping the candles. The memorial panel to his parents had been finished. There they were, Alessandro and Albera, pious, humble witnesses to the miracles of Santa Fina and San Galgano. A hundred years from now, no one would care that the witnesses were monsters who deserved places in the poet Dante's Seventh Ring of Hell, the place reserved for murderers, not recognition.

When he left the church he didn't notice Alberti's nephews sitting in the choir watching him. Andrea brought up the visit the next afternoon when he was visiting Francesco.

"Do you think it wise to honor your parents' memories with such a pretty thing as that panel Maestro Lorenzetti gave your church?"

"In a hundred years, no one will care," Francesco replied. "But I'll rest soundly in my crypt when the time comes, knowing I did my parents honor no matter their treatment of me. We're instructed to forgive those who do us wrong seventy times seven, is that no so?"

"Let me replace it with a tribute to better people and saints, with my daughter and you."

"I thank you, but no. My parents gave me life and that is enough."

"Some would think it an insult to your bride to have the girl saint of San Gimignano there, a saint whose name and appearance is similar to your lover's."

Lorenzo joined them as they walked down to the courtyard and passage into the Borgo. He whispered something to Francesco who barely acknowledged the message and waved him off. It wasn't missed by Alberti, however, who saw that the boy gave his master a letter.

"She is not my lover," Francesco replied quietly as he pushed open the gate to the street for Alberti and his servant.

"If she was, I would expect you to keep your promise to my daughter and I would expect you not to shame her and end it with the Giustini girl. She doesn't deserve such treatment," Alberti said as he departed. "You had best take this into consideration, my son."

"No, Serafina doesn't deserve such treatment," Francesco said when they were gone. He turned to Lorenzo and said, "My cloak and gloves. I'll be back before the curfew bell."

Again, Francesco went to Santi Apostoli and his family's chapel. For the longest time he studied the Lorenzetti panel and waited, his heart racing when he heard the footsteps.

"You do your parents' memory good honor."

Serafina's voice made it race faster and he turned to smile.

Before them, a statue of the Madonna smiled serenely and behind them plainsong floated up from the chantry. Dusty sunlight filtering from the trefoil windows behind Serafina shot webs of gold upon her face. Her plaits fell heavily over her shoulders like two silken copper cords. Francesco was aware of her in every pore of his body, in all of his senses.

"It's nothing of the kind. I mean only to smooth over guilt."

"Guilt? For what?" she asked, stepping near. It was spoken almost as a laugh, a light-hearted comment made at an *al fresco* supper in a garden on a summer's twilight.

"For my parents' sins. For breaking my promise to you." Francesco replied.

"How could you have known what happened to me?"

"I intended to do what is right and honorable. I made an attempt to steal you away from him when Gian Maria told me about the forced marriage. I failed. Then I tried to live a comfortable life to no one's comfort."

"No one will fault you for that. I will not." Serafina stepped closer and touched his face. The scent of wildflowers overtook him. "Know this," she whispered, "I will always be thankful for you!"

He leaned down and could almost taste her kiss when he suddenly and unexpectedly drew her away, pressed a finger to her lips, and motioned toward the choir.

Two of the Alberti had entered the church and now paused expectantly, as if searching. They approached the Romena chapel. With his free hand, Francesco silently drew his sword in case they wanted to provoke a quarrel. His hand still pressed against Serafina's mouth, Francesco watched and was relieved when they decided to go elsewhere and then finally leave the church. A bar of sunlight and then the creak and slam of a door confirmed this.

It was some time before Francesco released Serafina, precious moments that seemed endless when the feel of her body ignited his desire. But he unloosed his hold and stepped back self-consciously.

Serafina watched his face hoping for a smile or a look that would tell her everything was fine, that he loved her. "Have we nothing more to say to one another?" she lamented when his silence became unbearable.

"Believe me when I tell you it is not as it seems!"

And with a blunt nod, he slipped away. She watched him go and noted how the shoulders weren't carried as high as she remembered them, the head bowed. *See what becomes of us when we bow to tradition and the way of things,*

Serafina thought as she rode home and closed herself up in the solar to weep unseen and unheard.

That afternoon Niccolo entered solar at Serafina's castle without so much as a pronouncement, so used were the servants to his habitual arrivals. Serafina didn't bother looking up from her reading. She knew the familiar scuff of his boots, how the one trod more heavily than the other. She also knew the familiar touch of his lips on her skin and turned slightly when he bussed her cheek in greeting.

"Niccolo. How goes my money changer?" she greeted. Her brittle attempt at humor and the melancholy that accompanied it came as a surprise. Of late, she'd been dour, almost oppressive and abusive to him. The tears glistening on her dark lashes took him unaware.

"Better than most. The king of England has petitioned our London branch for a loan, and I've been called to London and will leave at month's end. You've never been to London, have you?" he answered.

"Nor do I expect to go there. But you may kiss farewell that precious new Arabian you bought in Milano, for you know the kings of England prefer to expel their Lombard bankers rather than make good on a loan."

An hour passed in silence before Serafina and Niccolo moved to their customary places on the window seat. Another hour was soon gone, as were the last rays of sunlight over the Arno Valley, leaving behind a soft vermilion wash on the horizon.

Serafina turned while they discussed her latest acquisition, a gyrfalcon, and all Niccolo could see was her mouth, her delectable, exciting mouth. In the new darkness, it was difficult to read Serafina's eyes. What filled his thoughts at that moment was easy enough to reckon. God, but he wanted to kiss her. He could taste her lips, just looking at them.

When he leaned forward, Serafina jerked away, almost hurling herself from the window seat.

"What troubles you? All I want is a kiss."

"No."

"Come, we're still friends, at least—"

"Don't touch me!" Serafina shrieked, and she backed into the wall. When Niccolo reached out to console her, she struck him soundly across the face.

"God's life, Serafina! What did I ever do to you?"

He tried to prevent her from leaving and took her arm gently. In doing so, the shoulder of her dress slipped, and he saw them: large, ugly bruises that had yet to lose their coloring. There were scars from a lashing, perhaps sliced by a dagger.

Serafina clutched at the dress and told him to leave. "You're not wanted here any longer. Just go."

"Serafina, did Romena do this? I would know so that he answers for it."

"Leave me!"

"What on earth did he do to you?"

"I said go!"

"I would know the truth!"

She shook her head then, and reached for the fur-lined cloak on the bed, using it as a shield. Niccolo persisted, and she finally sank down on a bench near the hearth. With hands locked around her knees, Serafina stared into the fire.

"Not Francesco. But he might have prevented it!" she said. "Who do you think?"

"Ranieri. So that's why he's dead."

"Imagine the worst one of God's creatures could do to another. Imagine everything depraved, despicable, unkind, unholy, and unbelievable. Imagine what horror someone might endure so that another might derive pleasure from it!"

"I've changed my mind, don't tell—"

"Can you not imagine? You're a man! I hear tell the worst is what lies in men's fantasies and how they want to conjure it, play it out in bed. Think! And then you'll know what I endured all those months locked up in Ranieri's castle! When he wasn't taking his pleasure of me, he gave me to his men, his sons, his vassals, his stable boys! I was kept locked in a bedchamber, kept in dark cellars, and he urged his mistress to use me in ways . . . but what do you expect? I'm only a woman and men rule the world and are men, and do what they want!"

"Not all men," Niccolo stated.

"Most," she said quietly.

Niccolo extended a hand and let it drop impotently to his side. He drew a breath and hesitated, then said, "Some, but not all. Not me. Not Francesco da Romena."

She looked up, startled. Color drew into her cheeks and she quickly looked away.

"I would never hurt you and would kill any man who would try," he said.

Serafina moved away to avoid his kiss. "Dream of it no more. Think on it no more. Let me be, Niccolo."

He did as he was asked and the next day the last person in the world Niccolo wanted to see waited for him at the Peruzzi offices when he arrived sometime after the noon bell. Holy Mother, but Romena looked ill, looked as if he hadn't slept all night. But then, Niccolo thought, neither had he. He only wished that the memory of his quarrel with Serafina would fade like afternoon sun on the flagstones, or that he didn't carry it on his shoulders. His sleep had been peppered with visions of what Serafina had suffered and he woke, screaming so that his mother and servants called for a physic to bleed him.

"Good morning," Niccolo greeted, taking documents from his worried clerk and settling himself behind the large desk in an officious and affected manner.

"The bells struck noon almost an hour ago. You've been abed all this time? I hope it was a lady that kept you from our appointment!"

Francesco's brotherly jest fell uneasily on Niccolo, who flushed and muttered "the lady was unwilling after all was said. Sad to say, nothing was done."

"Better to dream of the wench you cannot have than suffer the rejection of a wench who gave herself unwillingly."

Niccolo glanced up, his face the color of whey. "I don't know what you mean."

"Don't you? It was because of me you lost the affection of a certain lady."

"She was lost to me long before she knew Francesco da Romena!" said Niccolo with a laugh. He reached for the wine and poured two cups.

"What good does it serve us to bemoan those ladies we cannot have? I'm supposed to be the luckiest man in Florence, having the most beautiful and the wealthiest heiress as my betrothed." Francesco took one of the cups and drank quickly, wiping his mouth indelicately with the fine hem of his sleeve. "And my lady expects luxury."

Niccolo laughed, nodding. The other lady he knew would expect less.

"I'm to be fitted for a tournament at month's end," Francesco announced, and then added, "in honor of my marriage to Cunizza. I've invited the best knights in Tuscany to come. It's something to keep my mind off—look you, it's bound to cost more than my soul's worth. I need the loan of a hundred florins. Can that be arranged?" The last came hurriedly.

Niccolo nodded and took a sheet of new vellum from a drawer, writing just as quickly. "Even if you can't love her, you can play the part," he commented.

What if you loved someone and had to play the fool? The disinterested fool?

"Does it show that much?" Francesco asked.

"Not really, but I think I know you."

"Well, what you know you'll keep to yourself."

"Of course. Here's the note. I hear there's a new Milanese armorer on the Ponte Vecchio. He could fashion the best harness in a week. Take it, then." Niccolo pushed it towards Francesco, who studied it and nodded. It was some time before Francesco folded the note and secured it in his purse.

"Something else?"

"Yes," Francesco replied. His eyes met Niccolo's, and Niccolo summoned all of his courage to meet that gaze evenly.

"Ask and it is done."

"I think often of her. I have not forgotten. I only have regret and none where it concerns her."

He thanked Niccolo for the loan and extended a hand.

Niccolo stared at the hand, noting a small sapphire ring on Francesco's ring small finger. Why did he feel so much like a traitor?

Dream of me no more.

୬

THE LETTER WAS in Niccolo's own hand. Serafina knew it from the first; knew it was an apology, an outpouring of unwavering love, a prayer for forgiveness for their quarrel borne of his lust and desire to marry her. Three weeks had passed and she had not seen him, save for an occasional meeting in church or in the market square.

She smiled at the poor fellow who had walked all the way from Florence to Monte alle' Croci and told him to go below for ale and bread. His footsteps plodding on the wooden planks of the castle hall remained the only sound that autumn afternoon until she broke the letter's seal.

"Sweet Blessed Virgin!" Serafina swore, the letter trembling violently in her hands.

"Messer Niccolo's love poetry sets you to fire, does it?" Marghareta said jocundly and was taken aback by her mistress' cold stare.

"Fetch my cloak and horse and mind your tongue!"

Marghareta was of sound enough mind to keep her tongue while preparing for the journey to Florence, a journey that would be made alone she discovered when Serafina's horse galloped through the wood and down the spiraling road toward Florence's walls and into the town to The Rose and the Knight at the end of the Via Porta Rossa. Here Serafina drew up rein and slid off her sidesaddle, offering a penny to the boy who came running from the stables. Another boy gallantly opened the common room door and showed her to a table far from the noisy hearth where rustic travelers were bedding down on the floor, mindful of her gentility. Instead of ordering ale and supper, she called for the innkeeper and when he came to her table, she asked for the best of the private rooms above stairs and showed a purse to make it worth his while.

Only when the door closed behind her and she stood alone in the large bedchamber did Serafina think what she was doing was madness.

The innkeeper's wife had seen that the feather bed was new and the linens clean; the night's livery of wastel loaf and good red wine were set on a linen cloth laid out on finely wrought table near the bed. A bathing tub steaming with hot water and scented with roses sat near a brazier warming the room. A lamp glowed above the bolster and a tapestry brought from the Holy Land covered the only window; the Virgin smiled serenely from her devotional panel above the hearth.

"Madness!" Serafina whispered to herself as she removed her cloak and boots.

Surely this was madness, she thought as she undressed and slipped into the tub. She poured the warm scented water over her naked skin, drew the hand cloth out of the basin, and pressed it gently across her silken skin so that rivulets raced from shoulders to breasts and down the curves of her belly and beyond and the whole room was filled with the scent.

And all the while the Virgin smiled. She continued to smile when Serafina unbound her hair and let it fall heavily past her knees, she watched knowingly as Serafina threw off the drying cloth, letting the brazier heat warm her skin.

The Compline bell rang and then dissolved in the wind when there happened a knock, then a second. Serafina wrapped a fur-lined cloak carelessly about her and walked slowly to the door, opening it. She was not at all surprised to find Francesco da Romena though his wonder was evident.

The message he received from Niccolo was short and to the point:

> *Will you dice with me this evening? I have a fine room*
> *and entertainment at The Rose and The Knight. Tell the*
> *innkeeper who you are and he'll show you the rooms. I'll*
> *meet you after dusk.*

Having spent too many nights alone, Francesco was ready to lose himself in gaming and drink, perhaps a pretty, fresh-faced whore.

Now with Serafina before him, he saw the game Niccolo played.

"Should you decide to leave, I will understand. It is known that Francesco da Romena is an honorable man where it concerns his pledges," Serafina said timorously when the door closed behind him.

He didn't move. She might have been an apparition, or worse, a young whore whose face and voice were like Serafina's, a girl sent to drive Francesco mad.

"What pledge?" Francesco said when he had found his voice.

"You are promised to another. I will understand if you decide to honor that pledge."

"I am reminded of another pledge; one made to a girl at an abbey, and by a stream, on a winter's morning, and that pledge comes before all else."

"Niccolo has made a great sacrifice," she said.

"He said the lady was unwilling."

"Not unwilling, but afraid. Corrupted and bruised."

"I would never hurt you."

Francesco touched her arm and immediately felt her body go rigid, the rise of gooseflesh. Instinctively, he wanted nothing more than to retreat, to say that it was an accident, that he didn't mean to brush her arm, but then he saw her eyes. Imploring, seeking, trusting and fearing. Francesco saw all that in the glimpse. Now he brushed his lips against her brow and felt the warmth of her skin, how her breath drew inward and how she relaxed, the gentle buss of her lips against his chin. They stood together like this for the longest time, listening to the rise and fall of each other's breath, feeling heartbeats. Serafina was the first to move, and she slowly rode her hands across Francesco's chest, gliding over velvet and linen, feeling the sharpness of the fibers of gold embroidery on her fingertips and how they sank into the deep pile of the French velvet until they rested on Francesco's face.

"Perhaps this is the cure?" she asked.

Her warm, gentle, kiss stirred all of his senses. His hand went up to touch the shoulder that had escaped the fur-lined cloak and he found the skin warm and perfumed. His lips now sought confirmation and the girl came into his arms, yielding and soft, the fur-lined cloak slipping away to encircle them on the floor.

࿇

"HONOR ABOVE ALL."

"What my heart?"

Serafina shifted in bed and in his arms to reach for Francesco's hand and was reassured when he clasped hers tightly, left a kiss on the palm.

"It is my raison. 'Honor Above All.' I chose it as a boy when I saw how false were those who swore to uphold my rights. I pledged before the altar in the chantry of my mother's castle that I would forever live by that. By honor."

"There's not a man who'd deny that, Francesco."

"I have suffered and failed because of that. My promise to you is all that there is."

"I would be content to be your mistress."

"No more. I'll not be pushed by fear and threats."

"This is enough, Francesco. It is what others do, what is expected of a nobleman."

"But not me. The life expected of nobility is how my parents destroyed one another and everyone around them. It is not for me."

Serafina nodded and settled into the cradle of his arm, pulling the blankets around them tightly as if they were protection. She was afraid for both of them.

CHAPTER 36

AZZELINO ALBERTI'S SECRETARY, ser Bartolomeo, glanced up from his letter writing and scowled at the boy casting a shadow over his desk.

"Pietro, you're blocking the last of the sunlight. If you don't mind?"

"There's a man from Florence outside, Signor. He won't speak to anyone but you."

"Who is he?"

"A servant. Fiasella of San Galgano's man."

"Send him in."

A messenger more bedraggled than a soldier fresh from battle entered the library and knelt before ser Bartolomeo, who held a hand discreetly to his nose at the smell of horse and human sweat. "Get up man, I'm not the cardinal," the secretary snapped.

"I have a letter from Fiasella to the cardinal."

The messenger removed the precious cargo from his purse, horrified that Bartolomeo snatched it up, and was ready to take it back when the secretary broke the seal and unfolded the letter.

"I was sworn to give this only to the cardinal!"

"And so you have. Nothing goes to the cardinal without first coming to me. Wait here while I find him."

Brushing past the man, Bartolomeo hurried out of the abbey library and immediately skirted the herb gardens and cloister, almost ran through the chapter house, and finally burst into the abbot's lodgings. Before Azzelino had a chance to ask, the letter was thrown into the trencher before him and the vellum sank into the last of the gravy.

"Francesco da Romena has made a bargain with your stepfather, Eminence. He's agreed to marry your sister in exchange for Alberti castles and towns on the frontiers of his land. All else will be given to him. You've been disinherited. You're to have nothing."

Bartolomeo took several steps back toward the door and waited.

"Did he?" Azzelino barely whispered. His voice was controlled, but when he lifted the knife to skewer a game hen, he missed his mark and the knife was lodged in olive wood. "It's almost nones. I wish to pray. Abbate, your chapel is at my disposal, I hope?"

The abbot nodded his assent and showed the way. At the threshold of the chapel, however, the door was slammed in his face and the abbot listened in horror as the cardinal started to scream. The screams of rage, the destruction and desecration of priceless chalices, pyxes, patens, and holy relics continued for hours.

"He's been in there for most of the night; do you not think he may have done harm to himself?" the abbot said to Bartolomeo the next morning.

"We'd not be that fortunate!"

"Pardon, messer?"

"I'll go and see what's happened."

Azzelino was seated at the foot of the altar, his face streaked with tears. He held a flask of the sacristan's wine and was haphazardly pouring mouthfuls down his throat. The wine spilled over the fine linen fair cloth he'd stripped from the altar and used as a napkin. Bartolomeo gently removed the flask from his hands and brushed the golden tangle of hair out of Azzelino's eyes as a father might do for his child.

"There now, Eminence. You've done enough mischief for one night," Bartolomeo said as he lowered himself onto the altar steps below Azzelino.

"Don't treat me like a child!"

"Then don't act like one."

"You don't understand!"

"Well enough, I do, such as how you'd react to such news." Bartolomeo waved a hand at the wreckage surrounding them. "You've proved my point. Now you must do something quite out of character, Eminence. Show a glad face. Let everyone think you don't care. Think of what advantages this will bring you if Francesco should fall from his horse, or eat a piece of rotten fish. Who's to say what the future might bring?"

Azzelino's brows rose at this and he exhaled a sigh tainted by wine. "I suppose it could have been worse. He might have married her instead."

"Her? What lady do you mean?"

"Serafina Giustini. The only woman I've ever loved. Of course, I needn't worry about that now. She's living in a castle in the Garfagnana and my sister has a particular dislike of husbands who stray from her bed!"

"You didn't know?" The secretary saw Azzelino's frown and decided it was best left unsaid. He'd find out eventually. "I don't see why you should worry at all."

Now Azzelino turned to look at Ser Bartolomeo, and the secretary shifted uneasily when he saw how clear the cardinal's eyes were. Nothing of last night's rage was apparent.

"God help you for a fool, Bartolomeo! In all your years with me, have you learned nothing?"

Ser Bartolomeo agreed with him and said he didn't, adding they should not continue south to Avignon but leave for Florence as soon as possible as it was only a day's ride. It would be the perfect thing to have the cardinal bless the union of his sister and his enemy.

❧

THE FEAST OF the Archangels was chosen for the tournament in honor of the Romena-Alberti nuptials. A tourney yard had been erected in the meadow below the donjon of Castello San Galgano. Two pavilions stood beyond a palisade, the largest of these covered by a silk baldachin and spread with sumptuous tapestries and pennants. This was the court of the Queen of Love and Beauty, whom the favorite would crown. The second pavilion was smaller yet more sumptuously decorated and blazoned with the colors of Alberti and Romena. Bright vermilion and gold, somber murrey, dark browns, and mottled azure rioted against one another in the hot sun.

It was a glorious day for a tournament. Many said the weather had never been so agreeable since the Feast of the Baptist. Scarlet, gold, and green, the hues of autumn, made the day more festive. A hot sun shimmered off the murrey and or banners hanging limply on their staves outside Romena's tent. Seven smaller tents stood in a dusty clearing behind it, and here spectators dallied with the hope of meeting the famous knights from across Europe who'd come seeking prize money and favor.

The ladies nearly wilted in their heavy velvets and brocades as the sun climbed higher in the sky and broke through the seams of the baldachins. A murmur of approval followed Cunizza Alberti as she joined the other ladies in the Court of Love and Beauty. She was too old to be sitting among so many girls who still carried a virginal blush in their cheeks, but no one disputed her right to be there. No woman in Florence possessed hair so brilliantly gold nor eyes so deep a blue. When she smiled her teeth showed themselves straight and even, each one pearl in color, and that smile sent many hearts into a frenzy.

Francesco rode into the meadow late. Several knights greeted him with respect, knowing he was already the acknowledged victor of the day, but most hailed jests and exchanged rude comments about his prowess elsewhere, which made the ladies laugh.

Alberti scurried after his future son-in-law like a nervous mouse, watching the knights in fear and interest. Any one of them could unhorse Romena, or better still, issue a fatal wound. It was too much to think about. He was in a festive mood and wearing his most expensive garments in defiance of the sumptuary laws: a gown of green cloth of gold, sleeves of yellow cloth of gold. Of all the plumage worn by Florentine nobility that afternoon, Alberti's was the most high-flown.

"Where've you been all this time?" Alberti whined when he met up with Francesco.

"In a lady's bed," came the answer.

"Whoring?"

"Well, that's not what I'd call it, but men have different names for what pleasures them when they're forbidden to seduce and bed their bride."

"I'd laugh if it thought it amusing! I'd as lief you'd take up with the Giustini girl than shame my daughter with jades!"

"Would you now?" Francesco laughed, but took him by the neck none too lovingly, bringing him under the protection of his mailed arm, close enough so that Alberti could inhale the scent of sandalwood and rose, close enough to see that the razor had not done its work that morning, close enough to see the danger. "Now's the time to leave be," he murmured.

"As you will, but no tricks today, eh? No throwing yourself in front of a lance, eh? I heard that yesterday you were struck by the quintain in practice."

"No tricks," Francesco sighed in annoyance, absently rubbing his sore left shoulder at the mention of his accident.

"Ah, Francesco! Another thing. I had word from my son the cardinal."

"Damn you! I thought we agreed—"

"Easily! Don't bare your fangs to me! I had nothing to do with it. Your quarrel is with Fiasella," Alberti explained as he wiped his brow with a trembling hand. "Be easy and rest assured that he won't try anything. I am certain of that. Azzelino fears his sister above all others."

Francesco threw him a look that was easy enough to translate and turned to the hovering servants.

"Monsignore, you should prepare," Lorenzo said.

A commotion rose from the spectators as Serafina arrived, escorted by Niccolo Peruzzi. The lapis silk she wore glittered like a jewel and made her pale skin more incandescent. Peruzzi could not take his eyes from Serafina, and neither could many a gentleman in the crowd.

Francesco had to take a cup of wine to suppress a smile. Only three hours ago he'd left her bed at The Rose and the Knight. She'd promised to come after much persuasion and now Francesco was glad. By God, she outshone every woman under the baldachins! And she wore a dress made of the Provençal silk he'd given her a lifetime ago.

Let others speculate, she swore between their kisses, as their bodies grew hot for one another that morning, let others say she was Niccolo Peruzzi's betrothed, let others whisper the worst. No matter what, she was her own, Serafina pronounced when Francesco possessed her once more.

What man there and in his right mind did not wonder what it would be like in her soft, warm, bed? True enough, wagers were made matching her beauty to that of Cunizza Alberti. Gossip now replaced wagers, about her mother the infamous whore, about Serafina's marriage to Gherardo Ranieri and how, it was rumored, she had been kept a prisoner and used for perverse sport. Was it any wonder his widow dressed like any virgin of sixteen? She had suffered much. Wasn't it unfortunate that the conte di Romena could not have her? He was, it was whispered, still in love with her. All in all, such beauty was not meant for widowhood, and Niccolo Peruzzi was a fortunate man indeed.

"By my saints! This is not right, it is not well," Alberti groused. "Do they mean to proclaim the Salvemini brat before my daughter? This is Cunizza's day! Francesco, make it known that it is she you prefer above all others!"

Francesco merely smiled.

The two contenders for his affection, Cunizza and Serafina, diplomatically acknowledged one another with brief glances and pretended to ignore the acclamations for Serafina.

"Monsignore, you must prepare!" Lorenzo insisted, and as he spoke the *busines* sounded. Francesco ignored both, watching Serafina as she took a place beside Niccolo Peruzzi's sister in one of the lesser pavilions. Niccolo sat below Serafina and wrapped an arm playfully around Serafina's slender ankle in a familiar and loving gesture that made Francesco wroth. By God, Niccolo was playing his part too well!

"Monsignore, by faith—"

"Enough. I know it's time." Francesco sighed and buffeted Lorenzo affectionately on the shoulders, then submitted to the armorers' preparations during which Roberto entered the tent to wish Francesco good fortune, and came closer when Francesco suddenly asked to speak with him in private.

❧

THE BUSINES announced the first contest of the day and the crowd leaned forward as one body to watch the entrance of seven champions into the yard. As they paraded and gave reverence to the Court of Love and Beauty, another blast on the trumpets announced the arrival of Francesco and his two seconds. The crowd was on its feet as Francesco entered astride a spirited gray destrier. His golden armor flashing hotly in the sun, Francesco made one round of the yard and stopped at the smaller pavilion where Alberti draped a garland over the point of his lance. For a moment he did nothing except watch the crowd through the visor of his great helm, then walked the horse to the pavilion of the Court of Love and Beauty. The crowd fell silent, waiting for a customary speech that would proclaim Cunizza Alberti the queen. Instead, Francesco kept in the saddle and lowered his lance in tribute to his betrothed. A young girl was pushed to the front of the pavilion by Cunizza's women and recited pretty verses from Homer in Francesco's honor. Francesco offered the child a ribbon from his buskin and the crowd roared with approval. He lowered the lance again, this time letting the garland slide off the lance and into Cunizza's welcome hands. With a movement both graceful and theatrical, she removed her headdress and awed the spectators when her hair tumbled in a golden wash over her shoulders. She placed the garland on her brow and it was too much. The pavilions quaked with cheers and applause. Having done this, Francesco offered tribute once more and took a turn around the palisade to even more riotous cheering, never once acknowledging Serafina Giustini.

For Cunizza, that was the greatest tribute of all.

ॐ

THREE KNIGHTS IN turn had been vanquished under Francesco's lance. The day was cooler, now that fog drifted into the Mugello, but many complained that the afternoon was too long and hoped for a spectacle to relieve the boredom. The tournament had been predictable thus far.

Francesco asked for a fresh mount, and as he exchanged horses, the busines heralded the approach of a fourth champion.

The crowd grew silent and waited; only the sound of pennants snapping crisply in the wind rent the momentary silence.

"A priest!" One of the fellows sitting at the edge of the palisade laughed and the crowd joined in for it was Azzelino Alberti who came to challenge Francesco.

"Courage, ser Francesco, a priest on horseback has God on his side!" one boy gibed.

"Messer Conte, will you take the Blessed Sacraments from his eminence before he does you in?" another laughed.

Francesco ignored them and mounted a new charger. No one could see that he was shivering in a cold sweat or that his chest heaved in anticipation. This was something he had not expected.

Azzelino, dressed in silver French armor, now rode forward and circled Francesco once, coming round a second time and striking his shield with the point of his lance, rather than with a blunt coronel, making his choice of battle known. A joust *a l'outrance!* A duel to the death!

The trumpets blared twice and the contest was ready to begin. Francesco couched his lance and held his horse's flanks tightly between his knees as he issued a jarring blow on the first pass, splintering Azzelino's lance but failing to unhorse him. The crowd cheered Francesco's vigor as he made a second pass and gave his cousin another murderous blow. Azzelino still held and screamed at his men for new weapons, watching his adversary pace the yard on a tired horse. The golden armor was dented and dusty, the mail hauberk under his *chausses* spattered with his own blood.

When Azzelino was handed a broadsword, Francesco called for his own and then took up his shield.

The *busines* shouted again. Francesco muttered a *Pater Noster.* He hunched low in the saddle, charging forward, springing up as he approached and ready for the attack. The ringing of swords as they met vibrated in his great helm and numbed his hand. Again and again they met in the middle of the yard. Francesco's sword arm was tired, aching with every blow he cast. The cheering of the crowd was more and more like an insect buzzing in his ears. He heard his own breathing coming fast and hard, the pounding of his heart a drum.

Another pass and Azzelino was jarred. Francesco swung round unexpectedly and took a swing at him with an ax and now they were to it with more deadly weapons. Azzelino paused, walking his destrier as it foamed and snorted, struggled to keep it under control. He pulled up rein, calculating the risk he could take. Francesco waited.

"I don't like this," Niccolo told Serafina. "We should stop this."

"It's almost over, I know it," Serafina said and kept her attention on Francesco, who was slumping wearily, leaning on his shield propped on the pommel of the saddle.

Azzelino dug spurs into the horse's flanks and met Francesco in the center. Francesco was thrown when their swords crossed. The crowd did not like this sport and fell silent, waiting to see if their favorite would get up. When he did not, Serafina screamed and would have run into the yard if Niccolo had not gone first. All eyes, particularly those of Cunizza, fell upon her.

And then they noticed the blood, a rivulet oozing from the *aventail* under the great helm.

"Find a surgeon! Why do you stand there? Find a surgeon to bind up his wounds!" Niccolo screamed at no one in particular. He pushed away the spectators who thronged around Francesco. "You fools! Take away the great helm! Take it away! Give him air!"

One of the knights tore off the great helm, *bascinet* and *aventail*. A gasp went up and some shouts. Everyone was perplexed to find Roberto and not Francesco, lying unconscious, perhaps dead, on the ground. Alberti had rushed to join the circle, and upon seeing the other man bleeding to death, he crossed himself and asked Niccolo what was afoot. "I wish I knew!" Niccolo replied, and when he turned to reassure Serafina, saw Francesco watching the spectacle from the entrance of his tent.

Under the cloak of night, Francesco rode for Monte alle' Croci. Without a torchbearer, the journey was more difficult, for the path was steep that led up the hill to the basilica of San Miniato al Monte and beyond. The moon was full and gave some light, but his horse shied and snorted, tossing bit and scudding anxious hooves against the soft earth that was unfamiliar and dark, refusing Francesco's gentle urging. They climbed past the basilica and farther, above the church and episcopal palace, to a cluster of villas obscured from a traveler by well-groomed orchards and lanes guarded by cypress. And finally, they arrived at the castle on a protected hillock in the midst of an olive grove.

Francesco rode into the greater bailey and passed the reins to a sleepy groom who came from his bed to be of service. "I am Francesco da Romena," he announced. It was enough to gain admittance.

"Madonna Giustini will see you," Marghareta greeted him in the donjon, and led the way through a maze of corridors and stair casements and finally to the tower.

A door closed below stairs, and then Francesco heard whispered conversation. He turned from his vigil on the moonlit valley below them to discover billowing green sarcenet and velvet. He swung Serafina into his arms, bringing her mouth to his for a kiss.

"My God, Francesco! Why did you do it? I was so afraid! We all did think—Francesco, it was foolhardy—"

"We thought it would be a clever joke. It was foolish, but praise be to God, Roberto will live."

"Why did you do it?"

"Beloved, it was Roberto, and not Romena, pledging love to the Alberti widow before so many. Not Romena!" Francesco whispered, his mouth close.

"All's done?" she gasped between ardent kisses.

"It's done. Fina, I cannot wait. We can be married tomorrow. I can find a priest, two if you'd like! We can summon witnesses and lay a bridal supper. At sunset, as is the custom."

"What of Alberti's daughter? Do you think she will graciously accept your change of heart?"

"If we're married before she learns of it and after we've left Florence to the safety of one of my castles, what can she do?"

"You said Alberti's castles are near yours. We won't be safe."

"We will. I have men promised me from Lucca, Siena, Milano,"

"We won't be safe!"

"Then we go to England or France. Will you have me?" he whispered, using words as sensual as their lovemaking.

"Yes, I will."

He now offered promises and gratitude with kisses that fell haphazardly and happily on Serafina's face. Together they sat before the fire and were content to be in one another's arms and discuss a future that finally would be theirs until an explosion of noise below stairs brought them to their feet. Spurs and boots rang on floorboards, and servants began to beg for mercy, shouting woke the dogs. Francesco reached for his sword as Durante Giustini stormed into the bedchamber with Serafina's women at his heels, pulling at him and pleading for calm. They tried to hold him back, but Durante sought his quarry.

"Do you take me for a fool? I'll kill you in a moment!" Durante Giustini shouted as he pushed aside the servants and came at Francesco, who caught

Durante's blade before it was drawn from the scabbard.

"This is a family quarrel. Let's not share little secrets?" Francesco replied, and with a jerk of his head, dismissed the servants, even Marghareta, who protested until Serafina shouted her out of the room.

"When last we spoke you threatened me with death. I'm sorry your opinion of me hasn't changed, considering what I have to offer now," Francesco said when they were alone.

"What you have to offer? You pledge troth with Cunizza Alberti and in the same breath take my daughter for your whore! That's not much to offer!"

"Father, listen to him—" Serafina began, but shrank when Durante came at her. She gave Francesco a smile of thanks when her lover shoved her father into a chair gently.

"I pledged myself to this lady," Francesco said taking Serafina's hand, "long ere I thought to take the Alberti widow. You see that your bargains with the devil and threats to me have done little to alter this simple truth. Serafina has pledged herself to me and we shall be married tomorrow."

Durante hurled himself from the chair, the force of his movement knocked the heavy carved furniture backward into a table upon which precious trinkets and jewel casks sat. Serafina made a sound of dismay but made no move from Francesco's side.

"You promised me the right to choose another husband if I was widowed early," Serafina protested. "I have chosen. Be glad for me."

"Who's to say he won't kill you in your bed the way he killed his first wife? The way Alessandro rid himself of his first wife? Or murder his own sons the same way Alessandro did!"

Serafina looked at both men imploringly, frightened by her father's insinuations, but more frightened by the new aspect Francesco's calm face had taken. He was white—whiter than a lily or a newly washed bed sheet, the newest snow. And his eyes were blazing. Such a color green she had never beheld, and it frightened her. His hand was surprisingly calm. He leveled the sword at Durante and it barely moved in his iron-like grip.

"Take back your words!" Francesco hissed.

"Will you have me lie?" Durante laughed.

"Take it back! Before God and this woman I love, swear that you lie!"

"Everyone whispers and knows. It must be the truth!"

Francesco seized the Bible from the faldstool and held it aloft. This time, his hand was not as sure. The ribbon markers danced and swayed. Even the candlelight bowed. "I swear upon this holy book, I swear upon my love for this woman, I swear upon my infant son who died, I never did harm my wife! Nor would I have ever done so! Take back your lie!"

Durante's eyes slid to his daughter's and then he shook his head. "If you are slandered, God will right my wrong."

A glove of rich leather was flung to the rushes. Francesco never let his gaze falter and nodding, raised his sword in response.

"Oh no, you cannot, Francesco, no!"

Serafina's plea was ignored. Francesco beckoned toward the stairs. "Come, signor. Let us see whom God prefers!"

Space in the greater bailey had been cleared away of children and animals and a priest was fetched. Cresset lamps were hung from the windows and arrow slits, even from the trees. The bailey was light enough for daytime. The servants were assembled as witnesses. There was no armor, but Durante's soldiers gave up two brigadines.

Marghareta scrambled after her mistress, who seemed remarkably calm in spite of the knowledge that either her father or lover would soon die. "Surely this is more than madness!" Marghareta hissed in Serafina's ear. "I can send for Signor Niccolo. He'll make them see reason! For shame, madonna! You must not allow it!"

Serafina turned on the woman. "But I must! Who has done me more harm? Surely not Francesco!"

"For shame! You have a duty—"

"My duty is to the man I will marry!"

"Then you should stop them! Why would they do this?"

Serafina now gathered up her skirts and tried to keep up with Francesco, saying, "Why do men ever do what they do?"

A priest came from the episcopal palace and was told by Francesco to bear witness to a trial by combat.

"I will not! I cannot!" the priest protested.

"We ask no blessing, Father, only that you bear witness to a quarrel," Francesco replied.

"I cannot! I will not!"

"You will!" Durante growled and shouted down the priest's condemnation. Thus cowed to submission, he bade God hasten a decision for good or ill.

Francesco was strapped into a brigadine while Serafina watched. "Yet again I take up my sword for you by moonlight, sweetheart!" he jested. And under the disapproving eyes of her father, he gave Serafina a passionate kiss, one that bespoke victory.

The combatants met, offered courtesy. Francesco studied Durante's mocking face and smiled.

"God speed you to a grave," Durante said softly and laughed as he made a surprisingly vigorous thrust. Francesco anticipated the attack and equaled the parry with a feint more theatrical than practical. He heard applause and comments from the servants as if this was a tournament for sport and not to the death.

Francesco easily took on Durante but he had not expected such a vigorous opponent. He prayed that at the age of fifty-two he would have such vitality. With each *riposte*, Francesco's blade rang like a clarion and he felt their swords meeting in every sinew of his body.

Durante was spry and knew it. He welcomed each challenge and his eyes gleamed when the servants met his feints with approval. "Where is the strength I hear talk of, Romena? Are you not the finest horseman, the most excellent of knights, the most dread of warriors? Where is all that? I see none of it here!" Durante teased.

Francesco came at him then, hewing his way closer as if he were in the heat of a melee. Durante recognized the familiar bloodlust and his courage started to falter. As Francesco whirled and ducked, bent on a knee, and addressed each blow with new and frightening strength, Durante grew frightened.

"Stop! Watch out!"

A child had slipped through the ring of soldiers, and Durante looked behind him, stumbling on a tree root that caught his feet and projected him into the curtain. He fell and rolled onto his back as Francesco charged, and stood over him with sword raised. No one breathed. The hooting of an owl and the sobbing of a child for his bed pierced the silence. Serafina waited, her eyes sliding from Francesco to Durante and back again, and secretly rejoiced.

"Quarter! Quarter!" Durante gasped as he dug his heels into the earth and pressed closer to the stone of the curtain in an effort to escape.

Francesco kept the sword over the man's heaving, trembling chest. Behind them he heard whispers.

"Death!"

"He deserves it!"

"No quarter! Why should you?"

"Death, Monsignore!"

He ignored them.

The sword was shoved into the dirt to sway back and forth and tremble, throwing off flashes of light from the cresset lamps reflected on the metal. Durante closed his eyes and tasted his own tears, his own sweat. With a hand aching from his exertions, he made the sign of the cross and whispered a prayer of thanksgiving. When he opened his eyes, Francesco was crouching beside him. The countenance was grim but the eyes, Gesù! The eyes! Durante would never forget that look for as long as he lived and praised be to God and Francesco's uncommon sense, that would be for a long time to come.

"Tomorrow I shall be wed to your daughter," Francesco whispered in a voice only Durante could hear. "Bring yourself to terms with it?"

"Yes!" Durante answered in a rasping, uneasy voice. He needed a posset to stop the unnatural pounding in his head. He closed his eyes, begging

Francesco to let him rest and when again he opened them, Francesco was offering to help him to his feet and as they walked together to the donjon, the old man leaning on the younger, Francesco said low, again so that none could hear, "Now you know what my enemies know. Remember this."

CHAPTER 37

AS SOON AS the sun topped the trees of Monte alle' Croci, Francesco slipped out of bed and went down to the stables to see that the horses would be ready for their ride to Florence. When he returned, Serafina had risen, and they moved about the tower bedchamber silently and familiarly, getting ready for the day like a couple wedded twenty years and then some.

Marghareta didn't dare go up to the tower. Not after last night. She looked in on ser Durante and found him asleep at last. He'd kept her awake for most of the night. Between raving and fever Marghareta was certain madness or death would take him and hoped it was death, for if anyone deserved it, Durante Giustini would be that man. He'd answered to no one and cheated God and His angels for too long. What was he thinking to challenge a man as young and strong as Francesco da Romena? And over a slander about the conte's dead father! Deep in his cups when he made the invitation, no doubt!

He woke as Marghareta finished washing the spittle from the corners of his mouth and her presence gave him reason to continue last night's diatribe about Francesco. Lucifer and his minions were called upon to end Romena's miserable life. He'd think differently when the malady was gone, Marghareta thought, when the possets lost their effect and when he had to face Romena over a supper table. She told him that plainly and Durante began to weep and curse the day his daughter was born. They were all done for. The past could not be hidden.

Whether it was true, Marghareta didn't care. But something wasn't right.

She knew it for a fact when she climbed up to the tower and expected to be shouted down the staircase by Francesco da Romena or to hear the panting and sighing of lovemaking. Lovers stayed in bed 'til noon if they could get away with it!

Francesco da Romena was nowhere in sight. Marghareta first looked to the bed. No, the coverlets and sheets were just as smooth as they had been last night. The room didn't stink of a man's sweat or sex. Serafina was already dressed in a simple kirtle of tawny wadmal with a surcote of dark green wool. She was coiling her hair in plaits when Marghareta came round the bed curtains and found her struggling with the ribbons.

"Here, let me," Marghareta offered, and for once Serafina didn't protest.

"The conte di Romena has gone to Florence," Serafina answered the question on Marghareta's lips. "He'll return by noon. By then we shall be ready. You should gather your things. I want you to come with us."

"As you will, Madonna. Begging your pardon, where are we going?"

"To Castello di Romena."

"I'll see that one of the boys gets your father ready."

"*No!*"

The sharpness of the exclamation made Marghareta jab herself with a hairpin and then sucked noisily on her finger.

"My father will be brought to Florence. Francesco has men to watch over him, to see he does no harm to himself."

"You mean," Marghareta grumbled, still sucking, "to make sure he doesn't keep Francesco out of your bed!"

"My wedding bed. We will be married today." Serafina twisted around to look at her, and for the first time in years, Marghareta saw how vulnerable, how young the girl truly was. "Be glad for me, Marghareta! Never once have you approved of anything I've done. You said nothing when I was married by force and made a sex slave for Ranieri," she whispered huskily. "Can't you see how good this is? This is a good thing, and it is right!"

The girl's eyes were all that Marghareta could see at that moment, two large pools of violet that overwhelmed. Serafina was trembling and on the verge of tears. "There, lamb! There, there," Marghareta whispered and gathered Serafina into her arms. "It isn't fitting for a bride to cry on her wedding day!"

მ

THE CLERK MASSAGED his tired fingers and smiled meekly when Francesco spun round in his tour of the solar and began yet a fourth letter. Another letter that would be delivered within the hour. This was to ser Tommaso di Porciano. It was briefer than the other letters, praise be to God, but ended on a less than cordial tone:

> *No matter your feelings concerning this great enterprise of mine,*
> *we solemnly charge you with upholding those promises made*
> *some time ago, and your word is as gold to us. We charge you*
> *not to devise alliances with those who would do us ill, as we shall*
> *brook no interference. Heed our words well, that you may live.*

The clerk looked at Francesco uneasily, his unasked question answered with a smile. "I've no doubt that my uncle Porciano will keep his word. He has as much at stake as I do."

Before the clerk could pack up his instruments, Francesco bade him stay to scribe a final letter. "This to the captains of the garrisons in all of my castles, especially ser Roberto da Quintavale. Say this: all must be arrayed by nightfall and made ready against any eventuality."

❧

A CROWD OF curious and amused Florentines waited on the steps of the Duomo an hour before sunset that day. It was too impossible to be true: the widow Cunizza would at last snare Francesco da Romena in her web. Andrea Alberti received word just that morning that the Count of Romena wanted the marriage to Cunizza to be solemnized immediately. He had business in Avignon that made such haste a necessity.

Cunizza and her father marched into the Piazza del Duomo with a retinue as garish as it was scandalous. Noted first was the costly fabric of her gown, a glowing ruby-colored velvet brocaded in gold thread under which was a shirt of yellow silk, also embroidered with gold thread. Over this splendid gown was a surcote lined in gold tissue and blazoned with the heraldic crests of both the Alberti and Romena. One dressmaker remarked to another that the gown had been made months before and that at least Cunizza had the good taste not to wear her hair loose. Bride though she was, virgin she was not.

And so the bride took her place at the top of the Duomo steps, escorted by her father and the bishop of Florence, reigning over an expectant crowd that did not include the two men thought to gain the most from this unnatural alliance: Tommaso di Porciano and Azzelino Alberti.

❧

THE STREETS WERE quiet. In fact, Tommaso could not remember a day when he had sat at this window and heard nothing, nothing but the nickering of horses in the stable across the street, the fly buzzing about the chamber in lazy rectangles. Tommaso had been staring out the window for almost an hour, waiting for the sound of church bells on the other side of Florence, the signal that the deed was done. There was no one on the street. Were they all at the cathedral with Alberti and his daughter?

He started when Azzelino snorted and grumbled in his drunken nap. He'd been so quiet that Tommaso had all but forgotten his presence. Blest be Elisabetta for thinking ahead, to suggest keeping Azzelino drunk and under his watch until the marriage rites were done.

Tommaso stared down at Francesco's letter, taking particular interest in the fine signature. He picked it up and sighed, read it for what might have been the tenth time in an hour. For his silence and cooperation in this enterprise that would soon shake all of the Florentine to her stones, Francesco had promised a great deal.

"I'll go back to Avignon," Azzelino drawled and then belched, following it with a feminine, irritating, giggle. "There's no damage I can do here. Not when my cousin of Romena has purchased all the favor in Tuscany! Do you think, Uncle, he might have let me officiate over the marriage rites? Of course not! He chooses a bishop of little consequence over me. He might have given me that pleasure if I couldn't see him dead. No, I'll go back to

Avignon."

"That's a wise decision. Perhaps in time you and Romena can come to terms. Sometimes it's best to be reconciled with your enemy."

"Like you did?"

"If you behave yourself, perhaps Francesco will give you something for all your trouble."

"You sound like a wet nurse: keep your holiday robes clean and I'll give you a sweet! No, Uncle! It will take more than keeping my holiday robes clean for Romena to earn my cooperation in anything!"

Azzelino had staggered up from the window seat and was now swaying beside Tommaso, trying to steady himself on the old man's shoulder. He began to giggle when he saw the elegant cursive hand of Francesco da Romena on the letter Tommaso was holding.

"What's that? A love letter from one of your slatterns?"

Before Tommaso could hide the letter up his sleeve, it was torn from him. The reaction was expected and violent. Azzelino was out the door, Tommaso's pleas going with him. Elisabetta hurried into the room when she heard the commotion and gave an exasperated sigh when she found Tommaso alone.

"You didn't tell him! Please tell me you didn't!" she begged.

"I didn't have to. He saw Francesco's letter," Tommaso answered raising and dropping his hands in a universal gesture of helplessness.

"Oh, Tommaso! Why do you think I thought it best to keep him drunk and ignorant? This will be the end of us all!"

Tommaso nodded wearily and said they should go to the church and hope to arrive before the cardinal.

❧

SITTING ALONE IN the nave of San Miniato al Monte, Serafina tried her best to recite childhood prayers to comfort her, but no comfort came. The vespers bell rang and still there was no sign of Francesco. Even the priest engaged to perform the marriage was late.

Again she would be married in secrecy within the confines of the nave rather than on the steps of the church. The church doors would be closed against proper witnesses; no spring flowers strewn before the bridal couple, no music or happy children. The rite would be performed in haste so that no one could question its dubious legality.

Serafina wanted to cry, but she was too frightened.

She got up and took a turn around the empty nave. Once in the course of her stroll, she glanced down at the exquisite gown Francesco had delivered that afternoon, made of silver tissue and studded with gold cabochons among needle-worked trefoils. The bands at the wrists and bodice were of heavily embroidered tawny silk. At the center of the bodice was the silver falcon of Romena embroidered with diamonds and pearls.

The eye of the falcon was a blue onyx. She sighed and smoothed the cloth carefully. At this wedding ceremony there would be no one to admire the bridal clothes.

A door closed.

"Francesco?"

No, it was Niccolo and Marghareta instead. She closed her eyes and swallowed the lump in her throat.

"How lovely you are!" Marghareta gushed.

"He's not coming!" Serafina whispered.

"Patience, sweetheart," Niccolo replied as he bestowed a kiss on her brow. "I didn't give you up for naught."

Francesco suddenly swept in with an armed escort and two priests trying their best to match his long strides. Francesco's man Lorenzo hurried in next, followed by Roberto da Quintavale, who timidly offered Serafina a bouquet of fragrant roses. Francesco placed two of his soldiers at the great doors opening out to the porch and then strode up the nave, his cloak billowing behind him like a sail.

"Ah, there you are, Niccolo!" he greeted breathlessly. "I'm glad you delayed your trip to England. I've brought two priests. One to perform the rite and one to witness it. And our loyal servants. My men will see that the doors are kept open to ensure a proper marriage but detain any who should protest our work here." He now turned to the bewildered Serafina. "Well, Fina! Here we are." Francesco eagerly took her hands. "I've summoned my vassals and a few of the country folk in the neighborhood to witness this happy occasion," he explained, and brought her out to the porch where two dozen baffled peasants, each clutching a shiny new coin in a dirty fist, waited at the bottom of the steps which were strewn with flowers. Upon Serafina's arrival, a shout of praise and good fortune went up in the crowd and musicians struck a song in her honor. A ring of soldiers surrounded the piazza before the church. It was so ludicrous. Francesco and his bride stood on the porch and held hands, trying with difficulty to suppress their laughter.

"Well priests," he said to the clerics standing behind them, "do your work and do it quickly!"

❧

AT THE DUOMO, the bishop of Florence avoided Alberti's stares and loosened the clasp fastening his cope. Cunizza stood quietly with a proud face for show. No one left her at the altar, not even Francesco da Romena.

"He isn't going to come!" she said behind her smile and between her teeth.

"Be silent!" Alberti hissed, and as he said this caught sight of Tommaso di Porciano and Cardinal Azzelino running into the Piazza del Duomo. It was then Cunizza realized that she had indeed been made a fool of, and began to weep.

෨

A CROWD SCRAMBLED up the stairs to San Miniato as the bells started to ring. Alberti fell on his knees and began to weep and moan like a spoiled child. Azzelino pulled his stepfather up and dragged him along, scolding and berating the old man as if he was an errant child. Their foolish party had gathered numbers by the time they reached the piazza.

Francesco drew his sword when he heard the crowd and motioned to his men to stand ready. "You're too late; it's done," Francesco said when the bells were quiet.

"No!" screamed Alberti, his shout echoing through the trees and frightening kestrels that suddenly gave flight.

"I warned you. Pay homage to my countess and have done with it," Francesco ordered, motioning with his sword. Andrea and Azzelino stared at the girl trembling beside him and did nothing. The Florentines clustered at the foot of the steps began to spread the word that Romena had married his lover and a cheer went up in the crowd.

"There is nothing any of you can do," Francesco pronounced, looking directly at Azzelino. At the edge of the crowd he spotted Elisabetta and Tommaso, keeping a discreet distance from the rest.

"I swear I'll make you suffer for this!" Alberti swore. "We had a contract!"

"That contract was nullified the moment your stepson tried to kill Roberto da Quintavale at the tournament."

"It was Quintavale, not you! There! Azzelino did no harm to you!"

"But he thought it was me and we agreed that the cardinal would not interfere, and we had that agreement put to paper. His interference in any way would render the contract invalid. Your notaries and judges will agree with me."

"We had a contract! It is legal and binding!"

"And I was pledged to Serafina Giustini ere I agreed to take your daughter. It's done."

While Andrea continued protesting there was movement in the crowd and Durante Giustini pushed his way forward. Serafina glared at Marghareta, who began to protest her innocence. Francesco patted Marghareta's shoulder reassuringly and held a hand out to Durante.

"Father, I hope you are well this evening; better than last?" Francesco greeted.

"I am against this!" Durante shouted loudly so that all could hear. "I would rather see my daughter dead than married to this man!" He spat violently.

"And I shall see that that never happens," Francesco replied quietly.

"You!" Durante growled at a priest. "Did you perform the rite?"

309

The priest shrank away, stepping within the safe confines of the narthex as Durante came closer. Two of Francesco's soldiers made a protective curtain before the priest, Francesco, and Serafina.

"It matters little who performed the rite," Francesco said. "What matters is that it is done."

"No!" Durante screamed.

"I'll kill you, I swear it!" Alberti sobbed, crumbling to his knees.

"Try as you might, you'll be dead before you best me."

The bells of San Miniato al Monte once more began to peal, this time for the wedding of Francesco da Romena and Serafina Giustini.

CHAPTER 38

THE JANGLE OF coins dropped one at a time into a bowl was starting to wear on Tommaso's nerves. He turned from his meditation on the dying fire to across the chamber where Azzelino was slouched over a trencher of untouched food, his hand refusing to yield the flask of malmsey that had been its captive for most of the evening. Tommaso turned back to the fire and found more interest in the embers dancing among the white-hot logs. He reached out to shove one errant piece of wood that shimmered with liquid light and singed the toe of his new boot.

Again, the jangle of coins. An oafish laugh and then a sigh like the wind being pressed out of a swollen pig's bladder.

"Would you stop that?" Tommaso demanded.

"It's all I've got left," Azzelino drawled.

Tommaso grunted and pulled his robe closer to capture the fire's warmth. He didn't much like this room in the daylight; he despised it at night. Of all the rooms in his house, this room he'd never taken care to decorate lavishly. It was more storeroom than private chamber, with its naked stone walls and unadorned windows. The furnishings were little more than bales of unprocessed wool from the Cotswolds and tall ells of cloth that caught the firelight and threw off a myriad of hues, which at any other time would have been pleasing to the eye. Not now. Tommaso was counting the minutes until Azzelino tired of feeling sorry for himself and went elsewhere to sleep it off.

"Something has to be done."

"Eminence, admit defeat. Return to Avignon."

"Eminence? Eminence? You must be quarrelsome, Uncle, to speak to me with respect!"

Another laugh came from the dark corner and then the silence was rent by the crash of pottery and furniture overturning.

"What is it now?" Tommaso sighed.

"I should have killed him when I had the chance!" Azzelino snarled as he came at Tommaso like a wounded bear. The elder man leaped from his bench and sought protection behind a servant roused from his nap by the commotion.

"So close, so close!"

Azzelino continued to babble insensibly. Tommaso looked at him in disgust and signaled to the servant to bring a torch. It was time they were up to bed.

"I can send a man to kill him! What would she do then?" Azzelino started to giggle as they made their way through the dark house to the bedchambers above stairs. "I can see that he falls from one of his damned gray horses or trips on a sword! What would she do? She'd have no one!"

"Eminence, you'd surely be found out. It's foolhardy. We'll talk in the morning."

"No, damn you! Damn you for a fool!"

Tommaso winced in pain as Azzelino wrenched back his arm to prevent him from going into his wife's bedchamber. He was pressed into a cold wall so that he could feel the uneven grade of the stone that had built the house. And then Azzelino's face was close and his sour breath took what little wholesome air there was between them.

"You could have prevented all! I listened to you and this is what becomes of me! I will not sit idly and live to comfortable old age while Romena achieves all! He has the one thing he should never have been allowed to take!" Azzelino rasped, and as he swore profane oaths, he clutched at Tommaso's throat so that the old man couldn't breathe and struggled to free himself.

"What . . . do you . . . propose . . . to . . . do?" Tommaso gasped.

"When all's said and done, death is the balance, the righter of wrongs!"

Tommaso was afraid to look at this young man, to look at this son, this monster he'd made of his own ambition.

"Tell me you don't want something of the Romena fortune! Gesù! It's all you used to talk about!" Azzelino continued, the effect of the wine starting to wear. "Your sons are dead and your name's a joke because of your obsession for it. I can't believe you've ended your quarrel, given up so easily! Are you content to live a merchant? To count your bales of wool and defer to landed men? To be the titleless, landless son in a family bloated with princes?"

"It's what I've gotten used to. You should also. It's what comes from being born to the wrong son in the Guidi family."

"What are you saying?" Azzelino had released him, shoved him away as if he was rife with contagion. "What are you saying?"

"Why do you think all these years Alberti never cared a fig for you? It wasn't because you were some knight's by-blow off my sister Marietta!"

"What are you saying?"

"I'm your father!"

It took a moment and then Azzelino nodded, asking in a surprisingly calm tone: "And my mother? Who's she?"

"Albera da Susiana, the niece of the Holy Roman Emperor.

Alessandro's widow."

Tommaso expected to be shoved further against the wall, to be told he was lying; that it was a cruel joke, but nothing like that happened. Azzelino spat. He wiped his mouth on his sleeve and took a last look at Tommaso before leaving.

"You've only made what I've decided easier!"

"No one is less welcome than an unwanted brother!" Tommaso called after him.

Azzelino stopped, smiling. "That would depend on which brother is unwanted. Are you going to help me?" A pause, then, as if trying it on for size, "Father?"

Tommaso raised his hands imploringly and then dropped them just as quickly, letting them hang limp, sagging just as his shoulders did.

"I'll give you a day to think about it, and if by then you've not given me satisfaction, God help you!"

His ultimatum delivered, Azzelino found his way down the passageway and disappeared. Tommaso didn't move until he heard the slam of a door.

By the time Tommaso had risen the next morning, a letter arrived from Azzelino. There was no need to read it; the contents were already known. When Tommaso finally did, it sickened him to admit he'd taught Azzelino well. He spent the rest of the day locked in his bedchamber, shouting down the pleas of Elisabetta and the servants when they banged on the door. It was twilight when he finally emerged, and by that time the household was already in bed.

Elisabetta turned in the bed when she heard the door open. "Today I lit enough candles for you to burn down the cathedral," she sighed.

Shrugging in response, Tommaso pulled the small chair away from the hearth and sat down, pulling one of Elisabetta's annoying lap dogs into his arms. He sat there quietly, stroking the dog's warm belly and listening to Elisabetta's recounting of the day's events while she combed out her gilt hair. He noted there were streaks of gray among the gold and marveled that it was still breathtaking. For Elisabetta, though advanced in years now, was still a handsome, desirable woman. It was rare that he came to her bed these days. Would she think it odd if he stayed the night? Perhaps, when he explained what he'd thought about for hours, she would not think it strange at all.

"I think I should go to Castello di Romena," he said at last.

"If you've a notion to cause trouble,"

Elisabetta was shocked by what he did next. Tommaso took his wife in his arms and kissed her. Not a perfunctory, chaste kiss that bespoke years of marriage and inconvenience, but one born of need.

He had forgotten what it was like to make love to his wife. Of late, whores and serving girls had satisfied his needs; they were mechanical and impersonal couplings that left him angry. Now enveloped in Elisabetta's arms in the afterglow of climax, he was acutely aware of her scent, the softness of her skin, and wondered why he had ever strayed, why he had preferred the witch Albera to her.

Elisabetta drew the coverlets around them and drifted in and out of sleep, kneading Tommaso's tense neck with a hand. "What have you done, Tommaso, that requires such absolution?" she asked at last.

"I told Azzelino."

"Why?" she gasped, sitting up in bed. "He will destroy you as assuredly he would destroy Francesco! My God, Tommaso! None of us are safe!"

"When Gian Maria died, Francesco asked me to make peace. I told him to go to hell. And then there was another time and I ignored that, too. We made peace of sorts, but not real peace. See where that has left me? It's time I went to Castello di Romena. I believe the offer still stands. Would you like to come with me?"

❧

ELISABETTA WAS UNPREPARED for the sight of Castello di Romena. Her eyes misted when they rode up the orchard-lined road toward the barbican and were saluted by the watch as they rode through the gates. Fourteen great towers rose out of the mist and fog and cast slate-colored, early morning shadows over the contado. As in her childhood memories, each tower bore a pennon displaying the mulberry and gold of Romena. And now something else, pennons of blue and silver. The new contessa's colors. Garlands coiled round pillars and were stretched across the curtains. A fortnight had come and gone, yet Romena still celebrated his wedding.

The bridegroom was waiting for them on the steps to the donjon.

"Elisabetta, welcome home," Francesco murmured when they kissed in greeting. He turned and inclined his head towards Tommaso, who had dismounted and had joined them, then extended a hand towards the stairs to the solar. He leaned against the doors and waited while Tommaso and Elisabetta removed their traveling cloaks and stood by the fire warming themselves. "You'll have to forgive me for not responding immediately to your letter, Porciano, I am more accustomed to your declarations of war than peace," he opened. He motioned towards Lorenzo, who came with goblets steaming with brandywine.

"It takes us all by surprise," Tommaso admitted. He was distracted for the moment by the sound of women singing in the antechamber, the soft laughter of young girls, and he wondered which of the voices belonged to the young contessa.

Francesco knelt by the hearth began to take pains with the collar around his alaunt's neck, and Tommaso began counting the painted stars on the beamed ceiling, noting the brightness of the initials "S" and "F" among the decorations laid out so many centuries before.

"Please, make yourselves comfortable," Francesco said, gesturing toward the cushioned bench at the hearth.

"How is your wife, Francesco?" Elisabetta spoke up. Her smiled widened when she realized it was a fortunate question when Francesco's demeanor changed almost immediately. "She is Eden, I tell you," he gushed.

"I pray you will never have to go to war again, that you will never have to leave her side," Elisabetta said and leaned over to kiss his cheek.

"That will depend on a number of things," Francesco answered, and looked directly at Tommaso. "Perhaps now we should talk?"

"There isn't much to talk about. Everything I wrote in my letter is true. I never knew that I would ever be afraid of my own child!" Tommaso said.

"Whatever agreement we come to, Tommaso, it will all depend on you. I have no desire for betrayal of any kind. I've had my share of it and I'm sick to death of it. Truth is, we need each other now. We have a common fear."

"Whatever you wish. Give me the treaty and I'll sign."

"After supper, then," Francesco replied and raised his cup. "I never thought I'd see the day."

Tommaso nodded and placed the cup he held to his lips, but his hand was unsteady and his nerves so raw that when Francesco gently took the fine silver cup from him, he gasped.

"Be at ease, Tommaso. I keep a better garrison than I used to. Do you need my protection?" Francesco asked.

The angle of Tommaso's shoulders shifted so abruptly that Francesco knew he was correct in that assumption. Francesco glanced at Elisabetta and she nodded. "It's not pleasant is it? Not knowing from where your enemies spring. This family is remarkable for breeding malcontents and showing them how to hate their fathers."

"Will you help me, Francesco?"

It was the closest Francesco had ever heard Tommaso to desperation. It was the first time he'd heard Tommaso use his Christian name. The fear in his voice was genuine. Rather than dismiss the matter to another day, which he would have done a year ago, Francesco nodded. "You shall have as many men and arms as I can spare. I pray to God you shall not have need of them."

The bargain was sealed when Tommaso took Francesco's hand. Their eyes met briefly, and Tommaso knew from that steeled glance that Francesco expected from him no less than what he promised.

"And now, Nephew, let me bid a good morning to your pretty wife," Tommaso said and nodded in the direction of the antechamber door where Serafina stood.

అ

"THAT WAS A marvelous undertaking," Serafina remarked after Tommaso and Elisabetta left with an armed escort for Florence several days later. "To think old Porciano would build a chantry in memory of Gismonda. To think that he has become your champion! He owes you more than that, but it is one right against so many wrongs."

Francesco draped an arm around her as they walked from the gatehouse back to the donjon. "Do you approve?"

"Husband, we all have past loves. I was never so fortunate, but you were," she answered, kissing him.

"I am now," he whispered.

"I will be fortunate indeed if my father comes to call."

"All in time, Fina; see how long it's taken to work one miracle."

"Miracle? You'll be a grandsire ere we enjoy that second coming!"

Francesco forced a smile for her but kept his thoughts to himself. As much as he had tried in the last two weeks, his overtures of friendship had been rejected outright. As far as Durante was concerned, there was no marriage. He considered his daughter Francesco's concubine and no better than her mother. These endearing missives from Durante he'd managed to keep from his wife.

In time, Francesco thought. *See how long it took to work one miracle?*

". . . shall you keep your promise to me?" Serafina teased, skipping ahead of him.

"Which promise was that? I've made so many these past weeks," Francesco laughed, catching up. He thought of one in particular and kissed the base of her neck in hopes that would rouse her memory and other things.

"Shall we go falconing?" Serafina asked, offering a smile.

"You read my mind."

"For wagers, I hope?"

"If you'd like,"

"What is the prize?" Serafina asked, skipping alongside him.

"Do you have to ask?"

Serafina blushed and said they'd both come out the victor.

An hour later they were on a hill near the castle where Serafina removed the hood from her favorite gyrfalcon and watched as she circled and swooped in one fluid movement to claim her prey.

"Look how pale our lord of Romena is," Serafina cooed to her ladies, and they all burst into laughter, for Francesco had again lost the bet.

"I wager that's six florins you owe me, Husband!" Serafina said with a laugh when she rode over to where Francesco sat with his henchmen under a walnut tree.

"I wager I'll wager no more, Wife!" he said and helped her out of the saddle, loving how she slid languidly down into his arms, feeling every contour of her body against his, which made him long for privacy. He moved away just in time for the gyrfalcon to light on her mistress' gauntlet and demand praise for her performance. Serafina soothed the bird with gentle caresses and sweet words that Francesco would have sooner heard from his wife behind the confines of their bed curtains. She handed the bird off to the falconer so that she could deal with her envious husband.

"How shall you pay me?" Serafina teased, holding her hand out.

Feigning insult, Francesco pressed into her palm the amethyst pendant he'd claimed back from the goldsmith in the old market so long ago. "I know you wanted to throw this into the Arno," Francesco began.

"No, no!" she exclaimed, slipping it on. "Mother cherished it, but the suitor,"

"My father. And that is all that needs to be said, save that I am not my father and you are not your mother," Francesco whispered. "Let this be a talisman of good fortune and happiness!"

While Roberto organized a supper party in the meadow, Francesco lured Serafina towards a coppice away from the others and pulled her down into a soft tuft of grass. A willow's low-lying branches made a bower for their lovemaking.

"I'll be sun burnt and wind burnt and the sport of jests from my ladies," Serafina sighed, reaching for the shift Francesco purposefully held from her and inched farther away every time she was close. "You are evil!" she jested when he tossed it, forcing her to forget modesty and scramble for it among the wildflowers.

Francesco swore softly as he beheld his wife ambling naked like a woodland sylph in their hiding place. The sunlight and late afternoon shadows dappled her ivory skin and made each curve of her body more alluring, tempting him again.

"Gesu, but I have a fair and wanton wife!" he proclaimed when he seized her as she tried to flee. Serafina feigned anger and struggled only for a chance to press closer to his body, the torso she'd heard her women talk of in phrases and sentences she'd never think a lady would use; she knew them all to be gloriously true. She had the husband all women in Florence wanted and lusted after. Let them fantasize about what it would be like to lie in these powerful arms; she knew.

Serafina let him press her against the bruised and broken grass where they had lain for almost two hours now and wrapped him in her arms.

"Aren't you worried about a sunburn, Sweetheart?" he laughed softly.

"The sun will set in an hour!" she gasped when she felt his lips where she hoped they'd be.

"Monsignore! Francesco! Monsignore!"

The shouts came from the meadow. Francesco rolled off Serafina and swore hotly, grabbing for his clothes.

"Look; those are the banners of Florence," she murmured, pointing toward riders coming up from the south.

Moments later Serafina stood with her women and pretended to ignore their stares at her grass-stained and rumpled clothing, their comments with their double meanings, while Lorenzo, Roberto, and Francesco discussed something consequential that had occurred with the heralds. Serafina knew it was news of the worst kind. They were soon riding with all haste back to the castle.

Envoys from Florence waited in the bailey. They were exhausted, having ridden to Castello di Romena from Florence in so short a time and immediately followed Francesco and his men to the solar when they arrived. Serafina was left to pace the great hall. When she could stand the suspense no more, she went upstairs to join the men and was met by silence as soon as she opened the door.

"What are you doing?" Francesco barked. "Get out!"

"I would know what is happening!" Serafina protested.

"You'll know soon enough but not now."

"I would know now, Husband."

The gentle lover of only this afternoon had vanished and was replaced by a hard-visaged man of arms. She was dismissed without his usual tenderness or promises. When she demanded to stay and hear, Francesco barked at his knights to escort her to the tower as if she were a prisoner. Serafina went quietly, listening as her husband's voice rose in anger and the civil exchange between Florence's emissaries turned into a quarrel.

Hours passed when she heard horses leaving the bailey. She went down to discover what was afoot. "Francesco; husband, I—"

"Go back to the tower and stay there!" Francesco snapped, turning angrily at the sound of her voice. His face was pale and his eyes dark and angry. When she was gone, Francesco threw the sword he held on the ground.

"She'll have to be told," Roberto offered.

"What good will that do? Having her worry about my safety?"

"You have to do something. Porciano's towns along the Florentine frontier have already fallen and you gave a promise."

"Monsignore?" A forager had entered the solar fresh from his horse. Francesco glanced at him, questioning. The fellow knelt and said, "Our scouts have returned. Every town on the frontier from Arezzo to Florence has submitted to Azzelino Alberti. He rides at the head of a powerful army that swells by the hour."

"I can issue commissions for array," Roberto offered.

"Do that!" Francesco snapped, and turning back to the forager, said, "Anything else?"

"Not that you'd want to hear,"

"What is it, Coluccio?" Roberto asked gently.

"An army approaches Consuma and means to join with the cardinal. Durante Giustini rides at its head."

It was some time before Francesco spoke. "It is as you said," he murmured to one of the envoys. "I didn't think it possible." He turned to Roberto and added, "We'll not tell the contessa, shall we? Not yet, at least. There may be a chance to turn this around and make it work to our advantage."

Romena and Porciano towns within reach of the Florentine contado and those on the Aretine border had been plundered in quick, violent raids. Francesco carefully considered his moves. He arrayed his garrisons from Consuma to Poppi but wondered if that would be enough. How many men would be willing to fight against a man of God?

Serafina was already up from bed when Francesco returned to the solar after a night of preparation and war councils.

"Let me come with you," she pleaded softly.

"No; there is too great a risk in both of us going."

"I shall ask for sanctuary at San Miniato."

"You'll stay here with Roberto. I've left enough men to protect you. No arguments! Promise you'll not follow," Francesco said after they kissed.

"Yes," she answered dutifully.

"Cover yourself; here comes Roberto. Smile now."

"Francesco, everything is ready," Roberto advised and kissed the hand Serafina extended, looking up to smile at her sweet, sad face.

Serafina stood beside the window and watched as Francesco rode out of the castle with his retainers. It was an age-old ritual; women watching their men ride off to battle and then going on with their lives as if nothing out of the ordinary had transpired. Marghareta made this apparent when, an hour later, she entered and told her mistress there were several vassals waiting below to offer petitions. She was the contessa di Romena, and certain duties were expected of her, even in a time of uncertainty and war.

CHAPTER 39

"ABBATE, DO YOU not think it's the best course of action? After all, ten florins is ten florins and we can afford it."

The Abbate di Badia Prataglia couldn't believe his ears, and turning to the subprior and brothers said, "Do you think he is a common mercenary? He'll not be bought with ten florins."

"He'll not be purchased at all! He is a man of the cloth! A cardinal anointed and invested with holy obligations."

"Fra Pietro, of all the cardinals in the curia, how many are celibate, poor, and say their office?" one brother spoke up. "Such a calling is not for the pious!"

"For shame, Fra Agnolo! He is a man chosen by God! If the Lord so chooses, he could well become our next vicar of Christ!"

"Azzelino Alberti a pope?"

The comment brought laughter to the usually silent chapter house. Abbate Filippo rapped his knuckle on the stone bench and the fraternity grew silent once more.

"To the business at hand, my brothers. What we think of the cardinal is for God alone to know. To the business at hand. He'll not be purchased cheap. We have our orders."

"But no one's heard from Francesco da Romena for days."

"If ser Francesco was dead, I'm sure we would have heard something by now. We have our orders."

"What does the contessa say?" Abbate Filippo spoke up.

"His contessa! His whore!" spat an elder brother and nearly extinguished the candles with his breathy sigh.

"She is as much in the dark as anyone here," Abbate Filippo answered. He turned to the elder brother still carrying on about the contessa Romena and leveled disapproving eyes on him. "Choose your words carefully, Brother. She well may prove our benefactress!"

For that came a murmur of approval. The subprior nodded and studied each of the brothers in the chapter house, looking for assent. "And if the conte still lives, we'll have much to answer for if we do not obey and protect her."

The bell struck for matins, ending Chapter. "Well," Abbate Filippo sighed, "shall we go out and greet Cardinal Alberti?"

Azzelino Alberti had garrisoned his army at Corezzo and rode alone to the Badia, disappointed there were so few to honor him on the short progress. He knew there'd be trouble when he saw the abbot and his cadre of brothers assembled in the close.

"Welcome Eminence," Abbate Filippo greeted, kissing the ring of office thrust under his nose.

"Should I know you?" Azzelino demanded.

"I am Abbate Filippo, by the authority and good grace of the conti Guidi and bishop of Arezzo."

"I am now vicar of this holy see by authority of the pope."

"But which one? Eminence, I do not question the authority of our most worthy Holy Father in Rome or even Avignon, but it is customary for the lords of Romena to recommend to the Curia—"

Azzelino threw down a sheath of documents with papal seals dangling from each like gobs of blood. "The conte di Romena is dead. I am vicar of the holy see of Pratovecchio,"

"There is no holy see of Pratovecchio!"

"—which extends as far north as San Godenzo, to the south at Subbiano, to the east at Bagno a Romagna, and to the west at Borgo San Lorenzo," Azzelino snapped.

Abbate Filippo skeptically glanced at the documents handed to him. "That is the entirety of Romena lands!" he protested.

"It is no longer held by Romena, either by right or inheritance. If you had read the papal bull issued Saturday last, you would know. You would also do well to at least show respect, even if you cannot feel it!"

"My loyalty is to Francesco da Romena, Eminence; you may have authority and privileges as befit the office you hold, but 'tis known a cardinal's red hat may be purchased if a man has the money and influence."

Azzelino sighed and drew a sword. God's bread, but he'd have to be put out by a country priest! "Do you quarrel with me?" he growled.

"I stand for Romena."

The abbot's defiance was license enough for Azzelino, who slew him on the consecrated ground of the abbey close. When the impotent prior and subprior could only mouth whispered protests, Azzelino threw down his bloodied sword and dismounted. "I am Azzelino Cardinal Alberti, vicar of the holy see of Pratovecchio." Before entering the church, however, he blessed the murdered man.

Castello di Romena stood ready. Serafina sent word to the cardinal that he would never be welcome so long as she was *Castellana*, but he was soon at the gates with his army.

She stood at the barbican entrance with the household garrison. Francesco had taken most of his army and captains to Florence, leaving

Roberto in command. But Roberto had been sent to Florence yesterday to discover Francesco's whereabouts and seek help. Even the sweet and good Lorenzo was with his lord. Serafina knew it was a mistake to send her most trusted man so far afield, but she needed to know of Francesco's safety before all else. Now she stood with twenty household knights.

"I come with news of your husband!" the cardinal greeted.

"Any news you bring is at once suspect."

He dismounted and walked towards the barbican. Even from the distance between them, Azzelino saw those violet eyes blaze, and he relished the thought of bantering with her. Playing with his prey before he devoured it.

As expected, she attacked. "Stand where you are! Make no move or it will be your last!" The hiss and clang of swords taken from sheaths made Azzelino pause for a moment. He raised his hands and walked forward.

"A battle was joined at Campolombardo and Romena was vanquished," Azzelino said as he slowly approached. "Most of his army was either killed or set to flight. For all we know, he's gone to ground. Or dead. I know he was wounded. I saw the arrow he caught in the breast. With a wound like that, more than likely he's dead."

Serafina and her captains exchanged doubtful glances. Campolombardo was not so far. If it were true, surely a scout would have come back with news. Still, it would explain Francesco's unnatural silence these past few days.

"Madonna, you must yield. There is no other—"

Azzelino's words were cut off by her shout. "No! The Casentino, the Pratomagno, and Mugello belong to the conte di Romena! I could easily raise the entire contado and most assuredly I will do that if forced! I will not move from this place!"

"I'll take you by force if you don't come willingly."

"You will not," she insisted, her eyes nevertheless riveted to the column of knights and archers approaching. "I have instructions from my husband to stay here until his safe return."

"He'll never return," Azzelino laughed. "He's dead!"

"Then all of the Casentino will rise up. And Florence. You know how Florence loves martyrs!"

Azzelino was now at the portcullis. He threw down his sword and unloosed the belt gathering his scarlet tabard, dropping that too, arms splayed forth to show he was unarmed.

"You know better than to cross me, Serafina. I am your only protection."

"I will not disobey my husband."

"Then you sign your death warrant."

"I said I will not go!"

"You know I can realize ten times more soldiers than you see here and topple this castle to the ground. I have armies standing ready in Poppi and Stia," Azzelino responded, his cordiality fading. "I do not jest, madonna. You know me. I've done worse."

"Stay back!" Serafina shouted as he approached. "That's far enough! Remove yourself!"

"When I think of us in the heat of battle, this isn't what my mind conjures."

A buzzing caught Serafina off guard and she was pushed out of the way as one of her archers aimed for Azzelino and missed. That one arrow was answered by a shower and from under the cover of a shield and two of her captains, she watched her men struck down. No one was left standing except for her and her two captains.

"I yield!" she screamed.

Serafina's heart pounded in her ears. She could barely hear Azzelino giving commands to his men, but watched as his army quietly and without further violence took the castle. Francesco's loyal servants and the rest of the garrison led away to imprisonment and perhaps death. She had lost and now resigned herself to imprisonment, rape, and other horrors, until she saw Fiasella.

Fiasella was laughing at a shared jest with Azzelino as easily as if they'd been companions for years. The fear subsided and Serafina was now full of rage. As soon as she got him alone, the fool would wish it were an audience with Francesco instead! Fiasella dared to meet her gaze and found it frightening, promising vengeance. He turned quickly to bark orders at his men to take the garrison into custody.

Azzelino was speaking to her again. "I'll not carry out my threats if you obey, Serafina; you shall be treated with all the respect due your station."

"What are your promises but lies?"

Azzelino removed a glove and stroked the soft, white skin of her cheek with his hand. Again he kissed her, but this time it was not a courteous kiss of greeting. It was a kiss that brought laughter and approval from his men. "Give me half a chance and I'll prove you wrong!" he whispered. He offered his arm and escorted Serafina into the donjon.

❧

"MADONNA, HIS EMINENCE requests leave to dine in your company," Marghareta announced. She raised her brows inquiringly and waited for Serafina to finish playing before coming further into the solar. Azzelino had given his golden bird a magnificent cage, at least. She was under house arrest. The song Serafina played on the harp was one introduced by Francesco from Avignon; a Provençal jongleur entertained them with it at the 'love day' festivities. Serafina was always humming it.

"Tell the cardinal he would do better to go elsewhere," Serafina replied and continued to play.

"Thank you for not sending me to hell. It gets tiresome," Azzelino said as he entered the solar, for once without a bodyguard and the trappings of his holy office. He looked like a common soldier now.

"I know for a fact you were cast out. You were too expensive to maintain and too much competition for the devil," Serafina wryly jested. She ended the song with a lush chord and then turned to him. "Leave me. You're not welcome here."

"I've come to bargain with you."

"I do not make bargains."

"Then you must stay here until you see reason."

"Am I a hostage?"

"I suppose you are."

"Either I am or I'm not. But why a hostage, since there's no one to pay my ransom? What's it to be?"

"What you will. It will be what you wish it to be."

She plucked at the strings randomly, each note rich and clear, floating away distinct from its sisters, and then she smiled sweetly at Azzelino. "I wish you were dead."

Azzelino eased himself onto a cushioned chest and folded his hands as if in preparation for prayer. For a moment he was silent. Serafina kept her eyes on him.

"Come with me to Avignon! He's dead. I've instructed my clerk to draw up new contracts for the Romena lands and castles. Sign and you shall be free. You shall have any of the castles in the Casentino if you come to Avignon with me."

Serafina picked up a basin and hurled it, the crockery shattering against the bed dais. Azzelino bowed away, a triumphant smile curling his lips.

She heard their quarrels later in the night, the voices of Azzelino and Fiasella rising with the quantity of food and wine they consumed. She knew eventually they'd turn against each other, for when did renegades ever keep faith? Pretending not to care, Serafina instructed her women to keep playing their musical instruments and hoped it would drown the angry voices growing louder and more dangerous.

"Madonna?"

Serafina raised the book closer to her face in order to avoid confrontation with Marghareta, who had been whining for some time that they must all go to bed.

"It's been quiet for nigh on an hour."

"Perhaps they've killed one another!" came the barb, bringing nervous laughter from the tired women. Serafina noted the candles and saw they were three-quarters burned down. Dawn was coming on.

"Open the shutters. We will say our morning office with the new sun,"

Serafina said cheerfully.

"Yes, open them; this promises to be a momentous day." Azzelino came in and with a gesture dismissed all the women.

"I will not go!" Marghareta hissed. "I made a pledge to madonna's husband!" Her protests were stifled when Azzelino threw a backhand at her face and she ran after the others, vowing revenge.

The doors were bolted. Serafina moved toward the windows when Azzelino laid aside his cloak and gloves and made himself comfortable on the bed.

"Are you going to jump? That isn't like you," he laughed.

"You promised to leave me alone."

"I promised to spare your life. How I make you live it is another matter. You grew accustomed to one way of life in the Garfagnana."

All the fear she'd been keeping in check for days now came to the surface and Serafina started to tremble. It was there for Azzelino to see and take advantage of.

The smooth limestone of the window ledge was cold and damp from the morning air. Serafina's nails dug into the ledge as she waited.

"I swear you're going to jump!" Azzelino chuckled. "Come away, Serafina; you know me better!" She was closer to the ledge and Azzelino groaned, saying how it was like a woman to make things difficult. He shoved himself off the bed as if her threat were more amusing than real. "No! You're not going to do this to me!" He was at the window in a second, grabbing Serafina before she lunged outward. "Bitch!" he growled and cuffed her on the face so violently a bruise was immediate. "I have no desire to make this easy for you!" The struggle was short, for Azzelino had no trouble pinning Serafina to the bed.

She expected the worst now and silently vowed she would not show tears or weakness. She would become stone. She would be like the tranquil statue of the Holy Mother in the Lady Chapel. Her smile would be an etching in marble across her face. Her skin would be smooth, cold, uninviting. If he wanted to possess her, she would not make it easy.

Azzelino had secured her with a knee and held Serafina's arms above her head and against the bolsters. With his free hand he ripped open her gown, exposed her to the chill morning air.

"Did you ever lie abed and wonder about me, Serafina?" Azzelino whispered. "Even when I was a boy and we played together as children, I used to wonder what it would be like to have you! I was willing to give you a fine house and jewels, anything you wanted, but you paid no attention to me. You let other boys touch you, and kiss you, and you gave your virginity to Romena! He made a whore out of you, Serafina. Why else would Ranieri have sold you to his friends? To join in their sick, wanton, games? I heard that you were more famous than the whores of Venice."

While Azzelino spoke, he kissed her neck, and Serafina shivered when she felt his breath on her skin. His hand was kneading and stroking and his voice grew darker and huskier.

"I heard stories of sodomy and lovemaking so perverse, yet so pleasurable. My nights were tortured by dreams of you with those men. I used to stay all night in the chapel and pray, but the sanctity of prayer was tainted by visions of you lying in bed with other men. I wanted to be the sodomite with you! I wanted to be your lover! To take you in my arms and have you cry out my name, have you sweating in my arms and taste you! Some say that I am as handsome as Romena. Why would you not want to lie with me? See how gentle I am with you? I can feel your body relaxing now. You respond well to me, Serafina. Does this talk not excite you and make you wonder?"

And then he saw her eyes.

He'd not give her a reason to seek vengeance. He suddenly released Serafina. She curled up into a tight, defensive ball on Francesco's side of the bed.

The doors were unbolted and thundered as they closed again.

CHAPTER 40

NICCOLO HEARD THE clatter of horses in the street and turned over in bed towards the window to see if it was light. The bells of Florence were just striking four. Below, voices rose and fell in conversation like those in a dream; but no, there was shouting and cursing, mostly from his father. He stumbled out of bed and went down.

Gheta Peruzzi, Niccolo's stout mother, came from a chamber near the foot of the stairs. "An emissary from Cardinal Alberti is in the hall," she whispered nervously.

"So what?" Niccolo snapped as if the man's presence was her fault, his anger quick and misdirected.

"It concerns Serafina."

"It can wait until morning. She has a husband now to protect her," Niccolo replied quietly, and he started back upstairs.

"No, wait! Francesco da Romena is dead and God knows what will become of Serafina."

Niccolo swung round and nearly smote the torch in the sconce with his wash.

"What?"

"By Holy Saint Catherine, something is not right! All night there's been talk of a battle. Go below; you should speak with the cardinal's man."

The cardinal's secretary ser Bartolomeo stood when Niccolo entered and came to the point immediately. His weary, resonant voice was full of pomp as if speaking to an inferior, the voice of one too long at the papal court.

". . . and because of these momentous events, his eminence commands you to join him at Castello di Romena."

"Commands?"

"Your close association with the late conte gives you no choice but to go where you are commanded."

"Late conte? Do you believe that?"

Ser Bartolomeo sighed and passed a hand over his eyes wearily. "It is, Signor, just as I say. No doubt you've heard of the battle at Campolombardo,"

"No."

"A battle was joined and the Romena army was routed. When the dead were booked the late conte's household guard, his mount, squires, all were found among the slaughtered."

"But not the conte."

"It is said he was cut down fleeing from the field."

"Romena may yet live," Niccolo murmured, and then whispered as if to himself, "God help you all if that be so!"

"Please, signor. I have performed my office. Would you come with me?"

Niccolo stared at the shadows dancing on the flagstones, his mind working rapidly. "Get out." He noticed the secretary shifting uneasily and removed a ring from his finger holding it out. "You need not worry. I've no desire to be cut down in the street or murdered in my bed. Azzelino has a habit of ending friendships that way. Here is my pledge. Go."

Gheta was kneeling before a tabernacle of Saint Anne that occupied a corner of the hall when Niccolo found her. She met his eyes and asked, "So?"

"If the story is to be believed, we have much to fear."

"And Serafina?"

"If it is to be believed, then Serafina is once again a wealthy widow."

"My son, I know what you're thinking."

"No, you don't. I know what she feels for him. Serafina would as soon as take the veil than give herself to another man again."

Niccolo sat in his favorite place from childhood, the place he'd go to think and be alone: a recessed window seat almost as large as a room itself. He leaned his chin on his hand, watching the light change from blue-black to purple outside. Gheta quietly finished her prayers, her beads clicking with every whispered ave.

"Something must be done," Niccolo sighed at last. He turned and saw that his mother was smiling in agreement.

❧

MARGHARETA FOUND SERAFINA in Francesco's great chair beside the hearth. She yapped at one of the serving women to find the ewer and basin for Serafina's ablutions, and then pushed the arras to one side, saying the morning was sure to be cold. There was hoarfrost on the mulberry trees.

"What time is it?"

"The sun is just up. Have you been in that chair all night? You'll be all the worse for it—ah, praise be God! Signor Peruzzi!"

Serafina went to see for herself. Just so, it was Niccolo arriving.

He passed unmolested through the gatehouse, saluted lazily by Azzelino's scarlet-clad guards. The horse he rode was shivering, not from the chill morning, but from a breakneck ride from Florence that spared neither rider nor horse. She could see that the beast could barely carry its own weight, much less the slight Niccolo. And when Niccolo fell from the saddle the horse keeled, then swayed drunkenly and dropped dead.

Niccolo himself was helped to his feet and one of the guards offered wine. He refused, looked up and saw Serafina at the window, acknowledged her with a flickering eye.

"Tell the cardinal that Niccolo Peruzzi has arrived," Serafina instructed the guards when she came into the bailey. For once they didn't leer or smirk. One of them even bent at the waist in homage.

"Will you dine, Niccolo?" she asked.

"No," he sighed, accepting the arm she offered for support. "Let's walk. The exercise will revive me."

"This way," Serafina suggested. They completed four tours of the inner curtain before Niccolo had the wind to speak. Even then, Serafina didn't need to be told. It was evident by the speed of his journey and his milky pallor.

"If there was any other way to tell you this I would find it. But I can't."

For the second time in as many days blood pounded a heartbeat in Serafina's ears.

Niccolo was speaking, but the words made no sense. Then the air rushed from her lungs and she struggled to catch her wind, but no breath came. At last there came a shriek—not a woman's cry, but the howl of an animal, and it came from Serafina's throat. That sound sent the hair on men's necks standing on end. The guards rushed to Serafina's aide when she groped blindly for assistance and then at last swooned, the cloth of her gown swirling around her as she fell.

She was aware of the brilliance of the sky soon afterward. Such a splendid color marred only by the birds swooping in and out of trees. Again, she heard Niccolo's voice but couldn't make out the words. Something about Francesco. No, he had surely been mistaken in that. Francesco would be home by nightfall. He had promised.

"Help me, one of you!" Niccolo snapped at one of the guards. Serafina was brought to her feet and Marghareta was there, cooing and clucking about Francesco, admonishing her about her conduct. What would ser Francesco say to see his wife thus?

"No! He promised no harm would come to him! He made a solemn promise! He promised!" Serafina wailed. "What shall I do?"

The screams brought Azzelino to the entrance of the donjon and he stood amazed, watching Serafina's grief vent itself to frightening proportions. "It must be true," he murmured to Fiasella. He enjoyed the scene for a short while and then called his council.

In the bailey, Serafina was still far from being comforted. "Madonna, there's no use carrying on; you must show a brave face!" Marghareta chided. "Don't let him see you this way! Do you hear me?"

"He made a solemn promise! Now he's left me to their mercy! I want to die!"

"No, you won't!" Niccolo interjected. They were now heading toward the chapel, moving swiftly across the dew-kissed grass that soaked their shoes and the hems of robes and skirts. When one of Azzelino's captains approached just as swiftly, Niccolo held him back with a raised hand.

"The lady goes to be shrived and to pray for the soul of her husband. God's life, give her that much at least!"

The damp, earthy mustiness of the chapel filled their nostrils when the doors swung open. The only light came from narrow windows set with colored glass, the sun pouring through them, showering muddy hues on the flagstones. One of the windows was brighter than the rest, a new panel finished only weeks before, portraits of Francesco and Serafina as Saint Michael and Santa Fina. He said it was a wedding gift, but she knew it had been planned long ago, perhaps after their first meeting. The sanctuary lamp burned bright, a crimson eye illuminating the weary yet stern face of the Lord gazing down from the cross. Serafina remembered the chapel at Castello di San Galgano and a pair of cool, strong hands holding hers. And in that chapel she had silently sworn her life and her body to that man . . .

Serafina swallowed hard, looking up at the windows as if searching for friends. And she found them. She stared at the imperturbable face of Santa Fina smiling from her violet-strewn heaven, then at the handsome countenance of Saint Michael in his golden armor watching sternly. It was some time before she said, "This is what becomes of people who ask too much of life!"

"They haven't found him, madonna!" Marghareta whispered. "You heard Messer Niccolo. No one's seen him. There's still some hope!"

Niccolo agreed and drew Serafina into his arms and let her weep some more, then sat her gently on the sanctuary steps. "If you still have a man you can trust, we can send him to Roberto da Quintavale. Someone must have heard or seen by now. Serafina, you have to show a brave face no matter how painful it is. Once Azzelino sees how it's affected you, he'll take no quarter!"

She began to tremble like one seized with chills, and Marghareta swore an oath to the Holy Mother condemning all men to hell before she ran to find a physic. "I would to God it had been Azzelino's death and not my husband's! I am afraid to sleep, knowing Azzelino is so close," Serafina confessed to Niccolo when they were alone. "He attacked me. I don't know what could be worse—if he had succeeded, or nights wondering if he'll try again."

She heard his breath drawing inwards, his profanity whispered in her hair as he held her to his brigadine, so close she could scarce breathe, could feel the nails studding the leather and buckram, but unwilling to protest, so welcome were his arms about her.

For the longest time he held her. Outside in the bailey the garrison was waking and fragments of conversation, good-natured jests and laughing, the scud of boots on soft, muddy earth, the music of harness, seemed to come from another world.

"Let me go," she implored, gently freeing herself of Niccolo's arms.

"Are you sure?"

"I need time to think. Be at ease, Niccolo. I'll stay here for a while. Tell the cardinal where I am and ask if it would please him to send his chaplain. Masses will be said for my husband's soul."

Azzelino listened impassively to Niccolo's account and glanced at his captains, then back to Niccolo, saying, "If the contessa truly is in such a state, a posset can be made to ease her and make the journey comfortable."

"It would be a travesty, Eminence! Give her a day or two, even a week! To make her leave this place in such a morbid state would bring on something worse, even death," Niccolo argued, pushing away the trencher of food brought to him. "Put aside your prejudices and think what would be best for Serafina."

"A week, and then we leave for Avignon," Azzelino pronounced after some reflection.

"And will you promise not to disturb or harm her in any way?"

Azzelino started to laugh. "I'm a priest! What on earth did you think I would do?"

"When has being a priest ever stopped you?"

The week went slowly. On the day before their departure, Niccolo found Serafina where he'd left her every day: kneeling before the altar with only the sanctuary lamp and a lone candle for company. The rest of the household had gone to supper now that mass was done. Even the cardinal's men were somewhere else for a change, and that was a great relief. The pleasant scent of burned candles still hung in the air and a haze of incense still wreathed round the altar.

"Will you come to supper?" Niccolo asked, kneeling beside her. "Azzelino has promised to leave you to your prayers tonight if you'll join him. I've been asked to be your cupbearer."

Serafina, keeping her hands clasped beneath her chin, moved her head slightly. "You've been asked to keep an eye on me," she replied. "Poor Azzelino; he thinks I'm willing to kill myself out of grief. I won't give him the satisfaction."

"Don't fight him, Serafina, it's too dangerous now. Before, you might have won, but now,"

"It doesn't become you to play the cardinal's pander, Niccolo. Go on to supper."

Niccolo sent Marghareta to Serafina when his pleading and arguments came to no avail. Serafina turned when she heard the chapel door creak and groan and then thud with an echo.

"You may tell Niccolo it will do no good," Serafina greeted and resumed her vigil on the sanctuary cross.

"Oh my sweet girl," Marghareta implored as she knelt beside Serafina. "We all know what you suffer, all of us in the conte's household. But you must not act foolishly! Messer Niccolo told me three hundred men are waiting in the Campolombardo, more at Poppi. The Guidi of Davidolo have promised as many men as can be summoned."

In whispers Marghareta now told her of the plan to release them from captivity.

"I too, have a plan," Serafina replied. "It may be worth your while to listen. Between us, we can overcome him."

When Marghareta heard what Serafina was about she swore a violent oath, profaning the chapel with her words, and told her mistress in no uncertain terms that it would be impossible. Nay, dangerous. She would not allow it. Francesco, if alive, would most certainly not allow it!

"And what if the cardinal's foragers discover Niccolo's army? No matter the promises of Francesco's kin, they've been known to turn," Serafina argued. "Think on it, Marghareta! You know well that it has a good chance because we all know too well the over-mighty cardinal—"

The chapel door swung open. Serafina suddenly plunged in a curtsey and acknowledged the cardinal, who stood in the doorway with one of his German mercenaries.

Later that night Marghareta watched her mistress uneasily and stared at what was laid out on the bed. A new bed gown of blush-colored sarcenet, and a robe of a lapis-colored velvet and trimmed in black ermine. There was a bottle of scent, and the amethyst. The horrible, cursed amethyst that seemed to bring no woman luck! Yet there it lay on the bed, waiting to be draped around a young girl's neck.

All but the necklace had been wedding gifts from the conte di Romena, yet Serafina put them on now as if she was expecting her lord to appear; as if at any moment the sound of his sonorous, sensual voice would glide up the tower's winding staircase to announce him, his knee-weakening smile lighting up the darkest of chambers.

Serafina unlocked the door and now paced a circle before the hearth where the night livery was laid on a cloth-shrouded table. And it was no ordinary livery, not like the conte di Romena expected. Tansy cakes, ale, strawberries, and pears. Food of a sensual nature.

Serafina held out the necklace and Marghareta shuddered. "I beg of you, madonna, don't do this!"

"It is how one makes bargains."

"Have you learned nothing from your mother's life? Do you not know?"

"I know what I want to know and what I need to know. The necklace, Marghareta."

Marghareta fastened the clasp around Serafina's neck. "It is unnatural! If Messer Niccolo knew,"

"Go."

Marghareta made no further protest and trundled away, grumbling misgivings as she wound through the many staircases to the servants' quarters. Had she taken her usual route by the passageway that led from the south tower, she would have encountered Azzelino.

Serafina caught her breath at the sound of the knock. She lowered herself slowly into a chair and watched as the latch jerked up and the door creaked open. Azzelino entered alone. He said nothing and strolled across the bedchamber to pause before her.

"You've reconsidered?" he greeted. She controlled the urge to pull back as she felt his breath on her hand and then the kiss of courtesy. Their eyes met and for once his were clear, almost sparkling; his breath wasn't corrupted by ale or wine. He was quite sober.

"I've no choice. You've made that quite obvious. My husband is dead. I have to shift for myself and I'll not be the pensioner or pawn for anyone. I would not be weak in the face of my husband's enemies. And mine."

He studied her face and a clear indication of grief stilled his doubts. She was indeed a marvelous woman if she could keep her tears private and transact business as if this was any ordinary night. But Azzelino hoped it would not be that—an ordinary night.

"Believe me when I tell you I mourn for your loss."

"You're kind to play a farce. I know you don't mean it."

He shifted his weight and folded arms across his chest, leaning against the mantle so that he could feel the heat of the fire rising along his body. "The terms, Serafina. I didn't come for nothing."

"My dower. Have Ranieri's bastards give back my dowry. And if you're in a generous mood, give me Castello di San Galgano and this castle," she said quietly.

"Two castles out of many? There's nothing else?"

"If you're offering a house in Avignon, I'll take that, too. But I'll demand your word."

Azzelino now placed his hands on the arms of the chair and grinned at her wickedly. "You know I'll more than gladly arrange for a house."

"And your word?"

"We'll see."

"What else," she whispered, bringing her face close enough for a kiss, "would you offer for an accord?"

He swallowed hard, still grinning, the sweat starting to come to his palms. Sweet blood of Christ! Would it be this easy? Fiasella wished him good hunting when the summons came from the contessa. He expected a joust, not the acquiescent exchange that was staggering him now.

Serafina had shifted slightly and the robe and bed gown slipped to expose the round, high, silhouette of a perfect, magnificent breast. He caught sight of this and Serafina made no attempt to cover herself and slid out of the chair, reaching for the flask of wine on the livery table.

"Again I ask—what do you offer me for what I'm willing to give in free exchange?"

"Ask and it is yours. You have the castles and the house in Avignon. You can have jewels, servants, horses, just ask." he whispered, never taking his eyes from the contours of her lovely body highlighted and shadowed by candlelight to full advantage.

She smiled and nodded; poured two cups, offered one.

"I'll think about what I want when our business here is concluded. Then I'll tell you. Will you drink with me now to seal our bargain?"

Azzelino seized the cup and almost spilled the wine, pouring it down his throat. He wiped his mouth with his sleeve and watched as she poured a second cup and drank. This was unexpected, but what woman did not steel her courage with drink? What Serafina had done was indeed difficult.

"You're a man of your word, Azzelino? May I depend on that?" She smiled at him from over the rim of her cup, her eyes sparkling, the arch of her brow seductive.

"Upon my life."

When she proposed another cup, Azzelino all but begged for it and drank as if his thirst would never be quenched. "I'll make amends," he swore now.

"The list is long, even longer than my father's where it concerns sins against me. I have decided to forgive and forget."

He watched as the silken cords binding the velvet robe were unloosed and snaked around her waist and to the hips. The robe sailed to the sweet-smelling rushes. She walked easily across the solar to bolt the door.

The curves of her body, the blush of her breasts, and the soft mound of Venus were all revealed to him under the diaphanous shift that followed her movements, caressed each limb, and swayed with the breeze coming in from the window. She paused at the hearth to stir the embers and then turned to him.

"You have it! Anything you desire!" he swore, licking his dry lips, though why after so much wine they were in such a state, he did not know. "I will make amends."

"You will have to answer for your sins."

Serafina poured more wine into his cup and he swallowed all after one gulp. Azzelino was starting to experience the contentment and warmth wine always brought, the ease. Serafina was as clear-headed as if she'd only taken water. No matter; he hated taking women when they were drunk. There was no sport in it.

"My husband is dead," she pronounced quietly.

He laughed nervously. "Madonna, if you intend to take your revenge upon me, you do have me at a disadvantage."

"Do you confess to his murder?"

"If it was a deed done on the battlefield, I cannot take credit; I admit that if we'd met on the field, one of us would never have walked away."

"Thank you for your honesty."

"Let this be a new beginning for us."

Azzelino tipped his cup in tribute and drank. When one of the servants in the antechamber dropped a crockery ewer, he started and swore. Serafina touched his arm and let her hand ride down his sleeve, pausing at his waist. "Easily, Azzelino. You no doubt came here expecting an ambush, or something else."

"True."

"What good would your blood do on my hands?"

"True" Azzelino murmured, letting his lips graze her brow and when he sought to kiss her, she let him, even allowing him to pull her into his arms.

"I'll tell you what I want," she whispered. "What every woman desires is to have her own way. What I desire is to be left alone. After tonight, I shall seek the life of a contemplative. I know what you desire, Azzelino. Tonight I shall give you what you want in fair exchange."

He didn't answer, for his heart caught in his throat at what she did next.

Serafina walked to the bed and pulled back the finely woven coverlet, threw the silk-covered pillows against the bolster, and leaned against them provocatively. "You made it perfectly clear, Azzelino, what you desire most. And I am a widow yet again. After tonight, my body will be Christ's. Tonight it shall be yours." She opened a coffer at the bedside and took out a vial, which she unstopped and put to her lips.

"Not poison!" Azzelino objected.

"A philter I bought from an apothecary. A love potion, he said. Though I am of a mind to give you everything you want, I do need courage."

"Of course," he sighed with relief.

"Any moment now it will take effect," Serafina said and unlaced the cords to her shift, letting it fall.

"Sweet Gesu! I had hoped, but,"

"Why do you wait?" Serafina laughed softly as she stretched out on the bed; "surely there's no need to instruct you!"

The effect of the wine overtaking him, Azzelino tore at his clothes and made jests while struggling with points and laces, with buckles and boots. He climbed into bed and she slid into his arms, her sighs and moans promising ecstasy as they kissed and fondled her.

"I was told that this philter can prolong the moment. Surely you'll want that?" Serafina purred. She reached for the vial and let drops fall on her breasts. Azzelino wasted no time in licking them off and laughed when she poured the rest of it into his mouth. "Soon! It won't be long now," she whispered as his kisses moved from neck to stomach.

She was like velvet and silk. The scent and touch of her kept him aroused. She felt like fire, so warm to the touch. Azzelino laughed as she rolled him onto his back and straddled him as she would a horse. This would be interesting, for only the whores of Santa Croce were this adventurous. Oh, the curves, the scent, the ropes of silk that were her hair...

A dagger as deadly as it was beautiful was shoved at his breast.

"Call your men and it will be to no avail," Serafina whispered. "Does the fear arouse you, Azzelino? Do you like how the sweat comes and the dryness in your throat overtakes you, making it impossible to scream?"

Azzelino wanted to escape from the bed or try to take the weapon out of her hands, but suddenly he was thrown into another world, a delirium of distorted faces and voices, of bright, hot colors that bled one into the other. But Serafina was real. There was no doubt of it when she pressed the blade closer so that he felt the prick of steel against his skin.

The hot colors were searing, blinding, and white now.

The voices returned, a cacophony of shouts, bells ringing—no, swords—meeting.

Again, voices and hot colors.

"Shall I give you a taste of what you gave me? Indirectly, Azzelino. We both know you've never had me, but you married me to that monster Ranieri, you were responsible for all that befell me in that castle tower! Do you want to feel what I felt all those months in captivity? I heard that death is like the climax, that one can't tell the difference. With Francesco, it was rapture like none other. When he died, did he experience the rapture? Is death like the climax? Shall we see if it is true, Azzelino?"

"Serafina, what do you—"

And then the exquisite end.

The complete darkness.

Serafina held the dagger a moment longer until she was sure he was dead and then slowly and with difficulty withdrew the blade from Azzelino's chest. The blood began to flow immediately, and Serafina grabbed her shift and used it as a bandage against the dead man's wound, holding it there until the heartbeat ceased.

Although the room was stifling, she was seized with chills and pulled a fur-lined robe around her body. Then she knelt at her faldstool and prayed.

Below stairs the shouting had stopped. Off in the distance, she could still hear the swordplay. And she prayed that Niccolo would be the victor.

An hour passed before she looked at the man on the bed. Serafina touched Azzelino's neck. His face was gray, the mouth agape and caked with froth, blood, and bile. Disgusted, Serafina closed his eyes and threw a sheet over him.

When it was finally quiet, Serafina went to a window overlooking the ward and saw Niccolo and his men leading the vanquished to the outer bailey. She knew they would be executed without trial or absolution.

Niccolo came up as the midnight bell rang, bloodied and injured. One glance at Serafina and the body of Azzelino told him more than he wanted to know.

"What did you do?" Niccolo later asked. They were in the privacy of the solar and for an hour he'd endured her ministrations to his wounds and her unnatural silence. "Your woman said that you meant to give yourself to him."

"I am Francesco da Romena's widow. No man will touch me ever again," she answered. "I am not my mother."

He glanced at the cup in his hand and sniffed at it. Serafina had just offered a posset to ease his pain and she read his uneasiness swiftly enough, saying, "Niccolo, should I have ever wanted to kill you, it would have been when I was twelve years old and you kissed me and reached under my gown!"

"Thank the Lord you did not," he jested, and tried to get to his feet. "I need to take account of our night's work. The podesta of Florence expects word by tomorrow morning."

"You'll be no use to him dead. Sleep, and then we can send our tidings."

"Tell me what happened to Azzelino."

"I gave him a sleeping draught to relax him. I pretended it was a love philter and pretended to drink it. The rest you know."

When Niccolo looked as if he would argue, Serafina convinced him that he needed rest, not a quarrel, and made him lie down on Francesco's bed. She was still sitting on the bed chests when he woke hours later.

"What o'clock—?" he drawled, his speech liquid and slurred from the poppy juice tincture Serafina gave him for pain.

"You were tired and I let you sleep. Coluccio took care of booking the dead."

He reached across the coverlet and took her hand, surprised to find it freezing cold in spite of the stifling heat from the great fireplace.

"What do we do now?" Serafina asked, daring to meet his gaze.

Niccolo shrugged and said he didn't know.

CHAPTER 41

THE PLAIN OF Campolombardo, once a fertile expanse between Castello di Romena and Florence, the site of previous battles, was now red with the blood of men who had died fighting under Romena's banners. Five days before, the armies of Alberti and Romena had met in a bloody, mismatched campaign.

Francesco had expected to come up against Azzelino's companies of mercenaries and militia from his rivals' towns, but not the companies led by his father-in-law, and worse, by Edmund Clifford. Hours of negotiation and persuasion that came to nothing led Francesco to attack. He had no choice. Francesco engaged the enemy and lost against tremendous odds.

Roberto arrived at Campolombardo a day after the battle. When he saw the waste of life, Serafina's stricken face on the morning of Azzelino's arrival came vividly to mind. She had asked for news no matter the outcome. How could he explain this to her?

The discovery of another mutilated body or wounded knight made them less confident of finding Francesco alive. Roberto had never seen so much carnage. Of Francesco's host and household guard, two men were found whole, and they conveyed the epilogue of the contest when commanded to do so.

Romena's banner had gone down toward the end of the battle, and then his great grey destrier fell like a marble statue. It was then that the ranks of the Romena army broke and those who were still whole and had their wits about them fled only to be massacred.

Roberto wanted to believe that all this before him was a dream—the mangled, incredible shapes sprawled on the ground used to be men like him. They had wives and lovers, children; they were the sons of fathers most probably now wondering as he did if all had been for naught. Through the smoke and haze he'd seen hell, for nothing else could describe it. Only when he chased off a scavenger despoiling a corpse, or stumbled upon a woman cradling what once had been her son, husband or lover, did he give up hope. Still, he pressed his men on and they searched for nearly a day.

At dawn, Roberto gave orders to break camp and his disheartened band headed to the west under cover of morning fog, riding toward Castello di

Romena, about five miles distant. The party forded a stream and climbed up to the smoking ruins of an abbey, where all was still quiet, save a chilling noise—a lowering, guttural sound of one in pain. Screaming at the others to follow, Roberto unloosed his sword and ran towards the sound, into an orchard. There sat Francesco beneath a tree holding the body of the moon-faced servant, Lorenzo.

Embarrassed yet stricken by this unfamiliar show of grief, they circled him and did nothing for a time. Roberto at last knelt before Francesco and gently touched his face, wiping away encrusted blood and filth.

"Francesco? Do you know me?" Roberto whispered. "You've been wounded, signor. It's best to get you away from here in case there are foragers about. We'll see that the boy is buried and the rites are said; we can head towards Castello di Romena. We're on safe ground," Roberto whispered, helping Francesco to his feet. Francesco now turned and managed a smile.

"You're still with me, Roberto? I thought you'd gone with all the rest."

"I'd welcome death first."

Roberto instructed three men to see to Lorenzo's burial and then led them out of the orchard and towards the road. "Signor, are you sure you can walk? We can be at Castello di Romena by vespers."

"I think not," one of the others spoke up.

A Giustini scouting party had rounded the hill and stopped short, seeing their quarry. Their victorious shouts signaled a cadre of knights that now advanced.

"Make no stand," Francesco advised, adding "They'll want me alive for the ransom."

He freed himself from Roberto's protective arms and stepped forward to greet his captors thundering forward on armored horses, smiled weakly when the captain of the foragers recognized him. That smile faded into horror when he saw it was Edmund Clifford.

"Edmund, as you may see, I've blundered," Francesco jested bitterly. "I did not heed the advice of my wife to ignore a challenge."

"The best of advice is not often heeded."

"Traitor!" Roberto spat, and had it not been for two of Giustini's soldiers, he would have attacked Edmund. Francesco signed them away.

"He has always performed his office well. Isn't that what you're here to do, Edmund? On whose orders do you come?"

Edmund looked at the miserable band and was sorry to have come so far in his agreement with Azzelino Alberti. He was ordered to take no one alive save Romena. His men drew their swords and waited.

"Let the rest go. They're no use to you."

"Francesco, you can't!" Roberto protested.

"Be at ease, Roberto. I shall need a man to look after my wife."

Francesco looked at Edmund. "Surely you'll grant this last request?"

"Come," was all Edmund could say.

"When did you decide it wasn't worth the effort to kill me?"

"We don't have to discuss that now," Edmund answered, embarrassed. Damn Francesco for being so out of character as to make things difficult!

"When? Was it when you sent the man to Florence to kill me on Christmas Day? Or when you tried to kill me at Castello di San Galgano?"

"I said, come along. Now."

"Better still, when did you first betray me?"

"Francesco, we don't have to do this."

"I must know. You see, my conscience is safe, for I know what I've done wrong. What of yours?"

"You once said it wasn't about winning, but who was better at the game," Edmund remarked uneasily.

"I remember that,"

"The game is won."

Francesco laughed, then wiped the tears from his eyes, swallowed the lump in his throat. "For king, country, and the best whores in London," he said hoarsely.

"Francesco, don't,"

"What was it you used to say?"

"Enough! It won't help!"

"That I'm a fool for ever wanting what I can't have—and wanting what will kill me trying to achieve," Francesco sobbed. "Will you be able to sleep at night? Christ, Edmund! It's only a pile of stones! That's all it is! A castle for a life! You should have left me in that tavern in Chepeside. I could have looked after myself. We wouldn't have come to this!"

"Come with me now, Francesco. That's all I ask. You'll be treated fairly."

Edmund held out his hand and Francesco grasped it tightly.

Their hands trembled as Francesco clung, locking his sight on the other man. "I loved you!" Francesco whispered.

Edmund suddenly broke free and staggered back. Before anyone could prevent it, Francesco had taken Roberto's dagger and scored a crimson line across Edmund's throat. He held Edmund's body as it crumpled like a sack of grain and cradled the dying man in his arms, wept as he closed Edmund's eyes with a gentle hand and kissed his brow.

"Go!" Francesco screamed at his men as Edmund's soldiers moved in.

❧

FRANCESCO WASN'T GIVEN the satisfaction of an immediate execution. He was taken to Andrea Alberti's castle in the forest of Camaldoli.

As soon as Tommaso received the news, he locked himself in his bedchamber.

Elisabetta heard his labored footsteps; they'd echoed through the third floor living quarters for most the night. Just when she drifted off to sleep the scud of his leather boots on the wooden planks roused her. She knew when he had completed a tour of the bedchamber. He'd pause only for a moment, more than likely at the large window facing the Via Calzaiuoli, and then start again.

"It's more than I can bear, Husband," she sighed after she knocked and found the door unlatched. He didn't seem surprised to find his wife staring daggers; in fact, he smiled and offered her a cup of wine. Elisabetta closed the door behind her and strode across the bedchamber to the window where he stood. The cup passed between them silently.

"Ask," Tommaso said. He turned, waiting for her reaction.

"What I do not understand is why you will not do something!"

"I cannot. My hands are bound. If I do then we lose everything. Giustini and Alberti will see to that."

Elisabetta dismissed this with a shake of the head. She held her cup for more wine and drank deep. "What you are saying, then, is you will not. All of my sons are dead because of your obsession for Francesco's lands and titles! Yet now, when it would serve us to help him, you do nothing! Is it Azzelino? Have you made a pact with him? Whose colors do you wish to wear when you die, Tommaso?"

"I can do nothing to help Francesco."

The cup Elisabetta held was launched against the new tapestry on the northern wall. A ribbon of saffron-colored wine traveled down like tears on the face of a martyr.

"Tommaso, you must! He risked his life to come to your aid! No sooner had Azzelino's armies moved against you than Francesco was there to protect what was yours! He kept his word. You cannot pretend it matters little!"

"I would lose my life in saving his! Everything I have, we have, would go to Azzelino! And how would you like being under lock and key in a convent in the middle of nowhere? For that's where Azzelino will put you if he doesn't have it in mind to make you his concubine! Damn him! He should never have died!"

Elisabetta caught her breath and grabbed his arm, her nails digging deep until Tommaso felt them under his woolen robe and linen shirt. "Is Francesco dead? What are you talking about?"

"That stupid woman was so bent on revenge for his lusts!"

"Stop it, Tommaso! Francesco! Is he dead or not?"

"No! Alessandro! All this is Alessandro's fault!"

"Idiot! That was so many years ago."

"If he had only—God! We are done for. That's for certain."

"I asked you once to do something for me," Elisabetta whispered sadly. "Now I beg you, do it for yourself!"

Tommaso turned from the window and looked her straight in the eyes. She was amazed when he at last said he'd do it.

☙

FRANCESCO WOKE HE heard footsteps and a metallic jingle of keys on a warder's belt. He sat up and waited for what were sure to be his executioners.

Every night had been torture in this place, hours bathed in sweat, with each marked by a scratch on the slime-coated wall, while he wondered when the headsman would come, or when poison would conveniently find itself in a bowl of wine. No one thought to bind up his wounds. The smallest exertion was painful, and were it not for the wine one of the more sympathetic jailers had managed to procure against Alberti's wishes, he would have spent every waking moment in excruciating pain, instead of immured in a surrealistic place where only the bells of the nearby abbey told him he was still alive.

More than that, he worried about his wife. Strong-willed as Serafina might be, there were those who would bend her to their will. And the very idea of Serafina at the mercy of Azzelino . . .

Francesco waited as the door scraped open. The dark cell was dimly lit by moonlight barely able to find its way through the arrow slit. The man in the doorway blocked what little light he enjoyed.

"If you won't bring a candle, identify yourself. At least I'll know who's come to kill me," Francesco spoke up.

A flint was struck, and with the spark came a burst of light, then a pitch-burning torch banged into a sconce. The visitor threw back his hood and looked down at Francesco waiting on the pallet.

"You look well for one expecting death," Durante Giustini remarked.

"All this reminds me a little of my childhood," Francesco quipped. "It's something I've gotten used to." After a moment, he asked, "How is my wife? Do you have any news of her?"

"No. She can manage for herself, as you well know. I'm here against the wishes of the Alberti. They would have you executed tomorrow morning, and I want you to live. If you want to live, Romena, you only have to agree to certain terms. You know what the first is."

"No."

"I can renounce her, Romena. I can make a codicil to my will and disinherit her. Nothing would please me more than to give it all to Azzelino, and why shouldn't I? He's made some pretty promises and kept them. At least the last thirty years of struggle wouldn't have been for naught!"

"No."

"Would you like to see her wandering about the streets of Florence like her mother did? Where it concerns Serafina and her mother, the apple doesn't fall far from the tree! It wouldn't surprise me if she hadn't already given herself to Niccolo, Azzelino, countless others, before she found her way into your bed."

Francesco tried to lunge for him then, but Durante drew his sword and pushed Francesco back gently on to the pallet. He cried out in pain, for the sudden exertion had opened the festering wounds in his shoulder and breast and the searing pain made him nauseous to the point of fainting. Blood oozed through his torn, dirty shirt, making it cold and uncomfortable. Francesco reached for his blanket and used it to staunch the bleeding.

"You ought to have someone look at that," Durante whispered, sniggering.

"Say what you like about me, but dishonor the good name of my wife and should I live—" Francesco gasped.

"If you live, Monsignore. You will live only if you agree to my terms."

"No!"

Durante knelt before the pallet and yanked Francesco by the hair. "What is it, Romena? Do the men of your accursed family like martyrdom? Devotional panels and candles mean nothing! After a while, Serafina will dry her tears and forget and she'll take up with another man. Perhaps Niccolo Peruzzi."

Seeing Francesco's color fade and his pupils constrict, Durante smiled. "Do you think your good friend the banker isn't waiting for the day your body's brought back to the castle? You'd best be careful of that friendship, Romena!"

"No."

"Is it so much to ask? A marriage for a life? There are girls enough in the world. You found one to replace your beloved Gismonda. Why not Serafina?"

Francesco tried to attack him but fell back exhausted against the wall. "No," he whispered. He choked back tears and closed his eyes, waiting for the sharp, cold edge of the sword.

It never came. Durante shouted something at the guards, Francesco could not tell what, as he faded in and out of consciousness. The corner of the blanket was almost soaked through and Francesco pressed it closer, falling asleep when he heard Durante mutter, "He'll save Azzelino the trouble by bleeding to death come morning."

He slept; for how long, he didn't know. The clang of a bell threading its way from the abbey to the castle woke Francesco. Voices came to him and he could distinguish plainsong—or it might have been two men quarrelling. The bells continued with their painful ringing and Francesco thrashed about in his sleep, muttering "No more, no more!"

"Easily, monsignore! You're burning with fever. Hold still! There. Hold still while I apply . . . there! In a moment you'll feel the operation of the salve."

It must have been a dream, for Roberto da Quintavale was kneeling over him. He felt comfortable and warm for the first time in days. The cold, smooth edge of a cup was against his lips and he was being urged to drink. Francesco shook his head, protesting and crying out, "No more, no more!"

"Signor, I beg of you! Be at ease! You're no use to them dead!"

Francesco opened his eyes then and started, tried to get away from this apparition that was Roberto da Quintavale. He labored for breath and then reached out. No ghostly talon or icy chill of vapor, but a warm hand, a firm hand with a steady grasp on his. The face was in shadow, obscured by a hood but the eyes and smile were unmistakable.

"Roberto? You're alive?"

"Yes, and damn your unnatural luck, so are you!" Roberto laughed gently.

"How did you come here? How long has it been?"

"A while. We're taking you home. Now be silent."

"We?"

"Tommaso came with me."

"Tommaso is here?"

"Yes," said Tommaso as he thumped a fat candle onto the floor, lighting it unsteadily. Francesco turned toward the sallow light, his eyes meeting Tommaso's almost immediately. It was Tommaso who looked away first. "I made a promise to my wife. Seeing how I've offended everyone I know; I can't afford her disaffection." Tommaso said and knelt at the pallet, the bones in his knees creaking and his breath coming with difficulty so that Francesco felt the labored sigh on his brow. "I went to Quintavale and asked him to help me. We've gone to much trouble to free you; now I suggest you stop asking questions and let us finish the task."

They were dressed as mendicant friars, hoods pulled up to obscure their faces, yards of rough-spun wadmal covering sword belts and brigadines as Francesco felt when he struggled to sit up.

"We have to go. They'll wonder why administering medicine is taking so long," Roberto said. "How do you feel?"

"Help me to stand and I'll tell you for certain."

Using Roberto as a prop, Francesco heaved himself up, more surprised that he did it than by the pain catching him. Eventually the properties of the salve would go to work. He could already feel its warmth.

"You'll need these," Tommaso said and removed the habit and brigadine he wore, helping Francesco into them. Feeling warmth for the first time in days, Francesco welcomed the leather and metal plates against his damp shirt, the yards of dark cloth that turned him into a shadow.

After a glance at Tommaso Roberto motioned towards the door, saying, "You go first."

Tommaso flung open the door casually and stepped out into the passageway.

Roberto followed, supporting Francesco as best he could as they crept through a maze of corridors and stair casements, wary of the absence of soldiers. They started to believe that fortune was indeed blessing this enterprise when they heard the echo of voices, keys, and chain mail in one of the casements. Tommaso grabbed a torch from one of the sconces and threw it. The footsteps followed the direction of the light. They spun about and retraced their steps through dark corridors dripping with fetid water and slimy moss, clinging to the damp walls to find their way.

From out of the darkness came a face, the stench of garlic and decay. Roberto shoved Tommaso aside and attacked, plunging his sword into leather and flesh until it came away bloody. But no sooner had the first soldier toppled to the ground clutching at his eviscerated midsection than another appeared.

"Quintavale! Romena, behind you! Get out of the way!" Tommaso screamed, and suddenly lunged. From then on, Francesco and Roberto scrambled up from the maze of dungeons and managed to escape the castle, to find the road to Castello di Romena.

Only when he saw the fourteen towers of Romena did Francesco pause to rest, and then he wept at his good fortune. He swore he would forget the rest.

He would block the memory of Tommaso da Porciano dying at his feet from his mind.

❧

NEWS OF THE rescue found its way quickly to Florence. Michelino Groppa, serving yet another term as podesta of Florence, raised himself up on an elbow and glared past yellow candlelight to the clerk looking ridiculous in a nightshirt and cloak. A trio of guards stood behind him and four faces stared down apprehensively. At once Groppa was apprehensive. But no, these were his men, men who were known to him and were like brothers. Their business had to be urgent to wake him at such a disagreeable hour. While the podesta's sleepy mind wandered through thoughts of horror—from the burning of Florence to another outbreak of plague, to yet another French invasion—the clerk was unraveling a tale which, when concentrated upon, had something to do with the Conte di Romena.

Groppa waved a hand in frustration and bade the man start over again. The tale related was fantastic if anything, but given recent events, might be credible.

"Where is the conte now?" he yawned, heaving himself out of bed. "And what o'clock is it?"

"Almost dawn, messer podesta," a guard noted, looking at a candle wasting on the table.

Groppa clutched at a wine bottle sleepily and was relieved of it by the clerk who poured a cup, saying, "The conte di Romena is safe. He escaped Camaldoli yesterday."

"There's no trick to this, eh? No funny business about?" Groppa asked each man in turn.

"None we know of, messer."

"Where is he now? Does anyone know?"

"At Castello di Romena?"

"Are you certain, or is that a guess?"

"I don't know, messer. All I know is that he escaped."

"What of Andrea Alberti? And the cardinal! Where's the cardinal?"

"That we cannot say, messer podesta."

Groppa grunted, dissatisfied, and claimed his pillow again. "If the conte di Romena is safe we should all go back to bed. I don't believe the commune would protest if Romena dealt with them as he saw fit. After all, this happened outside of Florence. Do you think, messeres?"

There was a murmur of assent at this from all present.

Groppa was settling down to sleep again when he bolted up, knocking the candlestick over. Four men were on the floor trying to prevent the bed curtains from going up in flames.

"Send word to the cardinal. If Romena wishes to bring a charge against the Alberti, Florence will back Romena on this."

"The cardinal? He'll take it as a challenge," the clerk warned.

"The cardinal is not lord of Florence. No one, not even a cardinal, is above the law. The cardinal is not to interfere."

"As you will, messer."

"We've forgotten Tommaso di Porciano! Does anyone know if he has anything to do with this?"

The clerk's eyes slid to the guards, and then back to the podesta, whose brows were raised and made them look like two caterpillars.

"Porciano had no hand in this," the clerk answered. "All of Florence knows he's been quiet, kept to himself of late."

"Hmm. Well, get a message to him; tell him Romena has achieved all. If that doesn't end any designs, I don't know what will."

"Death," spoke up one man, which sent a ripple of laughter.

The podesta's brow creased.

The clerk intervened. "Death. Death ends all designs, doesn't it? He's dead."

"Is he? Well, one less matter to deal with."

"Yes, messer." The clerk paused, watching as the podesta settled into his bed again. "Messer podesta, don't you want to know how it happened?"

"What matters is that it happened. Come, is there a man in this room who's shed a tear for his end?"

"As you say, messer."

"I thought not. Oh, all right! *How?*"

"He was helping Francesco da Romena escape."

"Was he? Was he? Can this be true?"

The faint smiles on the faces of the men confirmed this to be true and the Podesta scratched his head, whispering, "Fascinating!"

Once again Groppa started burrowing into the pillows and once again he shot up.

"Oh, and one of you, send word to the Conte di Romena,"

"Yes, monsignore?"

"Congratulate him on the occasion of his marriage."

Finally alone in the safe confines of his blankets and pillows, Groppa began to laugh.

&

IT WAS LIKE waking from a dream, pausing after his difficult climb upstairs at the entrance of the solar, and seeing everything beloved and familiar through new eyes; things only yesterday Francesco thought he'd never behold again. The shutters had been bolted and black mourning cloth made the room even darker.

Crossing the solar, Francesco threw open the shutters to allow in sunlight. The black hangings embroidered with the Romena cognizance lifted and tumbled back gently with every breeze. In the morning light he could see that the table was still as he had left it. Paper and books, a chess game, trinkets from childhood that were still precious to him, such as the wooden poppet, his beloved statue of Saint Michael, were exactly where they'd been so many weeks ago. Next to the Archangel, however, was a brightly painted bowl overfilled with dying flowers. Someone had forgotten to clear them out and left them to drop papery leaves and petals on the table that now wore a fine film of dust.

Instead of his faithful hounds, a small spaniel dog lay by the hearth. It growled when he entered and then laid its head back down on a velvet cushion when, after sniffing the hand it would sooner bite, found nothing threatening. Its tail brushed lazily against the flagstones as Francesco moved on.

"Marghareta, where've you been? I sent a man to the village an hour ago—"

At once his heart began to race. Her wealth of copper hair was hidden beneath a widow's barbette and fought to stay within its confines; her lips were stained with rouge, but her eyes, those incredible eyes. Red-rimmed from weeping though they were, they lit immediately when she saw him. One sight of her had the power to erase days of uncertainty and death.

"How is it with you, sweetheart?" he said laughing when Serafina was in his arms.

&

SERAFINA DREW BACK the tent from around Francesco's bathing tub so that Roberto and Niccolo could join in the conversation, taking a small stool nearby in case he would have need of her. He was tired and the wounds he had received to his shoulder and breast at Campolombardo, not to mention the superficial scrapes and bruises acquired in his escape, caused discomfort, though he would never admit it.

They spoke of the battle as if it were nothing more than a squire's exercise, discussing the notable dead and the reparations owed to Francesco for his men and arms, the spoils that would eventually be divided. And while they talked, Serafina's eyes could only behold Francesco. She quietly motioned to the servants when they forgot something or made their lord uncomfortable, whispered instruction and remained unobtrusive while the men talked of war. *No more*, she thought to herself, as cups were raised to Francesco's fortune, *no more!*

"Here's something you might want to think on," Roberto spoke up while Niccolo and he, acting as Romena's chancellors, opened letters and dispatches and read them aloud. "There's to be a tournament in Florence on the feast of San Giovanni. The Commune desires that you ride as champion."

"Maybe that's something you'd like," Niccolo remarked and prompted laughter all around.

"There's time enough to decide," Francesco answered, reaching for Serafina's hand and his near-empty bowl of wine. "I do think that my wife would prefer I stay off a horse and out of harness for a while."

"To la contessa Romena," Niccolo said softly, and Roberto echoed the tribute. Francesco turned her face to his and in the look he offered to his wife was even greater tribute.

An hour later Francesco slept soundly and Serafina thought it safe to leave him for now. She closed the curtains round the bed and tiptoed out of the solar to meet Niccolo on the winding staircase that led up to her tower.

"He sleeps?" Niccolo queried with an easy smile.

"Through the night, I pray," she answered as they walked up and paused on the parapet that looked out to the southwest and Florence. The sky was beginning to turn with night colors and the stars were speckling a clear, rich sky. Serafina leaned against the rough stone and trembled, and then released an ugly sob.

"Hush, dearest! He's home," Niccolo whispered, and embraced her gently as if she was made of the most fragile Venetian glass.

"Thank you," Serafina said when she found her voice again and the strength flowed again in her weary, brittle soul. "Not once have I said thanks for what you did. Without you, God knows what might have happened."

"There's nothing more to be said. I've been repaid for my loyalty and sacrifices," Niccolo admitted now, offering another smile. When Serafina gave him a quizzical look he continued, "I am now his second. Seneschal and chancellor."

"I'm glad for you," Serafina cried and bestowed a kiss on his unshaven cheek. "And Roberto? What laurels for him?"

"The captain of his garrisons. Romena's marshal."

"How neatly everything has fallen into place," she murmured, and then took Niccolo's hand as they watched the coming of night.

How neatly everything had fallen into place.

CHAPTER 42

IN A DRESSMAKER'S shop in the Via dei Cimatori, the proprietress, mona Gherarda Fiasella, put aside her ells of French velour and went to the door to see what the commotion was about. People were laughing and hugging as if it were a feast day, as if Florence had been delivered from a great catastrophe. Gherarda caught the arm of a clerk running from one of the Romena shops and asked, "What has happened? Is the German emperor dead?"

"Better than that, Signora! Francesco da Romena is alive!" the man cried happily.

"Beatrice!" Gherarda called, and peered round the door when her daughter did not come from the workroom. "Beatrice! Ah, there you are! Mind things here, I'm going to the Duomo."

Wrapping herself in a black widow's mantle, Gherarda set off for the cathedral. She was not alone, for many Florentines had thought it meet and right to offer prayers and candles in thanksgiving. Kneeling on the pavement of the nave, Gherarda began to laugh and weep alternately.

There were few *magnati* who were as benevolent and fair as Romena, especially after what Fiasella had done and how her late husband met his end. Romena had been generosity itself. She had refused his kind offer of a pension, saying she would rather earn her living by her needle and not be remembered as the wife of a traitor. In spite of her protests, he gave her a gift of forty florins to start her enterprise and told her she should not look at them as pieces of silver.

No one deserved his death more than Fiasella. How fortunate it was that he should be found dead by his own hand. It would have been worse if Francesco da Romena had pronounced the sentence, for no matter how benevolent and compassionate he might be, a man who knew and suffered the evil that men did was not inclined to show mercy. There was no honor in taking one's own life, and certainly no mercy from God, but to face the executioner at first light, well, it was no matter now. Gherarda was glad her husband had finally done something honorable.

In the month that had passed since Fiasella's death she had found peace and a sense of well-being. She had a purpose, supplying the great ladies of Florence with dresses the like of which had never been seen. Her reputation was spreading in the grand townhouses and castles. So it came not as a surprise when Andrea Alberti's daughter, the legendary widow Cunizza, came to the shop in the Via dei Cimatori that afternoon when the excitement had died down.

Gherarda returned from the Duomo and settled in to embroider pearls on a cap before the sun set. When the light changed she looked up and saw a groom staring at her. He stepped back and waved towards the door. Upon seeing the great lady with her train of servants Gherarda whispered a prayer of thanksgiving. It was said Cunizza had loose purse strings and her commission today would surely pay to add another room on the house at the back of the shop.

"Are you the wife of Edmund Clifford?" Cunizza had to repeat the question, for Gherarda was, as were most people, overwhelmed at the sight of her.

"Edmund Clifford? No, Madonna; that is my daughter's lot. She's Edmund's widow."

"Widow? So I remember. I wish to speak with her. Is she about?"

Gherarda nodded, and without taking her eyes from Cunizza, motioned to a girl seated by the window, stitching a pattern of fantastical flowers on a dress. Beatrice looked up when she heard her name and smoothed her apron to make herself look somewhat presentable.

"Beatrice Fiasella? Am I correct?" Cunizza demanded. As always, she surveyed the younger woman and assessed the competition. There was a little.

"Yes," Beatrice finally answered, putting down her handiwork. "What would madonna require today? Many of the dresses are already spoken for, the holy day at week's end, you see, but we would be glad to embellish something already made," Beatrice said, trying her best to avoid Cunizza Alberti's gaze.

"I have a business offering," Cunizza replied, coming closer. "You'll hear me out, for it may better your condition."

Beatrice motioned to a workroom, a little afraid, but mostly intrigued.

"You and I have been slighted and shamed outright by Francesco da Romena," Cunizza said when the door was closed, and she was seated comfortably with a cup of wine to cool her against the warm June sunlight that streamed in through the only window.

"Madonna, whatever you may think, the conte di Romena was not entirely to blame at least where it concerns my situation," Beatrice confessed.

"Do you think so? Then you are stupid or naive. I would like to think naive! Romena killed your husband! He killed your father."

"My father took his own life, which is against the Lord God's commandments. He was found by the contessa's men after soldiers of the

Commune freed her."

"The contessa!" Cunizza spat; "A creature even worse! And your husband! He was Francesco's friend! What friendship is that, that makes one man murder another?"

"My husband, rest his soul, died honorably on the field. What is it you wish to say to me?"

The girl's opinion of herself was too high, Cunizza thought, and said what she felt aloud. "You're in no position to play the great lady."

"I don't understand why you've come," Beatrice whined in exasperation now, her customer's reputation nothing to the frightened girl. "I have work to do,"

"Don't you wish to see justice done?" Cunizza asked.

Beatrice's eyes slid to the purse Cunizza placed on the table.

"I don't understand,"

"Hear me out," Cunizza purred as she pressed the purse into Beatrice's trembling hand.

❧

"YOU'LL HAVE TO do something, Father," Cunizza sniffed at supper that evening. She moved her trencher away from Alberti, unwilling to share. Very carefully and methodically she sopped up gravy with manchet bread and sucked on it. "Do you know, I dreamt last night . . ."

"So do most people," Alberti growled, watching his daughter finish her meal. He noticed that almost all of the men in the hall were doing the same. Only Cunizza could make eating simple fare a sensual, erotic thing.

"I dreamt of the Feast of San Giovanni. So many people in Florence! The music, the feasting, entertainments not to be believed," she went on, and one by one licked her fingers with a pouting mouth made more inviting by lip rouge. "I dreamt the contessa di Romena was one of the gypsy girls that dance for their supper on the street corners and soldiers of the Commune took her away to ravish her and make a public mockery of her. I dreamt that Francesco da Romena died in the midst of a crowd and no one noticed."

Alberti paid no need to his daughter's rambling and turned to help his old brother Silvio, who was having trouble with his broth and spilling it over the dogs.

"Something will have to be done, Father!" Cunizza shouted.

"For shame, Cunizza!" Alberti hissed. "We know that you've been slandered and made a fool of. But what's done is done and we must now look to other matters."

"And if it were you? You'd not sleep for weeks thinking of ways to get even!"

"Do you think I haven't? God's teeth! There's nothing more we can do!"

"I will not be made a fool of!" Cunizza screamed, and with an arm she swept away the costly plates and cups, the bejeweled knives and fine linen napkins. In any other house, this violent gesture would have brought silence, but in Alberti's great hall, it was just another supper with Cunizza and a few heads turned, but not most. Cunizza reached for one of the knives nearest her father and before he could protest, watched as it was stabbed into the trencher before him.

"Are we going to do something?" she hissed. "After all, you always say once a thing is done, it's finished."

"In. Good. *Time!*" Alberti shouted. "Enough! Leave me now or else."

"You never carry out your threats, Father," Cunizza said as she spun about and left the hall.

The stairwell to the private quarters was dark and Cunizza shouted for lights when she was halfway to the first landing. "Lights! I want light, damn someone!" she yelled. Soon there was the scrambling of footsteps and torchlight dancing like fireflies as a servant hurried to do her bidding. Cunizza turned when she saw the light and her foot caught in the hem of her surcote. Before she could right herself, she fell, tumbling down, the sparkle of jewels and embroidered fabric catching in the torchlight. By the time she landed at the servant's feet, a scarlet ribbon of blood trickled from her mouth. She was dead.

⌀

THIS WAS HOW it must have been for Edmund, Beatrice thought, staring at Francesco seated in his great chair at the end of the great hall. Surrounding the conte were his wife, Roberto da Quintavale, and Niccolo Peruzzi. The old woman named Marghareta was seated at a window seat, lazily occupied with needlework, but nevertheless interested in her surroundings, judging by the cat-like movement of her eyes. Beatrice came forward and made an awkward obeisance. The swiftness of the movement banged her knees hard against the stone floor and she caught her breath to suppress tears. They'd see the blood when she rose. If they let her live.

"Signora Clifford, you will forgive me if I do not seem overjoyed to see you. I thought about not receiving you at all. The counsel of my wife and my friends changed my mind."

"I was seduced by Edmund and convinced that you were not the kind and generous man all swore you to be."

"You know me well enough. Why would you think otherwise?"

Beatrice muttered something imperceptible, and when Francesco leaned forward to hear, she said, "I remembered a promise."

"I made no promise to you, madonna. What happened between us was nothing." Francesco's eyes slid towards Serafina now. She was studying the bejeweled cincture at her waist and her hands were trembling. "Well, you've made too much of it. It should never have happened, and I am sorry to have offended you."

The response was callow, and Beatrice's eyes shot upwards in disbelief. Francesco's eyes were still on his wife, who had lost all of her pretty color. Roberto da Quintavale leaned down and whispered, to which Serafina replied with a shake of the head.

"You've come a long way; what is your business?" Francesco now asked, shifting slightly on his chair and summoning a man to bring refreshment.

"My mother bade me come," Beatrice answered, gazing down at the scuffed points of Francesco's soft leather boots, the traces of mud on the soles. Strange, that the usually immaculate conte should be so imperfect.

"Is she in need? I have heard that her enterprise does marvelously well."

"She lacks for nothing, signor, thanks to your generosity. Another man would not have been so kind."

"This is so. You should remember that."

Beatrice looked up and saw that all eyes were on her. "What I ask is nothing more than what you have given my mother—consideration. I ask for your pardon for the sake of my husband, rest his soul, who was once your great friend, and to be allowed to do you good service." Looking at Serafina, she added, "And your contessa, who never did me any harm."

"How would you accomplish that?" Roberto spoke up, stepping forward.

"I am a dressmaker, I know how to ply my needles. I would gladly be a lady-in-waiting. Hear me, please. I am not welcome in my mother's house. I have nowhere else to go."

Francesco stood and was at his wife's side, his arm encircling her waist possessively and lovingly. "It is for my contessa to decide."

"If mona Serafina can find it in her heart to forgive, I would gladly speak for you," Roberto said.

Beatrice's eyes widened.

"Signor? My late husband was your greatest detractor! Why should you be so generous?"

"Need you ask?" Francesco commented, winking at Roberto.

Serafina now intervened, for the audience was turning more uncomfortable as silent minutes slipped by. She stepped forward and kissed Beatrice and clasped her hands tightly. "Beatrice, you will have rooms close to mine, and I shall find a girl to help you. It will be good to have a friend in this household of men, especially one close in age to me. Come with me now so that we can discuss my clothes for the Feast of San Giovanni. Did you know my husband will ride in the tournament?"

Beatrice nodded and said she had. As she followed Serafina to the second-story bedchambers in the castle overlooking San Miniato al Monte, the purse of coins hidden in her gown grew heavier and heavier.

❧

THE PONTE VECCHIO was teeming with people for the holiday: country folk dressed in holiday clothes, peddlers and merchants bleating for customers while shoving silks and pretty trinkets at pedestrians and singing the praises of their quality, jongleurs competing with buffoons for an audience. Pretty girls sold aromatic sprays of flowers and herbs. The good, intoxicating scent of meat and garlic roasting on spits wafted from one of the butcher shops on the bridge and invited revelers to come and partake.

Francesco, Serafina, Niccolo, Beatrice, and Roberto, all on horseback, had ridden from Serafina's castle to prepare for the feasting and tournament in honor of San Giovanni.

Francesco and Serafina laughed and conversed happily with the crowd as they pressed on. Serafina heard her name and looked up at the shop windows. A trio of young men pelted her with flowers. Francesco caught a rose and presented it to his wife, which made the fellows cheer. They had a difficult time staying on their horses, though, for the crowd was pressing too close and children surged forward begging for pennies.

They were separated at the foot of the bridge. Francesco caught Serafina's attention and shouted over the din, they should meet at the other side, in the Via Pigna.

Men came from hiding places as Francesco approached the statue of Mars in the Oltrarno. One of them leapt in front of his percheron. Francesco tried to wheel the horse away from bystanders scrambling for safety. His escape was blocked by two men dressed in Alberti livery. They came at him with clubs.

There was confusion in the crowd; someone shouted there were soldiers marching on Florence from the south. The holiday was soon forgotten as revelers pushed their way to the safety of the Lungarno. To add to the confusion, a fire had broken out in one of the shops and was spreading. People were leaping over the side of the bridge into the Arno to escape the smoke and flames.

"Niccolo! Give me a sword!" Francesco screamed while fending off his attackers with a baselard. Serafina saw what was happening and forced her way through the melee. "Go back to the castle!" he shouted, but she ignored him and pushed forward.

Niccolo dismounted and fought the surging crowd to reach Francesco, his vision impaired by acrid smoke spewing out of the burning shops and the people closing in as they ran into the Oltrarno or back into Florence. When he had a clear line of sight, Niccolo froze in horror. The assailants had succeeded in dragging Francesco from his horse. He was paralyzed, unable to move as the crowd became suffocating. People trying to escape death, sent hurling backwards, buffeted him as he tried to reach Francesco. Over the din of the crowd he could hear Serafina's shrieks and pleas for help.

He drew his sword and grabbed a second sword from a dead knight and managed to reach Francesco, fighting off the attackers and dragging Francesco to his feet. From there they escaped to a butcher's shop on the bridge near the Via Pigna. The poor tradesman looked quite unhappy to see the infamous conte di Romena standing in his hall, bloodied but alive. Outside it seemed as if a hundred men were pounding on the door. How long before they broke it down and took the intruder by force?

"You certainly took your time!" Francesco screamed at Niccolo, heaving for breath against the bolted door.

"You're welcome; I'm sure you'd have done the same for me," Niccolo snapped.

"Where's Serafina?"

"I'm sure she's safe."

"Did you recognize any of them?"

"Alberti's men."

Francesco turned to the astonished butcher and threw him a purse of coins. "I have no intention of disturbing you or your trade more than I already have. I assure you I shall be only a moment, if that at all. Have you a man to assist us?"

"Certainly, monsignore!"

"There'll be more if your man finds my wife and brings her safely here."

The butcher nodded eagerly and looked down at Romena's arm dripping blood into the straw. "I can have my wife take care of that."

"No need! My wife,"

Nodding, the butcher shouted behind a curtain. A greasy-faced boy of no more than sixteen appeared holding a cleaver in his hands, his apron bloodied with entrails.

"What's your name, boy?" Francesco demanded.

"Giovanni, messer."

"My son, signore Romena," the butcher introduced.

"My wife is caught in the brawl outside. Bring her here safely and that is yours," Francesco said, nodding to the purse in the butcher's hands.

By this time the crowd outside was in complete pandemonium. The fires were spreading. The bridge would be gone, up in flames, by midnight. Giovanni peered out a window and shook his head. Muttering something unintelligible he went back to the room behind the curtain.

"There's another door," the butcher explained.

"Your arm," Niccolo said, motioning to Francesco with his own bloodied sword.

"Leave it, Niccolo," he snapped, but supported it with the other hand now that it began to throb and burn. "What takes the boy so long?"

"With that crowd it will take time."

"The bridge will be gone!"

A full half hour passed before Giovanni appeared from behind the curtain with Serafina and Beatrice.

"I told you he'd be safe," Serafina said to the other girl.

Beatrice said nothing and watched as Serafina embraced her husband. *What had she done?*

❧

ANDREA ALBERTI SPREAD himself a fine supper. The best of the pantry lay before him: mutton, beef, fowl, and fish all in savory sauces or broth. The cooks were still at it by the time the first three courses were done and it was sure to be a long night. The master had a reason to celebrate. The conte di Romena was surely dead by now. No one could have survived such an assault.

The solitary celebration was interrupted by pounding at the downstairs door. Andrea shouted for a man to see what the matter was and returned to his joint of fowl. A few moments later his steward ran in, as deathly pale as a man could be and still breathing. Before he could utter a word Francesco da Romena entered, his arm still oozing blood, a sword ready in his good hand.

Andrea stood quickly, holding the chicken in his hands like a weapon. He opened his mouth to speak but nothing came. And then there was the crushing pressure on his chest, as if the air was being sapped out of his lungs. Francesco da Romena was towering over him now, screaming, but Andrea heard nothing. The pressure was too great now. Clutching his chest, Andrea collapsed on the floor.

"He's dead," the servant pronounced a moment after checking for signs of life.

❧

"MONSIGNORE, THEY HAVE another conspirator."

Francesco waved away the surgeon and servants hovering and acknowledged Roberto. Michelino Groppa, sitting on a bench close at hand, blurted out: "Is he still alive?"

"He was trying to escape, messer podesta. Didn't get past the Porta San Frediano."

"Where is he?" Francesco and Groppa asked in one voice.

"The Palazzo dei Priori."

Now Groppa took a pen and parchment freely from Francesco's cluttered desk and began scribbling, his words barely legible. The letter was thrust at Roberto.

"Go there and see that he's kept there! No bargains."

"And the spy?" Roberto queried.

"What spy?" asked Francesco.

"We told no one of your plans to come to Florence. Someone had to

357

tell Alberti where you were."

Francesco screwed up his face in pain and then rubbed a hand wearily over his eyes. Beatrice, standing quietly out of the way, waited. As yet no one turned to look at her. Surely they must know by now, she thought.

"Find out," Groppa ordered. "Do what is required."

"There's one thing more," Roberto spoke up. Heads turned in his direction, surprised he was still there. "The conspirator is one close to you, messer conte."

"Who?" Groppa demanded. "Out, man!"

Roberto's eyes again slid towards Serafina and he begged permission to speak to Francesco alone. When his request was denied, Roberto said quietly, "Durante Giustini."

Unwilling to hear any more, Beatrice slipped away, behind the arras and through a doorway that led into the Borgo Santissimi Apostoli.

Francesco reached too quickly for the cup of wine a physic held, causing searing pain to his wounded arm. He swore as the wine spilled like new blood on the death warrant the podesta's clerk had just prepared, the ink still wet and now streaking the parchment in mottled purples and blues. He controlled the trembling of his hands by thrusting them into the wide sleeves of his robe and knew every pair of eyes in the room watched.

But his eyes were only for his wife.

❧

NO ONE PAID attention to the girl hurrying along Via Porta Rossa. She might have been a servant trying to get home before the curfew bell rang. Twilight was high, the crowded streets a result of the fires still burning on the Ponte Vecchio. Another girl running through the streets with purpose was nothing peculiar on that night.

A mob was gathering at the Torre Alberti. As the girl ran past she failed to notice the ransacking of the great townhouse at the end of the street, the servants herded out into the street and mocked by neighbors, who, only a day before, feared the master of the house. He was a felon and had died, was the rumor; what was once Alberti's was anyone's for the taking.

Someone grabbed the girl's arm as she tried to press through the mob. "Don't I know you? You're one of Alberti's maids!" he bawled drunkenly.

"Let me go!" the girl cried and she tugged away, though escape would have been impossible in such a crush of people.

"Leave her!" another fellow remarked. "I know the girl to be Edmund Clifford's wife. She's Romena's whore."

Hearing this, the crowd respectfully fell back and allowed Beatrice Fiasella passage. Never looking over her shoulder, she continued on until she reached the river. There at the quay she fell on her knees and wept. How long before they discovered her disappearance and came after her? Francesco would show no mercy. She had betrayed him not once, but twice.

Men on horses suddenly appeared at the end of the Via Pigna. Their silhouettes in the flame-lit sky fell the length of the street.

"Beatrice!"

It was Roberto's voice! They were coming for her. The girl began to sob uncontrollably. She whispered a paternoster and threw herself into the river. The horsemen paid no attention to the rippling water of the Arno as they galloped past.

೨

THE CROWD GATHERING outside the Palazzo dei Priori grew in numbers as the hours passed. Michelino Groppa shook his head and wondered if the prisoner would be safe to bring to execution. No doubt this rabid mob would tear him to pieces.

"Perhaps if we wait until tomorrow," he said.

"It will only grow worse. Give the Florentines something to remember. Perhaps it will wash my father out of their memories," Francesco answered. He had joined the podesta at the window. The crowd recognized him and started chanting his name as if he were their champion.

"Tell them we're ready," Groppa said to a soldier waiting in the doorway. The execution would be held in the courtyard of the municipal palace. It too, was crawling with people. This would be no private affair. As soon as Romena appeared the spectators grew quiet and then suddenly exploded with acclamations of support. A guard of eight men, his own household knights and those of the podesta, surrounded him. The only man so well protected in the courtyard was Durante Giustini, now being led to one of the upper story windows. Francesco and his host waited on the stairs. Again the crowd fell silent as a priest offered to hear Durante's last confession.

"What sins do I have?" mocked Durante, and he spat in the priest's face. The rope was secured round his neck and tightened, and then he was hurled out the window. Durante's body pounded against the wall of the palace like the clapper of a bell, weaving back and forth as it convulsed in death throes. Blood stained the hard stones where his broken body struck them.

It was over. The crowd went away feeling a little cheated. The podesta signed that the gates should be closed and sighed, running his fingers through his hair wearily. Now that Durante was dead, Alberti dead, Tommaso murdered, what sport would there be in Florence? They had provided entertainment for the better part of thirty years. By the end of the month the jongleurs would be recounting their sordid lives in the halls of great men. Francesco da Romena would become one of those heroes young boys worshipped. In market squares and courtyards, children would choose sides and one would be Romena, the other Alberti. Young girls would weave flowers in their hair and walk with eyes downcast, playing at being

Serafina Giustini and dreaming of a handsome conte just like Francesco da Romena, and this would go on until the next pair of lovers and their quarrelling families came along.

Groppa dismissed these thoughts from his tired mind and now glanced at Francesco. The young man's face was ashen, the color of newly hewn marble. "Go home, messer conte," he said. "The quarrel is over."

Francesco turned slowly and looked at him as if seeing him for the first time. Nodding, he walked down the steps and out of the courtyard. Not once did he glance at the body of Durante Giustini still swinging on the rope, not during the execution or after.

It was indeed over, this quarrel.

Serafina waited for him in the courtyard of the Torre Romena. She came down the stairs from the second-floor landing, her women disappearing respectfully into the shadows. Roberto and Niccolo went off to find something to eat, Roberto saying that revenge made for appetites, and left Francesco alone.

As soon as he passed the colonnades and under the arched passageways, Serafina was in his arms. Wordlessly they stood in an embrace, gathering strength from one another as they cleaved, receiving from each other a powerful life force for a future no longer dim, a future they could claim together.

The End

ABOUT THE AUTHOR

A NATIVE of the San Francisco Bay Area, Ellen L. Ekstrom makes her home in Berkeley, California. Ms. Ekstrom's growing library of work includes *Armor of Light, What She Wished For...A Cautionary Tale ("A Knight on Horseback"), The Midwinter Sonata Series*, which includes the companion novels *Tallis' Third Tune* and *Scarborough*, and, writing as Caitlin Luke Quinn, *St. Edmund Wood*.

Coming soon: *Ascalon* – the sequel to *Armor of Light*, the third book in the *Midwinter Sonata* series, *The Shambles*, and a tale of the events of 1066, *Swannsaeld*.

※